Family
The Unworthy Cosmos Anthology

P. MARCELO W. BALBOA

BALBOA.PRESS
A DIVISION OF HAY HOUSE

Copyright © 2024 P. Marcelo W. Balboa.

All rights reserved. No part of this book may be used or reproduced by any means, graphic, electronic, or mechanical, including photocopying, recording, taping or by any information storage retrieval system without the written permission of the author except in the case of brief quotations embodied in critical articles and reviews.

Balboa Press books may be ordered through booksellers or by contacting:

Balboa Press
A Division of Hay House
1663 Liberty Drive
Bloomington, IN 47403
www.balboapress.com
844-682-1282

Because of the dynamic nature of the Internet, any web addresses or links contained in this book may have changed since publication and may no longer be valid. The views expressed in this work are solely those of the author and do not necessarily reflect the views of the publisher, and the publisher hereby disclaims any responsibility for them.

The author of this book does not dispense medical advice or prescribe the use of any technique as a form of treatment for physical, emotional, or medical problems without the advice of a physician, either directly or indirectly. The intent of the author is only to offer information of a general nature to help you in your quest for emotional and spiritual well-being. In the event you use any of the information in this book for yourself, which is your constitutional right, the author and the publisher assume no responsibility for your actions.

Any people depicted in stock imagery provided by Getty Images are models, and such images are being used for illustrative purposes only.
Certain stock imagery © Getty Images.

Print information available on the last page.

ISBN: 979-8-7652-5219-2 (sc)
ISBN: 979-8-7652-5218-5 (e)

Library of Congress Control Number: 2024909506

Balboa Press rev. date: 07/16/2024

Contents

A word from the Author 1
   Double Ninjas 3
   Lost Opportunity 19

Concept Art 35
   Klark And Kimberly 59
   My Mother's Our Father 73

Shadow War 85
   Slug Shot 97
   The Horrid Play That Is 115
   The Magical Munchgalumptagans 119

My "Studio" 321
   Rise Of The Queen Of Shadow 338
   The Forgotten Path 363
   Scin'd And The Forbidden Forest 373
   The Plain Of Hollow Dreams 396

Kit Bash Projects 399
   Red Snow 402
   Itty Bitty World 408
   Wisdom of the Golden Guardian 410

Cosmic Journey, Family Edition 499
   Thank you… 501
   Vincent's Life 536
   World Peace 539
   Hall Of Legends 541

Thank You All, ... 545

About the Book 547
About the Author 549

A word from the Author

As an author I am excited to create worlds and characters that readers around the world can get to know and follow on their journey. But along the way I have made characters with backstories that have not been told. I was more than happy to publish many of their stories in the Epic Tales of King Hudson but there were more that developed after this book as well. So I found myself reaching for new ideas. How can I incorporate these characters into new adventures? I analyzed each of them and it occurred to me that they had captivating stories with a correlating topic. Family.

In the past, I have written my books based on ideas inspired by things that happened in my life. But I haven't leaned into the complexity of family. Yes there are a couple I can say I am good not knowing but there are so many I am grateful I have had in my life. In their honor, I created this anthology in my collection of work. I looked for the common thread and found that these stories allowed me to break down my definition of family. The name stuck as I wrote each draft. As I completed the initial drafts I found that there were more stories I had to tell that were inspired by the stories I wrote in this book already. So I added them. Some are a part of the table of contents. Others are hidden gems that I inserted as a token of my affection for the topic. My family is so complicated and yet so much like many other families in this world. Although my early work was inspired by pain, it is the love of many of my family members that has filled every chapter in this book. I dedicate this book to them.

Double Ninjas

Petey was a naïve child. His parents were distant communicators but great as teachers of how to live life right by example. And they were close to family across the street who had a daughter a year younger than Petey named Noila. She was a beautiful little girl with golden brown hair and hazel eyes. Whenever the parents would get together, they would let the two go play. Their best spot was the park downtown. They loved to pretend they would go on cosmic journeys together.

Sometimes they would be Martians, while other times they would simulate talking trees. Most of the time, they were ninjas who could move swift and stealthily climb anything. Unbeknownst to their wild imaginations, they were completely visible to the naked eye as their parents could immediately identify them on their adventures through the playground. Still, to them it was real, and they built a bond that was strengthened with every memorable experience they created in their minds.

Noila visited the playground alone one day. She sat in the sand in silence as she looked at the children playing. Little by little, she could see her and Petey play. They had a song, "You gotta eat your spinach, baby, cause that's the only thing to do, or choose." She smiled at the thought of their enthusiasm about the song. Not a care in the world. Her heart warmed to the laughter she remembered they shared. She remembered a time that called to her. She rose up and ran to him. There were monsters attacking a village that only the double ninjas could defeat. They were off.

Petey was in love with Noila. Not for her looks or her family's success. His mind was pure, and his love was too. Noila was in love with him to. They were convinced they were going to marry someday. They were too young to understand this was not possible. They were too naïve to understand what platonic love was. They were simply two souls who knew they loved each other's soul without judgement or physical attraction. And it was this innate bond that complimented their like-minded imaginations.

When they approached the village from high ground, both were there in their imaginations. Both could describe something, trade thoughts and fill each other's missing images. They looked out at the surrounding darkness and studied the terrain. "We need to talk to the villagers to find out what is going on." Noila said. "Right. But we can't just rush in. The threat is near and could attack us at any time. We must be quick and remain invisible." Petey remarked. "Right." Noila responded.

The double ninjas moved fast. Nothing moved around them as they hopped to each checkpoint. Then a monster attacked them without warning. "Look out Petey." Noila yelled out. Petey turned just in time to see a great beast of epic proportions pursuing him ferociously. His instincts were on point as he evaded the initial attack. These double ninjas needed no weapons. They had each other and their super-duper ninja skills. "Wayakatapatapata" Petey yelled out as he performed some of the most amazing unscripted, naturally performed techniques anyone at that playground had ever seen that day. Including him.

"Hang in there." Noila yelled as she jumped into the fight with her audaciously spectacular fighting motions. She was sure of every spontaneously choreographed technique she performed. Although her body remained in place. They imagined a large version of the mean dog that barks at them from next door at Noila's house. They talked about how scary he was a few days ago when he spent the night at her house. It was such an angry bulldog. They were not sure why, but they agreed it made their spines tingle. Not today. Not on this mission. They were ninjas and the village people needed them. The monster was too big for their speedy footwork. Just as fast as the monster attacked, they were able to run to the entrance and seal the doors shut.

"Holy moly dude that was a close one." Noila said. The two breathed their hearts out in simulated terror. "Are you alright? I hear those mutant dogs are cursed." Petey panted. Noila checked herself for any wounds. "Nope. I'm too fast to get eaten. How about you?" She asked. Petey checked himself as she spoke, almost instinctively knowing what she was going to say. "He almost took off my leg, but my ninja skills were too quick." He said.

"I saw you. You were so fast." She responded. "What do we do now?" Petey asked with enthusiasm. Noila looked at him with joy as she could see he was so pure in his passion. He invited her to be free of any judgement. "We need to talk to the leaders and find out where those monsters came from and how to defeat them." She said. "Right. Let's go." He responded.

The double ninjas hopped to and from the monkey bars until Petey slipped. Noila ran to his aid and saw bruising up the backside of his torso. That wasn't an injury that came from slipping. And Noila was smart enough to know this. He pulled his shirt down. They were too young to communicate what they were feeling at that moment and continued to play. Noila snapped out of the memory and tussled her feet in the sand. She remembered that moment in frustration. "Why didn't you say something to him Noila." She asked herself. She cried softly. "I always knew something would happen." She said in her head.

She dusted the sand off her butt and feet then walked to her car. It was a black jeep with tinted windows. Not far different from her father's jeep. As she drove home, she remembered going on vacation with her cousin. She looked back in her rear-view mirror and got lost in the memory of Petey and her playing tag. They had just gone to the beach on the last day and her father let them lay down in the back like a bed. They were naïve to the dangers of their horseplay. Playing tag with your feet in the back of a jeep wasn't going to fly with Noila's father. As her father stopped the car and yelled at them to get out, they were caught off guard.

"So you want to kick each other huh?" He asked with an aggressive tone. The two were confused. "Turn around." He said as he turned them around by one arm each and began kicking them like they were kicking each other but harder. Noila remembers the sadness she felt but didn't realize Petey was being abused at home by lawn service man Sharlene. His sadness would never yield as this incident changed his bond with Noila and her parents. He was colder. He didn't talk to her the same. There was an uneasy quality about him. He was antagonistic and hostile yet hid it with a smile and subtle insults hidden in cryptic statements.

Pretty soon she didn't love him like she did and found him to be a bother. Little did she know he was fighting monsters in his life no child should endure. She didn't realize her father became one of those monsters that one day. She didn't realize her reaction to him only added to the alienated world he was creating in his head. Petey was never the same after that experience with her father. But that wasn't the end of the double ninjas. When she returned home, her children were just returning from school. Noila prepared a tasty dinner. Kind of.

She splashed flour on her cheeks and ordered pizza, but the kids were never wise to the secret ingredients. Kind of. They saw the pizza boxes in the trash outside as they went out to play every pizza day, so they played along. It was pizza day and mom had her make up on. Everyone was on board. Pizza day was always on Friday. And Friday was always the best day of the school day. Mark and Mica were the best of friends and siblings all in one. They were just a year apart and had fun outside every day. Noila had told them about her adventures playing ninja with Petey and they took it to the next level with their own outfits.

They cut up half gallon and full gallon plastic milk containers and turned them into armor. To an outsider this may seem silly, but they knew this armor was enchanted. Nothing could penetrate the unbreakable creation of theirs. But all good times come to an end. This Friday was different from any other. It was a sunny day with beautiful clouds. This day was not over but it was coming to an end too quickly. Clouds darkened and deepened with an unpleasant look to them. The lightning that came from them flashed blood red. The rain was dry and hot. Each drop smoked upon contact.

The siblings didn't run. They looked at each other and stood strong. "The time has finally come Mica." Mark said as he looked up in ninja stance. "This isn't good Mark. We need to tell mommy and daddy." Mica responded. "Let's go." Mark responded. Just as the siblings ran to their house, a bolt of lightning struck the house. Their ears rang as they tried to see through the smoke and fire. "Mica? Mica?" Mark yelled. "I'm here. Are you hurt Mark?" She asked. "No, but my tummy hurts." Mark said. "Are you bleeding?" She asked. "No. But I can't see anything. I think my eyeballs are cooking." He said. "It's the smoke. Don't worry. Your eyeballs aren't hurt. Can you come closer to me. I can't see you through the smoke?" She yelled.

Noila screamed out a terrifying sound. "Mommy" The siblings yelled out to her. Noila wept and screamed. Then there was no sound but the thunder, lightning and carnage occurring all around them as far as the eye could see, if they could see. "Mommy" The siblings yelled out again, as they ran to the last place they heard the scream. Parts of their home crashed down in flames as the front of the house lay in rubble. The siblings found their mother and each other but there was nothing to be happy about. Their father was crushed under the rubble with only his arm visible. Their mother, Noila, was staring at the sky with tears in her eyes. They thought she was gone but she turned to them. "My double ninjas. I love you." She said with her final breath.

"Mommy" Mica screamed out as she ran to her. Mark dove at her, pulling her just before a large piece of lumber crashed down. Mica didn't flinch as she reached out for their mother. "Mommy" She cried out. More of the house crumbled onto their mother's remains. Both cried out in sorrow. The neighbor heard them and ran to their aid. "Come with me children." Ms. Wilkins told the two as she grabbed their arms and pulled them out of danger.

The double ninjas were too distraught to fight back. They entered Ms. Wilkins vehicle along with her 6 cats, 4 dogs and a parrot. "I'm sorry for your loss little ones. I saw parts of your home crumble as your father entered the house. I heard your mother scream. I am so sorry. I lost my parents to at a young age too. It was hard. But you can't give up. You hear me?" Ms. Wilkins said as she drove to a shelter.

While Ms. Wilkins was trying to avoid the meteor fragments still falling along with swerving through the chaos the exploding debris was causing, the children were finding solace in the kisses the cats and dogs were giving them. They giggled in tears as the parrot reminded them, "Can't give up. Wok. Can't give up." "That's right Dragon. They can't give up." Ms. Wilkins agreed. "You named him Dragon?" Mica asked. "He named himself dragon." Ms. Wilkins said. "I'm a Dragon. Wauuuhk. I'm a Dragon." Dragon said. The children giggled. Ms. Wilkins noticed a barricade surrounding a medical relief center. "There we go. We can pull around and stay here. My babies need to get to a safe place." Ms. Wilkins said. Just as Ms. Wilkins turned right to enter the lot, she was blind-sided by a truck that was out of control and on fire. Mica and Mark were wearing their seat belts, as Ms. Wilkins made sure not to forget. However, in the chaos of calming her pets she forgot hers.

Mica and Mark awoke as paramedics tried to free them from their belts. The flames were growing and there was little time to lose. Just as they were cut free and separated from the vehicle, it exploded. "Ms. Wilkins." Mark screamed as he watched the parts of her vehicle land in random places. "Where's my sister?" He asked the paramedics. "She is unconscious with a few scrapes and bruises, but she will be fine." The paramedic answered. Mark didn't know what unconscious meant but he was hopeful the word fine was a good thing. "Can I see my sister?" He asked politely. "Oh sweetie, that's wonderful you love her that much. But let me get your leg fixed first then you can spend all the time you want with her. Ok?" The paramedic said as she wrapped Mark's broken leg.

Mark was in such shock he didn't notice the bone sticking out of his lower leg. "Owww!" He screamed. The pain kicked in. "It's going to be alright child. You are in the best place to get all fixed up. Don't think of the leg. Fight the bad moment with thoughts of really good moments. Ok?" The paramedic said as hospital staff rushed him to the Emergency Room. "Ok." He said as he squeezed his eyes shut in pain. "Look at you. You are a strong one. I can tell." The doctor said. "Really?" Mark responded. "Oh yeah. I've seen big bear size men cry over little cuts compared to your injury. I can tell you are very strong." She said. "Now, I'm going to have to take some of this stuff off to get to the broken leg. This may hurt a little." One of the nurses said. Mark's spine straightened a bit as he clinched his fists in pain. "I am a ninja. That's why I have my armor on." He said.

The nurse patted Mark on the shoulder. "That armor kept the bone from tearing out of you further. You are a lucky one." She said. "I don't like talking to strangers. I'm Mark." Mark said. "You're a smart one. Well, I'm Nurse Bennet. Glad to meet you." She said as she took Mark's armor off. Another nurse walked up with a needle. Mark wasn't a fan, but he knew it was good for him. Before the nurse could say a word he said, "Just do it." as he squinted and looked away. The nurses looked at each other, impressed by the little guy's maturity. "Alright. It will be really quick. What's your name?" Nurse Ratko asked. "Mark" He responded. "Great job Mark. All done." She said. Mark opened his eyes. "All done?" He asked. "Yep. The doctor will be in soon. For now I'm going to put this mask on you. You will fall asleep and wake up much better." Nurse Bennet said. "I am strong. That's why I can take shots." He told Nurse Bennet. "You sure are." She giggled.

The doctor walked it. Mark was slowly succumbing to the sleeping gas. He could see the name tag of the doctor. "Well what do we have here? I knew there was a kid under that stuff. That leg looks easy to fix. Nurse Ratko, can you get me…" Mark heard Dr. Wolfe say before he fell asleep. "Well that's not too bad. I hear you're a strong one. I'll have you out and about in no time."

Family

Mark heard as he opened his eyes. "Really? Can I see my sister too?" Mark asked half asleep. "I'll make sure you are placed in the same room. What was her name?" Dr. Wolfe asked. "Mica." Mark responded. "Mica. Got it." The doctor said as he walked out.

Shortly after Mark was rolled to another room for a second surgery. He was scared but hid it as he looked around. People were lined up in the hallway crying, bleeding, or wrapped on beds. "Where's Mica?" Mark asked the medical staff rolling him. They looked at him then talked to each other. Their masks hid their faces but Mark knew these were different nurses. These were unfriendly nurses in a rush as they were rolling him to surgery. "Stay calm sir. We will take care of your injury as soon as possible." One of the nurses said. The stern tone of the nurse intimidated Mark. He didn't say a word. As he was rolled into a scary medical room with sharp tools and a particular scent in the air, Mark grew a deep need for his parents. But he was strong and didn't cry. He reminded himself, "You are strong. You will be all right. They are hospital people. Hospital people help people."

As he told this to himself, the medical staff put a mask on him that sprayed an air that made him feel better. He started feeling happy. A big smile came over his face as he began to fall asleep. "When you wake up you will be all fixed up, you hear Mark?" Dr. Wolfe said as Mark dosed off. Mark was relieved to hear the kind voice as the sleeping gas took effect. Screams and crackling debris opened Mica's eyes. She was in the dark but the fire from the hallway was light enough for her to see the hospital was falling apart. She jumped out of bed and ran to the hallway. Mark was in the same room but still knocked out. "Mark? Is that you?" She asked, still affected by the strong painkillers she was provided.

They brought Mark to her in her sleep. She had no idea he was there. With smoke filling the air, it was hard to see if it was really him. "MARK?" She yelled in overwhelming joy as she ran to him. She jumped onto him and hugged him. "Whoa, whoa, whoa Mica. My leg was just fixed. Careful." He said. She pulled back thoughtfully. "I'm so sorry. I'm just so happy to see you." She said. "I missed you. I don't think I like this place." He said. "Me too. Mark, you need to get up. We're in trouble. The hospital looks like our house did before it fell apart." She said. "We shouldn't stay here." He said half awake. "I know. We need to get out of here." She said as she helped him sit up. She ran to get a wheelchair. "Here, get on. We'll get out faster with you on this." She said. "Yesssss! Finally I get pushed on the wagon." He said. Mica smiled as she remembered always making him push her or pull her on her wagon their father bought her for her birthday a year earlier.

"It's our ninja wagon." She said. They laughed as she raced through the chaos as arms tried to grab out for aid. The sight was heart breaking. Still, the urgency was clear as the building itself could be heard giving in. Mark didn't say it out loud, but it was a fun ride. He had a difficult time enjoying it with all the bleeding, crying, or open-eyed sleeping people on the way to the exit. "There's the exit." Mica yelled. As they neared, a middle-aged man ran up to them and asked, "Can I have that wheelchair for my daughter. She's lost her leg." Mica was about to keep running but Mark stopped her. He stood up, "Take it." He said. "But..." Mica started. "It's alright Mica. I'm strong. We can make it. The man ran to his daughter but as the two exited, he yelled out, "Hey." They turned around.

He handed them a crutch. "Thank you." Mica said. Mark took it. "Be strong sir." Mark said. "Be strong." The man responded as he went his way with his daughter. "I love you Marky." Mica said. "Love you too sis." He answered. "Now let's get as far from this place as we can. It's going to fall apart." Mark said as they ran to safety. The siblings ran through smoke and fire, wreckage, and debris as they tried to find refuge. "I miss mommy and daddy Mark." Mica said. "Don't Mica. Remember when mom told us about her adventures as a double ninja. We can do it for real." Mark said. Mica smiled. "And their silly song." She said. "You got to eat your spinach, bayyyybehhh." She began. "Cause that's the only thing to do or choose." Mark chimed in. The double ninjas laughed.

"Why did they sing that? It's spinach, gross." Mark said. "It was never about the spinach yah goof. They were happy and singing and loving being with each other. The words didn't matter. They just loved being happy together." Mica explained. "Oh." Mark instantly understood. "Well I'm happy even with all this because I have you. We are the new double ninjas right?" Mark asked. "Yes we are. Look, there are a bunch of people up there. Maybe we can find some help." Mica said. From afar they could hear the collapse of the medical building they were in along with countless other buildings near and around their current position. The ground shook as smoke clouded the air from all directions.

Car alarms, people screaming dreadful screams, ambulances, fire trucks, and police vehicle sirens rang through the air as darkness covered the landscape for quite some time. "I'm scared." Mica said. "No you're not. We're ninjas. We're strong. Don't be scared." Mark said. "Right. Right. Ninjas. We're ninjas. But this isn't pretend. We need to get somewhere safe and fast." Mica responded. "If we make it real then it's real. You are what you believe. Ninjas are quiet. If we are quiet and listen maybe we can find the right way to go." He said. She paused in the darkness. The horrible sounds still surrounded them as they waited for an idea or something to happen that could give them a fighting chance.

"We're double ninjas and we have to find a way. Come with me." She said. "Ninjas vanish in smoke right? Let's follow the sounds of people. Then we might find a safe place to get out of this weather." He said. They ran through the darkness helping each person they came across. The group of people they helped grew little by little. When one seemed to give in the other pulled their counterpart along. The group became excited as they heard numerous voices ahead. They would emerge from the smoke to find tents with people helping people. They ran up to participate and were welcomed with open arms. They received food and drink, making sure Mark and Mica were attended to first. There was medical aid and bunks to get well-deserved rest. "We did it Mark." Mica said. "The Double Ninjas always come out on top." Mark said. They gave each other a high five.

After some time telling their story and hearing the stories of the new friends they helped along the way, the double ninjas fell asleep in peace. The peace didn't last long as their dreams became riddled with nightmares. Mark was floating over his parents bodies. Monsters were throwing flaming balls from a ship in outer space. He punched the flame balls away, but a vampire slug came from behind him and tried to turn him into a vampire. He woke up from the dream to find Mica was gone. He limped around until he heard her voice. "No, stop." She screamed. But her voice seemed muffled. He limped as fast as he could only to find an old man trying to do something that didn't look right. "Hey, stop it." Mark yelled. The old man looked at the boy and laughed as he tried to continue. Mark limped to the man and swung his crutch. The man grabbed the crutch and swung it at Mark's head.

Mark hit the ground but tried his best to get up. He was dizzy but could hear his sister scream. Then he heard another man's voice. "What are you doing you sick son of a." The man said before a fight broke out. Mica ran to Mark and helped him up. She looked back and saw the heroic man beat up the old man. She looked away as she noticed the man didn't stop hitting the old man. "Serves him right." She said in tears. They returned to their bunks and a guard was set up to watch over the children from that day forward. Mark and Mica were able to find their friends and other family on their father's side. Over several weeks, Mark was able to heal enough to walk and run without any issues.

Then the military arrived, and everything changed. The lower ranked soldiers were rough spoken and had little answers for their actions. They seemed more concerned with finding weapons, ammunition, and recruits. They exchanged food, water, and information but before long they were gathering everyone up who was able bodied to help fight off what they feared was an alien invasion. "Mica, I think we need to get out of here." Mark said. Mica looked over at the old man who had never stopped his gaze of her since that horrible night. "Let's go now." He said. They grabbed their backpacks, filled them with items that looked like they could help them with surviving a long journey, then departed while everyone was asleep.

They ran down into a ditch then under a train track bridge then through a park until they were able to find a place to rest in a closed mall. It was abandoned and had plenty of hiding spots. The double ninjas picked a high spot in the toy department upstairs. Their nightmares followed them. Mica couldn't get that evil man out of her head. He followed her like a snake. Sometimes he was a snake, like this nightmare. She ran through her house but never could get a step ahead of him as he found a way to pop up in front or beside her. She would run in the opposite direction only to be stunned as he popped up in front or beside her again, and again. She began to freak out the moment he finally caught her.

"I got you Mica. I got you." He said. She screamed. "Stop screaming, he will hear us." He said. She thought her brother was coming to save her like the last time. Her only option seemed to be to scream louder. The snake man shook her and shook her until she woke up. "Mica, we have to move. He found us." Mark whispered. Mica was half-asleep as her brother tugged at her. She resisted. "Let me go." She said. Her instincts held onto the possibility it was not reality. "Mica, that old man. He found us. He heard you scream. Come on, he's getting closer." Mark said. They exited the toy store and not a moment too soon as the old man crept over to the area he heard Mica scream.

Family

    Mica was immediately triggered at the sight of him and his despicable facial expression. A deep seeded festering desire to do irreparable damage to her body was seeping out of his bulging eyes and drooling mouth. His hunch back gave her chills as she remembered him leaning over her, grabbing at her private areas with his scaly stretchy skin hands. She cried silently. Mark held her while trying to take a protective position. "We need to move faster. Remember, ninjas. Just like mommy was." He whispered. "Just like mommy." She whispered. "Come on." He said as he picked her up by the shoulders.

    The double ninjas moved as if they were in their back yard. Swift and quiet. Smooth and athletic. The old man didn't have a chance. They were out of the mall and on their way as soon as the old man realized they weren't in the toy store anymore. They were awe struck at the sparkling night sky. It wasn't the same. Normally, the sister planet Rezandria decorated the night sky. It was moving while beautiful clouds of colors they never dreamed could be in the sky took its place. All that beauty did little to take away from the destruction that surrounded them. They continued on as they felt the old man's eyes behind them. They ran until they were convinced they escaped him for good.

    "I need to rest Mica." Mark said. Her memories of what happened and what could happen pushed her. Mark didn't have that same drive. She looked at him and empathized enough to calm her perception of the potential threat. "Over there. The firefighter house has fire people who came to school one day to tell us to stop, drop, and roll. They can help us." She said. A forth of the way they stopped in their tracks. They were struck by terror as a great being visible from outer space reached out for their planet. It's grip was wide and so threatening the two chose to stand in ninja pose. They didn't have any chance of defeating this foe, but they were the Double Ninjas. They were strong and ready to fight till the end. Inside they were frightened and missed their parents.

    Even with all their fright, they stood firm as enormous pillars grew from the ground and stretched out to the hand that now covered the planet, causing great darkness. "Why can we still breathe?" Mark asked. "I don't know but our planet is alive and seems to be fighting back." Mica said. Terrified souls who were still alive to witness this event simultaneously screamed. Mica and Mark gave into their ninja mindset for a moment and held each other tight in the darkness. They were unable to hide the fear that struck their hearts. The screams were worse than the night of the meteor shower. They cried as the humanoid planet vibrated. Buildings still weakened by events prior crumbled to the ground. More lives were lost in a deep darkness that covered the gripped side of the planet.

"What do we do Mica?" Mark asked. "I don't know. I'm just a kid." She said. "I'm scared." Mark responded. "Mark, we need to stop this. We promised to be strong. We can't give up. Remember?" She said. Mark wiped away his tears. "Yes." He whimpered. "Stand up." She said as she stood to her feet. "We are Double Ninjas right?" She said. She knew better but she needed to be strong for him as he had been for her. "Stand up Mark." She said more confident. He stood up while wiping his tears away. "Get out your flashlight." She said. Both did so. They turned them on. "Let's find a safe place from the falling buildings." She said. "Right." He responded. They ran until they found a forest area. There they made a camp area where they tried to get rest. For some time they managed to survive until their supplies began to run low over time.

"I've noticed an area with big lights. We should go there to see if we can trade for some food and water." Mica said. Mark didn't disagree as he put on his backpack and started walking. When they reached their destination they saw there were people inside quickly constructed shelters with power from generators built by local mechanics. This community had built a system in response to the potential end of the planet. Mica and Mark would grow up and become the leaders of tomorrow out of this small group of survivors. They would miss their parents and the loved ones they would come to meet and see pass away but their memories would guide their actions. Through their lessons, the Double Ninjas would help a new world grow stronger than it ever was.

The day would soon come when all would find out what really occurred. Nuwa, the creator, merged two universes. Earth and the planet of the Guardians were set to collide had the planet of the Guardians not imploded. The large meteor fragment that remained flew through space. As the merger began, they were set to tear Rezandria apart. However, Rezandria was unexpectedly pushed out of the way leaving Mark and Mica's planet. Such a collision would destroy all life on their planet. The Guardians, bound by responsibility to a fallen planet and plagued by passed failures, realized this truth. The universe had expanded enough that no other planet, star, black hole, supernova, etc. would come close to each other during this phenomenon. Due to this fact, Nuwa had no issue with the collision as life was temporary. Not to mention few on the planet had committed enough good in relation to the atrocities they had done to each other during their planet's existence to warrant protection. Deemed unworthy, the merger took place as planned.

The implosion of the planet of the Guardians didn't take the lives of the Guardians. Leaving them to dwell on what remained of their failure. Brea returned after the emergence of the Guild, the rise of the planet Rezandria and the impact his Cosmic Guides were now making across the cosmos. The large meteor that was once their planet served as their meeting ground. "Greetings brothers and sisters. I come to you in good health, but I fear in poor timing." He began. His brethren were seated in waiting as they could feel him drawing near weeks in advance. "Welcome brother. We are eager to hear the news whether good or bad." Sol said. "I am pleased to see all of you. I called upon the one all exists within for the opportunity to travel the cosmos and learn. I wished to become the leader we needed to make right the wrongs of our past. I was tested, passed the test, and earned the right to travel all of which exists within the one all exists within. I tell you this day, we are but a grain of salt among a sea of salt. I was humbled by the powers many in existence possess. I was horrified all the same." Brea began.

The Guardians leaned forward. Nine once sat in the great hall. Four turned on their creator and sought to enslave the land they were created to protect. One changed his mind and turned on the other three soon earning his place back in the Kingdom of the Clouds. The greatest of them all, in good faith, sought to correct the flaws of the past but his perception was misguided. Many years of woe would follow the actions of these fallen Guardians. A weight too heavy for the others to bear. A weight Brea felt obligated to carry for them all. "But my travels lead me to enlightenment. I saw the errors of my ways. I too thought of what I felt would be right. Much like our fallen brethren. I was wrong. For the Unworthy Cosmos do not revolve around us. We too are flawed like the planet we watched over. And believe this... There are so many planets out there with great beings much like us along with planets with far worse problems than ours that if I were to repeat my steps with each of you and reach out to triple more planets we would still be unaware of a thousandth of a portion of the existence that are within my unworthy reach." He continued.

"What is this speech for? Have you come to bring sorrow upon our existence? Do you wish us to believe we are a mistake?" Kobay remarked. "I do and I don't brother. You have seen much but I have seen more. And we are in the biggest moment of our existence yet." Brea continued before taking a drink of his wine. "Speak brother. If we are to learn of something bad and it allows us to do something good then speak of it. Why stall?" The Guardian of Weather said as a storm grew above the Kingdom. As he spoke, his brothers and sisters listened. With Bello, Catalyn, Karlo, Reeza, and Kayfus gone. There was little doubt the lives of other brethren would not endure the details Brea revealed.

Seph, the Guardian of Weather, and Erious, the Guardian of Atmosphere, knew something was wrong. With the knowledge their universe was set to merge with another now understood, they sought to correct the environment as it altered. Sol, the Guardian of Land, combined efforts with Kobay, the Guardian of Metal, to create a child of their hidden love and admiration for each other's gifts. Losyabok was the name provided to this golden entity with the inherited capabilities of both parents. However, not to the full extent as the two Guardians would have hoped. Nonetheless, a great being made of pure gold was now in full representation of both entities.

The planet of the Guardians was far smaller due to the devastation of so many hardships forced upon it. It was now a floating rock surrounded by debris. That debris became bullets that shot at Mark and Mica's planet. Millions of lives were in danger as the merger began. To many other planets across the universes, this merge was beautiful, breath taking to say the least. To these two planets, it was the beginning of the end. That is until Seph and Erious rose up with the aid of Losyabok to control the change in the atmosphere that would have taken the air from Mark and Mica's planet, killing all life almost instantly. As the meteor set its course on colliding with their planet, Sol held on to as much of the larger debris as he could. Brea, the Guardian of Travel, recruited a being that was part planet who could transform into a humanoid and help protect Mark and Mica's planet.

The Moon created an unexpected shift in currents which forced Seph to fight the change in weather to the point she merged with Erious to become space itself. Transcending the physical form of their old capsules, they became something else. Not more than what they were but more capable of reaching their full potential. 'They', who were no longer they were, could feel the space of the cosmos. This new entity was one with the space but free from its constraints all the same. In it, as it, this new 'They' was able to construct the necessary environment around both planets that would ensure every life form could survive. The only issue that lay before them was the inevitable collision of said planets. Sol did well but small fragments still broke free. After creating metal shelters for the remnants of life forms still walking the planet of the Guardians, Kobay came to Sol's aid and stopped whatever debris remained that could do more damage than had already been done.

Brea would depart then return just in time with another transforming planet. The merge itself drew upon the Guardians greatest efforts. Life drained within them just to fight off death as it lingered at every moment of the merge. Their existence was never more necessary than this very moment. As the planets grew closer, Brea's friend transformed from a planet into a humanoid. It was far larger than the two planets and the meteor put together. With a gentle reach the humanoid planet grabbed the two planets as the smaller humanoid planet reshaped the meteor into a moon to orbit the planet of Rezandria. Kobay extended metal as Sol extended land to create enormous pillars as touch points that would prevent the grip of the larger humanoid planet from crushing any life. Losyabok aided the Guardians in this, the great feat no one on either planet could comprehend.

The merge was complete. The planets survived. Losyabok, Sol, and Kobay developed the new moon into a flourishing smaller version of their former planet. 'They' created separation that allowed the new moon to rotate around Rezandria while not affecting Mark and Mica's planet. Now, they could look upon the stars they were gifted and view Rezandria and their new little sister planet they would name Angel-Land. It wasn't what it was, but it was enough for the Guardians that remained to look after as it rotated around Rezandria from the day of the merge forth. The Guardians didn't bother Mark and Mica's planet but were visible when their planet's rotation gave their adopted sister planet a perfect view. And it was plain to see the Guardians looked like the Angels of Earthly religions. Brea sought to teach Losyabok the lessons of the past so that the Golden Guardian may emerge as the leader of the Guardians someday. With Brea's blessing he was off to his ongoing Cosmic Journey.

P. Marcelo W. Balboa

    Losyabok became aware of the hardships endured by past conflicts of his planet's sister planets and sought to aid them in recovery. The Golden Guardian came down upon the planets and provided aid wherever aid was within the Golden Guardian's capabilities. The people were so appreciative new religion grew. Losyabok would learn of this and sit with the worshipers to give them the lessons provided to him by Brea. A female leader by the name of Mica wrote of what the Golden Guardian said in these events. The lessons are written in a small book she published called, Wisdom of the Golden Guardian.

Lost Opportunity

Raja Ali was born pre-mature and didn't want to eat. His mother was worried he would pass as the nurses put tubes through his nose to force vitamin milk to keep him alive. When he finally opened his mouth, it was a relief to everyone. This iron will to prevent anyone from feeding him was innate. It served him well as the defensive in for his college team. They were one defensive stop away from going to overtime.

Raja looked to his left, then his right. He looked at the quarterback. His eyes were focused on the left side. However, the play was familiar. The offensive line was set for a pass to their star receiver but there were two players out of place. Raja did his homework. He knew this team's plays inside and out. "Hike." The players began their motions. Raja faked left, lowered his shoulders, drove his body into the offensive lineman and spun the opposite direction into the running back. At the moment he received the ball he didn't see Raja running at him.

"BOOM!" The crowd cheered as the ball came flying out of the running backs arms. Raja was a strong man and loved to make contact. He ran through the running back so brutally he didn't lose stride. With a few lucky bounces of the football, he was able to catch it and run with all he had to the end zone. Unfortunately, it was not to be as a wide receiver ran up behind him. "BOOM!" The crowd cheered again. Raja's best bud was there to save the day as he blind-sided the receiver, ensuring a touchdown. The fans ran onto the field as the game ended. Raja was a senior and a champion.

The night was wild as they celebrated. Everyone was at the Nick-Nack Bar and Grill. The linemen were famous for their large orders and this night was a definite must. All the linemen sat across from each other. Offense vs Defense. Raja looked to his right and where his best bud always sat. "You ready?" Raja asked. "Get it." Allen said. They tore into the inhuman pounds of medium rare meat like wild animals. All the students cheered them on.

The bar was going crazy as Raja and Allen did it again. Another come from behind win as they stood up and bumped chests.

Later that night, or was it the morning, either way the lady of the night was there, and Raja knew tonight could be the night. Allen was well aware of their silent dance but found this night to be his night. He stood up from their table, walked up to Shelly, and let his best game fly. Shelly was captivated. She was disappointed in Raja who Allen said was not interested as he unleashed the game of the century on her. She wasn't sure he was telling the truth but when Raja left she didn't have much of a reason to disagree. This night marked the birth of a marriage the two never saw coming. In fact, most students who knew them thought Raja was the one.

Raja would go off to become an outdoorsman. Hiking, biking, swimming and any other outdoor experience he found worth trying. His online videos called Champ-Life were popular as his wild ways provided entertaining moments. As his finances increased, he decided to settle down and buy a home in The Hills. It was a very wealthy part of town he grew up in. To his dismay, just a block away were his old friend and crush. They were married without children as their careers took hold of their lives. They found throwing parties to be the way to deal with the lack of relatability in their personal lives.

This truth was not revealed for some time. Raja spent most of his off-time hunting. Sitting in the rain but not touched by the rain as he cooked a steak over an open fire. His dog, Bull, was always patient to get his piece. Raja loved laying back with a full stomach and relaxing to the steady fall of raindrops. It was a matter of time when his return fell on the same days as his old friends' get together. Raja arrived home, dropped his gear at the door, and went to the bathroom. It was a ritual he had created. Turning on the water, stripping down to what he was born in and taking a shower was a great feeling.

"Welcome home" He would say. As he finished up, and dried his hair off the doorbell rang. "Who the…?" He thought aloud as he got dressed. The doorbell rang once more. "I'm coming. Hold up." He said, light jogging down the stairs. When the woman stood close to the door, Raja stopped in place. The clear window did not give an image he wanted to believe. He reached for the door and opened it. There she was, Shelly, who had grown to become a breathtaking woman. As he admired her, she found his physique to be eye catching and didn't hide it. Remembering she was married, both corrected themselves.

"Please, come in." He invited. "Actually, I need to get to all the rest of our neighbors before dark. But thank you. I just wanted to invite you to our wine tasting party tonight." She said. He was happy to hear her voice then thought about Allen. "Um... I don't..." He began. "I know Allen would love to see you again. He speaks about your football days to everyone. You should come." She interrupted. "Well.." He hesitated. "For me." She said with a sweet voice. Raja looked at her. He never dreamed he would see her again let alone be in her home. "What time?" He asked. "Yessss. Uhh, we usually start the festivities around 6 but you should come a bit later, so you don't have to sit around with our neighbors and wonder who everyone is." She said.

"I'll be there, late and fashionable." He said. He clapped with delight. "What a night it will be. I've missed... Allen and I have missed you. We can't wait to see you tonight." She said. They waved goodbye but there was this unspoken desire not to leave one another. "Can't wait either." He said, closing the door in awe of the moment. "Oh shit." He said. He ran upstairs hooting and hollering. There was a party in just a few hours and the girl of his dreams was going to be there. Married or not he was happy to be in her life.

He had no idea she could hear him. She wasn't far off in her reaction to seeing him again. She was lost in her marriage. The new yet old face brought joy to her spirit she hadn't felt in a long time. She could hardly remember visiting the other houses in the neighborhood. When she walked up to the last house, she rang the doorbell, forgetting it was her house. Allen answered the door, "Is this a joke? You know I have a lot of work to finish before the party Shelly, come on." He said. His usual attitude was enough to snap Shelly out of her daydream. "Sorry. I was out of it." She responded.

"Well get it cause I want the appetizers to be better than last time. You over cooked the shrimp. You know how much..." He began. "I know, I know you LOVE the shrimp." She spoke over him as his voice faded into the background. He didn't appreciate her attitude either. "Watch it Shelly. I'm not playing with you today. Get it." He said. She thought to herself, "GET IT, GET IT. I'm not your stupid football teammate jock." She quietly went about preparing the appetizers, forgetting for the moment that Raja was coming.

Allen and Shelly had fallen in love as they went on to their careers. She saw his hard-working attitude and discipline to work toward a life that was luxurious. But she didn't count on the ego or drunken rage. Allen was only attracted to one thing. Shelly was the hot girl and Raja could never have her. That flimsy foundation exposed itself as their careers became more important than their personal lives. They almost became robots. To help them find peace, they came up with these parties. Partly to show off their lives to the neighbors and partly to find a reason to enjoy each other's presence without arguing at some point.

Raja on the other hand was a secluded soul. When his crush found her partner for life, he wasn't interested in the idea of anyone else. His passion was nature. He loved the forest, the mountains, the rivers, and the ocean. Camping, hiking, and many other outdoor trips became his life. With social media expanding, he purchased the equipment needed to document his experiences. Partly to keep his mind out of the loneliness that was growing inside him. He dreamed of what could have been on many occasions. It was only a matter of time until his popular internet channel took off. His waking hours were scheduled for outdoor events, filming from multiple angles, and editing. Lots and lots of editing.

Then the door knock changed his entire life around. A face that filled his dreams was a reality again. Never was there a day he saw it possible that she would be in his life. Then, in an instant she was standing in front of him, just as beautiful as the last time he saw her. Older, but aged like wine. Shelly and Raja were busy preparing for the party while their minds flowed through what could have been. Neither could tell what the other was thinking but both were feeling something they shouldn't feel. She was married and he was not her husband. Yet their minds were unable to relive where they went wrong.

The party couldn't come fast enough. Raja sat by his clock and whittled a present for his old friend. When his alarm went off he almost ran down the stairs. When he arrived, there were people in the backyard and inside the house. Shelly opened the door to Raja almost at the moment he walked up. "Well hello stranger. Long time no see." She said. Her dress was casual but showed she was still in great shape. "A pleasure to see you. A sight I thought I'd never see again." He said. She stepped to the side, inviting him in. He was nervous. There was another face still to come. Before he could remember his old friend, "Holy shit! Shelly told me she saw you, but I can't believe it's you." Allen yelled obnoxiously.

Family

They shook hands but the men they became were different. As Allen walked his old friend, he patted Raja on the back. "She's a beauty isn't she?" Allen asked. Raja was caught off guard. "Sure." He responded. They stopped in front of Allen's barbeque pit. "My cooker my man. The best there is. I can cook for a thousand guests and make the best tasting meat you'll ever eat." Allen declared. "That's... That's really cool." Raja said. He wasn't impressed but remained cordial. It wasn't his thing with the minimalist lifestyle he lived himself. "I saw some of them internet videos you do. Cute. But you make pussy meat. This..." Allen began as he opened one of his grills to reveal several large pieces of meat, simmering and sweating. "Is meat." Allen said. His body language almost took Raja back.

"Some things never change." Raja thought. "Wow. That is impressive Allen." He decided to say instead. "You're damn right fella. And believe you, me. It tastes better than shaved pussy after a shower." He said as he nudged Raja. "You're a dick." Raja said in a playful manner. Not so playful in his head. "I could cook one of them too if they tasted as good as steak." Allen responded and laughed as if he told the best jokes anyone could ever hear. "That's funny." Raja said. "Well I have to attend to other guests bud. Have a tour and enjoy my house. Maybe you can pick up some ideas to make your house better." Allen said, walking away half talking to Raja and half talking to everyone else.

Raja looked around. Like radar, he locked onto Shelly who was talking to a few women in the neighborhood. He didn't feel comfortable intruding, so he found a seat inside to sit with other neighbors watching the game in the living room. "Hey, aren't you that guy who does outdoor videos?" A young woman asked. "I do create outdoor content and post it on the internet. I'm not sure if I'm the same person you have seen." Raja answered. "No way. You definitely are. Raja Ali. You climbed the second highest mountain in the world then shot down the other side on skis. That was so inspirational." She said. "I'm grateful you enjoyed my experience. I almost fell off the cliff twice. I saw my life flash before my eyes." He said. "I bet. Where do you get the..." She began. "Did I flash somewhere in that life?" Shelly said softly in his ear.

The young woman immediately read the vibes and left Raja alone. Raja turned to see Shelly standing with two glasses of wine. "Have you gone on that tour of the house yet?" She asked. Raja stood up. "If you're the guide, I'll take that tour for sure." He said. Allen was almost drunk but not enough to

23

miss his wife walking upstairs with Raja. He let the worst thoughts marinate instead of walking up to them and joining them. He half wanted to find out if she felt the same for his old friend. He chugged two more bottles of beer. "Son of a bitch." He blurted out. Then he threw his beer bottle in a rage, jumping over obstacles to chase his wife down.

They were standing over the pool on the balcony Allen custom built to look over, or down on, the guests from time to time. "You have done well for yourself." Raja said. "You aren't doing so bad yourself. Still in great shape. Seeing the world. Living free. I've watched your videos often wondering how much fun it must be." Shelly said. Raja paused to look into her eyes. She was already looking at him. "The living being was never meant to be alone. Secluded in these beautiful places in the world is great but when there is no one to smile and enjoy it with, it sucks." He said. "I would give anything to be free and go see the world. I live vicariously through your videos. Sometimes I pretend I'm with you." She said but paused as she realized where she was going.

Raja didn't say anything. She didn't either. Just as he was about to inquire, "What the fuck are you doing up here? You two trying to fuck?" Allen accused. They turned around, Raja was confused but Shelly was already used to this behavior. "Are you kidding me? He's your friend. We were talking, that's it." She yelled. "You… I know you were trying to fuck. I'm tired of your shit." He said, slightly slurring. "Oh, go take a shower. You're ruining another party. Before long we won't have any friends." She said. "I think I'll head out now." Raja said. "Oh yeah, you try to seduce my wife and leave… Right. I'm the bad guy." Allen said. As Raja walked downstairs Allen tore up his bedroom in yet another drunken rant.

Guests followed Raja out the door. Shelly tried to apologize but no one was hearing it. Before long, no one was in the house but them. Shelly went upstairs and grabbed her clothes. She packed in the guest room as Allen stormed around the house looking for her. When he finally found her, he saw the luggage. "What's that?" He asked. "I'm done." She said. He grabbed her right arm as she continued to fill another suitcase with clothes. "What are you doing?" He asked. "Let go." She said. "No. You're not going anywhere. You were the one acting like a slut, not me." He assumed. "Me? You have the nerve to accuse me of doing something wrong. Look at you. You think I don't know about Trudy, Erica, Yvonne?" She accused back. "What? I…"

Allen stumbled over his words. "Yeah. I knew. And then you drink all the beer and set yourself up for embarrassment then you accuse me of making a fool of you. Let go of me, you're hurting me." She said.

Allen pushed her to the ground. "You leave me, and I'll kill you." He said. She saw his eyes. Allen scared her but this time it was different. Raja had an effect on both of them. Allen's reaction to Raja living so close was not healthy. He began drinking early. The result left him unable to handle his emotions at this point. Shelly didn't say a word. The clothes, make-up, personal items meant nothing at that moment. She walked past him and walked toward the stairs. "HEY!" Allen yelled. Shelly didn't lose a step. "Hey bitch, I'm talking to you." He yelled. Her stride remained true. Allen ran up and pushed her. His strength was superior to hers, but drunken rage added more than he meant. Her little body flew over the rail, hit the wall, then rolled down the stairs.

The crack at the end was just as frightening as the rag doll landing her body made. "What have I..." He asked, struggling as he tried to run down the stairs drunk. A sober realization mixed with a drunk regret made it difficult to accept reality. "Shelly wake up. Wake up. Please." He pleaded as he shook her body. He looked around for help. Every part of him wished there was a way to take everything back. "Fuck man. Fuck. What do I do? Shit! Fuck! What the fuck? Awe man, shit. I fucked up. Oh shit I'm going to jail." He babbled, running around the house looking for something to make his mistake disappear. His blind fear didn't help as the world was enduring something far worse. Shelly opened her eyes. She sat up and turned to the noise Allen was making.

Allen searched the kitchen for a few large trash bags and a large knife. "I'm so sorry. Fuck. This is so fucked up." He said. Hiding the body would be difficult but slicing it up and eating it might be the only option. Or so he thought. He turned around to start the delusional solution and Shelly jumped at him and tried to bite his neck. "What the fuck is your problem?" He screamed. He was so happy she was alive he forgot he was planning to cut her into pieces. Then he looked at her and realized she was not the same. Her eyes were blood shot, and her neck was broken. Her speech was replaced with a sound that wasn't her. It was choked and strained. "Stop your shit Shelly." Allen yelled. She didn't listen. He didn't know how to react until her jaws took meat off his shoulder.

With one clean stab, he penetrated her cranium. She rolled her eyes back and went limp over him. He threw her to the side as he removed his shirt. It was covered with coagulated blood and white bubbling drool. "What the fuck? How the hell is her blood all fucked up already. I just killed her." Allen said. The words disrupted his comprehension of the moment. "I killed her twice, but the second time wasn't right. Fuck! That first time wasn't right. Both times weren't right. What the fuck?" His mind rambled. Her body twitched, freaking him out of his mind.

He punched her face, tearing her skin. Seeing her skull tipped him over the edge. He fell into a daydream as he stared at her. Screaming and wreckage filled the air outside, but his mind was gone. He couldn't figure out what went wrong. He looked at every possibility and found the reason. "Fuckin' Ali." He said. He grabbed the knife and pulled it out of Shelly's skull. The skin on the side of her head was removed with it. With it already loose, her face also came along with the blade. Allen was so gone he took it as a sign to wear the face of his wife as his face so he could be her and she could be alive again. He put it on. No words. No explanation needed. "You're a dead man." He said.

The young woman talking to Raja before Shelly took him on a tour escorted him home. In that short distance she was able to pick up there was nothing there. He was in love, and she wasn't the one. So she kissed him on the cheek and left him at his doorstep. "Here. If you ever change your mind, give me a call." She said as she handed him her number. "Thank you." He said. He walked into his house and walked upstairs. He removed his clothing and let each one drop where it dropped. He stepped into the shower, turned the shower on, and then curled into a ball. His tears and the water masked the carnage spreading throughout the neighborhood. His heart was confused. Broken would be a better word but he wasn't with her. He just wished he had been.

"Why didn't I just go up to you?" He cried. "I know you loved me. You still do. I love you too. Forever." He cried. Two punches at the shower floor followed. He put his hands on his forehead and combed his fingers back, through his hair. He thought about what he was saying and caught himself. "Get your shit straight. She chose him. I lost an opportunity to be with the love of my life. Tough shit. Their married you asshole." He began. A crash of glass downstairs startled him out of his depression. "What was that?" He whispered. Without hesitation, he exited the shower and put some shorts on. He ran to his shoes, put them on, then grabbed his hiking stick. Many wild animals were fended off over the years with his trusty stick. Hiking made it a third leg and a worthy weapon.

Raja leaned his head into the hallway. He could hear noises downstairs. He stepped into the hallway and made his way to the stairs cautiously. The crashing noises were unnerving but the noises the intruders were making were bone chilling. "Allah give me strength." He prayed. His grip tightened as he took each step one by one, crossing his legs with each step. The intruders suddenly ran into the room at the bottom of the stairs. One looked up at him almost instantly and screamed. "What the hell?" He said. The deteriorated being that looked partly humanoid ran at him. A swift swing to the head tore into the weak bone, crushing the side of the skull in. The being's body fell to the ground, but the conflict drew the rest to Raja like a magnet. A few more skillful swings left several bodies piled up along his stairway. He jumped to the ground level and landed athletically. He stood up in shock as he noticed the face of one of the intruders. She was his escort home.

He walked to his living room and sat down. He could hear the screaming outside, but he didn't want to accept what was happening. He wasn't into horror movies, so this wasn't something he ever dreamed to be prepared for. He turned on the television, switching channels until he found a news network. "Sources say there are cemeteries around the world experiencing the rise of bodies buried which were previously presumed deceased. In addition, religious leaders are calling this the end of days as demonic possessions have allegedly occurred in major cities..." Raja turned the television off, cutting off the news reporter.

"This doesn't make any sense. How is this even possible?" He pondered. The bodies behind him didn't take long to fill the room with its stench. "What are those things?" He asked the air as he looked at the pile of corpses. He checked his body for wounds. There didn't seem to be anything to worry about. "Alright. Everything is where it's supposed to be. I need to get these things out of my house." He said. His cellular phone had trouble finding a connection. With the stench getting worse, he decided to get the bodies out and explain himself later. The skin on the bodies were decomposing quickly. Raja had to get low and carry the first body to the front door to place it in the front yard.

He dropped the body abruptly as the face of his childhood sweetheart stared at him with the body of a grow man. "Allah give me strength." He whispered in tears. Allen had found the time to put on a long black coat and some fancy loafers. The blood on his hands and his wife's face disrupted the classy wardrobe. "I've come dressed for success my friend. It is my best attire for the funeral." Allen said. Raja had no words to express what he felt. "You took my wife. I have brought her back. We agree you need to pay. Pray for forgiveness for your sins old friend. Today, this day, right now, your life has come to its end." Allen said before charging at Raja.

Raja wasn't ready to deal with this. He ran inside his house and slammed the door. Allen ran into the door, but it held up. "A fucking door isn't going to save you from your fate Ali. We want you dead bud. We want you dead." Allen said. The door was falling apart with every ram of Allen's shoulder. Raja could see it was only a matter of time, so he ran upstairs, passed the corpses, rushed along the hallway, then shut the door to his room. Crash! Allen tore through the door. "Raja. You're a coward. I took your dream girl. Come down here. Deal with me like a man. I knew you wanted the bitch. I married her just to spite you. Come out of your hiding spot. Face me. Let's prove who the real man is." Allen said.

Raja walked out of his room and looked down at Allen. Shelly's face looked up at him. A chill ran down his spine at the sight of the eyes piercing through the holes of the face of the woman he loved. Death and mayhem flooded the neighborhoods surrounding Raja's home. This moment, as Raja walked down the stairs, drowned out everything. They never took their eyes off each other. Raja's anger grew in response to the death of his lost love. Allen's delight grew as he finally had the opportunity to take his lifelong jealousy for Raja out on him. No words. The two friends attacked, holding nothing back. Raja did what he could but found Allen's knife made a few more holes in his body than he realized. He retreated.

Allen didn't rush. He walked slowly, soaking in the victory he wished for since Raja got all the glory their championship year back in college. "Run, run, run, run, run." Allen said. Simulating the start of an engine. "I'm gonna gut you Ali. I'm gonna put you on my grill and make you into a nice meal." Allen said. "What the...?!?!" Raja whispered in disgust as he hid in his laundry room. Allen's footsteps could be heard just outside the door. "I can hear you bleeding. The bubbles are dripping. The iron is strong within you." Allen said. Raja tried to keep conscious, but he blacked out. The crash of Allen running into the door woke him up. Before Allen could break down the door, Raja rose to his feet and ran at the window. A clean dive landed him on his roof. He rolled then jumped to the ground level.

The fall was loud, but the swimming pool was kind to Raja as he landed on his floating recliner. He passed out from blood loss. "Ahhhhh!" Allen screamed. Raja opened his eyes and looked toward Allen, who was pleading for the possessed neighbors to stop ripping him apart. Raja sat up but couldn't move as he floated safely at the center of the pool. He dove into the water, peeking his eyes out over the water while remaining under the floating recliner. He watched as his old friend was ripped into several pieces. The small group of possessed neighbors looked in his direction but didn't smell him anymore. The heard screaming in the streets drew their attention. They ran back to the front yard to participate. Raja floated quietly as his mind rambled.

"Praise Allah for your mercy. Praise you in your glory. Praise Allah for saving my life. I am unworthy of your gift. Praise Allah for giving me a chance to prove my worth." He whispered in complete shock. He floated in silence for a few seconds in his mind but a few minutes in reality. The sky was dark, and the clouds were sinister. The air was alive with the carnage and chaos surrounding him as far as his ears could hear. His eyes never left Shelly's face. She was looking at him. That is, Allen's eyes pierced through a face with torn eyeholes of a mask that resembled Shelly. The moment he found the courage to get out of the pool, he swam to the edge. Small and sudden sounds made him dive underwater a couple of times. When he finally had the nerve, he slowly exited the pool. "My love. My lost opportunity. I'm so sorry for not fighting for you. You didn't deserve this." Raja said as he took Shelly's face off Allen and walked inside his house.

He searched the house for any threats then began gather items to pack his back for another outdoor adventure. He cherry picked the best tools of the trade in his arsenal. With a lifestyle like his, he had the best of the best supplies to survive even the end of the world, as he knew it. He looked over his items as he packed them away. "Let's see… multi and cutting tools, got em'. Cooking and lighting combustion devices…" He said as he set out several options. "Got em'. Coverage material… let us see… got em'. Alright… cords, ropes, wires… there we go." Raja said with a little bit of a thrill all his outdoor work had meaning now. He brought together cups, bowls, plates, and other containers for storage he used often on long trips. "Got you, you, and you. Oh, and you too little guy." He said. Next were clothing, cloths, and repair tools. He had a method for storing everything to maximize usage in the smallest storage space possible for long treks. With a few navigational tools to place inside the small compartments in his bag, he was set.

He reacquired his walking stick then went to his balcony and climbed atop the roof. His eyes burst into tears as he looked in all directions. Fire, smoke, death, and horror were all around him. He sat down and cried as he held his hands to his face. "Praise Allah for your mercy. Praise Allah for allowing me to keep my life. Praise…" He prayed but stopped at the sound of a girl screaming. Grabbing his binoculars he looked in the direction of the screams. There she was. A little girl on the roof of the house across the street from Allen and Shelly's house. He stood up with a new motivation. The carnage and chaos was as far as he could see, and his path was clearly dangerous as the possessed ran rapid an all directions from all directions. He descended from his roof then made his way to his front door. A possessed woman was in his living room. She rushed at him with a loud war cry. In one motion, he sidestepped and struck the back of her skull.

Her body twitched as it fell. Raja continued on his path without hesitation. Each possessed neighbor who ran at him flailing his or her arms and drooling distracted his sight. Yet, his steps never deterred him from his chosen path. The little girl saw him as he tore into the horde. "Over here. Please, help me. My mom and dad are sick." She yelled to him. Raja hastened his steps as he saw that the possessed parents of the child were pushing on the window their daughter used to gain access to the roof. "Don't open the window. I'll be right there to talk to your parents. Don't open that window." Raja yelled out.

The little girl screamed as her father's arm broke the glass. Raja swung at the horde of possessed all the way up to the door of the little girls home. He opened the door, entered, closed it then locked it as fast as he could. Not because anyone was chasing him, but to make sure no one could escape. He walked through the living room without any issues. Then he made his way up the stairs where the younger brother could be seen standing still across the hallway. The darkness that covered the land made the hallway dim. However, the eyes of the child had a yellowish red glow. The boy held a teddy bear in his left hand.

"Hey there. Are you all right? I'm here to help." Raja said. The boy swayed from side to side. "Please forgive me Allah for what I am about to do." Raja prayed as he prepared for the possessed boy to attack. Without warning, the mother burst through the door behind Raja. Raja turned around to defend himself. The little boy ran at him with vigor. Raja used his walking stick to maneuver the mother so she would be in front of the boy. The boy jumped at the wrong time and Raja's stick knocked him over the railing. The mother didn't beat an eye at the death of her son. Raja was all she wanted and what she wanted wasn't good.

Raja rolled back and kicked her off him. The father entered the fight at the worse time as the wife ran at Raja. Raja sidestepped and the two ran into each other. With two well-targeted strikes, Raja was able to continue without resistance. There was blood everywhere leading to the window. He looked out through the broken glass to communicate to the little girl, but she was not there. Then he heard her. "Help." She said. Not like before. Her voice was softer, with more of a struggle. He looked down and took a big breath. Part of him didn't want to look. Nevertheless, he did. To his right was the little girl. Her body was still intact from the waist up. But her legs were somewhere else.

He ran up to her. "I'm here. Don't worry. I got you now." He said with great remorse. "I don't feel the pain anymore." She said. "And you won't have to anymore because you're safe now." He responded. "Why did my daddy do this to me?" She asked. "Your father loves you. I am sure of it. Sometimes parents do things we can't understand at that moment but know that if he had to do it over he would have protected you." He said. She smiled. "I knew my daddy still loved me. I thought I did something bad." She said. "No. No, you are wonderful. And your parents love you and your brother with all their heart." He said. "Oh. O.K. I underst…" She smiled in her last words. Raja closed her eyes.

He walked down the stairs and opened the door. The little girl's legs were there to greet him. He was so far gone he didn't notice them. The chaos continued all around him. His mind was on one thing. He pulled Shelly's face out of his back to fix it the best he could. The front door of her beautiful home was open. In clear sight, he could see her body. He took her to the back yard and buried her. "May your days be renewed before the magnificence of Allah. Praise to Allah for creating such a beautiful live for this world to experience." Raja prayed. Lost in his guild he lay beside her. The sky was frightening but it wasn't what he saw.

He envisioned a life with her. One with children and a home of their own. Birthdays and vacations. He danced with her in the clouds as she swayed effortlessly with the music. He closed his eyes and dreamed a good dream. This was short lived with all the horrific sounds that never stopped. He sat up, walked through Shelly's house, wishing he were the man who lived in it with her. He washed up in the kitchen then found a way to get to the top of the roof. There he sat as he snacked on some celery and ranch dip from the kitchen. The world was gone. It was a new one he was not interested in living in.

He reached into his pocket and pulled out a necklace. It was the one he gave Shelly their senior year in college. She never stopped wearing it. He noticed it the moment he saw her at his door. It was by her body before he picked her up to bury her. He put it on, finished his snack, threw the paper plate he was using in the trash in the kitchen, grabbed a cup, opened the kitchen door, poured orange juice two-thirds the way up and looked out of the window above the kitchen sink. He drank slowly, looking forward in a daydream. "I failed you my love. May Allah find favor in my effort to meet you again in the afterlife." He said. He put the orange juice back and washed the cup before returning it to the cupboard.

Raja walked out the front door to face the horrors head on. He hesitated then walked back to his house. He opened his garage door. There was his canine companion ready to save the day. Not one bark. "What a guard dog you are." He said. Together they went out to face the world. No strike was without maximum effort. Anyone he could help he would, placing his life in danger at every turn. Never did he hesitate or think of his own safety. His life now belonged to his lost love. Although he intended to die in battle, he found out quickly he was very skilled at what he was doing. Life after life that should have not survived now breathed air into lungs that should never have held air again.

He would travel the world giving aid to all who were in need. When the time came, a greater calling was presented to him. At this time, he would be introduced to a man who was destined to become his best friend, some might say a brother... perhaps. Padre Merrio Ully and he would go on memorable spooky adventures, with their fellow journeymen Pep and Tec, across the cosmos. In his pursuit of death, Raja would be blessed with a journey that found lives and saved them. His name would be etched in the Hall of Legends on the planet of Rezandria for all to remember his great deeds.

Concept Art

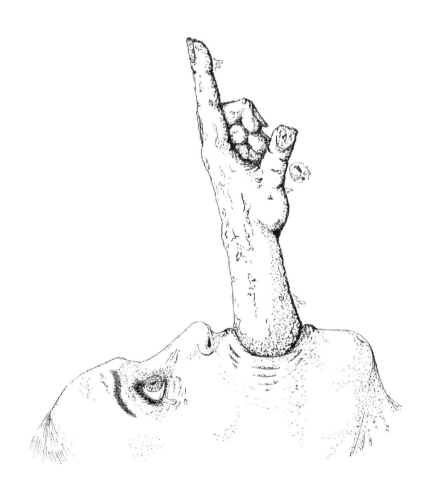

Family

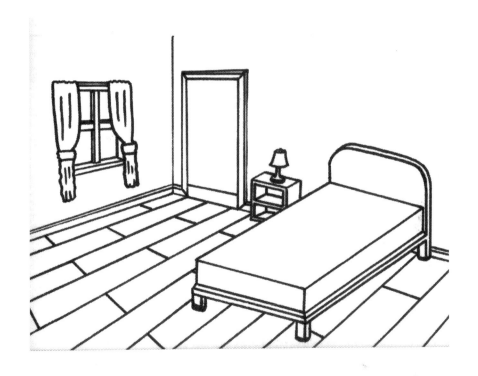

P. Marcelo W. Balboa

Family

P. Marcelo W. Balboa

Family

Family

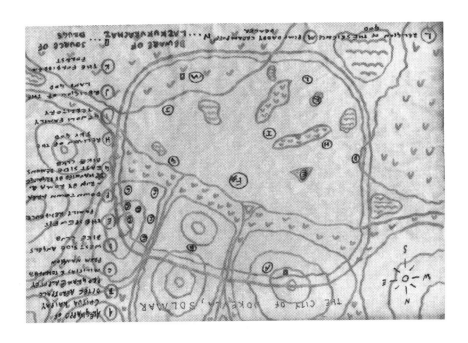

P. Marcelo W. Balboa

Family

P. Marcelo W. Balboa

Family

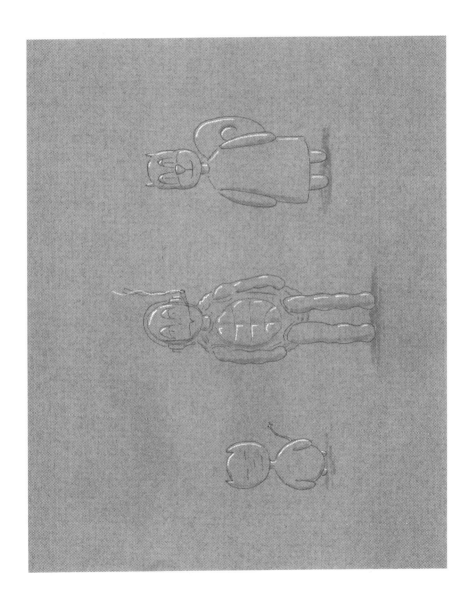

P. Marcelo W. Balboa

Family

P. Marcelo W. Balboa

Family

Family

Family

Family

Klark And Kimberly

Klark was a naive boy. Even as a seventeen-year-old, he had the mind of an elementary school student. Destined to be a child man, he lived sheltered by hard working parents. Anything he desired he could get with a hissy fit or two. "Mom, can we get the new stuffed burger at McDooglebee?" He asked. "Are you talking about that fake meat stuff that was on the television ad?" She responded. "Please Mommy… Pleeeease." He said. "No baby. We don't need that kind of food." She answered. "This isn't fair. I'm going to commit a crime so I can go to jail. At least they have burgers there." He cried. "Really? My goodness that was so unnecessary and drastic." She reacted as she placed her right arm over her breast.

It was a valiant effort that resulted in a quick visit to that restaurant in order to get the burger that day. But it wasn't a walk in the park. Klark had a shady neighbor who couldn't handle him having anything better than her child. Lina was a cruel woman who happened to be a nurse at the hospital Klark visited consistently due to his random seizures. It was there where Klark's mother and she became friends, sharing their parenting techniques and adventures as mothers. It was also were jealousy and envy grew over the toys and pampering Klark received. Lina hated Klark as she saw her son as more deserving, but she was to selfish to buy him the same things.

"When you visit, take whatever you want. That little hoodlum doesn't deserve those toys if he doesn't even know they're gone." She never missed a chance to recite these words whenever Klark would invite her son over. Growing up was confusing for Klark as his mother was a submissive person while his father was a military man. He saw the great war of the fallen guardians. He lost many friends and loved ones. It was the main reason his father consumed unhealthy amounts of alcohol. Where his mother would give in, his father wouldn't hold back. The 'Woopins', as his father would call them, were brutal.

The tears tore his mother apart almost always inspiring her to get him what he wanted to sooth his pain. And when his toys went missing he would get in more trouble. "Do you know what we paid for those things?" His father would yell. "Answer me." He would scream. Klark learned any answer was wrong, as it was another reason to get a beating. So he would just stay quiet, tighten up, and take it. Watching his mother watch the abuse and do nothing would make him frustrated with her. 'Not doing something bad and letting it happen is just as bad as doing something bad.' He taught himself.

In relation to his unhealthy relationship with his father, he tended to mirror the rage of his father with his mother. Klark tended to act this way when his father was at work or not around, of course. This manifested into the man he became. His choice in females had no foundation to build from creating an easy hole for toxic relationships. Frika was the answer to his antisocial tendencies. She was strong and forward with an uncanny ability to ignore shame. The beginning was great until the crazy in her revealed itself. He was no walk in the park himself. His inability to express himself in tense moments mixed with his anger management problems were the ingredients that fit perfect with Frika's insecure, antagonistic, scarred personality.

The breakup was smooth, but the aftermath was heart breaking. The child within Frika was wanted but it was destined to be born without unity from its creators. Klark was more to blame. He chose to go on his own rather than work on the toxic relationship and the rough relationship with his in-laws. Frika thought he wouldn't leave since she was pregnant. Seeing him leave her without an afterthought hurt her. And that fury turned to rage. She accused him of assault and put a restraining order on him to keep him from being present at their child's birth. He was more than happy to pay child support but never saw his child in the early years since Frika left the state.

"You know, you're just like your father." These were the last words she said to him as he left. His father left his family. The cycle continued and it killed him to know what it felt like. His daughter was out there somewhere, and he wasn't there to raise, teach, or protect her. He knew her name was Lealosa but he had no idea what she looked like. He never heard her voice. He dreamed of a child that had to grow up trying to figure out the world without the guidance needed. Then the phone call of his life came. "Hi." A beautiful little lady's voice spoke. "Hello. Um… Who is this?" He asked half

Family

in hope and half in disbelief. "I'm your daughter." She said. "Lealosa?" He asked. "Yes. How are you?" She asked.

Klark's mind was blown. "I'm great. Great. Uh… How have you been? How are you? You sound so mature." He said. She giggled. "You sound nervous Dad." She said. Chills ran down his spine. 'Dad!?!' He thought. "I am. I never thought we would ever meet let alone talk." He said. "Yeah, me to. I'll be honest, this was my mom's choice. She told me I had to call you." She said. Klark's heart dropped. Reality set in. "I understand. Kind of. I'm pretty sure your mom doesn't like me." He said. "She doesn't want me to say why but she is making me call you. To tell you the truth, I think you're a dead beat, so I don't really think we need to talk. Ow… Why'd you hit me? I'm talking to him aren't I?" She said.

"Who hit you?" Klark asked. "My mom. Here, she wants to talk to you." Lealosa said. The phone made noises that sounded like smothering and talking. "Hello?" Frika spoke. "Hello. Long time." He responded. "Yeah, it has been. Are you doing well?" She asked. "What is this all about? All of a sudden. You lie about me, keep me away from my daughter, and now she is forced to … she doesn't even… I'm done." He said. He was going to hang up, but Frika yelled out, "I HAVE CANCER KLARK." Klark stopped in motion. "You could have let me see my daughter a long time ago. I know I messed up, but you weren't perfect either. Now the guilt trip. Come on Frika." He said.

She began crying. Lealosa grabbed the phone. "Look you ass. My mom is a butt head, but she is still human. She wants us to try to connect before she dies because she feels bad for keeping me away. But you need to think about why someone would do that. Jerk." Lealosa said. "She cheated on me and her family threatened me every time we visited. I didn't even know you were mine until the blood test. Remember there are two sides to every story big mouth. Call me when you want to call if you want to talk to me." He said before he hung up. Regret set in but it was too late. The call was anonymous, and he didn't know how to make contact with them again since he didn't ask where they lived now.

"Idiot." He yelled at himself. For days, he struggled to sleep. He called in to work enough that he was placed on probation. He looked like crap daily. In the middle of the night a knock at the door turned into a bang. Klark was drunk and hungover all in one. He didn't even hear Lealosa walk into his room. "Hey. Wake up." She yelled. When that didn't work she pushed him several times. In frustration she kicked him. Nothing. "Grrr." She grunted. "What a loser." She said. Hours passed. Morning came. Klark woke up in pain. "OW." He yelped as the pain from the kick to his back computed in his brain. He walked to the restroom and let the water fall loose.

"That's so gross." Lealosa yelled out. Klark staggered and sprayed all over the kitchen floor. "What the…" He said as his feet slipped around. "It's the kitchen you sicko. You're really that messed up that you couldn't tell you're pissing in the sink?" She asked. "I leave the lid up… Wait… What the heck are you doing in my house? How did you find me? Wait. Where's your mom?" He rushed in speech as he washed his hands in the sink. "She dropped me off and left. So be a dad. I'm hungry." She answered. "There's food in the fridge." He answered. "There's two ketchup packets and a hotdog half eaten. Eww." She said. "Damn, I forgot to finish that. Right. You're right. I need to get some food. Can you heat up my hotdog while I get ready?" He asked. "As if! You're the dad. Heat it up yourself. I'm hungry. Feed me, DAD!!!" She said.

Klark rushed to get some clothes on. "Let's go mouthy. We need to take you to your momma." He said as he walked out the door. "No way. I'm not getting into anything with you STINKY." She responded with an attitude. "This is too much already. I'm done with you. Just wait in the car and I'll be back." He said. She followed him back into the house and sat on his couch. "Where's your remote? There's nothing but trash all over the place. How do you live like this?" She asked. "Grrrrr." He grunted. "I'm done. You need to go yesterday." He said as he prepared a quick shower.

Lealosa fell asleep on the sofa in the living room. Klark rushed to get dressed then grabbed his keys. "Hey! Naw, no way dude. Get up. I'm not doing this. Hey!" Klark said. Lealosa pretended to be knocked out. "Come on dude. This isn't right. You call me, act like a spoiled punk then show up at my door… IN MY HOUSE. Wake up girl." He said with a desperate tone. Klark took some pain medication and went back to bed. "You've got to be kidding me dude. NOT cool. Totally NOT cool." He said. Within seconds his sleep apnea kicked in. Lealosa could hardly sleep with all his choking and near-death experiences. She looked for the controller under all the boxes of eaten food and found it.

"Eww, g-Row-ssss!" She exclaimed. The whole house was what a single lazy guy's house would look like. Underwear and food in places that, to the

Family

naked eye, look misplaced but to the bachelor everything is where he meant it to be. Lealosa wasn't having it. She started cleaning the living room up. She found his vacuum and started doing chores. He was gone. The vacuum only altered his dreams, but he didn't wake up for hours. By the time he opened his eyes the living room and kitchen were ready for an open house. He sat up from a horrible dream his baby's mamma dropped their kid off at his house out of nowhere and she became a zombie trying to suck his blood with an ant eater face that sounded like a vacuum.

The faint sound of his television made his dream feel as if it was still going on. "Shit." He said, slapping his forehead. "Oh, damn. That hurt." He whimpered as he fell back onto his bed. As he stared at his ceiling fan spinning, he listened. Lealosa was watching 'Stupidness', a show about videos showing people making stupid decisions and failing in funny ways. He sat up and walked to the living room. She ignored him, laughing and making comments at the stupid people before they did stupid things. He smiled, agreeing with her. Even though he wasn't happy she was there, mind you. "Oh come on. You can't be that stupid. The bull is literally scraping at the ground. Why would you taunt it?" She asked. Klark laughed as the stupid guy took a horn in the butt. "Oh, ouch. That's gonna hurt in the morning." He said.

Lealosa wasn't impressed. "I'm still hungry." She said. Klark slowly got up. "Come on. Let's get some fast food." He said. "Really?" She asked. "You said you're hungry. Don't make me repeat myself. I'll just take you home empty..." He started. "Let's go. I got shot gun." She said. He stared at her confused as she passed him intent on that seat. "There's no one else. What are you talking about?" He asked. She hopped into his car. She wasn't happy about it though. There was junk all over the place. And there was an odor of sweaty man in there. He opened his door and she faked puking. "Dude, what the hell? What's your problem?" He asked.

She looked at him as if he should know exactly what the issue was. "Whatever." She said. He pulled out of his driveway quickly. "This is getting really old." He said to himself but loud enough for her to hear. "Real old." She responded. "What's your issue? I never did anything to you. I don't even know you." He said. "That's what a dead-beat dad would say." She answered. "Dead beat... Dead beat dad? Really? Look, Ms. Wet behind the ears. I tried. Your mother was something else. And her family was always threatening me because she made them think I took her 'Flower.' I had a choice to live as their bitch or say goodbye and find a new life." He explained. "So you ran out on my mom and me. Thanks DAD!" She interrupted.

"Yeah. I was young and stupid and made some mistakes." He said. "So now I'm a mistake?" She accused. "Whoa dude! Chill the fuck out. What I'm saying is I made decisions I would have made different but that's the life I lived. I can't go back all I can do is learn from every decision. I have hated not being in your life but if I was and stayed you would have had a bitch of a father." He said. "Better a bitch that a missing lazy smelly ungrateful stranger." She responded, crossing her arms, and looking out the window. "I'm sorry I left. I'm sorry you had to grow up without a father." He said. "Oh I had a father figure. Grandpa was there when no one was. And he..." She began but teared up.

Klark pulled into the fast-food restaurant drive through. "Welcome to Bizzy Burger Buns. Would you like our grilled cheese sausage burger?" A voice said from a worn-down intercom. "Sure. And I'll take two large Loopty Juices and a delight meal." He said. "Really? I'm not a child. I'm a teenager. I don't want the delight meal." She said. He pulled up to pay. "You're thirteen. I have ball hairs older than you." He said. "Guh-Row-ssss!" She said. He looked at her and laughed. "What's with all that?" He asked. "What?" She said with a smirk. "That accent with all that gross stuff. Where did you get that shit from?" He asked, pulling up to receive his food.

"I don't know. It's what I say. Some stuff is 'Ug'. Some stuff is 'Ew'. Some stuff is 'Whatever'. And you're 'Guh-Row-sss'." She said. "Whatever your whatever. You don't smell too good yourself." He said as he pinched his nose. She pushed him laughing. "As if. You stink so bad skunks pinch their nose." She responded. "Oh really? Well you're so annoying I'd dreamed of having a drop of water dripped on my head, starving in a concentration camp and I was relieved because I thought you were the nightmare." He said. She sat back. "Whatever." She said. He noticed that was too much. "I'm sorry. I was just playing." He said. "No you weren't. It's probably why you left me." She said to herself but loud enough for him to hear.

The drive through staff gave Klark the food he ordered. "Thank you." He told the staff. "Here you go." He told Lealosa. "I said I didn't want a D'light meal." She said. "The D'light meal is for me. I'm collecting the Star Battle set. Lord Diki is the next toy." He said. Searching for the toy, he finds his treasure. "Here we go." He joyfully voices to her. She looks at him in part embarrassment and part annoyance. Yet a smirk breaks through her sassy demeanor. "You think I'm a fool, I'll show you a fool." He said in his best attempt to re-enact the epic line from Lord Diki in Star Battle 4. Lealosa stared at her father, or little brother, and raised an eyebrow.

"You're stupid." She laughed. "You think I'm stupid, I'll show you stupid." He responded. She curled up as he tried to tickle her with his new toy. "Come on dude. This is the best. Lord Diki, the great villain of Star Battle. You can't tell me you aren't into kid stuff. You're thirteen. THIRTEEN." He said with childlike happiness. Her expression changed. There was history in her eyes he could see was serious enough to let the issue go. He put his toy back into the D'light meal case and continued on. "Where is your mom? Did she stay at your grandmas?" He asked. She didn't answer. "Lealosa? You're mom dropped you off and went where?" He asked. She took a bite of her delicious burger and looked out her window. "Lealosa, I'm trying here. I'm sorry. I see you have a lot on your mind and there is stuff I don't know about that's troubling you, but this silent treatment is... Just tell me where your mom is." He said.

"Why are you so ready to get rid of me? I'm here. Mom wanted us to get to know each other. So why are you trying to throw me away again?" She asked. Klark exhaled. "Look. I'm sorry. I know... I'm just not ready to be the dad you need. I'm in a bad spot right now in my life. You won't find anything in me you will want to know." He admitted. "How do you know? Maybe I just want... Maybe I needed a dad." She said. "I get it. I don't even know my real father and my stepdad wasn't great. He was short-tempered, distant, and mean but I was never in need of anything. I get I failed you. But whatever you might think you can get from me at this point is not enough. I'm sure of it." He said.

Lealosa looked at her father in disgust. "You don't know anything about me. Who are you to judge what I need. I needed you a long time ago. Where were you? I had to endure... Ugg!" She said then turned away. She looked at her burger and picked up the packet of mustard. "I forgot to put this on my burger." She said as she fondled with it. Klark noticed as he tried to pay attention to the road. "Don't." He said. "What?" She asked, jiggling the packet up and down. "Lealosa, I'm warning you." He warned... technically. "Dad, I'm just thinking if I should put my mustard in my burger. What's your issue?" She asked. "Alright. Try me. I'm telling you I'm not the one." He said. She began to giggle.

The sky began to turn dark red. They didn't notice at the moment as the sky in front of them looked normal. Lealosa threw her packet right at her father's face. Smack! He almost instinctively poured his freezing cold drink on his unsuspecting daughter. "Oh my God!" She gasped. Her breathing was intense. Every bit of her father's drink spilled onto her. "I freakin' told you I'm not the one." He laughed. She panted, "So…Worth…It…" She said. He laughed louder at her reaction. She laughed too. She needed the release. Both of them did. However, the moment was short lived as a piece of burning coal crashed a few yards in front of them. Two vehicles crashed. Klark pulled over as other vehicles began to lose control.

"What is that?" Lealosa asked. "I don't know. Get in the car. We need to get to your mother. Where is she?" He asked. Lealosa didn't answer. "I'm not playing right now. We need to get you to your mother." He insisted. "Those damn Guardians are probably…" He said to himself. "What way do I need to go?" He asked Lealosa. She didn't answer. The sky turned completely dark and lit up red and orange around light yellow bolts of lightning. "Fuck it. I'm taking you to your grandma's." He said. He drove through crashing vehicles, falling debris, and panicking citizens looking for answers. "Why do we have to go to grandmas? She doesn't even like you." Lealosa asked. "I'm not in the mood Lealosa. Just shut up. I need to think." He demanded. "Whatever jerk." She responded.

Another vehicle crashed into the back of his car sending them into an uncontrollable spin. Lealosa wasn't wearing her seatbelt and shot out of the car into some bushes. The car rolled and barely missed crushing her, but her right shoulder slammed into the root of the bush, dislocating her arm. "Ahhhh!" She cried out. Klark was bleeding from his forehead and the steering wheel pinned his right leg down. The sound of Lealosa screaming woke him up. Being partly drunk made his body roll with the vehicle. A slight kink in the neck was popped away with a turn of his head. Crack! "Damn. What the hell is going on?" He asked. Lealosa's scream drew his attention.

He noticed his leg was stuck but not broken. Her screams lit a fire in him. "I'm coming sweetie." He yelled. "Dad, my arm. Owww! Help me." She yelled out to him. Klark found something inside him that motivated him

Family

to push, pull and whatever else until the wheel loosened enough for him to exit his car. The glass was everywhere, cutting him as he slid out through the roof. His car was drilled into a food mart wall, upside down and on fire. He limped to Lealosa. "Dad, please. Owwww! My arm, it's broken." She yelled as he ran to her. "I'm coming sweetie." He yelled out to her. A flame tore through the sky. Klark dove at his daughter. He could see she was all right for the most part.

"I need you to trust me." He said. "What? No way... OWWWW!" She said. He popped her shoulder back into the socket. "Shhhhh! There's a fucking dragon spitting flames." He whispered. "What are you..." Just as she began to speak, a large dragon flew over their position. Hidden in the bushes, she could see it, but it couldn't see her. Her expression went from disappointment in her father to awe at the sight of this gigantic flying monster. "See?" He whispered. Both stayed silent for a minute. "I hate my name. What would you have named me?" She whispered. "What? Are you serious?" He whispered. "Yeah. If you were there when I was born, what would you have named me?" She whispered. He paused in thought.

"Lealosa is a cool name, but Kimberly is my mother's name. I would have named you after her. You would have loved to meet her." He said. "What happened to her?" She asked. "My parents passed away hugging each other. My father was already on his last days and my mother couldn't live without him. They just left." He said with wet eyes. "That's beautiful. Kimberly. Not bad." She said. Klark looked around and saw the dragon was far away. "Hurry, we need to move. This place is getting bad. We need to get to your grandma's as fast as possible. I have a buddy close by. We can borrow his ride. He owes me big time." Klark said. Lealosa followed him instinctively.

The neighborhood was sketchy, but Klark knew the right streets to pass through. With all the damage the dragon caused the two didn't notice there were warlocks on foot and witches flying along with more dragons. Terrifying displays of dark magic filled the land and sky on their way to Klark's childhood friend. An old rival noticed Klark and called to his crew. They ran out and called Klark. "Hey weeso, remember me?" The rival yelled. Klark turned back. "Oh shit. Run." He said. "Run? Why?" Lealosa asked. Klark yanked her left arm, almost pulling it out of socket again. "OW! Stop. You're hurting me." She yelled. A gun fired. The whistle of the bullet changed Lealosa's response. Suddenly she was running faster than her father.

"Why are they shooting at us dad?" She asked. They turned the corner to the right at the end of the block. "Run back there, behind the house." He said. "What? I'm not leaving you." She responded. "You're going to run and hide, let me take care of these guys. Please. Just do what I say." He said. She listened. As the three men turned the corner in pursuit of Klark, they lost him. "What the hell way? Where is he?" The leader looked around confused. A witch flew down and snatched one of the three. Klark ran from their blind side and elbowed the weaker of the two who remained. He remembered them. They were brothers and his friend was getting bullied by them. He was older than them and bigger, so he had an edge. Now they were bigger. Well, bigger as in compared to when they were children. Klark was still a little bigger.

As the elbow chopped into an unsuspecting neck, knocking out the youngest brother, the oldest had time to turn in Klark's direction. "You fuckin' cheap shot motherfucker." The older brother reacted. Klark faked going low to tackle his rival, causing his rival to drop his guard. Klark threw a perfect overhand right at an unsuspecting chin. The one's you don't see get you the worst. Lealosa watched in shock. Her father was a beast. Klark searched the unconscious brothers and found a switchblade, butterfly knife, and a revolver. "One bullet short but five deep, ready to go. I like it." He said. He looked up at his daughter who was watching him like a deer in front of headlights.

"Get over here." He said. She ran to him. He handed her the switchblade. "If something comes at you, trust it's to kill you. Stick the tip of this into its eye, stomach, or groin. Do you understand?" He said as he pointed at those exact spots on his body. Lealosa was thirteen mind you. Her mind wasn't ready to grasp puberty let alone the end of days. "Hey, wake up. Do you understand?" He asked again. She snapped out enough to hear him. "Uh, yes. Yes, I'm... I understand." She responded. "Good. Follow me." He said. They made their way more cautiously in route to his friend's house. By the time they arrived, the neighborhood was in shambles. People were loading their vehicles or driving away while they were alive to do it.

Klark ran into his friend's house. "Chris. Chris, you home?" He yelled. A warlock shot bolts of black flame at neighbors a few blocks away. "Chris." Klark yelled again. He searched upstairs and found every room empty, cleared out, or in shambles. "I'm exhausted dad. Can't we rest?" Lealosa asked. "Are you serious? No. Didn't you see...? Look. Go to the kitchen, see what you can find." He responded with a short temper. "I see what your dad was like." She said. "Get the fuck out of here with that shit already Kimberly. Lealosa. Not right now, OK? Just go to the kitchen and don't make too much noise. We don't know what the hell is going on and we may have to defend ourselves." He said.

He continued to search the first floor as she went to the kitchen. She dropped the jar of cookies causing a huge crash. The Warlock ran into the house and began shooting flames at everything. She hid under the kitchen sink and closed the cabinet doors. Klark ran out with his friends automatic rifle. He barely dodged an incoming fireball. He aimed between the Warlocks eyes and pulled the trigger. The chrome-plated revolver sporting a wood grain handle burst forth a .357 round from its four-inch barrel. The bullet was firm, penetrating the Warlocks seemingly unbreakable skin. In a state of disbelief, the Warlock tried to scream. Mid scream, he fell. "Lealosa? Lealosa, are you OK?" He called out. She ran out of the kitchen. "I'm fine dad. I'm sorry. I just wanted something sweet. That burger... I only had a bite." She said.

They walked to the kitchen and sorted items that were good for travel. Klark ran upstairs to his friend's room and grabbed his camping bag still in the closet. He ran to the sister's room and emptied out her backpack. "Here, put whatever you can in this." He said. She looked at it and instantly knew. "I'm thirteen, not eight. What's with the flowers?" She asked. "Lealosa, just... I'll be back. Don't make any more noise." He answered. She gave in with a little attitude to boot. He paused, handed her the revolver, and ran to the restroom. He grabbed some medical and sanitary items from his friend's mom's restroom. She was a single mother but took good care of her kids. As a nurse for twenty-three years, there were plenty of supplies around the house.

When he returned to Lealosa, she was enjoying a sandwich with the revolver set on the ground beside her. Her attention was focused on the sky and her ears were slowly becoming traumatized by the screams and destruction caused by the evil beings. "Hey, you good?" He asked, touching her left shoulder. Startled she swung her switchblade. "FUCK!" He yelled. The tip of the blade went across his face, slicing a clean line across his face. Superficial but enough to put Lealosa in a panic. "Oh my God! Oh my God! I'm so sorry. I didn't mean to. Oh my God!" She repeated. "Don't leave the gun just laying around. We could have to run, and you might leave it on accident." He said as he pulled out an alcohol wipe. "Sorry. I never used a gun before. I don't know what to do with it." She said. He put some ointment on. "Can you put the bandage on my cut?" He asked. She did as he asked. "There we go. Good as new." She said. "Good. Now… Let's get to your grandma's." He said. He walked to the front door where the keys to his friend's mom's truck were at then went to the garage.

The driveway door opened slowly, revealing a world that was not the world they last saw. He drove out quickly to avoid the burnt humanoids now victim to the black flames and fire spit from the throats of dragons now filling the sky. "Daddy, I'm scared." Lealosa said. Her unfamiliar gentle, fragile voice woke up something deep inside Klark. He knew right there everything and anything was going to die if it messed with his daughter. Lealosa was scared but not like before. She had seen enough to know inherently that her father was there. Something was different. Still, her body shivered. Death spilled into their view from every corner. Klark had little issue driving through the rubble with little to no life controlling the vehicles in flames, ripped apart, or in positions they were never built to be in.

"Why is this happening Dad?" She asked. Her voice, her spirit. All of her daughterly instincts kicked in. "Something we won't learn for some time. I can say that much. This isn't supposed to be real. Last time crap like this happened the Guardians of our planet turned on us. All I know is we need to get you to your grandmas." He said. "Why? Why do we need to go?" She asked in tears. He looked at her. The question wasn't in the same tone as before. He couldn't help but take a moment to correct himself. A moment of irritability stalled at the sight of a daughter he had never met before. "I… I don't know sweetie. I'm not sure what I want. I don't know what to say. I have no manual to help me here." He said. "Mom's dead." Lealosa said.

A dragon spotted the moving vehicle and darted at it. Flames spouted from its mouth at full throttle. The vehicle flipped and landed on top of a vehicle repair shop. The roof was weak from the damage already applied to it, caving in almost seconds after they landed. The vehicle fell onto one of the high shelves then slid between them. There was enough friction to slow the landing but little time to react. The dragon tore into the roof dramatically. Klark released himself then cut Lealosa's seat belt to free her. "Follow me. Stay low. Stay quiet. Stab anything that grabs you. Got it?" He whispered.

Family

She nodded yes. Any lack of trust in him was gone. They escaped the vehicle moments before the dragon reached for it with its mouth. Its bright red orange scales complimented its bright red orange flaming mouth. With a single separation of its arms, the vehicle was torn in half.

Lealosa looked back for a second to see the dragon torch the inside of the vehicle. The fire breath lasted long enough to incinerate anything inside. What was just a few seconds, felt like an eternity from Lealosa's perspective. "Come on. Get your head right." Klark said. Lealosa turned to him and followed. They ran out the back door cautiously. With nothing in view that looked like it would try to kill them, they ran to the next store beside the repair shop. A fast stop market with little supplies left served a party of two quite nicely. Klark grabbed two backpacks from the apparel section then grabbed all the essentials. Fire, food, fighting, and fixing items. Lealosa copied her father. When he was done, she was done. When he moved, she moved. They found a place in the back to lock themselves in to eat, rest, and recover.

By morning, the sounds had gone further away. They used the restroom, cleaned up then headed out the front door. The sky was still dark. The dragons and witches could be seen flying in the distance. Flames were still bright, but many areas were spewing black smoke. Burnt flesh rained ever so lightly. The smell was not like a cookout. There was a sweet, iron smell to the air. "What is that smell?" Lealosa asked. "You don't want to know." He responded. "Why?" She asked. "Let's keep moving. We should be able to get to your grandma's within a few hours if we don't stop." He said. She didn't follow him. He looked back. "What?" He asked. "Why?" She asked. He threw a tantrum, looking up at the sky while placing his hands on his waste. "Do you have to be difficult every moment of every day? This is ridiculous." He said. "Why do we have to go to my grandma's? I want to stay with you." She said.

He looked at her, intrigued by the idea but intimidated by the responsibility. "What do you want from me?" He asked. "To be a dad. You're my fucking dad. Just be my dad." She yelled. He looked around for danger. "What is all this? You tell me your forced to talk to me. Then you tell me you got dumped on me. Then you tell me your moms dead. Now you don't want to go to your grandma after bashing me as a father. Not to mention tearing my living choices down. What is all this? I'm doing you a favor." He said.

"No. You're doing you a favor. I ran from my mom. She said she was going to give me to my grandparents. My grandpa molested me. When I told my mom she took his side. My grandma knew and even though she was upset she didn't do anything." She cried. "I'm…" He began. "And where were you? Safe in your fucking big house. Plenty of space for me. You could have looked for me. Tried. Something." She interrupted.

"I didn't even know where…" He tried to respond. "Oh whatever. Look at all you've done to get me to my grandma's. Look at you. We've faced death multiple times. You protected me. Guided us. Look around us. Everything is dead. But not us… Why couldn't you come get me? I needed you to protect me like this years ago. All these monsters are nothing compared to the monsters that exist inside humans. People are the real monsters. You should have been there to…" She cried. He walked up to her and hugged her. She cried more. Deep down inside her soul a heart-wrenching cry took over. Klark cried too.

He knew the feeling of needing his parents at the most trying stage of his life. The world was broken after the second fall of the Guardians. His parents passed away together but it was because of the weak structure of the building they were living in. He snuck out with his friends to get high when the building caved in. When he returned home there were ambulances and police surrounding the wreckage. He would find out later his parents were under rubble hugging each other. They passed in their sleep. He had shut down then started drinking. Frika entered his life at the wrong time. He left her and his job to start over in another city. Soon enough he found himself homeless then jailed for missing child support. After spending enough time in jail and being released early due to good behavior, he sought out to do right. He started small with part time jobs then got a break with a construction company. Soon he was able to build good credit, find a home and buy a car. Not the best but he was happy with what God let him earn.

Nevertheless, he always felt bad about his daughter. He focused on paying back his missed child support and just as he paid it off, Frika pushed the courts to require him to pay higher monthly payments. He never felt upset because he never regretted making a life. Now here she was in his arms. "I'll go wherever you go daddy. Just please let me stay." She cried. "I got you Lealosa. And I'll never let you go. Let's find a place to crash out then head home." He said softly. "Kimberly. Call me Kimberly." She responded.

My Mother's Our Father

Grandma: Be careful my babies. I don't want you to get hurt.

Joseph: Yes Ma... ((Wack!))

Kevin: For Sparta!

Grandma: Alright my babies, are you ready for a sweet dream story?

Larissa: Oh yes, please!

Kevin: Rrrahhh!

Joseph: I want to Gwa... ((Wack!))

Grandma: Well you need to calm down first silly goose.

Kevin: WINNER!

Grandma: Great! Now I need all of you to lay down.

Joseph: I'm alweady down.

Grandma: Oh my, I see.

Kevin: Did you see me win?

Grandma: Yes, it appears you did. But if you want to hear my story, you need to lay down.

Larissa: Oh yes, lay down. I'm on it.

Grandma: You sure did my darling angel.

Family

Joseph: I got it! Kevin, get over here!

Kevin: Tiiiimbeerrrrrrr!

Larissa: Ok, I'm ready.

Grandma: Good girl. But I need everyone to lay down for this story.

Kevin: D-Did you see how high I flew?

Joseph: Did you see me win too Gwandma?

Grandma: Wow, my strong babies are warriors. Are my little warriors ready for a sweet dream story now?

P. Marcelo W. Balboa

Grandma: Oh my! What an entertaining evening, right?

All the Children: Yes mam!

Grandma: Well done! Now my story isn't a story but a history of sorts. One that spans the time of all that has been created.

Kevin: By wh-who?

Joseph: Go with the flow bro.

Kevin: Right. S-Sorry?

Grandma: That's alright. As I was saying. Long ago there was nothing but Adonai. And for the curious minds in attendance, that means the one and only.

Family

Grandma: Now relax your minds my babies. See yourself falling into a deep sleep as you go on this sweet dream.

Joseph: Off to sweet dweams.

Larissa: I love this part.

Kevin: I d-don't. It makes me dizzy.

P. Marcelo W. Balboa

Grandma: For the physical, astral, and metaphysical realms are being formed by Nuwa, the creator of all creators.

Larissa: Oh, that is such a beautiful name.

Grandma: Yes my dear. She is a beautiful sparkle in the endless darkness.

Joseph: Dawkness is spooky.

Kevin: But think of all the alien adventures J-Joseph.

Grandma: Spooky Adventures are a guarantee. In the darkness, Nuwa made magical things happen. 'POOF', there were things that made light, so we could see the things that could never be seen.

Family

Grandma: There were planets of all types that were revealed. And countless landscapes possessed breath taking views.

Joseph: Like mountains?

Larissa: And Clouds?

Kevin: A-And oceans?

Grandma: Why yes, of course! And many more planets like ours. Extending farther than our eyes can see.

All the Children: WHOA!

P. Marcelo W. Balboa

Larissa: So there are all kinds of homes for cute kitties right?

Grandma: Yes, kitties and puppies and so many more life forms.

Kevin: C-Can there be birds t-too?

Grandma: Definitely.

Joseph: And fish to swim in the oceans?

Grandma: You know it. There are so many life forms our planet is only a few of the variety created. There could be as many as the stars we see at night.

All the children: WHOA!

Kevin: You mean there are other types of people?

Grandma: Humans, birds, fish, kitties, you name it. In the endless void that carries the stars called the Abyss, there are other types of everything.

Joseph: Gwandma, do othew Joseph's exit?

Grandma: Oh my darling. Do you mean exist?

Kevin: We are t-twins. I AM the other y-you.

Everyone together: Hahahahaha!

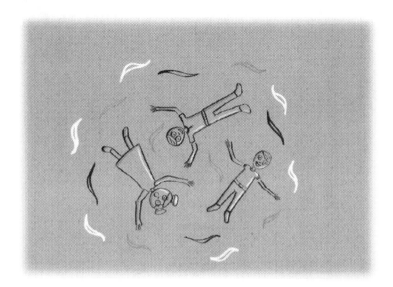

Grandma: Yes, you do look alike, but you are not the same. And that is why you must be thankful. You are the only you that has ever been or ever will be. And in this existence, there is so much to be thankful for let alone being blessed to experience it all.

Larissa: I love being created.

Joseph: Me too.

Kevin: M-me four.

Grandma: Oh dear, where's the third one, hahaha!

Grandma: Alright, it's time to float away into your sweet dreams.

Larissa: Before we go off into our magical dream world, can we give thanks to the one who made everything?

Grandma: Of course. Our Father…

Everyone: Who art in heaven, hallowed be thy name. Thy Kingdom come; thy will be done. On earth, as it is in heaven. Give us this day our daily bread and forgive us our transgressions. As we forgive those who transgress against us. Lead us not into temptation and deliver us from evil.

Grandma: Amen.

All the children: Amen.

Shadow War

An epic battle for the Kingdom in Shadow

The Prince of Darkness was a beautiful angel at one time. He walked with the one before all as a son walks with his father. Yet in all his beautiful spender he could not remain content. He saw himself as a valuable being who deserved the worship his father received. In his arrogance, he sought to talk to other angels. It was a matter of time but soon he found a number of angels that agreed with his beliefs. He took his beliefs to the one before all. This didn't sit well with his peers. Theories evolved into disagreements. Disagreements turned into arguments. Arguments broke up the angels into separate factions with various ideals. This friction gave rise to other angels who thought themselves as equal if not greater than the one before all.

Angels that stood loyal to the one before all were in greater numbers than the broken factions were. Moreover, in comparison to the rest, among the most loyal were the most powerful and wise of all the angels. An uprising would lead to war. A war for the future. When the selfish and arrogant angels stood against the loyal angels, they were banished from their place on high as the aftermath of their defeat unfolded. These rejects tried to find some resemblance of the life once lived in the Astral Realm, but most fell into the dark abyss that became known as Shadow Dimension. Many went to great lengths to destroy their existence, creating areas in shadow that were poison to anyone's spirit who entered. All having their own effect on any poor soul that ventured too far in the Astral Realm.

Of those angels that fell, some found a way to enter the Physical Realm while others found a way to haunt the Physical Realm. Of the angels that chose to regain some copy of the life they once lived, five territories were established. The Kingdom of the Prince of Darkness became the most powerful. His rivals were Karlo, the fallen guardian of the damned, Whoe, the mother of the rotten, Ku, the scorched being, Lump, he who starves, and Shoog, the boiled blob. Each of these fallen angels lost their beauty. They were especially offended that the Prince of Darkness kept his beauty. After complaining more than anyone, he sat back and watched everyone else fight. It didn't sit well with the fallen angels. But they were weaker than him at the time. Still not as strong, they devised a plan to take the Prince of Darkness down all at once. They waited for the right moment. Due to the acts of two unlikely heroes named Tec and Nieka, these fallen knew their time had come. They grew weaker with the fall of Karlo at the hands of the Forgotten, giving them more incentive to attack sooner rather than later.

Any one of the four remaining armies attacking the Kingdom in Shadow will cause a cataclysmic effect that will catapult the Astral Realm into self-destruction should they win. These fallen angels are ruthless and set on destroying far more than just the Kingdom in Shadow. The Prince of Darkness isn't the best choice but if Tec and Nieka are successful, the path of Shadow will be altered for the better for all who enter. But they need protection as they enter the Kingdom in Shadow to rescue a damsel in distress and face the Prince of Darkness head on. A great traveler of the Astral Realm, Ike, is aware of this and calls on the forces of light to aid him in assembling an army worthy of defending the Kingdom in Shadow.

The Shadow Dimension aka 'Warzone'

Let the game begin.

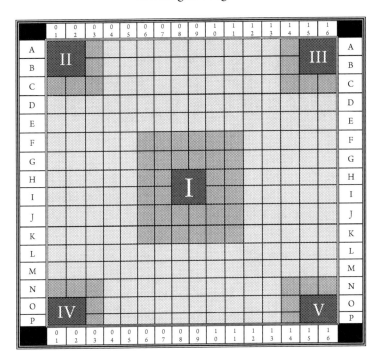

Ike is fighting for a better future. Every other army has an agenda that could spell doom for the Kingdom in Shadow and the Shadow Dimension. (I) is the Kingdom of Shadow the great traveler, Ike, is set to defend. (II) is the Army of the Torched Souls. (III) is the Army of the Boiled Souls. (IV) is the Army of the Starved Souls. (V) is the Army of the Rotten Souls.

P. Marcelo W. Balboa

The Art of 'Warzone'

- The map is set for five players, but 2 to 4 players can play.
- Each player starts with one army on their respective head quarter, (HQ), located in areas I through IV.
- The best player always represents the center HQ.
- All other players start at any one of the HQs located at the corners of the Warzone.
- Any inactive HQ at the start is out of gameplay.
- To settle any challenges for a certain HQ, roll D20. Higher number wins.
- Rotate turns according to the HQ number.
- The entire map is accessible, but movement is limited to one of any of the eight spaces surrounding an occupied square space.
- To challenge another army, the targeted army must be in one of the eight spaces surrounding the challengers occupied square space.
- Players can only be challenged by one player at a time.
- Avoiding matches is a violation and subject to the loss of HQ protection.
- HQ protection simply means that all armies must be defeated before the player's HQ can be challenged.
- For matches to begin, one army must move into a square space that is occupied by an opposing army.
- Each chess match will result in the permanent removal of the defeated army from gameplay.
- A turn can be used to move an army around the Warzone or the create another army within HQ.

The Battlefield

8A	8B	8C	8D	8E	8F	8G	8H
7A	7B	7C	7D	7E	7F	7G	6H
6A	6B	6C	6D	6E	6F	6G	6H
5A	5B	5C	5D	5E	5F	5G	5H
4A	4B	4C	4D	4E	4F	4G	4H
3A	3B	3C	3D	3E	3F	3G	3H
2A	2B	2C	2D	2E	2F	2G	2H
1A	1B	1C	1D	1E	1F	1G	1H

The Battlefield is represented as follows; it can be on a piece of paper, cloth, napkin, or whatever platform is available. The pieces can be wood, plastic, glass, metal, or whatever is available. As long as the match itself follows the rules of chess. As a reminder:

- The limit is 15 armies in total for each player per game, with only 10 allowed to be active in the Warzone at a time.
- If a player has met their army limit and all the armies have been defeated, their HQ can be attacked. This match is best out of three.
- If an HQ is conquered, the player is eliminated, and the HQ can now be used to generate new armies for the conquering player if the player in control of multiple HQs has not met the army limit.

P. Marcelo W. Balboa

The Warriors in Conflict

(1K, 1Q, 2B, 2N, 2R, 8P)

(K) *The key piece. Capture it and the army has lost.*

(Q) *The most versatile piece. Move her diagonal, up, down, left, or right as far as the Battlefield allows. But if an opponent's piece is in the way, the Q is forced to stop just short of that position. If the option is there, the Q can take the position of the piece and the piece is captured into the opponent's war camp for the rest of the battle.*

(B) *These 2 pieces move diagonally as far as the Battlefield allows. Still, much like the Q, if any piece is in the way a decision must be made to move to (but not through) or away from that direction of the piece or take the piece.*

(N) *These 2 pieces are odd but can cover the entire Battlefield if the right positions are chosen. Move two positions up, down, left, or right then turn to move one position to the left or right in relation to the initial direction originally chosen at the start of this piece's motion.*

(R) *These 2 pieces move up, down, left, or right as far as the Battlefield allows. Still, much like the Q, if any piece is in the way a decision must be made to move to (but not through) or away from that direction or take the piece.*

(P) *The seemingly most useless piece has the numbers. With 8 lined up at the front of the army, it moves one space forward at any time. It can never move backward, left, or right but it can capture pieces if they are in a position directly diagonal to their position within one move.*

Family

Behind the Scenes

The Game Build

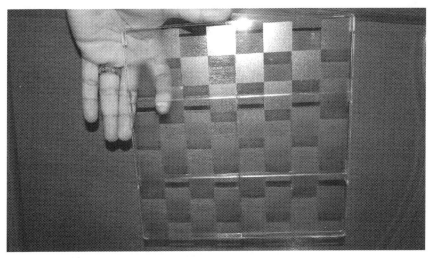

I came across some clear plastic boards that served well for the territory the pieces would be tactically moving around on.

The battlefield was easily replicated with a board game's letter tokens and a square cloth I could customize.

To engage in play I was forced to play a computer. I simulated the opponents movement by rolling a D8 to dictate what direction the army would move and a D10 to choose what army would move. As I continued to win, the dice number reduced as well. I just realized I want to call it the warzone. I'll re-edit this chapter later.

The "Warzone"

Family

Each set of chips, tokens, or whatever you want to use to represent your army, will start at the farthest corners with the main army at the direct center.

Movement is limited by the squares surrounding any particular army represented by the black or white tokens shown here. Up to ten armies per player can exist in the Warzone. If a player keeps running, any army can attack their HQ. If your skill allows it, you may not even need to generate ten armies. Up to four may be all you need.

P. Marcelo W. Balboa

When an army attacks a square occupied by another army, the token is placed atop the defending army token and the battle will commence.

Understand that an army can be surrounded and attacked repeatedly but if there is no defeat, they can maintain the occupation of the square they currently possess. This is in effect on all squares, especially the HQ square which is the starting and generation point of any army.

Family

Feel free to make or buy dice that can accommodate you in your game play. D = Dice. D20 = Dice with 20 sides.

Here's me trying some different ways to play the game.

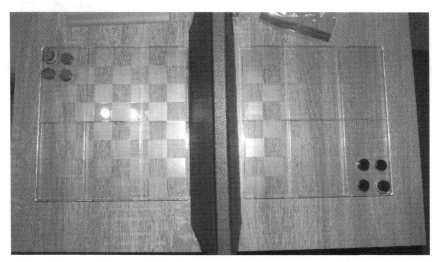

I thought it might be fun to blind the attackers, but it felt too distracting. I love chess and want to play with a little extra on the line to encourage more games.

Still, it was fun trying out other avenues of play. I would encourage anyone creating something for the fun of creation to defy limitations. We created the tools that enhance music and art. So I say, create tools that increase your experience when doing things you love.

Slug Shot

"AAAAHHHHH!" Terrible screams could be heard down a dark hallway in an abandoned hospital. The flesh of a young man had been skillfully removed. The depth was just deep enough to reveal the muscle fibers yet not so deep as to take the poor souls life. He stole money from a former drug dealer's liquor store and had to pay with his skin. Doctor Fister had performed many torture procedures for his boss and made a lot of money in the process. Although he was sick and twisted enough to love what he did to people, he would have done it free. Still, it was nice to be under the payroll of the infamous Ale Gwappo because he always received a bonus for his excellent work. Ale Gwappo was a skillful drug pusher in his early years who recently stepped away from the life to pursue less incarcerable ventures. Laundering his money through legal businesses made Ale Gwappo a very powerful man. And with such power came affiliations in the political realm that would set him up for life. It is hard to believe it took one man to stand between him and his ultimate goal to rule the world. This is that man's story.

But to get there we must go back many binary planet rotations ago...

A young girl by the name of Romanita Gabrioni, is adopted and raised by a family with tremendous pull in the city of Sheek. Many referred to them as, "THE Family." A city that fell apart in the great war of the worlds. That story is for another epic tale. This story needs the role of Roma explained. She was a very sweet girl. Blonde hair, blue eyes, and skin as white as snow. Her siblings were competitive as their family was spread within the community with deep roots in powerful positions. She wasn't a push over though. She was intelligent and learned the ways of her family. Then the great binary planet war tore the city into fragments.

The major countries involved with their sister planet's habitation program united against the military threat that came from space. The distraction left the laws of the land unmanageable. Ale Gwappo used the war to take the lands of natives in the northern mountain region. A plant grew in those lands that, when processed, created a powerful powder drug. The natives spread to lands not their own but vowed to take their land back one day. Until then, they warned the people of lands they spread to about the potential threat. No one listened. This time of unrest created territory wars across the world. The sister planet's superior military destroyed the major cities as civil war dismantled any chance of the minor countries rising to superpowers. The only surviving land, Jokevla, which was north of Sheek, was the one that sided with the sister planet before the war started. But assassinations and split factions prevented a quick recovery.

As the sister planet secured victory, Roma's planet was left in shambles. Gwappo's growing empire in the mountain region helped the 'The Family' develop a program to feed the hungry and shelter the homeless in a political effort to gain favor in Jokevla. It was a distraction to say the least. There was a dangerous biker gang before the war that split into two clubs. To the east, one club pushed prostitution and low-grade drugs for a pimp that ran the southeast called Pimp Day-day. The plant that grew in the forest area to the far east was an addictive drug that made him enough money to run the streets. The other club controlled the West where illegal guns were sold. A religious group grew through the leadership of three powerful leaders. But they too could not agree on what to do in the end of days and divided into three holy entities. Gwappo saw an opportunity and assisted one of the religious leaders. He financed the build of a grand cathedral to the northeast of Jokevla while building an affiliated convent in the snowy mountains. It was a perfect business to launder more of his money. To the dirty south was The Family's territory. They didn't interfere with the low-grade pimping to the east. Their business with the biker club to the west ensured security in the city of Sheek. These separate factions tried to respect territory boundaries as business began to improve.

To be clear, the city of Jokevla was small but flourishing before the assassinations. It was Roma who could see that there was descent in the ranks. Through her connections she made contact with Ale Gwappo. They would come to an agreement which would finance Roma's political career. One of her methods toward securing political power was to anonymously pay media to advertise propaganda that pit sides against each other. Which led to the assassinations. Once everyone was fighting, she would present herself as the solution. With Gwappo's assistance, any rivals would be kidnapped by his henchmen, 'The Lazkukurachas". Pimp Day-day paid well for those disposable bodies. It gave life to an underground human trafficking business that made him rich. The few areas that united to build strong communities would be nullified with the help of 'The Family'.

In her personal life, she fell for a married man and seduced him into leaving his family for her. When he found out about her corrupt nature, he reached out to his brother, Lando. Lando helped him build a shelter under his garage so that he could hide with his family. When his ex-wife, Brit, went missing he left his children in the shelter then went to find her. Within a day he was caught by the Lazkukurachas. Roma would have killed him, but he escaped. Next in line was Brit. She was taking chances trying to find out what Lando was talking about after he revealed what he knew. Roma caught wind of the problem and had her kidnapped too. But her fate was far worse as Gwappo found her to be pleasant and had his way with her. He refused to release her to Roma but agreed to send her away when he was done with her. He sent her to Doctor Fister then the convent in the mountains. It was a front. The nuns there were former prostitutes he recruited to hold, torture, or eliminate people. Their leader, the mother, often performed sacrifices as a practicing witch. Brit's fate was like many females caught in the human trafficking trap as she was repeatedly enjoyed by many of Gwappo's henchmen before they delivered her to the nuns. That is another matter altogether. For this story, what must be understood about Roma has been explained. Let us continue on with the story of the man who stood against the infamous Ale Gwappo.

The story officially begins in the room of a nerdy kid with dreams of comic book stardom. Just before the great binary planet war began.

"Hurry up. I haven't got all day." Mr. Bricks yelled out to his son. "I'm coming dad. Give me a second." Jon Alex responded. His costume was a year of work, ready to display to the world. The comic world, that is. The Buck City Comic Convention was under way. He saved a serious portion of his allowance to get a ticket and wasn't about to miss it. Jon Alex ran to the car while trying to put the rest of his costume on. Mighty Martial Arts

Master Brice Lane. He loved his movies and cartoons. A child at heart, Jon Alex couldn't get enough of his comic book life. And Brice Lane was born in comics. He owned four copies of Mighty Martial Arts Master Lane. And at least two copies of his first run. The actor who plays him is a guest at the convention.

Arriving at the convention was exhilarating for Jon Alex. The culture is welcoming, and anyone can be whom they choose without judgment. He had the V.I.P. Pass so no lines for him. With an hour head start to walk the grounds, he was able to get several limited-edition figures, a convention exclusive item and even a signature from a well-known actor walking the grounds as a fan herself. By the time the doors opened officially, he was ready to go eat with his cosplay friends. They sat in the open courtyard decorated for spooky ambience. Each had a great find their counterparts absolutely drooled over. After a fun get together, they walked the convention like celebrities. Kids and adults alike asked for pictures. It was a welcomed display of affection toward all their hard work making their costumes. By the end, the panels began, and Jon Alex made sure he sat in the first row. There were movie teasers, star actors, artists, writers, and cosplay contests for multiple ages. The first day was amazing for Jon Alex but the weekend was all he needed to feed a yearlong wait until next year's convention.

When he arrived at school for his first class the next day his best friend and fellow weirdo Shila, Brit's daughter from a previous marriage, had to know the details. She had to stay at her aunt's house because her father was out of town. But it meant the world when Jon Alex revealed he bought her a highly sought-after replica of her favorite comic character. She gave him the biggest hug in the library. They often requested a soundproof room between classes to group study. Like clockwork, they were secured. "Oh my gosh, you shouldn't have Jon." She almost yelled out. "It's the least I could do. You got me that retro Cosmic Journey shirt last month, so I felt like you needed the right thank you." Jon Alex said. "You planned this the whole time and didn't tell me." She asked as she pushed him. He fell off his chair. "Oh my gosh, you're stupid." She laughed. He repositioned himself as he usually did after falling when she pushed him. "I hope we can find a better solution to our scheduling. Last year I missed the convention when you went. It was huge." He said. "I know right. I was able to meet Norway Blockbomb. She was sooooo beautiful." She responded. "Norway? You are ten time more beautiful homie." He said. "Awww. You're so sweet. Too bad your ugly. I would love to smash you." She joked. He tackled her and tickled her for saying that.

Their relationship was as awkward as her relationship was with her father. She didn't behave with her mother so when the divorce happened, she stayed with her father. They were fine until he began dating. She looked so much like her mother it affected how her father treated her over time. Jon Alex gave her a similar distance. But she didn't care. She knew he was her man and wasn't letting him go. He didn't have any clue as his passion for art and comics were first priority. For all he cared, she was a dude to him. So, when she nipple twisted him, he nipple twisted in retaliation. "What the hell? I have sensitive nipples." He laughed as she rolled him and took top position. "I feel no pain butt head. Twist all day, I can take it." She laughed. He gave in as his nipple sensitivity was too much to bear. They laid down beside each other laughing. The whole time they didn't notice people running to the large window wall on the opposite end. Star ships were hovering over the skyline. A war seemed imminent, but the origins had not been revealed.

There had been no warning on the news or speculation of a potential war brewing among rival nations. Someone was kind enough to knock on their door. Shila sat up as she attempted to regain some sort of dignity. She opened the door as Jon Alex rolled on the floor like a baby in pain. "How may I help you?" She asked. "You two need to see this. I think we're in danger." The student said. Shila looked over at Jon Alex who was collecting himself. "Jon, you wanna check this out?" She asked. "You go, my nipple hurts." He said. She grabbed him by the arm. "Oh shut up you little baby. Come on." She said. He was a bit smaller than she was, but he packed heart. Unless it involved his sensitive nipples.

"Do you really have to be so rough Shila?" He asked. She had no response. Neither did he once he caught a sight of the skyline. More warships had arrived the likes of which no one on the planet had ever seen before. "What do you think is happening?" A student asked. "Alien invasion." Jon Alex responded. No one laughed. "Let's get home Shila." He said. She followed him without any doubt. He was sharp and innovative. Growing up, he always created contraptions that were able to move on their own and perform tasks. Shila was always captivated by his know-how with little to no instructions guiding him. Her parents were poor, so she had nothing to offer but friendship. By age 9 she was in love with Jon Alex. By his 9th birthday, she gave him the ultimate gift. They were together ever since.

He never misled her to think he was into her more than his art and she never got in his way as he grew into the educated man he was becoming. His goal was to be an engineer for the national space program. The habitation program on the sister planet fascinated him. He loved creating concept art for new space adventures he dreamed of experiencing. He studied any material that covered the subject of space and space travel. The great traveler, Brea, had already visited their planet and introduced the reality of other life-bearing planets. The imaginations of the artsy-fartsy citizens of the world were inspired to dream new dreams and create more lavish creations. Hence, Jon Alex found his calling.

The two found their way down the stairs even with other students pushing and bumping beside them. They jumped into her truck and burned rubber. She was a crazy driver already, but this day called for it. In all directions, there were war ships, jet fighters, and paratroopers dropping in high numbers. "It's a fucking war." Jon Alex gasped. Shila passed stop signs, red lights, and almost crashed twice. When they arrived at their house, they ran to his room to get his survival kits he made for them then hid in the cellar. From there they called their parents who were coming home as they spoke. "Right. We're safe in Mr. Brick's wine cellar. Right. No problem daddy, just hurry. And be careful." Shila said. "How far is he?" Jon Alex asked. "Not too far, what a blessing?" Shila said. They were relieved when their parents returned.

The blessing was this wasn't an invasion. Shila's father came to pick her up and they went home safely. It turned out it was the new high-tech army of the sister planet. A revolution had arisen in response to the high taxes the governments of the world were allowing to keep rising to make the rich who lived on the sister planet more powerful. At first, this was a universally accepted idea when the world leaders sold it as a new habitat to secure the future of the leaders of tomorrow. It was described by the media as a chance to expand living space for all to benefit from. The majority of puppets in society believed everything they heard without question. The skeptics were shunned for having their doubts.

As the middle class dwindled and the poor grew poorer, the voices of those shunned skeptics were getting heard. And as the majority began to influence the government, this couldn't be tolerated. Things only escalated as the rich refused to allow the poor and middle-class citizens to visit the sister planet. The status quo had been working for those in power. Now troublemakers were dealt with immediately. For years, if a citizen didn't meet certain criteria they were turned down. Soon enough the "Old Planet" became the working class, and the "New Planet" became the authority on everything. But as living costs skyrocketed out of control while resources continued to trickle to the New Planet even the puppets had to accept they were tricked. They became the troublemakers. With less work, there were fewer resources to provide to the New Planet.

With a strong-arm method, the new world was ushered in with brutal law enforcement implemented on behalf of the "Authority" managing the police on the Old Planet from the New Planet. But the divide between the poor and rich on the Old Planet became more evident as Jon Alex and Shila entered their final semester of college before they would get their associates. They changed their majors some time back to criminal justice. They wanted to deal with the crime that was rising. The poor were running rampant in what was considered the "Unfortunate living areas." They actually took the time to build a game plan on policing crime on their own. To build hours of on the job training they tried to fight crime on their own.

"Do you have your pepper spray?" Jon Alex asked. "Yes. And my camera's battery is fully charged. I'm ready." Shila answered. They were excited, fully dressed in black. They watched police movies to get themselves mentally ready until the evening arrived. "You ready?" Jon Alex asked like a character in the movies they watched. "Ready." Shila responded. She wasn't too far off from his perception of reality. They went for a ride, and it was as expected. No law-abiding citizen went outdoors after dark, and no one was safe in unlit areas. Shila drove cautiously. Jon Alex was focused and intent on fighting crime on night one. And with luck, they found a guy trying to break off a chain to steal a bicycle in the park. Shila pulled over and Jon Alex ran out to stop him.

Shila began recording. "Sey man, whatcha doin'?" Jon Alex yelled. The guy looked at Jon Alex then continued trying to pry the bicycle loose. Jon Alex tackled the would be crook. They fought a little and it drew the attention of some people in the recreation center across the street. One happened to be the owner of the bicycle. He jumped in and helped Jon Alex subdue the guy.

The police were called, and he was taken to jail. They were heroes. When they returned home, they threw a two-person party and celebrated their new career choice. The next night they saw a motorcycle getting stolen. Jon tried the same tactic. Shila recorded the situation, but Jon would return to reveal the motorcycle belonged to the person. They almost dropped out of college that weekend to pursue this career up to that point. That situation created second thoughts.

Jon Alex searched through his father's old riot gear then snuck out with some pepper spray shots along with his father's shotgun. "What's that for?" Shila asked. "We need to be ready for anything. I'm not fighting every night." Jon Alex responded. Their nerves showed as they realized what they were choosing to do for the near future. "I'm not ready for this Jon. Let's take it slow then work up to shotguns." She said. "I'm not getting killed out there. But we can't make this our full-time job if we don't' take it seriously." Jon Alex said. He pulled out a small handgun. "I'm going to keep this on me at least. For my safety." He said. Shila thought about it for a moment. "For safety." She affirmed.

He hugged her. "Thank you Shila. Now let's go do this." He said. Partly to break the moment's jitters but mostly to get out there and fight crime like the heroes he read about all his life. "I have a new camera I bought this weekend. It attaches to the dashboard so I can take pictures too. We can document our experience for future law officials to study and improve their methods with." She said. "Dang. That's a great idea. See, we're already making a difference." Jon Alex said.

The night proved useless as crime was not in the areas they were performing surveillance on. What is important to add is they were very selective in choosing the spots. There were criminal activities near many areas they pulled over, but they weren't ready to deal with those dangers yet. Still, choosing this line of work means danger can find you if you look for it too long. And by the second week they walked into a robbery. "Shila, stop. Pull over." Jon Alex said. "What?" Shila asked as she pulled over. "The gas station over there. I love the coffee they make. I know the manager. I can get us a discount." He said. She pulled into the station then parked. She sorted out her equipment as Jon Alex prepared to go inside. "Do you want anything?" He asked. "A French vanilla coffee." She said. As she checked her hand-held camera screen, shots rang out. Shila wasn't sure if it was Jon Alex who shot or someone else. She waited in shock.

Inside, the cashier frantically called the police. "Yes, I want to report a robbery. Shots have been fired. I think someone is hurt." The cashier said. "OK. Where are you?" The emergency receptionist asked. "I'm on Willow Avenue. The store is Rickster's Gas and Stuff. Please get someone over here. The robbers are gone but I don't know if they will come back." The cashier said. "Stay at a safe distance and we will get to you as soon as possible." The receptionist said.

When the initial gunshots took place, two hooded figures ran out of the store. Shila waited in shock but exited her vehicle when Jon Alex didn't come out. Jon Alex exited slowly as he was bleeding from his mouth and nose. There were red dots all over his arms and face. "Jon, oh god." She cried. He fell to his knees as she ran at him to catch him in her arms. "I.. I love…" Jon Alex tried to speak. "Stay with me Jon. Stay with me OK." She said. In a desperate effort, she tried to stop some of the holes in Jon Alex's body from bleeding. There were too many. He nearly bled to death before the ambulance arrived.

The first responders would save Jon Alex's life, but the great war of the worlds would take place while he was in a coma.

Crime was far worse with Roma in power. Her great city, Jokevla, sucked the life from the cities trying to rebuild around hers. It grew and she grew. But her paranoia grew just as much when she decided to cut ties with Ale Gwappo and 'The Family'. Ale Gwappo was a superpower in his conquered mountain lands, so it didn't mean much to him. But 'The Family' were not happy about the betrayal. They caught wind of the affair and found out that Roma's love interest had a child named Layla who went to school in Sheek High School. She had gone missing along with his three other children. Ale Gwappo was more than happy to lend Lazkukurachas to them for assistance in the matter.

When Jon Alex opened his eyes he was in a hospital, but the hospital was quiet. He looked around. The windows were busted, and the ceiling was ready to cave in. He sat up. No one was there to tell him he just woke up from a coma. His will to live kept him breathing without food or water for days. The hospital Jon Alex just woke up in was just another casualty of the reign of Roma. His memory was foggy, but he would find it in him to get food and drink before making his way home. He would learn about the loss of his parents soon after.

In the days to come, he would attempt to reunite with Shila. He learned from a video Shila left to him that she went back to college and received a degree in criminal justice with a minor is psychology. The field her mother studied. The recording also let him know she had moved on and left to Jokevla. Jon Alex was broken. He never lost his bond. His life was derailed but there seemed to be a chance that he could get it back on track, then this. He took time to recover and went into his dad's shed to sort through his supplies. A neighbor came to visit. It was Tod. He was a family friend who chose to stay as most of the community left during the war. But Jon Alex didn't want to talk. Tod gave Jon Alex a box his mother left before she passed. His mother had remained good friends with Brit even after the divorce. She was the only person Brit could trust before her abduction. Jon Alex's mother looked into what Brit had revealed to her and collected information she had found on her own. When Brit went missing she gave the box of information she had to Tod's parents. Tod's father was killed in the war and his mother overdosed leaving him on his own. In his sorrows he found the box and opened it. Jon Alex closed the door and opened it. What he found inside was nerve wrecking.

He was deathly afraid of what he knew was in the future, but he had to know what happened. The first step was to retrace her steps. He went to Tod's house. A knock at the door of his parent's friend was met with kind gestures. "Please, come in. We have a lot to talk about." Tod said. Jon Alex walked in casually but with intent. "I'm so glad you came to visit. Your parents talked so much about you. I saw pictures of you, and I remembered you were in college to be a police officer." He began. "Is that what they told you? I guess they weren't wrong." Jon Alex said. "You don't remember? I'm Tod. I was in a class with both you and Shila but had to leave college for a few years. I didn't know what I wanted back then. I'm glad I made up my mind. I got Shila hired with the agency years later. She told me all about you. I'm sorry…" Tod said in a sad tone recognizing his parents were gone.

"When I woke up, I learned a lot about the war and the political issues but the loss of…" Jon Alex choked up. Tod put his hand on Jon Alex's shoulder. "I know." He said softly. "I am not one to sit back and watch life happen. She was a brick where others are pebbles. When they drop in a lake, they make little ripples. When she drops, she affects the entire lake." Jon Alex said. "What do you mean by that? I don't sit back. I make changes every day." Tod spoke up. "Then I ask you to do this very thing and let me in on information that can help me find out what happened to my parents." Jon Alex said.

"Would you like some coffee?" Tod asked. "I'm not thirsty." Jon Alex responded. "I'll get some coffee for us both. It's going to be a long night." Tod said. Jon Alex smiled. Tod was a bit like Shila. A strong mind and a quick wit. "Thank you." Jon Alex said. When Tod returned, he had a different box with several files inside. He passed Jon Alex a small pitcher of coffee and two cups. "I've been on this case for a while. I wasn't supposed to open the box, but I had to know what was in it. Learning what you have, I investigated myself. It may cost me my life, but I will prove a political figure was helped by a drug cartel and a mafia family to obtain her position." He began. "Do me a favor and start from the beginning. I'm a bit foggy on the past." Jon Alex requested. "With the rise in crime the citizens have been up in arms about issues that weren't issues before. Social media has clouded the judgement of people willing to believe whatever they hear." Tod said.

Tod excused himself to go to the restroom. Jon Alex sorted out the files and took quick glimpses of the material Tod accumulated. Reports of widespread human trafficking were joined with sporadic cases of a mafia family involvement in criminal operations. Over and over the same name came into play, Roma. And Brit was on most of the evidence accumulated in that box. Tod returned. "Sorry about that. When you gotta go." Tod said. "I understand. You said that there was a rise in crime. Is Roma the one responsible?" Jon Alex asked. Tod paused. "One could blame her, but she is just a part of a bigger issue. To get to her is to get to the political problem we face today. To get to Brit, we have to figure out who Roma needed to help her get rid of the problem Brit was creating." Tod said.

"The Lazkukurachas." Jon Alex said as he pointed to a file about them. "Yes. Who better than the henchmen of Ale Gwappo to get rid of issues?" Tod said. "Then he's my guy." Jon Alex declared. "Hold up superhero. That little fire in you is what got you in a coma. You need to think. It's a much more dangerous world than the one that tried to take you out. No one gets to Gwappo. No one gets to Roma. You just can't. They are protected with all the money to pay all the right people to make bad things happen to you and those around you." Tod said. A vehicle burned rubber outside.

Gunshots followed. They ducked as the house was torn apart by bullets. Jon Alex crawled up to Tod to guide him to a more protected spot, but Tod was leaking blood out of the huge hole in his forehead.

Jon Alex shoved the files into the box and made a dash to the back yard. By then the vehicle had left. A message was sent to the right person at the wrong time. Jon Alex had two holes in his body he wouldn't realize were there until he passed out. As he opened his eyes, he could see the stars. Pain in his right shoulder and left leg woke him up completely. The bleeding had stopped but it was enough to weaken him severely. Both bullets flew clear through his body. Regardless, he almost passed out on the way to the hospital. He parked as if there was nothing wrong and walked into the hospital to sign in. His loss of blood left him almost delirious. Nursing staff rushed him into the emergency room for surgery. With his long hair and beard out of place, he looked homeless. After some questioning from police he walked out of the hospital before he was fully healed.

Not but a moment after stepping outside, he was grabbed by masked men and taken away in a black van. He didn't fight back. This was an opportunity to get closer to the chance of finding out what really happened with his parents. So, he fell asleep. The Lazkukurachas were more than happy they didn't have another fighter. They hog tied Jon Alex and left him alone for the remainder of the ride. An hour later, they pulled him out and dropped him in a hole. Concrete splashed on Jon Alex's face as the henchmen began pouring the fresh supply on him. "What the... Oh come on, really? My story doesn't end here. I must have gotten too close for you to..." As Jon Alex spoke, gunshots sprayed across the opening as the Lazkukurachas ran out of sight. Silence followed.

A few bikers cleared a debt of unpaid weapons this group of Lazkukurachas decided not to worry about. By luck, Jon Alex was able to reach into his pocket and find his multitool. He climbed out slowly, looking around at the dead bodies, making sure no one was playing a trick. There was no one else around. The construction site was for a new building Roma intended to use for her own space program. Bodies found their way into the foundation from time to time. Courtesy of Ale Gwappo's sick sense of humor. But it was still a dangerous area. Roma would be forced to halt construction when the dead bodies of Ale Gwappo's henchmen showed up on the news the next morning. Jon Alex was making a name for himself, and

Family

he needed to shed it quickly. He returned to his parents' home to grab his father's riot gear but chose to hide out in homelessness.

On his travels he befriended a mountain man who made his own tools and weapons out in the wilderness. The man said little and wore no clothing. Jon Alex traded his father's gear and labor for apprenticeship. When he was ready, he departed to find an infamous dealer of Pimp Day-day's drug supply. He sold a marinated version that competed with Pimp Day-day's business. Pimp Day-day put many hits on him. He survived all of them. Now he lived secluded right under Pimp Day-day's nose in the eastern forest. He cut his hair and grew his beard out. It was always in a long thick ponytail. He wore turquoise scrubs as if he was medical staff. Jon Alex searched far and wide for the dealer Tod's files identified as Kreeper. He spent time in prison for playing a part in Pimp Day-day's human trafficking business. The drug dealer life was a side hustle that became successful on accident. With persistence, Jon Alex found him. After almost getting shot by Kreeper, Jon Alex would find his next step toward Ale Gwappo. He befriended Kreeper, convincing him he was just camping out on vacation. They had a great night smoking a substance Kreeper called "Foggy Pillow". For someone hiding from certain death, Kreeper had a big mouth. Before Jon Alex knew it, Kreeper was telling him everything about the human trafficking, the church of fake nuns, and Pimp Day-days prostitution hotel along with his involvement. Jon Alex didn't say it, but Kreeper had put himself on Jon Alex's short list of villains. The Foggy Pillow would eventually take hold of Jon Alex, and he passed out. "What the fu..." Kreeper began but didn't finish as he stumbled to the floor. The room was still spinning as he closed his eyes. "Damn it Kreeper. You're shit is too strong." A random woman said. Kreeper passed out. Jon Alex sat up. He looked around confused. He was mixed with the sleeping bodies of half a dozen men and women. He shook his head. "I better not have... Damn it." Jon Alex said in frustration and regret.

He staggered out the door and went to his tent. He opened the box he took from Tod's house months ago and placed his notes inside a random truck that still had keys in it. He broke down his tent, put everything into the beat-up truck, then drove to a nearby biker club he was familiar with. He traded the truck for a dirt bike and a leather bag he could put his files in then rode away to the next destination. There was a trap house that had members of Pimp Day-day's low level drug dealers Kreeper bragged about robbing.

This was the beginning of a series of kick doors Jon Alex performed, causing Pimp Day-day to put a hit on him. It wasn't going to be hard to find him was he left shotgun shells everywhere he went. Without any identification the hoodlums began referring to the serial killer as Slug Shot.

One evening, after clearing another trap house, Slug Shot sat in the living room to clean his shotgun. Watching the news, Slug Shot learned there was a missing child named Vincent. The sister, Risa, was very overcome with emotion. It gave Slug Shot a greater purpose than just revenge. Instead of killing everyone, Slug Shot began questioning the dealers before disposing of them. He was able to find out the new location of Pimp Day-day's human trafficking hotel. He cleaned out the place and saved several children including the little boy he saw on the news. He was able to reunite him with his family before continuing on his mission.

He returned to the trafficking hotel, after clearing out a few more places, to talk to the landlord, who he left tied up on the roof. Slug Shut began to load his shotgun quietly. "Wait... Wait a minute. We can make a deal here. No need to kill me. I'm just the numbers girl for Pimp Day-day. I make sure no one steals. No one runs away. That crap. You'll have no problems from me. Trust." She pleaded. "I want Day-day." He said in the coolest voice he could muster up. "Where is he?" he asked. The woman looked around in fear. "I don't know anybody who comes through here." She said. He struck her in the chest. "Ow... what did you do that for? I don't know him. I just get paid to keep business in house. My hotel makes no money because of the crime around here. It's my only source of income and it's good money. I'm telling you the truth." She cried.

"You will join the rest of these losers if you don't give me something. I know you Peylee. I know your daughter is sick and you want her to grow up better than you. Help me and you will see her grow. If you lie to me one more time she will go where I'm sending you." Slug Shot said. "There's a building two blocks from here. You can find what you need there. It's called Paco's Tacos. But he may not let you in the secret entrance in the back room." Peylee said. He struck her in the neck. She choked. "Why did you do that? I'm telling you the truth. Please, I want to live. Leave my daughter out of this. I told you everything." She cried. "I killed everyone there. I found out you were the one with the names of everyone who is pimped out and contacts for new prospects. I want the damn list, or your daughter will have to meet you in another life." Slug Shot said.

Family

Peylee's face changed. A goon fired at Slug Shot from behind. The bullet hit Slug Shot in the left shoulder. There was no need to fire back as the goon was already dying from the slug that tore his stomach apart. He hit the floor. Peylee had managed to finally untie herself and used the moment to run. Before she made it to the door, her right leg flew out from under her. "Oh my god. WHAT HAVE YOU DONE? WHAT HAVE YOU DONE?" She screamed in shock. Slug Shot put his foot over her neck. She looked at him holding her book of bodies labeled as units. "You fucking pimped out babies?" Slug Shot asked. She spit at him. From a distance the shotgun could be heard releasing one more round.

The next morning the newspaper headline would read, "THE TWELVE GUAGE SHOT GUN ASSAILANT BRUTALLY CLEARS A NEIGHBORHOOD SHATTERED BY POVERTY AND CRIME. HERO OR FOE?" Slug Shot was annoyed by the title as he drank some coffee at gas station nearby his next destination. After getting some news in he pulled out Peylee's ledger. The list had names of people that connected the dot's in Tod and Brit's collected information. Some people or 'units', he knew, recently went missing. Then he discovered Brit was housed there. It was difficult to take in but also finding out that the convent Kreeper talked about was housing tortured women with Brit's name listed as one of the transports there was gut wrenching.

Then the impossible happened. Slug Shot's eyes almost popped out of his fact. Shila's name was a prospect to be kidnapped and brought there. And there it was, her address. He didn't waste any time. He jumped on his bike and went straight to her house. She wasn't home when he arrived, so he snuck in to surprise her. She almost shot him when she got home. Their bond was still there though. After catching up, and going over the annoying name Twelve Guage, the two intertwined. All the time Slug Shot worried for her. The next day Shila headed out for work. Slug Shot went to get ammunition and supplies. He was set to protect her. When he returned to her house later that evening she wasn't home. Her car was in the driveway, but the door was open. Inside, everything was torn apart. In her office lay a folder with the name, Ale Gwappo. That was the final draw. Slug Shot was more determined than ever to get to Ale Gwappo and finish him once and for all.

To get the job done he would have to get help from his old friend. The mountain man knew how to track, hunt, and kill every animal known to hunters across the region. His visit didn't need a welcome. When the door opened, they exchanged a few words then Slug Shot walked in, and the door closed. "Claymon, I don't want to take up too much of your time. My friend is in danger, and I need to find her and free her." Slug Shot said. "Jon, try this new moon shine. It's the best I've ever made." Claymon said. Slug Shot took a drink. "Whoa." Claymon chuckled. "Enjoy the rest of that glass. Tomorrow, we get started." Claymon said. His tone was enough. Claymon spent the night fashioning the perfect tools for the job.

By morning, Claymon was ready. "Let's go." He said. Slug Shot struggled to get up. "I feel like I fell off a cliff." Slug Shot said. Claymon laughed. "Been there." He said. They collected some gear and headed out. Claymon had his own motorcycle. They chose a great day to hit the road. The sun was out but the weather was cool. The condensed forest area opened into a swirling road as they climbed up a hill leading to the mountain. The land was a sight to see as they rested on a deep edge along the mountain side. As nightfall approached they took the time to enjoy the scenery. "Nothing more beautiful than the sun glistening across a river, huh?" Slug Shot said. "Yup." Claymon responded. By sunrise, the open road welcomed them as they traveled on a common pathway along the mountainside.

Claymon made a few phone calls. He was secluded but not out of touch. Soon several motorcycles met up with them. They cleared the way for the two men with intent to join in the fun. It was a sight to see so many motorcycles riding as one. The long swirling road up the mountain complimented the display. For each member of the club, it was what they lived for. Riding free and taking in the views of the world untouched by war. Before they made it to the convent, they took time to enjoy their potentially last moments alive with a drink. It was a good night. The stars glistened in the clear night skies. The New Planet could be seen from afar. Slug Shot was well known by this point, and it didn't take long for one of the bikers to realize who he was. The bikers returned to them and surrounded them. The display was not what they expected. Slug Shot had cleared out their competition. They didn't wait until morning to continue on. The entire club provided what they could to allow for the two men to survive such difficult terrain. Once they arrived Slug Shot took Clamon's gun. "This is my path. Thank you for coming with me. I couldn't have made it up here without you. But there's no need for you to come any further. From this point on only I should risk my life." Slug Shot said. "Shut up Jon. I'm going with you." Claymon said. Jon Alex didn't budge. "Really my friend. I couldn't live with the fact I put your life in danger and survived. This is my path." Jon Alex said. Claymon gave him his grenade launcher. "I wish you the best Slug Shot." Claymon said. The two parted ways.

Jon Alex was able to approach the convent with ease. Getting in was not as easy. There were armored nuns with sophisticated weaponry. Taking them out was a blessing in disguise. He put on the gear of the large guard and looked for a better entryway than the front door. The place seemed empty until he heard screaming. The mother had a knife in her hand to stab a young woman. Nearby were Kreeper and a young male. He aimed his rifle and shot Kreeper. He was a provider for Peylee's units. Getting unsuspecting people high was his trick. The shot startled the nuns as the mother tried to kill the young woman. "For our lord." She yelled out. While firing his shot gun, Slug Shot threw a knife into the mother's eye. After clearing the sacrificial chambers he took down a hallway full of nun guards with the bombs he took from the guards at the front door. His actions helped the young woman and the young male escape. The explosions broke open the door to the room the nuns were sacrificing another girl in. Tied up nearby was Shila. Slug Shot wasn't about to see her die. He lost his composure as he cleared the area like it was a trap house.

The nuns pleaded for their lives, reciting biblical text, calling Slug Shot evil names and crying for their salvation. Nothing could quench the thirst of Slug Shot. He helped the young girl and Shila escape then turned back and shot until his ammunition ran out then threw bombs in every direction. The explosions weakened the foundation. Claymon was nearby and helped them get to a safe place. Slug Shot didn't know it at the time, but Shila had been raped to near death and had been forcefully overdosed with Ale Gwappo's signature drug. Claymon did what he could to keep her alive. To Slug Shot's amazement, the mother was still alive. Fragments had lacerated her neck, just missing the jugular. The cut was deep but not enough to kill her. As Claymon took Shila and the young girl to a nearby hospital, Slug Shot collected information.

It took a day to get to a medical facility. Shila was not the same. Her body was ravaged from what she had to endure as a sex slave before she was provided as a sacrifice the nuns. The tortured her and would have killed her had Layla, the young woman about to be sacrificed by the mother, not fell into their grasp days before. Her mind was shattered from the experience. It took years for her to piece together remnants of the person she once was. No matter. Jon Alex let go of his past and married her, remaining by her side for the rest of her life.

Loyal reader, as much as I would like this story to end here, I made a promise at the beginning I need to keep. Shila would take her life. All the pain and anguish living through nightmares and post-traumatic stress was too much. Jon Alex would have left well enough alone. Losing her sent him over the edge. He joined a war led by the young woman he saved named Layla and her future husband, King Corey Hudson. They aimed to dethrone the corrupt politician Roma who was outed for having direct affiliations with Ale Gwappo. Slug Shot's presence was felt in many regions. His bloodthirsty tactics spread fear in the Lazkukurachas who he eradicated in his pursuit to find Ale Gwappo. Slug Shot would find a small army of natives to the mountain region to the north who aided in his search for and elimination of Ale Gwappo. Every move he made was out of the love he had for Shila she could never experience again. At the war's end, Jon Alex, aka Slug Shot, would be recognized in the Hall of Legends for his contributions. Every year following the victory over Roma, Jon Alex would visit Shila on her birthday and have a romantic pic-nick with her. He would talk to her about what happened throughout the year. Little did he know, her spirit was always present, listening to every word.

The Horrid Play That Is

Karlo's Existence

P. Marcelo W. Balboa

Innocence Lost

Hello there, valued reader. It is with regret and sorrow that this story be told. Yet as this anthology requests family oriented subject matter, such a story must be included. As betrayal of brethren and jealousy over bloodlines are a valid part of Karlo's existence. If you choose to skip it, do as you may. Such an existence is folly, useless, and a menace. Enough has been said of warning. Let us begin.

...

Many who experienced the Guardian of Electrical Currents would say he was a villain but the brethren among the Guardians in the Kingdom above the Clouds would disagree. It is hard to judge the path of those who find themselves misled, betrayed, and undervalued. Karlo did not mean to become what he did, nor did he mean to hurt those he had but there was no one there when he needed someone. Moreover, when he tried to help those he valued they turned on him at the first sign of failure. With a broken spirit and no support, there was nothing for him to build a positive point of view. So, at the lowest depths of his life, he became determined to take that, now worthless, life into his own hands. He decided to make a life where he could be what he viewed himself. In three acts his foul story will be told.

ACT I

The love triangle

There were nine Guardians created to tend to the goings on of a precious planet created by a demigod. Each were gifted yet limited to the control of certain elements needed to help the planet flourish. The Planet of the Guardians was beautiful. The colorful plant life, vibrant minerals and water, and beings that caried life blood filled the lands. But jealousy and envy consumed Catalyn, Guardian of Fire. She seduced Bello, Guardian of Souls, and manipulated Karlo, Guardian of Electricity. Together they fell from the Kingdom Above the Clouds to become the dominant species of the land they viewed themselves to be. Catalyn would set brother against brother resulting in a humiliating defeat both ruining the plans of the fallen and their place among the brethren in the Kingdom. Catalyn would turn her back on Karlo in his defeat.

ACT II

The antisocial failure

Karlo fled in shame. Bello and Catalyn would dominate the lands for some time leaving him no place to show his face. So he dwelled in the ice-covered lands to the north. He secluded himself, becoming basic in existence. Eat, sleep, hunt, repeat. He killed a beast and took over his cave. There he wasted his existence away.

ACT III

The hunter and the daughter

Karlo's deterioration became instinctive. A quick kill then back to hibernation. Until one day came when his pathetic hunt was disrupted. A young boy was setting out to bring food home to his grandparents. Karlo was about to attack when an arrow hit his meal first. He watched the boy strap it up and take it home. Karlo swooped in and took it from the boy then followed him home to kill him and his grandparents. He lived in the cabin until he saw a little girl playing near a river. His impulses took over. The child was provided an unwanted seed. He thought nothing of his actions but grew annoyed of her constant screams and cries. In his shame he took the child to the nearby house that matched her sent. The mother screamed. Karlo reacted maliciously. The father came to her aid but was dismantled all the same. The little girl held her little baby brother in her arms and shielded him with her body. He meant to discard her from existence but held his strike. She did not cry or scream. Her eyes were filled with riverbeds but there was no fear. Not anymore. Her love of her brother fueled her courage. "If I must die then I will die, but you will not take my brother you monster." She declared. Karlo realized at that moment she had just done what he couldn't. In a burst of emotion he retreated deeper into the Iceland Region.

An End… But not The End

The Magical Munchgalumptagans

The Back Story

It all begins on a little cookie shaped planet called Flubberboober. There was a magical land with various beings who possessed different gifts and abilities. The land was lush with vibrant plant life that grew from a special nutrient-giving crystal sand. The waters glistened with a clear golden blue liquid. The bare crystal sand rested underneath the gentle waves. Their existence came to be after the creator of the planet made Munchgalumptagans then added Humilumpkidans to the mix. Nuwa then created Munchaglumptagans with magical powers of different types. When holes tore into the sky bringing discord across the cosmos, the planet Flubberboober fell right in line with a warmongering race of metal worshipers called Maglurians. This led to all-out war the magical beings didn't want to take part in. With all their combined magic, they caused their magical land to disappear from the eyes of the non-magical beings. Over time visions haunted those with the gift of foresight. A gathering of elders led to the creation of a prophecy. That one would come from afar, greater than all the magical beings on Flubberboober, to bring peace to the land and prevent the magical land's extinction.

A Short Story of a Supernatural Fox

The Guardian of Travel, Brea, assembled a group of gifted characters that called themselves 'The Suntento Crew' to help a Munchgalumptagan, Tec, on his quest to find a weapon that would help him save his life partner Pep. A story for another chapter. The Suntento Crew would eventually veer off into a side mission to aid a betrayed elf princess. Perhaps this too is better suited for another chapter. As for this story, the crew would venture onward in pursuit of other miscellaneous activities to help the princess find her powerful familiar. Bonded with the princess, the familiar was stolen then hidden by the princess's conniving sister. The princess named her Star, a six-tail fox who sparkled like a fairy as she effortlessly flowed through the air. The Suntento Crew's actions became the catalyst that led to a fight between a grand dragon and star. Their combined energy upon collision was so powerful it tore a hole in the fabric of space that shot them from the Astral Realm to the Physical Realm. Both Star and the dragon were sucked into the void of space, directly in the path of the planet Flubberboober. These supernatural beings broke through the magical veil with ease, causing incredible harm to the land. What would be left is an Island with small land masses scattered around it. Remnants of the vast land that once was, fulfilling the prophecy and changing the course of the land the magical Munchgalumptagans affectionately called Wuhoohoo.

And now, a sneak peek at the first draft of the page-by-page plots of a comic book called...

The Stupendulously Spectacular Island of Magical Beings

WUHOOHOO

The Page by Page Story Outline

Page 1: *An arial view of the magical land of Wuhoohoo.*

Page 2: *Panels reveal magical beings and their abilities.*

Page 3: *A view of the star lit sky from the beach front.*

Page 4: *Space bends, a portal opens revealing a dragon.*

Page 5: *The dragon passes through the portal but is in conflict with another being.*

Page 6: *A dark elf queen witch is riding the dragon but is cast from it.*

Page 7: *A six tail fox can be seen shooting sparkles at the dragon.*

Page 8: *A great magical war takes place in midair.*

Page 9: *The sky is lit up with magical explosions that vibrate the air.*

Page 10: *As the elf witch falls unconscious, she hits the golden sand.*

Page 11: *The dragon senses this and loses its composure.*

Page 12: *The fox will not relent as the dragon supercharges.*

Page 13: *The fox is hit so hard it is knocked to a far moon.*

Page 14: *The magical land hides the elf witch's magical energy, confusing the dragon.*

Page 15: *The dragon crashes into the waters in a rage causing a tsunami unlike anything that has been seen on Flubberboober.*

Page 16: *The magical Munchgalumptagans try valiantly to save each other and their land as it is ripped apart from grand scale earthquakes caused by the dragon shooting magical supercharged energy into the land underwater.*

Page 17: *The dragon emerges to set fire to the beings trying to survive as the land breaks apart and sinks underwater.*

Page 18: *The fox awakens in a crater her impact created on the distant moon.*

Page 19: *An arial view of the magical land cracking apart, sinking into the water with fires rising from the areas the dragon has attacked can be seen through her eyes.*

Page 20: *Magical beings fight to save their land and each other but cry in dismay as they realize their last day has come.*

Page 21: *The fox charges up causing three more tails, wings, and a sing horn grow.*

Page 22: *The dragon is fierce and relentless but doesn't anticipate the return of the fox.*

Page 23: *As a family is about to be scorched, the fox spears a ray of sparkling magical energy at the dragon.*

Page 24: *The impact drives the dragon into the ground.*

Page 25: *As the dust settles the dragon emerges but weakened. It tries to strike her again but the fox is fast and dodges the dragon then counters with fireworks of sparkling energy.*

Page 26: *The dragon is fatally wounded as it shoots to the damaged moon the fox made a crater in.*

Page 27: *The fox turns her attention to the drowning magical land. Few survive but a fraction of the land is preserved with the combined effort of the surviving magical Munchaglumptagans.*

Page 28: *An arial view shows a smaller piece of dry land that carries on the name Wuhoohoo. Small land masses surround the little island.*

Page 29: *The survivors praise the fox.*

Page 30: *The survivors join their magic to repair the island and make a shrine to the fox.*

Sealed in a magical veil, Wuhoohoo is home to a secluded community. Yet it would come to pass that someone would break through the magical veil yet again. His name is Kane, son of Connell, and he will lead the world into world peace. But that story is for another day. The story that is for this day happens to occur on the other side of the planet. Tec's story, as promised. Enjoy another sneak peek at the comic-by-comic descriptions for a series called…

P. Marcelo W. Balboa

The Original Story Outline of ...

Pep and Tec's Spooky Adventure

The 50-issue series

1) Pep, *a spunky squiralumpkidan from the planet Flubberboober*, pulls Tec, *a laid-back computer loving turtlumpkidan*, into a paranormal adventure that forces Tec to gain access to the *'Plain of Lost Treasures'* to find a weapon that can save her. When he uses the weapon to stab a monster possessed by the Prince of Darkness, *a beautiful fallen angel and ruler of the Kingdom in Shadow*, his heroic act nearly kills the prince and draws the attention of Brea's Guild. Such an act is not forgotten by the dark prince who retreats to the Shadow Dimension to recover.

2) Brea, *one of the nine Guardians created to watch over the Planet of the Guardians*, recruits Pep and Tec along with two other members, Padre Ully and Raja Ali, and establishes roles for his new paranormal team. Pep is possessed by Remi, *a minion of the Prince of Darkness*. The team shows their worth by fending off the intruder, sending her back to the Shadow Dimension.

3) Time has passed. Devonte, *a genius brought along to help the paranormal team learn how to operate advanced technology*, returns to his home planet Rezandria as the team visits a hospital on the sister planet.

4) Padre Ully, *a foreseeing divine practitioner*, fights a foul spirit named Sharlene while Raja, *a warrior and skilled survivalist*, fends off Cultists, *poor souls kidnapped for the possession of shameful souls that committed suicide in their previous lives and want to live again*, allowing Pep to save a baby they were trying to sacrifice named Neika, *the rejected spawn of the Prince of Darkness*. Tec tracks it all with cameras and data recorder robots.

5) Padre Ully conducts his 1st exorcism of a Lost Light, *souls that never had the opportunity to live due to premature deaths possessing willing bodies*, on a new planet as Tec finds out about baby Neika.

6) Tec learns the intricacies of fatherhood on the carrier the team lives in while on their cosmic journey. Brea sends the team to another

Family

planet with a haunted past. It turns out Cultists and Lost Lights, *both groups loyal to the Prince of Darkness,* have caused descent in the people's will to live and ambush Raja and Ully during their investigation. Raja's fighting skills are the only reason they escaped with their lives.

7) Pep gets rest as Tec loses sleep taking care of Neika. Later, on another planet, the team encounters a Demon Tick, a *minion of Karlo bent on defiling all that is good in the world.* If it attaches to the back of your neck it can control you. Their victory reveals the threat that is growing from Karlo who, *during this series,* has gained access to the Physical Realm from the Astral Realm.

8) Tec plays with baby Neika but loses her when she hides in the vents. Neika remains in the vents as she overhears Raja and Ully intelligently discuss their conflicting faiths in the God of their understanding, unintentionally teaching Neika.

9) Raja defeats an entire Demon Tick nest on their next spooky adventure. Afterward, Pep and Neika play dress up with Tec.

10) Padre Ully's exorcism of another Lost Light reveals their lair. While on their journey to the lair, Pep plays with Neika and loses her in the vents as well.

11) Within the Lost Light Lair, Padre Ully barely escapes as Raja is fatally wounded by Karlo. Karlo made a deal with the Prince of Darkness to help him repossess his former Guardian body in order to kill Raja for destroying his army of Demon Ticks.

12) Raja passes away and goes to Elysium but turns it down when he learns about his lost loves soul being trapped in the Plain of Sorrows in the Shadow Dimension. He decides to go on a quest to save her. Neika, *who grew to love and respect Raja from the vents,* learns the pain of loss and the value of life.

13) Brea recruits Antawn, *the long-lost son of King Hudson* and *grandson of Reeza, the Guardian of Liquid.* With an inherited ability to be able to turn himself into living liquid, Brea is sure Antawn can help them on their paranormal quest. Unfortunately, the team must navigate losing a teammate and accepting a replacement.

14) After their next paranormal encounter displays the ability of Antawn before the team's eyes, Padre Ully blesses Antawn turning

him into living holy water. Tec and Neika bond in route to the Lost Light Lair, *where Raja's body remains*. Antawn give a maximum effort destroying the Lost Lights hold on their willing bodies. Padre Ully is able to retrieve Raja's remains and get it to the team's shuttle. Karlo was defeated by a vengeful assassin who goes by the name of 'The Forgotten One' before they arrived.

15) The team encounters their most dangerous opponent yet as a giant monster releases havoc on an innocent community. Remi is sent by the Prince of Darkness to kill Padre Ully. She possesses this destructive being to draw the attention of Brea's Guild. On their way, the team completes a side mission the results in Antawn saving Pep from a serial Killer. Upon their arrival Antawn is separated from Padre Ully by Cultists who distract him, giving Remi enough time to kill Padre Ully before inevitably falling in battle to Antawn.

16) Padre Ully is reunited with his wife and child in Elysium. Ike, *the great Astral traveler*, and *great grandson of Brea*, contacts Brea in the Physical Realm from the Astral Realm with the help of his sister Elliana, *great granddaughter of Brea*. They discuss the growing impact of an assassin only known as 'The Forgotten One.' She is interested in joining Brea's Guild.

17) The Forgotten One, *aka Forgotten*, joins Pep and Tec's paranormal team. They are hesitant, still healing from the losses of Raja and Padre Ully but give in when Brea tells her story. Neika, whose existence has already been revealed to the entire team, runs out to greet Brea. In a terrible misunderstanding, Forgotten attacks Neika thinking she is a demon that snuck on the carrier. Pep jumps in front of Neika to protect her and is killed by Forgotten, *who is the child of the fallen Guardian Bello*. She inherited an ability to push a soul into the Astral Realm or pull a soul out of the Astral Realm. Even her own. Neika, standing behind the impact of the attack, is pushed into the Astral Realm alongside Pep.

18) This event shatters Tec. Brea dismantles the team in response. Haunted by her regretful act, Forgotten pulls Tec into the Astral Realm to save Pep, *who's soul has been captured by the Prince of Darkness*.

19) Tec learns about the dark prince and his Kingdom in Shadow. It is protected by a small division of guards. Tec circles the Kingdom to find another entrance as Forgotten attacks the guards. With the unexpected aid of an enormous purple winged demon, Forgotten is able to defeat them and in an unexpected twist, get information about her father.

20) With critical information, Forgotten leaves without waiting for Tec to return. Tec, unable to find another way in makes his way back to the front to see the aftermath. There he meets a highly evolved version of Neika. Crossing paths with Forgotten, Ike learns of Pep and Tec's situation.

21) Ike finds Tec and Neika and takes them on a tour of the developing dimensions in the Astral Realm. Already familiar with Tec on a previous encounter, Ike sends Tec and Neika to the Plain of Lost Treasures, *within the Shadow Dimension of the Astral Realm*, to get whatever they can find to save Pep.

22) With the help of Elliana, *who inherited the ability to help thought waves travel to and from any Realm*, Ike reaches out to their bloodline for aid. Tec and Neika prove to be worthy of saving Pep when they return from the Plain of Lost Treasures with everything they need to succeed.

23) *As other rivals of the dark prince smell blood*, Ike protects the front gates of the Kingdom in Shadow as Tec and Neika traverse the first level of the nine gates known only as, 'Dark Soil'.

24) *As the rivals build their armies*, Ike's bloodline unite in preparation to fend off any potential threats, *creating the grounds for a warzone*. Tec and Neika traverse the second level of the nine gates called, 'Dark Air'.

25) While Tec and Neika traverse the third level of the nine gates, 'Dark Flames', Wollis, *son of Elliom*, leads his corps of soldiers to the first battlefield to fight 'The Starved Souls'.

26) Elliom, son of Brea, leads his corps of warriors to fight 'The Rotted Souls' while Tec and Neika traverse the fourth level of the nine gates, 'Dark Liquid'.

27) Tec and Neika traverse the fifth level of the nine gates, 'Living Stairs', as I'yudan, *nephew of Brea*, leads a navy on the battlefield to fight 'The Boiling Souls'.

28) Ike leads a corps of souls tortured by Remi to fight off her army of 'Mutated Souls' although she is nowhere to be found. Tec and Neika have no idea there is a warzone outside as they traverse the sixth level of the nine gates, 'Labyrinth of Shifting Walls'.
29) Tec and Neika traverse the seventh level of the nine gates, 'Sticky Sludge', as Eli, *twin brother of Ike*, leads a corps to a battlefield where 'The Scorched Souls' await.
30) The winding internal portions of a demon worm lead to an anal pathway where Tec and Neika are able to enter the eighth level. Ike's bloodline return from their battlefields in victory, reuniting to finish off what is left of the mutated monstrosities fighting tooth and nail at the front gates of the Kingdom in Shadow.
31) An acid spitting minotaur rams through the path of swirling goo mixed with worm poo to find the exit, *continuing its chase of Tec and Neika*. Ike's army enters the Kingdom of Shadow.
32) After Neika defeats the minotaur, Tec sits at a chess table in the center of a cathedral like atmosphere. Tec wins chess match which opens the ninth gate revealing Remi and 'The Army of the Damned'.
33) Tec and Neika are no match until Ike arrives with reinforcements. Tec and Neika are able to continue their quest to save Pep while Remi is distracted.
34) Ike finally defeats Remi, *the illusive villain of the Astral Realm*. What seemed like the end only led Tec and Neika running into a living darkness where they lost each other.
35) Tec finds Pep but their escape is stopped by the dark prince. Neika finds her surrogate parents in time to stop the dark prince from killing them.
36) The dark prince fights his unwanted daughter as Ike, his bloodline, and the victorious army arrive. The breathtaking display results in Neika earning the title of Queen of the Kingdom in Shadow. She reigned with the unjudgmental, welcoming love and care taught to her by Pep and Tec along with the wisdom she attained while listening to Padre Ully and Raja Ali discussing the lessons and values of their beliefs when she would hide in the vents.
37) Tec visits Pep's grave often following the end of his epic adventure. But his story was not over. Pep calls to him, encouraging him to go on one more adventure with her.

38) Pep shows Tec the history of the abyss, the realms, and the new dimensions & their plains.
39) She reveals the future of the realms and the threat of Brogus, *aka Death Incarnate*. Tec's courage is tested as Pep attempts to convince him he is the one chosen to stop this evil demigod.
40) When Tec finally agrees to take on this obligation, Brogus is already in cosmic conflict with Yaboklos, *the defender of the abyss*.
41) Tec meets other trainees who are put through strenuous preparation to fulfill their roles in the pursuit of stopping Brogus. Brogus has changed his external image to reflect that of Yaboklos after consuming the golden angel. Tec's training comes to an end just as Brogus tears down the gates of heaven.
42) Many angels fall to cast Brogus out of heaven. Micheal would remain at the gates until Brogus was no more. Brogus conflict continues with that of Odin himself and the Vikings in Volhalla. The legendary warriors here were quite the match. Brogus would not remain there long.
43) Antawn joins Tec in training to motivate him to keep going as a collection of hundreds now became a handful of trainees. Brogus, in the meantime, chose to bring cosmic conflict to Zeus and his Spartans protecting Elysium. What seemed like an easier contention with fewer to oppose him, Brogus found it just as daunting a task to eliminate the existence of these warriors and departed.
44) Brogus conflicts with Kagutsuchi and the samurai defending hell. Brogus had his way with them. In defeat, the surviving samurai dispensed themselves. Bello, fallen Guardian of Souls, would rise as Hell's general after Kagutsuchi falls.
45) Brogus conflicts with Morrigan and his Celtic warriors in Tartarus as Antawn proves to be the better choice to fight Brogus.
46) Tec failed almost every challenge. Unwilling to quit but confused why he was still being trained, he would eventually learn he was chosen for being the least of any choice of warriors to show the power of Adonai, *the one before all*. Brogus conflicts with Mictlatecuhtli and the Aztec warriors in Naraka.
47) Brogus conflicts with Anansi and the armored legion defending purgatory.

48) Forgotten rises up with gladiators from Limbo when Brogus attempts to pass it. Thinking the dimension to be pathetic, he assumed there was no fight to be had nor energy worth wasting on it. She failed but her efforts earned her passage to the Metaphysical Realm.
49) Brogus would then conflict with Shinigami and ninjas in the Shadow Dimension. Tec wakes up from the vision of each of Brogus' conflicts to find it is time for him to face his fate.
50) The unstoppable Brogus would find the end of his path to destroying Nuwa, *his creator*, at the doorsteps of the Munchgalumptagan Tec. When his moment finally arrived, Tec was permitted to get the help of a micro-civilization that made him a new shell with technology so advanced there is no name that can be written in this book to explain how it works. Since it was his creation, along with Devonte, Tec was able to bring D.R.O.P.A., his trusty paranormal recording robot with him. Tec had no chance but the will of Adonai ensured every act of Tec succeeded against Brogus. The unstoppable force, death incarnate, Nuwa's unworthy creation fell to Tec. As Brogus' remained stunned at his utter failure to such an insignificant being, Antawn dove into Brogus' physical form and seeped to the core where Brogus' light dwelled. He sacrificed himself to trap Brogus' light-source of life. Understanding what Antawn's life purpose would now be, Nuwa took a piece of him and bonded it with a piece of her to create a life for that would live on in Antawn's name. Tec's courage and determination under impossible odds earned him a place in Eden, *where his entire race was brought back along with Pep.* There they would live happily ever after.

This cosmic conflict is the foundation of what would be modified into a five comic book series on Pep and Tec's Spooky Adventures. The story of an unlikely mother and father whose lives fall into parenthood of a child meant to be killed just before birth drives these five issues. Enjoy...

Family

P. Marcelo W. Balboa

Pep and Tec

The Spooky Adventures

ISSUE # 1 SCRIPT

PAGE ONE

NOTE: A MUNCHGALUMPTAGAN is a being with the head, feet, hands, and tail if they have one of the animal that begins the description of their type of being. For example, A TURTLUMPKIDAN is a turtle with humanoid limbs and torso.

The FORSAKEN OMNIVERSE is a beautiful yet hauntingly vast existence in outer space. In an effort to defile all that is good in it, the PRINCE OF DARKNESS attempts to gain power, feeding off the souls of the living. Although he thinks he is free from any interference, a spunky SQUIRLUMPKIDAN with a curiosity for the paranormal gets in the way.

SPLASH PAGE:

Long shot. Ext. Outer space – Night. Shooting stars, constellations, and galaxies spread along a vast void of darkness.

    1 NARRATION (CAPTION)

        The Unworthy Cosmos are filled with wonders beyond the imagination of any mere mortal.

    2 NARRATION (CAPTION)

        Life exists across countless universes as the great traveler Brea creates different teams of various abilities to aid planets in need.

3 NARRATION (CAPTION) (CONT'D)

> Of the several hundred paranormal teams he brought together and set out to fend off the forces of evil, only one team survived. This is their origin story.

4 NARRATION (CAPTION) (CONT'D)

> Enjoy valued reader as you ride along a shuttle carrier that goes by the name, Kobay G.O.M. S081.

5 LOCATION (CAPTION)

> Forsaken Omniverse
>
> Daly Universe
>
> Planet Flubberboober

P. Marcelo W. Balboa

PAGE TWO

The UNWORTHY COSMOS are frighteningly vast and immeasurable to the human eye. That is what surrounds the planet of the Munchgalumptagans called FLUBBERBOOBER.

SPLASH PAGE:

Extreme long shot. Ext. Planet Flubberboober's Orbit – Night. The planet Flubberboober floats, seemingly, alone in the vast space that is the Unworthy Cosmos.

    1 NARRATION (CAPTION)

        A few days ago.

PAGE THREE

Very scary things start happening across the Unworthy Cosmos because of a DARK WITCH named SCIN'D. Sensing opportunity, the DARK PRINCE attempts to capitalize on the cosmic dismay. After choosing a planet with the purest souls to taint, the dark prince settles on YANA, a FEMALE HAMSTERLUMPKIDAN ADULT, to possess. If his uprise is successful it will affect every Munchgalumptagan on the planet.

PANEL ONE:

Wide angle shot. Ext. Planet Flubberboober's Orbit – Night. The planet is cookie shaped but has the live and colors of any living planet as it floats in the abyss of space.

> 1 NARRATION (CAPTION)
>> The forces of darkness have begun to impact planets all over the unworthy cosmos. The delicate Planet Flubber Boober would not go unscathed.

PANEL TWO:

Long shot. Ext. Surface of the planet – Dawn. A green landmass is surrounded by a blue ocean.

> 2 YANA (V.O) (CAPTION)
>> I'll get you...

> 3 YANA (V.O) (CAPTION)
>> ...tasty little thing.

PAGE FOUR

Within a haunted castle is a horror story come to life as, SHAY, a small MALE KITTILUMPKIDAN CHILD who snuck into the castle with some friends is left behind to fend off Yana who is playfully stalking him.

PANEL ONE:

Establishing shot. Ext. Haunted Castle – Daybreak. A thunderstorm grows above the castle but nowhere else.

PANEL TWO:

Close shot. Int. Haunted Castle – Daybreak. Yana's teeth are crooked, sharp, and unbrushed.

    1 YANA

        Hahahaha!

PANEL THREE:

Bird's eye shot. Int. Haunted Castle – Continuous. Shay is running frantically through a long decrepit hallway.

    2 YANA (O.S.) (CONT'D)

        Run little thing.

PANEL FOUR:

Close shot. Int. Haunted Castle – Continuous. Yana's deteriorating hamster-like face has a menacing expression as she drools with anticipation. Her eyes are glowing yellow with red veins. It is clear she is possessed.

    3 YANA (CONT'D)

        RRRRRUHHN!

PANEL FIVE:

Close shot. Int. Haunted Castle – Continuous. Taking refuge under a bed, Shay cries all alone. His kitten-like face is adorable yet frightened with swelled up with tears. He peeks to his left, but doesn't actually look back, as he hears Yana get closer.

   3 YANA (O.S.) (CONT'D)

      I'm going to get you.

PANEL SIX:

Wide shot. Int. Haunted Castle – Continuous. Yana reaches for Shay's left leg with her long, lanky right arm. Her skinny, bony fingers with unclean long nails look like they are almost walking like a spider toward Shay's leg.

   4 YANA (CONT'D)

      GOTCHA!

P. Marcelo W. Balboa

PAGE FIVE

PEP, the spunky squirlumpkidan, is a go getter who lost all her loved ones during the portal invasion war. Convinced they are still with her, she dabbles in any potential paranormal activity that may present itself. Normally it's a fail, but she has a lead on something big. As usual, she recruits her life partner TEC, a laid back turtlumpkidan who goes with the flow, to come with her. She always finds a reason he needs to be involved. He lost all his kin before he was old enough to know it. Surviving on his own made him grow up faster than most. All his anger and pain is subsided by Pep's joyfully rambunctious approach to life. He may not say it, but he loves her to death. She doesn't need him to. She knows they complete each other. He'll go to the ends of the earth with her if she asked.

PANEL ONE:

Long shot. Ext. Under a waterfall – Sunrise. Pep is on her knees, shaking Tec's shell.

    1 PEP

        Hey Tec! Are you inside there?

PANEL TWO:

Medium shot. Int. Tec's shell – Sunrise. Tec wakes up grumpy, still laying on his couch. Pep's rattling his shell and the inside shakes like it's an earthquake.

NOTE: Yes, this doesn't make sense but in this world he can shrink into his shell.

It is clear that Tec's shell serves as both a mobile home and a protective suit of armor.

    2 TEC

        Gimme a sec Pep. I'm coming.

PANEL THREE:

Group shot. Ext. – Under a waterfall – Day. Tec's head and limbs spring out of the openings of his shell. Pep leans back slightly, catching her off guard as usual.

3 PEP

    Oh, you're up! Great! Wanna see something?

4 TEC

    Seriously Pep?

5 PEP

    I need you to come with me really quick. I got something I wantcha to see.

PANEL FOUR:

Wide shot. Ext. Pathway ascending a hill – Twilight. Pep and Tec are walking across a beautiful natural landscape in route to a location Pep believes there may be paranormal activity. The couple walk side by side with mountains complimenting the background.

6 PEP (CAPTION)

    Have you heard of that haunted castle in Kreptland?

7 TEC (CAPTION)

    That isn't close Pep. What were you around that territory for?

8 PEP

    I heard some kids snuck in there and one never came out.

9 TEC

    You're still in this paranormal investigation phase, huh?

PANEL FIVE:

Over the shoulder group shot. Ext. Atop a grassy hill – Dusk. Pep and Tec are laying on their bellies. Pep is focusing on Yana's estate through binoculars. It looks every bit like a haunted castle. The gates surrounding the haunted castle have sharp spears atop each metal beam. A crow sits atop one, staring directly at them. The sky is cloudy, but only above the castle itself.

10 TEC (CAPTION)

> What a distance? I'm pooped.

11 PEP (CAPTION)

> What a view you mean. By the way, do you have that old camera still?

PAGE SIX

NOTE: Tec can shrink things he is holding to bring them inside his shell. Pep never asks. She wants him to invite her.

PANEL ONE:

Long shot. Ext. Atop a grassy hill – Night. Tec's limbs and head shrink into his shell. Pep maintains her view of the haunted castle through binoculars.

    1 TEC (V.O.) CAPTION

        Yeah! Let me check on that really quick.

    2 PEP (O.S.) (CAPTION)

        Thank yooooooooo!

PANEL TWO:

Long shot. Int. Tec's shell - Night. Tec searches his former baby shell which he now uses for storage. He throws things out of his baby shell just to find the camera for Pep.

    3 TEC

        Alright. I know you're in here somewhere. Nope. Uh, nope. Wow, been looking for you.

PANEL THREE:

Long shot. Ext. Atop a grassy hill – Night. Tec shows he can choose individual holes to exit out of as his left arm reaches out with a portable camera. Pep holes the binoculars' focus on the haunted castle but takes a peek at Tec's camera.

    4 TEC (V.O.) (CAPTION)

        Found it.

    5 PEP

        Awesome! That's it.

PANEL FOUR:

Extreme wide shot. Ext. Castle front door – Night. Pep isn't satisfied with a distance study and decides a hands-on approach would be better. Tec walks up to the haunted castle right beside her.

> 6 PEP
>
>> It doesn't look so bad now that I see it close up.
>
> 7 TEC
>
>> I don't like how that crow is staring at us.

PANEL FIVE:

Medium shot. Ext. Castle front door – Continuous. Looks up, studying the haunted castle.

> 8 PEP
>
>> I think I can climb up to that window. Is your camera still linked to your computer?

Medium shot. Ext. – Castle front door – Continuous. Pep looks down at Tec's camera.

> 9 TEC (V.O.) (CAPTION)
>
>> Nothing is broken so it should be. Just be careful in there. I'll be on your heels if things go south.
>
> 10 PEP
>
>> Love you too.

PAGE SEVEN

The castle looks just as haunted up close as far away, but Pep is fearless when Tec is around. Tec isn't fazed. He is ready for anything.

PANEL ONE:

Long shot. Ext. Castle wall – Night. Pep climbs up to an open window.

    1 TEC

        Dang Pep! If only I could climb like that.

    2 PEP

        We need to get audio devices. I can barely here you.

PANEL TWO:

Medium shot. Int. Castle window – Night. Pep hops into an open window cautiously.

    3 PEP

        Whoa! This place is creepy.

PANEL THREE:

Long shot. Int. Castle – Hallway – Night. Pep begins her search as she sticks her head out into a long hallway. She is looking toward the reader, unaware of the silhouette of Yana behind her at the end of the darkened hallway.

    4 PEP

        Looks like the coast is clear.

PANEL FOUR:

Group shot. Int. Castle – Hallway – Continuous. As Pep reaches the end of the hallway she takes out Tec's camera to keep record of her search.

Little does she know, Yana is following her, crawling like a spider along the ceiling.

    5 PEP

> I hope your camera still broadcasts Tec. Cause you need to see this wicked place.

PAGE EIGHT

This situation is new for the love birds. Normally, they investigate sounds in the forest, or leaky pipes. This time, the threat is real, and they feel the tension.

PANEL ONE:

Extreme long shot. Ext. Castle – Night. Tec runs to a safe area to get in his shell as a thunderstorm begins.

NOTE: Munchgalumptagans are between four to five feet at their tallest measure. But there are wild and domesticated animals on this planet. They are what would be understood as normal size for earth.

    1 TEC

        Oh crap!

PANEL TWO:

Split shot. Ext. Castle – Atop a grassy hill/Crow from atop the castle grounds entrance gates – Night. Tec overlooks the haunted castle with Pep's binoculars as the crow maintains focus on him.

    2 TEC

        Seriously? Just when Pep gets inside huh?

PANEL THREE:

Long shot. Ext. Atop a grassy hill – Continuous. Tec pulls his head and limbs into his shell as the crow attacks him.

    3 TEC (V.O.) (CAPTION)

        You're jackin' up the plan bird.

PANEL FOUR:

Extreme wide shot. Int. Tec's Shell – Night. Tec runs past his couch and gaming set up, then his weightlifting bench, to get to his computer area.

NOTE: DEVONTE, boy genius, created the 'Cosmonet' which connects every charted planet to one technologically advanced reception control center on his home planet of Rezandria.

    4 TEC

        You better be broadcasting. Come one trusty Cosmonet.

PANEL FIVE:

Long shot. Int. Castle – Hallway. Pep has walked a short distance through the hallway as she peeks into open doorways along the hallway with Tec's camera. She has no idea Yana is on the ceiling directly above her.

    5 PEP

        I hope this old thing is capturing all this. This place has got some real paranormal vibes.

PANEL SIX:

Long shot. Int. Tec's Shell – Continued. Tec's computer set up is impressive and captures the live feed from his camera.

    6 TEC

        Yowza mcbowza bebby! We're in business.

PANEL SEVEN:

Close up. Int. Tec's Shell – Continued. Tec watching attentively but notices something out of place.

    7 TEC

        This place is sick. We're raking in viewers.

PAGE NINE

This is the point we can see Yana in her entirety. Her possessed body is eerily long and crooked with bad intentions.

PANEL ONE:

Reverse over the shoulder shot. Int. Castle – Hallway doorway – Night. Pep points the camera at herself to talk to the viewers. Yana is behind her twisted with lanky stretched out arms to grab her.

    1 PEP

        This is a scary adventure to say the least. There has to be a ghost somewhere. Maybe that lost kid is just scared and hiding too.

PANEL TWO:

Wide shot. Int. Tec's Shell – Continued. Tec runs back past his weight bench and gaming area.

    2 TEC

        Crap, oh crap. What the heck was that?

PANEL THREE:

Long shot. Int. Tec's Shell – Continued. Tec jumps down a hole in the floor, exiting the internal portion of his shell that is the living area.

    3 TEC

        I'm coming Pep.

PANEL FOUR:

Birds eye shot. Ext. Tec's Shell – Night. Tec's head and limbs exit the appropriate holes as the crow circles his shell.

PANEL FIVE:

Arial shot. Int. Castle – Hallway – Night. Pep runs frantically from Yana as she playfully stalks her.

    4 YANA (O.S.) (CAPTION)

        Run, run, run little thing. I'm coming for you HAHAHAHA!

PANEL SIX:

Medium shot. Int. Castle – Stairway – Night. Pep's legs are stumbling down a winding stairway as she tries to evade Yana. The right ankle has twisted.

    5 PEP (V.O.) (CAPTION)

        OUCH! This is not good. Oh my this is not good.

PAGE TEN

Pep's fate seems just as sealed as the lost child. Tec isn't as skilled of a climber, but it won't stop him from protecting Pep. The tension is high as neither are sure what fate will befall them.

PANEL ONE:

Close shot. Int. Castle – Stairway – Continued. Pep stops to catch her breath and record herself.

> 1 PEP
>
> If this is my last moment on Flubberboober, please know I didn't want to die.

PANEL TWO:

Yana's POV. Int. Castle – Stairway – Continuous. Yana's lanky arms reach out from behind an unsuspecting Pep as she continues to record herself.

PANEL THREE:

Extreme wide shot. Ext. Castle grounds – Night. Tec runs to aid Pep as the crow attacks him.

> 2 TEC
>
> You gotta be kidding me bird. Get outta here. I'm not playin' with you. I'm not the one.

PANEL FOUR:

Long shot. Int. Castle – Night. Tec closes the open window as the crow hits the window from outside. His body is covered with bumps from the attacks of the crow. Some of the wounds are bleeding.

> 3 TEC
>
> SHIT! What the fuck?

PANEL FIVE:

Long shot. Int. Castle – Hallway – Night. Tec jumps out into the hallway ready to fight.

    4 TEC

        PEP. PEP, WHERE ARE YOU?

PANEL SIX:

Long shot. Int. Castle – Hallway – Continuous. Tec is unaware something is approaching from behind.

PAGE ELEVEN

Pep's injury slows her down as she gets lost trying to retrace her steps back to the window she entered. From behind, Yana simulates a crying child, yet it sounds like it's in another room.

PANEL ONE:

Long shot. Int. Castle – Floor level hallway – Night. Pep limps along as she enters another hallway that looks exactly like the one she walked through at the start.

    1 PEP

        Holy moly! I think I found my way out. But what room did I come in from?

PANEL TWO:

Over the shoulder shot. Castle – Floor level hallway – Continuous. Pep walks in the direction she believes the cries of a child are coming from.

    2 SHAY (O.S.) (CAPTION)

        Help me! Waaaah! Owww!

    3 PEP (CAPTION)

        Oh my goodness. No way! WHERE ARE YOU? Holy crap what if?

PANEL THREE:

Medium shot. Castle – Floor level hallway – Doorway – Night. Pep peeks into the room where she believes Shay can be heard crying. She is partly confused and afraid but determined to help the child if she can.

    4 PEP

        Hello?

PANEL FOUR:

Long shot. Int. Inside the room – Night. Pep approached a crib to look inside. Terror is in her eyes. She has no idea Yana is behind her.

    5 SHAY

        Whaaaah! Whaaaaah!

PANEL FIVE:

Arial shot. Int. Castle – Inside crib – Night. The skeletal remains of Shay in order but not attached lay motionless in the crib.

    6 SHAY

        Whaaaah! Whaaaaah!

PANEL SIX:

Close up. Int. Inside the room - Continued. Pep can hear the sound of Shay crying from heard from behind her. Her eyes water up as she realizes she's been duped. Just in view, to the right, behind Pep's head is a part of Yana's face smiling insidiously.

    7 YANA (CAPTION)

        Whaaaaah! Hehehe! Whaaaaaah!

PAGE TWELVE

With just one more soul, the dark prince will have enough power to manifest himself in true physical form. Like a cocoon, Yana's body will by ravaged but from within her will emerge the most beautiful angel ever seen. Pep's sacrifice will be appreciated.

NOTE: Munchgalumptagans have the hands of their animal origin, but this Hamsterlumpkidan is possessed by a fallen angel with fingers. She is slowly taking his form as he grows stronger.

SPLASH PAGE:

Long group shot. Int. Castle – Floor level hallway – Continued. Upright, Yana's possessed frame stands at a lanky eight feet. Her long witch like fingers hold Pep by the skull, she glides to her destination as if floating all while Pep's body dangles. Pep keeps the camera pointed to her the best she can.

    1 PEP

        Tec. Help me!

PAGE THIRTEEN

Tec's path is offset by Shay, who has returned from the Astral Realm with a message.

PANEL ONE:

Group shot. Int. Castle – Hallway – Night. A ghostly figure tapping on Tec's shoulder.

    1 SHAY

           Hello there.

PANEL TWO:

Close shot on Tec. Int. Castle – Continuous. Tec is startled by the ghostly figure.

    2 TEC

           Whoa! Dude, what the fuck? Warn a guy.

PANEL THREE:

Medium shot on Shay. Int. Castle – Continuous. Shay holds his hands up to show he means no harm.

    3 SHAY

           Please forgive me. I am Shay. I died here what is long ago for me but a day ago for you.

PANEL FOUR:

Long shot. Int. Castle – Continuous. Tec stands battle ready but is open to dialogue.

Family

4 TEC

    Look, I'm just here to get my friend and leave. I don't want trouble.

5 SHAY

    I believe we want the same thing.

P. Marcelo W. Balboa

PAGE FOURTEEN

Pep's situation is revealed as she is captured by Yana who is now fully revealed.

SPLASH PAGE:

Long shot. Int. Castle – Castle dungeon – Night. The silhouette of the dark prince can be seen encapsuling Yana's body as she straps Pep onto a concrete bed with spooky symbols all over it.

    1 PEP

        I don't want to die.

    2 YANA (V.O. of dark prince) (CAPTION)

        You're sacrifice will give me the energy I need to break through from the Astral Realm. Thank you for your gift.

PAGE FIFTEEN

As time runs out, Shay is burdened with the quest to help save Pep.

PANEL ONE:

Group shot. Int. Castle – Hallway – Continued. Tec is confused but listening.

1 SHAY

Where do I start? Your friend is about to be killed. You can't save her without killing the dark prince.

PANEL TWO:

Medium shot. Int. Castle – Hallway – Continuous. Tec is normally laid back, but he want to save Pep and breaks character with a look of concern.

2 TEC

We're wasting time then. What, where, how? Let's get it done.

PANEL THREE:

Long shot. Int. Castle – Hallway – Continuous. Shay begins to enter Tec's body.

3 SHAY

To get where you need to go, you will need to be where I have been.

4 TEC

What are you doing?

PANEL FOUR:

Establishing shot. Int. ASTRAL REALM. Tec falls to what seems like his death in a red orange atmosphere filled with other falling bodies. Some souls are already exploding as they crash to the maroon rock, grave, and sand covered ground.

    1 TEC

        Shit, shit, shit!

PANEL FIVE:

Long shot. Int. Astral Realm – Continuous. Tec shrinks into his shell.

PANEL SIX:

Angle shot. Int. Astral Realm – Continuous. Tec crashes into the maroon sand causing a huge dust cloud.

    3 SFX

        Whooosh!

PAGE SIXTEEN

Back in the PHYSICAL REALM, Pep is facing her own quest to stay alive. The time is near for the rise of the fallen angel, the prince of darkness, LUCIFER.

PANEL ONE:

Long shot. Int. Castle – Castle dungeon – Continued. Yana cuts her bony hand with a knife engraved with cryptic symbols. The bowl is filled with the coagulated blood of multiple lost lives.

> 1 YANA (V.O. of dark prince) (CAPTION)
>> Bello, guardian of souls, I call to you to aid my cause. Now is the time. Answer my call. SEND ME YOUR AID.

PANEL TWO:

Group shot. Int. Castle – Castle dungeon – Continuous. Yana raises a text with ancient runes decorating it's exterior with a strap to lock in hanging open between her long bony fingers. Her other hand holds the engraved knife, ready to stab down into Pep.

> 2 YANA (V.O. of dark prince) (CAPTION)
>> GIVE ME THE POWER to break free of the Astral Realm and become whole in the Physical Realm.

PANEL THREE:

Wide shot. Int. Castle – Castle dungeon – Continuous. Pep is strapped down tightly though she still attempts to struggle free. Her expression acknowledges certain doom is at hand.

> 3 PEP
>> 3 PEP
>>> Scary lady, please don't do this. I don't want to die. PLEASE!

PAGE SEVENTEEN

The moment has come. The dark prince will be whole. Until...

SPLASH PAGE:

Group shot. Int. Castle – Castle dungeon – Continuous. As the dark prince shares the body of Yana, they raise the knife to strike down. Her eyes are glowing red, and her mouth has a long snake like shape to it as it sticks out of her bone chilling smile.

    1 YANA (V.O. of dark prince) (CAPTION)

        BELLO, FREE ME NOW!

PAGE EIGHTEEN

Pep screams as a blade penetrates its target. The power of Bello surges through the blade instead of Yana's body.

SPLASH PAGE:

Group shot. Int. Castle – Castle dungeon – Continuous. Tec has thrusted a dark ancient sword through Yana's torso from behind as Pep reacts with the purest happiness and simultaneous relief.

    1 PEP

        OH MY GOHHHHHHSH!

PAGE NINETEEN

The Dark Prince's plans are shattered. His soul is not only returned to the Shadow Dimension in the Astral Realm, but his soul is also near permanent death. He must seclude himself to his personal chambers past the ninth gate in the Kingdom in Shadow to recover.

PANEL ONE:

Group shot. Int. Castle – Castle dungeon – Continued. Pep sits up from the altar as Tec unties her. She looks broken. Tec looks like a barbarian warrior with apparel made from the beasts he slayed.

    1 PEP

        Thank goodness you came. I was so close to the end.

    2 TEC

        Not if I can help it. Now let's get the hell outta here.

PANEL TWO:

Long group shot. Ext. Castle front door – Daybreak. Tec holds onto Pep as she limps out the front of the castle.

    3 PEP

        How did you find me? And you look so handsome. Where did you get all that armor?

    4 TEC

        Well, to make a long story short.

PAGE TWENTY

A montage of Tec's adventure through the Astral Realm shows his talk with the child's spirit, the introduction of IKE, the ASTRAL TRAVELER, and the aftermath of his long cosmic journey.

PANEL ONE:

Long shot. Int. Castle – Hallway – Night. Shay fully enters Tec causing Tec's body to glow blue.

    1 TEC

        It wasn't easy. That kid that went missing possessed me.

    2 PEP

        What?

PANEL TWO:

Long group shot. Ext. Astral Realm – Smoking wall of the PLAIN OF LOST TREASURES. Tec stands in front of a wall of smoke beside Ike, a priestly looking fellow with full religious garb on.

    3 TEC

        Don't worry. It allowed Ike, Brea's great-grandson to pull me into the Astral Realm.

PANEL THREE:

Long shot. Int. Plain of Lost Treasures. An environment filled with living and forgotten things lost in time. Everything is some shade of gray. Even the air has a gray quality to it. Tec stands on the other side of the smoking wall, unsure where to go.

    4 TEC

        I had to traverse deep in the Shadow Dimension to enter the Plain of Lost Treasures.

PANEL FOUR:

Medium shot. Int. Plain of Lost Treasures. Tec squats down trying to stay warm next to a blue gray flame.

    4 TEC

        I journeyed for months, learning how to survive.

PANEL FIVE:

Long shot. Int. Plain of Lost Treasures. Tec stands over a defeated monster.

    5 TEC

        I had to make food, clothes, and basic tools out of the threats I was forced to slay.

PANEL SIX:

Long group shot. Int. Plain of Lost Treasures. Tec finds the sword he will save Pep with as his two friends, a Rabbitlumpkidan and a Deerlumpkidan who have discovered their own treasures.

    6 TEC

        I was able to make friends and discover treasures like the sword I used to save you.

PAGE TWENTY-ONE

The story continues with an epilogue of sorts. Setting up the rest of the series.

PANEL ONE:

Establishing shot. Ext. Planet Flubberboober's orbit – Day. An image of the planet Flubber boober with a carrier floating at a distance in outer space. A shuttle can be seen whisking away from the carrier.

> 1 NARRATION (CAPTION)
>> Present Day.
>
> 2 NARRATION (CAPTION) (CONT'D)
>> A shuttle with unrevealed guests prepares to land on the planet Fubberboober.

P. Marcelo W. Balboa

PAGE TWENTY-TWO

The spooky castle incident has been over for several weeks. Life has returned to normal, somewhat. Pep hasn't lost her fever for the paranormal but has taken a break to appreciate life. Still, there is this fire deep inside that pains for the proof that her loved ones aren't truly gone. Learning about the Astral Realm only solidifies her beliefs. Tec would have to retell his story of the spirit child and the astral traveler more than he would like to admit.

PANEL ONE:

Close shot. Ext. Open field – Day. Pep's healed up with a fresh Squirlumpkidan face.

> 1 PEP
>
>> I still can't believe you went on such a crazy adventure for months and it was only a few minutes in this realm.

PANEL TWO:

Close shot. Ext. Open field – Continuous. Tec is still healing but there are scars not yet healed on his face. As usual, he's smoking FLUBBERLEAF.

> 2 TEC
>
>> You were in danger Pep. I'll pass through the depths of darkness for you.

PANEL THREE:

Long group shot. Ext. Open field – Continuous. Pep and Tec are laying down on a fancy cloth, looking up at the sky. They're enjoying a pic-nick with a basket of food and beverages.

> 3 PEP
>
>> I'm sorry to put you through so much. I just know our friends and family are out there. That child's spirit only proves my case more.

PANEL FOUR:

Medium group shot. Ext. Open field – Continuous. Pep points at something streaking above them as she remains laying down on the cloth.

    4 PEP

        Do you see what I see?

    5 TEC

        Yup. It's about time.

PANEL FIVE:

Long shot. Ext. Open field – Continuous. A futuristic aircraft descends onto the open field.

    6 PEP (O.S.) (CAPTION)

        What does that mean? Were you expecting someone?

    7 TEC

        Why else do you think I would suggest a pic-nick?

    8 PEP

        To be romantic yah goof.

PANEL SIX:

Over the shoulder group shot. Ext. Open field – Continuous. The aircraft doors open to reveal BREA, the Guardian of Travel and founder of BREA'S GUILD. He has the look of a wise aged wizard. He also has a patch over his right eye. Behind him are two silent men. One is in a priests uniform and the other is dressed like a Sufi scholar.

    9 BREA

        Pep and Tec, is that you? I am Brea, traveler of the Unworthy Cosmos.

PAGE TWENTY-THREE

It's an epic moment. Pep and Tec's lives are about to change forever. What seemed like a long distance to travel on their tiny planet while going on spooky adventures will now grow into a journey of cosmic proportions.

PANEL ONE:

Wide shot. Ext. Shuttle entrance ramp – Day. Brea steps off the shuttle to greet Pep and Tec.

    1 BREA

        Little friends. You have proven your worth. Perhaps you would be interested in experiencing paranormal activity across the Unworthy Cosmos.

PANEL TWO:

Group shot. Ext. Shuttle entrance ramp – Continuous. Pep runs up the ramp, passing Brea, as Tec follows in a relaxed walking pace.

    2 PEP

        You better believe it. We can get to know each other on board. Tec let's go.

    3 BREA

        Whoa, well then. Good to hear.

    4 TEC

        Right behind you.

PAGE TWENTY-FOUR

PEP AND TEC'S SPOOKY ADVENTURES are about to begin. They are mesmerized by the sights of outer space without looking at it from the perspective of their cookie shaped planet.

PANEL ONE:

Extreme long shot. Int. Forsaken Omniverse – Night. The shuttle enters the carrier before it sets to soar off into outer space.

    1 PEP

        Our planet is so small. And it looks like a cookie. Isn't that the cutest Tec?

    2 NARRATIONS (CAPTION)

        Brea departs without the need of a ship as the team is left to get to know each other while living aboard the Kobay G.O.M. S081.

    3 (CAPTION)

        Forsaken Omiverse

        Undewer Universe

        Tur Galaxy

P. Marcelo W. Balboa

PAGE TWENTY-FIVE

A variety of planets are on display as the Kobay G.O.M. S081 displays its ability to cover great distances.

SPLASH PAGE:

Extreme long shot. Int. Unworthy Cosmos. The Kobay G.O.M. S081 passes by the Cha Solar System consisting of four our planets, a moon, and a star.

1 PEP (O.S.) (CAPTION)

    TEC, TEC! Look at these oddly shaped planets. Aren't they beautiful?

2 NARRATION (CAPTION)

    The newly assembled team travels through.

3 LOCATION (CAPTION)

    Forsaken Omniverse

    Weila Universe

    Kodey Galaxy

    Cha Solarsystem

4 NARRATION (CAPTION) (CONT'D)

    As they set out to rendezvous with Brea the cosmic journey provides wonderous sights such as these Planets.

5 LOCATION (CAPTION)

NOTE: The planets are visible from nearest to farthest in this order.

            Arbi
            Tola
            Niktaka
            Sheelee & Rock

       Star

            Marso

Family

Sneak peak of the Kobay GOM S081 traveling through the Unworthy Cosmos.

ISSUE #2

PAGE ONE

Traveling the Unworthy Cosmos is not a small feat. The distance from the Weila Universe to the Daly Universe allowed the members to get to know each other and the layout of the carrier. An unspoken truth that should be kept in mind.

SPLASH PAGE:

Establishing shot. Int. Daly Universe – Night. Unique constellations fill the page. The team's carrier looks small as it travels through this uncharted universe.

> 1 LOCATION (CAPTION)
>> Forsaken Omniverse
>>
>> Daly Universe
>
> 2 NARRATION (CAPTION)
>> The Unworthy Cosmos are filled with wonders beyond the imagination of any mere mortal.
>
> 3 NARRATION (CAPTION)
>> Life exists across countless universes as the great traveler Brea creates different teams of various abilities to aid planets in need.
>
> 4 PEP (O.S.) (CAPTION)
>> Guys, look outside. Isn't it beautiful?
>
> 5 NARRATION (CAPTION)
>> Of the several hundred paranormal teams he brought together and set out to fend off the forces of evil, only one team survived. This is their origin story.

6 NARRATION (CAPTION)

Enjoy, valued readers, as you ride along within a shuttle carrier that goes by the name, Kobay G.O.M. S081.

P. Marcelo W. Balboa

PAGE TWO

The team has had enough time to get the hang of being on the Kobay GOM. Now they must rendezvous with Brea so that he can provide them with their quest. He also needs to introduce an adviser that can help the team learn the major mechanics of the ship and their paranormal equipment as the ship has been running on auto pilot to get them to the orbit of PLANET KIR.

PANEL ONE:

Extreme long shot. Int. Planet Kir's orbit – Kobay G.O.M. S081 - Day. With a closer view of the Kobay G.O.M S081 orbiting planet Kir. The team welcomes Brea's arrival.

> 1 BREA (V.O.) (CAPTION)
>
>> I am pleased to see you have grown close on your travels. I have brought you together because you have particular talents.

PANEL TWO:

Close shot. Int. Kobay GOM S081 – Briefing room – Day. Brea's appearance is visibly different from when he initially picked up Pep and Tec some time ago. Stronger and more vibrant. The patch is gone displaying a glass right eye with a scar over to under the right eye.

> 2 BREA
>
>> Individually, you have proven your worth. Yet, as a group you will make a tremendous impact on the Unworthy Cosmos.

PANEL THREE:

Medium shot. Int. Kobay GOM S081 – Continuous. Brea's wardrobe looks angelic. He has clearly been on an epic adventure of his own.

> 3 BREA
>
>> In due time you will all realize this to be true. And the forces of light will be in your debt.

PAGE THREE

This will be the introduction of Devonte, but his role will not be official as he will be there as a temporary partner.

PANEL ONE:

Medium shot. Int. Kobay GOM S081 – Continued. Tec remains relaxed, smoking flubberleaf. He's playing a handheld game but puts off playing with it out of respect.

> 1 BREA
>
> To begin with, Tec, I plan on utilizing your unpolished passion for computer technology.

PANEL TWO:

Group shot. Int. Kobay GOM S081 – Continuous. Standing behind Brea is Devonte, kindly waiving.

> 2 BREA
>
> This is Devonte. He is a very intelligent young man who will aid you in maximizing you potential. When you are ready to be on your own, I will need him back.

P. Marcelo W. Balboa

PAGE FOUR

Everyone is familiar with each other at this point. They know each other's stories and have an idea this may be why they were brought together. Still, each of them remained respectfully attentive as they knew the spooky adventure to come would need details.

PANEL ONE:

Close shot. Int. Kobay GOM S081 – Continued. Brea smiles for a mement.

> 1 BREA
>
> And dear sweet Pep. To be in the presence of the dark prince and survive. I need say no more.

PANEL TWO:

Close shot. Int. Kobay GOM S081 – Continuous. Pep is wearing her best loop earrings for the occasion.

> 1 BREA (O.S.) (CAPTION)
>
> Even as you faced certain death you remain unbroken. Your relentless curiosity for the paranormal makes you a perfect lead investigater.

PAGE FIVE

The Kobay GOM is a living breathing entity by itself. As the backdrop the group can hear the steady hum of its technology operating while Brea speaks.

PANEL ONE:

Close shot. Int. Kobay GOM S081 – Continued. Padre Ully looks confused but tries not to come off disrespectful.

   1 PADRE ULLY

      My apologies great traveler. May I say a word?

   2 BREA (O.S.) (CAPTION)

      Certainly Padre.

PANEL TWO:

Medium shot. Int. Kobay GOM S081 – Continuous. Padre Ully's habitually descriptive with hand movements.

   3 PADRE

      Thank you. I apologize if I come of rude. But would I not be the best choice as the lead?

   4 BREA (O.S.) (CAPTION)

      As a gifted seer of astral threats in the physical realm with extensive experience in exorcisms, you are a pivotal member good man.

PANEL THREE:

Medium shot. Int. Kobay GOM S081 – Continuous. Brea is patient in his words and body language.

4 BREA

> And yet you cannot see that not every threat will need exorcisms. There will be false calls or non-paranormal situations mind you.

5 BREA (CONT.D)

> But be patient. You're one side of the blade if not the tip, I tell you.

PANEL THREE:

Medium shot. Int. Kobay GOM S081 – Continuous. Raja's life leaves him at a loss for words. As a lonesome outdoorsman, he is fine with listening and absorbing his environment.

6 BREA (O.S.) (CAPTION)

> And both sides will cut deep. It is Raja Ali who will be by YOUR side. He will ensure your protection, I have no doubt.

PAGE SIX

Brea's Guild was established on the planet of REZANDRIA. The sister planet caught up in a binary planet war that required the aid of one of Brea's team. With a place to train and build elite forces to fight the darkness looming over the cosmos, it was only a matter of time until the prince of darkness would step in. Though recovering, his eyes were one Pep and Tec. And he wasn't going to stand by as they gained confidence from their cosmic guide.

NOTE: REMI makes her first appearance. She is a mutilated soul with limbs reattached to the wrong areas and a face missing everything but an eye. Her entire body is resown with skin grafts not matching.

The PLAIN OF SORROWS is a place souls go in the Shadow Dimension when they pass away in the Physical Realm in a horrifying way. Still in shock, their souls are sad and haunted.

PANEL ONE:

Close shot. Int. Kobay GOM S081 – Continued. Pep's face is distorted much like Yana's was.

    1 PEP

        Uh, guys... I don't feel too good.

PANEL TWO:

Group shot. Int. Kobay GOM S081 – Continuous. The paranormal team experiences their first encounter. Pep Floats as everyone turns to her trying to figure out what's happening to her.

    2 PEP

        Something is wrong inside me. Everything is turning black.

3 PADRE ULLY

> Something is pulling her into the Astral Realm. PEP, FIGHT TO STAY WITH US.

PANEL THREE:

Long shot. Int. Kobay GOM S081 – Continuous. Pep's body has twisted, taking the form of the foul spirit overtaking her.

4 PEP (V.O. of Remi)

> FUCK OFF PRIEST. The little shit is in the Plain of Sorrows with the rest of her loser friends.

PAGE SEVEN

The team gets their chance to show each other what their contributions are worth.

PANEL ONE:

Group shot. Int. Kobay GOM S081 – Continued. Tec pulls out his sword, which looks like a long dagger to the others as he stands less than five feet tall. Devonte points a device that looks like a television controller but has electrical energy glowing at the tip.

PANEL TWO:

Group shot. Int. Kobay GOM S081 – Continuous. Raja Ali is in a fighting stance with his walking stick at the ready. Padre Ully opens his book and prepares to splash holy water from his flask.

PANEL THREE:

Long shot. Int. Kobay GOM S081 – Continuous. Pep's possessed body floats as Remi speaks through her.

> 1 PEP (V.O. of Remi)
>> I see you gave your priest a bodyguard. Too bad for the rest. Learning your lessons a little late Guardian?

PANEL FOUR:

Medium shot. Int. Kobay GOM S081 – Continuous. Brea's arms are crossed with an unimpressed expression.

> 1 BREA
>> Bite your tongue foul spirit.

PANEL FIVE:

Group shot. Int. Kobay GOM S081 – Continuous. Father Ully stands before Pep's possessed floating body with his left are stretched out with book in hand and his flask cocked back ready to splash holy water.

    1 PADRE ULLY

        Do not respond to this conjurer.

    2 PEP (V.O. of Remi)

        I'M HERE FOR YOU, Turtlumpkidan. The dark prince will have your little damsel. And your team will die like the rest have.

PANEL SIX:

Close up. Int. Kobay GOM S081 – Continuous. Brea's expression is furious. He knows most of his paranormal teams are already losing the war against darkness.

    3 BREA

        THAT'S ENOUGH, Remi. Be gone before you are made to flee by the archangel you witless minion.

PAGE EIGHT

As Remi sends her master's message, Brea holds back his wrath to let the team figure out a solution on their own.

PANE ONE:

Group shot. Int. Kobay GOM S081 – Continued. Pep looks away, shielding her eyes from the light energy shining from the book Padre Ully raises in her direction.

    1 PADRE ULLY

        Be gone Remi of the Kingdom in Shadow.

PANEL TWO:

Long shot. Int. Kobay GOM S081 – Continuous. Remi struggles, swirling around, trying to keep control of Pep's body.

    2 PEP (V.O. of Remi)

        NOOOOOO! I'll find your wife and child and torture
        them for eternity PRIEST.

PANEL THREE:

Close shot. Int. Kobay GOM S081 – Continuous. Padre Ully shows not fear as he performs the exorcism.

    3 PADRE ULLY

        Depart from this vessel for you are not wanted here.
        In the name of all that is good…

PANEL FOUR:

Over the shoulder group shot. Int. Kobay GOM S081 – Continuous. Pep looks at Tec as Remi fades away.

4 PEP

> Before I leave... know this. Your precious Pep will be tortured for eternity in the name of the dark prince... GRRRHHH!

PAGE NINE

Remi won't leave without a fight. But the fight is one the naked eye can't see. Everyone is confused except Brea and Padre Ully.

PANEL ONE:

Full page – Long shot. Int. Padre Ully's body. Remi and Padre Ully fight for his body. They are surrounded by light since Padre Ully is good.

    1 REMI

        Fine. I'll take your body.

    2 PADRE ULLY

        This isn't my first rodeo Remi. And I know your weakness.

PANEL TWO:

Close shot. Int. Padre Ully's body – Continuous. Padre Ully pulls Remi's eye out.

    3 REMI

        AHHHHHHH!

PAGE TEN

NOTE: How you act in the Unworthy Cosmos doesn't go unnoticed. Who you are when no one is looking has an effect on your soul. There are places to go in the afterlife. If you are good, bad, neutral, it all gets judged. And within your body grows the essence of the place you will go. Because Padre Ully's heart is pure and his actions good, he will go to Elysium when he dies. So around him is the essence of Elysium.

PANEL ONE:

Long shot. Int. Padre Ully's body – Continued. Padre Ully knows a living soul is stronger than a dead soul. He throws Remi's eye into the portal Remi came from.

> 1 PADRE ULLY
>> I call on the forces of light to aid in the departure of Remi.

PANEL TWO:

Close shot. Int. Padre Ully's body – Continuous. A radiant arm reaches out to grab Remi.

PANEL THREE:

Group shot. Int. Padre Ully's body – Continuous. Remi is pulled into the portal.

> 2 REMI
>> You will pay for this priest. I'll make you PAYYYY! ...

PANEL FOUR:

Padre Ully responds kindly.

> 3 PADRE ULLY
>> You may return to your prince in darkness.

PANEL ELEVEN

A visual of the Astral Realm shows the fallen souls crashing. The heavier their burden the more violent the crash. Many souls carry so much burden their souls are too weak and disintegrate. Under cosmic construction, the Astral Realm will be the platform to hold multiple dimensions with multiple plains within those dimensions. This area is the universal arrival point for all burdened souls.

PANEL ONE:

Establishing shot. Int. Astral Realm. Remi falls through the foggy red atmosphere as other bodies falls all around her.

> 1 NARRATION (CAPTION)
>> Screams of the falling souls fill the dead space as they fear instant collision in the Astral Realm.

PANEL TWO:

Long shot. Int. Astral Realm – SHADOW DIMENSION – Eternal Night. Remi walks to a destination unknown as bodies fall all around her. The ground is maroon gravel with spikey hills in the distance. She lands brutally. Her eye awaits a few feet away.

> 2 NARRATION (CAPTION)
>> The mutilated humanoid Remi lands in the Astral Realm as bodies pop from impact all around her.

PANEL THREE:

Establishing shot. Ext. KINGDOM IN SHADOW – Eternal Night. The environment is dark gray and black with things hiding. There are various colored, numerous, glowing eyes watching. Remi walks a dark grey gravel path leading toward a black castle in the distance. She is still putting her eye back in.

1 NARRATION (CAPTION)

> She make her way to the Kingdom in Shadow within the Shadow dimension. The atmosphere is stale. Around every corner lurks a menacing presence.

PANEL FOUR:

Extreme long shot. Int. Kingdom in Shadow – GREAT HALL OF THE SHADOW KINGDOM – Eternal Night. Remi bows to the dark prince within the dark hall before an unseen leader.

2 REMI

> I return to you humbly my lord.

PAGE TWELVE

Demon guards line the great hall. They stand at the attention as Remi entered. She is a highly ranked member of the dark prince's counsel. Yet even she is aware of the superiority of the dark prince and shows homage.

PANEL ONE:

Medium shot. Int. Kingdom in Shadow – Continued. Remi has dropped to a knee, even though her body is resown together with a leg as an arm and an arm as a leg.

   1 REMI
      Your message has been sent my prince. I pray I have pleased you.

PANEL TWO:

Over the shoulder shot. Int. Kingdom in Shadow – Continuous. The prince speaks from his flaming thrown several feet higher than the ground floor.

   2 DARK PRINCE (O.S.) (CAPTION)
      All has gone according to plan. Let them marinate on the dangers to come.

PANEL THREE:

Bird's eye shot. Int. Kingdom in Shadow – Continuous. A glimpse of the hall that houses the throne of the dark prince has a daunting presence as the two speak with a grand echo.

   3 DARK PRINCE (CAPTION)
      Pep's nightmare may have freed her friends, but she will surely be damaged emotionally. I have more important things for you to do.

PANEL FOUR:

Medium shot. Int. Kingdom in Shadow – Continuous. Remi looks up at her master.

    4 REMI

        Karlo?

PANEL FIVE:

Long shot. Ext. Open field – Daybreak. A glimpse of Karlo, a fat minotaur with his head twisted upside down after a second fight with an old rival goes south. He is leading his army of DEMON TICKS, six armed two-legged creatures with suction mouths and tentacle tongues, down a hill. The backdrop is a red sky with orange sunlight.

    5 DARK PRINCE (V.O.) (CAPTION)

        No. Let the warmonger think rivaling the one before
        all is attainable. In the end he will only help my cause.

PANEL SIX:

Close shot. Int. Kingdom in Shadow – Continuous. Remi's stitched up, loose one-eyed face has no expression.

    6 REMI

        Then what would you have of me my everything?

PAGE THIRTEEN

The carrier passes through breathtaking cosmic structures on route to the next spooky adventure.

SPLASH PAGE:

Establishing shot. Int. KODEY GALAXY – Night. The image of an electromagnetic tube of lightning streams across outer space as the Kobay G.O.M. S081 travels to its destination.

    1 LOCATION (CAPTION)

        Forsaken Omniverse

        Weila Universe

        Kodey Galaxy

        Event B7481

PAGE FOURTEEN

The battle of the forces of light and darkness have become uneven as portals around the cosmos have allowed entities from the Astral Realm to create havoc on the Physical Realm. The dark prince is not the only threat.

PANEL ONE:

Group shot. Ext. Kingdom in Shadow – Shadow Dimension – Eternal Night. Within a dark gray fog, glowing balls ingulfed in gray-blue flames float freely.

> 1 DARK PRINCE (V.O.) (CAPTION)
>> I need you to lead the lost lights.

PANEL TWO:

Over the shoulder. Int. Kingdom in Shadow – Continued. From his thrown, the dark prince raises his right arm as he speaks.

> 2 DARK PRINCE (O.S.) (CAPTION)
>> I have cults spreading around the cosmos with members ready for possession.

PANEL THREE:

Close shot. Int. Kingdom in Shadow – Continuous. Remi bows her head.

> 3 REMI
>> My lord, can we trust the vengeful Suicide Souls? Once they possess those bodies there's no telling...

> 4 DARK PRINCE (O.S.) (CAPTION)
>> I have that matter taken care of. You will be reassigned when the time is right. Now go. The Lost Lights are growing restless.

PANEL FOUR:

Extreme long shot. Int. Unworthy Cosmos. The Kobay G.O.M. S081 travels through constellations to their next destination.

> 5 NARRATION (CAPTION)
>> The paranormal team's shuttle departs from the carrier for the first time.

PANEL FIVE:

Long shot. Int. PLANE XZIBRON'S orbit – Day. A lush green planet is the destination for the paranormal team. A shuttle flies away from the carrier.

> 6 LOCATION (CAPTION)
>> Planet Xzibron

> 7 TEC (V.O.) (CAPTION)
>> Head's up everyone. Prepare for landing in 5, 4...

PAGE FIFTEEN

The team has landed in a peaceful land but there are reports of missing people. Pep and Tec's team are requested by Brea to investigate.

PANEL ONE:

Wide shot. Ext. Open range – Day. Pep walks up on a path that leads to a log cabin further on in the background.

> 1 DEVONTE (V.O.) (CAPTION)
>> The hologram message from Brea said the inhabitants have been going missing.
>
> 2 PEP (CAPTION)
>> I hope these robots you guys made work.
>
> 3 TEC (V.O.) (CAPTION)
>> The data recorders should help us get a read out of the inside the house before you enter.

PANEL TWO:

Long shot. Ext. Log cabin – Day. Pep stops at the front of the house, opening the case holding the data recorders.

> 1 PEP
>> Got it. Alright, here we go.

PANEL THREE:

Close shot. Ext. Log cabin – Day. Pep's open case shows little robots with sensors exiting.

> 2 PEP
>> Go get me some data tiny robots.

3 DATA RECORDERS

>Get data, get data, get data...

PANEL FOUR:

Long shot. Ext. Log cabin – Day. The data recorders of paranormal activity look for any entrance, finding a path inside through the chimney.

4 DATA RECORDERS

>Get data, get data, get data...

PANEL FIVE:

Over the shoulder group shot. Int. Kobay GOM S081 – TEC'S DATA RECEPTION ROOM – Day. Devonte guides Tec through the technical aspects of the multiple screen, advanced computer terminal.

5 DEVONTE

>Press F4 to pull up data recorder seven, eight, nine, and ten.

6 TEC

>Eeeee-fffourrr... There we go.

PAGE SIXTEEN

Padre Ully and Raja Ali are sitting at a monitor in the lobby, waiting for their chance to help. Tec and Devonte play their part with the documenting and recording of the events. Leaving Pep to do what Pep loves best. Inquire.

PANEL ONE:

Group shot. Int. Kobay GOM S081 – Continued. Devonte calmly guides Tec.

    1 DEVONTE

        F7 on screen 2 and F12 on screen 3 please.

PANEL TWO:

Close shot. Int. Kobay GOM S081 – Continuous. Tec looks calm, cool, and collected as he communicates with Pep. He knows she's going to do something unscripted.

    2 TEC

        Pep what are you doing?

PANEL THREE:

Medium shot. Ext. Log cabin front door – Day. Pep pulls the front door open to peak in.

    3 PEP

        Hey guys. The door is open.

PANEL FOUR:

Group shot. Int. Kobay GOM S081 – Continued. Devonte's worried and confused is opposite of Tec's usual docile expression. Tec knew Pep enough to know she was going to go inside before they received intel from the data recorders.

4 DEVONTE

>Wait, what?

5 TEC

>Pep, the data recorders are picking up some deceased bodies hidden in the walls. Wait for Raja.

PANEL FIVE:

Close up. Int. Kobay GOM S081 – Continuous. The monitor displays the deceased bodies cramped in a wall is on the large center monitor.

6 TEC (O.S.) (CAPTION)

>Raja, we're getting feedback from data recorder seventeen. We could use your service.

7 RAJA ALI (V.O.) (CAPTION)

>On it.

P. Marcelo W. Balboa

PAGE SEVENTEEN

Off screen Raja Ali is rushing to Pep's position. Padre Ully is praying. Devonte and Tec are helpless as their role is to monitor and document the events for the HALL OF LEGENDS DATA ENTRY CENTER, in Rezandria.

PANEL ONE:

Medium shot. Int. Log cabin – Day. Pep's eyes are wide open in horror at what she's looking at.

> 1 PEP
>> Oh my goodness!

PANEL TWO:

Long shot. Ext. Log cabin front door – Day. Raja Ali is entering the doorway hastily.

> 2 DEVONTE (V.O.) (CAPTION)
>> Raja, what's your twenty?

> 3 RAJA
>> Almost there.

PANEL THREE:

Close shot. Int. Log cabin – Continued. Pep covers her face in sadness.

> 4 PEP
>> Oh no, oh no.

PANEL FOUR:

Group shot. Int. Kobay GOM S081 – Continued. Devonte looks sad. Tec looks stoic.

Family

5 TEC

    That sucks! The image just came through.

PANEL FIVE:

Long shot. Int. Log cabin – Continued. A gruesome image of a man sitting on an old rickety chair with the top of his head exploded onto the wall behind him. He's half holding a postured shotgun still pointed at his head area.

6 RAJA (O.S.) (CAPTION)

    I think Pep found the person responsible for all the missing persons.

PAGE EIGHTEEN

The Kobay G.O.M. S081 has only one purpose. To get the team where they need to be safely. Along the way there are beautiful and horrible things. The team will learn this in time.

SPLASH PAGE:

Extreme long shot. Ext. NUGGET CLUSTER REGION – Night. The carrier travels through large clusters of rocks and meteors.

> 1 NARRATION (CAPTION)
>> The team would get more than enough time to recover from their shock.
>
> 2 LOCATION (CAPTION)
>> Forsake Omniverse
>>
>> Nugget Cluster Region
>
> 3 NARRATION (CAPTION) (CONT'D)
>> Taking in the scenery on their way to their next mission.

PAGE NINETEEN

A short montage of the spooky adventures.

PANEL ONE:

Wide shot. Int. Kobay GOM S081 – Tec's data reception room – Night. Tec is alone, navigating the team with the camera monitor, infrared screen, schematic screen, electromagnetic screen, audio screen, and monitor with typed records of events occurring.

    1 NARRATION (CAPTION)
        In time each member grew comfortable in their roles on the team.

PANEL TWO:

Wide shot. Int. House in the woods – Bedroom – Midnight. Padre Ully is performing an exorcism on a pregnant woman.

    2 PADRE ULLY
        I call on the forces of light to return this foul demon back to the depts of hell, whence it came.

PANEL THREE:

Wide shot. Int. Quaint apartment complex – Living room – Daybreak. Pep reassures a family of purple parents and little boy as they sit huddled together on their couch.

    3 PEP
        You have a rodent in your wall. It had babies. Have no worries, there is no haunting going on here.

PANEL FOUR:

Wide shot. Ext. Cemetery – Night. Raja Ali fights off the undead AFTERLIVES in a foggy cemetery. He swings his walking stick with expertise.

>4 NARRATION (CAPTION)
>
>>Every member had their moment to carry their own weight.

PANEL FIVE:

Wide shot. Int. Kobay GOM S081 – Cafeteria – Night. The team sits around an oval table with a variety of food and beverages. Their laughing, drinking, eating, and having a merry time with each other.

>5 NARRATION (CAPTION)
>
>>It would be refreshing to find that on their down time, they loved spending time with each other.

PAGE TWENTY

Each member brought something as a person too. Padre Ully's view of the cosmos was in depth. Very humbling. Raja Ali's input was adventurous. Epic stories of his days trekking uncharted territory. Devonte's digital expertise brought extensive information, music, movies, video games, and so on from across the cosmos. Tec's flubberleaf smoking, whittling, and chess playing brought a peaceful solitude to everyone's everyday living. But all that testosterone needs a break. And having Pep was an unspoken pleasure.

PANEL ONE:

Wide group shot. Int. Kobay GOM S081 – OBSERVATION DECK – Night. The team takes a moment to stand at the thirty-foot by sixty-foot observation deck to appreciate the Unworthy Cosmos. Stars, constellations, and colorful gases decorate the vast darkness of the abyss.

    1 PEP

        After so many spooky adventures, I'm still mesmerized by such a vast existence. It's so terrifying yet so beautiful.

    2 RAJA ALI

        It's still astonishing to think so much life exists so far away from our home planets.

    3 TEC

        We need to stop at a planet with gentle streams and a cool breeze. That would be nice.

PANEL TWO:

Medium shot. Int. Kobay GOM S081 – Continuous. Padre Ully's hair has aged, and his beard has grown. He wears his glasses more often now.

    3 PADRE ULLY

        There is a reason for everything in existence, yet I find myself in awe as well.

P. Marcelo W. Balboa

PAGE TWENTY-ONE

Small intelligent bugs look on as they see the Kobay G.O.M. S081 pass by their planet through other colorful systems of planets and stars surrounding the tiny planet.

SPLASH PAGE:

Over the shoulder group shot. Ext. ROCK CAVE – Night. Bug-like life forms look up at an unidentified flying object, the Kobay GOM S081, passing by their planet.

    1 TALL THIN BUG

        Glopnic toric.

    2 SHORT HEFTY BUG

        Nok nalk.

    LOCATION (CAPTION)

        Forsaken Omniverse

        Keya Universe

        Planet Jooklet

PAGE TWENTY-TWO

As the team has become one, Devonte's time has come to participate in other adventures. He contacts Brea with a heavy heart.

PANEL ONE:

Close shot. Ext. Kobay GOM S081 – Departing aircraft – Day. Devonte tears up trying to get out the words.

    1 DEVONTE

        It was a blast while it lasted guys. I wish you the best.

PANEL TWO:

Long group shot. Int. Kobay GOM S081 – Briefing room – Day. Everyone is huddled up on the jumbo screen to say goodbye to their dear friend.

    2 PEP

        We'll miss you Devonte.

    3 TEC

        Keep in touch.

    4 RAJA ALI

        Live well young man.

    5 PADRE ULLY

        Remember that your past does not define you. Your life's story is the entire book not just the first few pages.

PANEL THREE:

Long shot. Int. Kobay GOM S081 – Continuous. Brea appears through on the hologram projector. Behind the hologram is the large screen with details of the next spooky adventure with the location title of OLECIRAM. To the left of the hologram, on the same table, is a 3D simulation of the facility the team will be infiltrating, created by an ever-changing group of small magnetic beads that can take any shape the computer program tells it to.

6 BREA

> Well said everyone. Team, we need your help. Rezandria's sister planet, Oleciram, is in danger. Pep, I'll send the details to your tablet.

PAGE TWENTY-THREE

The team has to rush their goodbyes. Even as Devonte is returning to Rezandria they are already preparing to land just next door the sister planet, Oleciram. There is a sinister spirit that will haunt the planet if not dealt with immediately.

PANEL SIX:

Long shot. Int. Kobay GOM S081 – Briefing room – Midday. Pep stands in front of briefing table with Brea's hologram to the left side of the table and the next mission on the magnetic 3D simulator taking up most of the right side of the table. The large screen hangs from above with the image of the binary planets the Kobay GOM S081 is hovering between with a backdrop of outer space.

> 1 NARRATION (CAPTION)
>> Brea and Pep go over the game plan as Tec, Raja Ali, and Padre Ully make their preparations. The team moves like a well-oiled machine.

PAGE TWENTY-FOUR

The team's shuttle heads to Oleciram as Devonte enters Rezandria's atmosphere.

PANEL ONE:

Splash page – Establishing shot. Int. Planet Oleciram's orbit – Day. Planet Rezandria is visible at the top of the page. Planet Oleciram is visible at the bottom of the page. Outer space is visible in the background as the carrier hovers in space.

> 1 NARRATION (CAPTION)
>> Devonte's shuttle departs for Rezandria as the, now seasoned, paranormal team's shuttle is in route to the sister planet Oleciram.
>
> 2 LOCATION (CAPTION)
>> Forsaken Omniverse
>>
>> Brizie Universe
>>
>> Xzina Galaxy
>>
>> Binary Planets
>
> 3 LOCATION (CAPTION) (CONT'D)
>> Planet Rezandria
>>
>> Planet Oleciram

Backstory Break

Sharlene and Lovetta were lovers who plotted the deaths of a wealthy family they worked for. It would turn south when Lovetta turned on Sharlene's plans when the child, Petey, was next to die. Lovetta's daughter, Layla, ran away after experiencing Sharlene's abusive nature. Lovetta would try to chase her down to stop her but failed. Feeling remorse, Lovetta called the police and admitted everything while she drove back to the house of the family she participated in murdering.

The police would arrive first and shoot Sharlene who was beating Petey to death. Lovetta, still in love with Sharlene, tried to stop them and got shot as well. All three were transported to the emergency room. None would survive. Not due to injuries from the gunshots or beating but from the hospital getting bombed during the war that occurred as they were being hospitalized. Sharlene's soul woke, stained in the Physical Realm, determined to finish the job. Lovetta's soul awoke, stained in the Physical Realm, worried for Petey. Petey's soul would wake up in the children's section of the hospital.

And it was his soul the dark prince wanted. His unwanted spawn was a female. He wanted a male heir. The cult of the dark prince prepared for the second coming of their master. All they needed was Petey's body. He hoped to swap them, but Petey died from the ceiling falling onto his body. Now Petey is left to roam a vacant hospital, running from Sharlene, who, if he gets him, will feed on his soul yearning to feed on the souls of children from this day forth.

ISSUE #3

PAGE ONE

The shuttle lands on an open field in front of a war-torn hospital. Raja Ali has become accustomed to going with Pep. One side mission had no threat, but their guard dog almost ate her.

PANEL ONE:

Long shot. Int. Oleciram's Orbit – Nightfall. The shuttle flies over a storm cloud as it comes closer to its destination.

   1 TEC (V.O.) (INTO PHONE)

       Alright everyone. Get strapped in cause we are about to enter the planet's atmosphere.

PANEL TWO:

Long shot. Int. Hospital parking area – Night. The shuttle has landed. Pep uses her data recorder case as an umbrella as she runs to the war-torn hospital. Raja Ali giver her space but follows at a safe distance.

   2 PEP

       My goodness it's pouring. The hospital looks spookier with the thunderstorm.

   3 TEC (V.O.) (INTO PHONE)

       Be careful. Raja's ready to go if you have any issues.

PANEL THREE:

Long shot. Ext. Wartorn hospital – Entrance driveway – Night. Pep dries off in front of the hospital as she peeks into the hospital front window doors.

1 PEP

> The IN-side looks JUST as spooky as outside. Ooooohoohoo! I just got chills.

2 TEC (V.O.) (INTO PHONE)

> Focus Pep. Keep your eyes open. The information I've downloaded on these cultists describe them as loyal to the dark prince.

3 PEP

> Really? Yah wanna tell me just as I'm about to walk in. Seriously?

PAGE TWO

Many parts of the planet are still severely damaged due to a war that occurred between the armies of what were referred to as the 'Old' and 'New' planets.

PANEL ONE:

Medium shot. Ext. War-torn hospital front door – Night. Lightning strikes as Pep tries to pry open the hospital doors.

    1 PEP

        Ok everyone. I'm going in. Grrrhh! Uhg! Raja.

    2 RAJA ALI

        On it.

PANEL TWO:

Long shot. Int. Wartorn hospital – Front lobby – Night. Lighting strikes as Pep walk through the front doors of the hospital as Raja holds them open.

    3 PEP

        Thank you!

PANEL THREE:

Medium shot. Int. Wartorn hospital – First floor hallway – Night. Pep opens her data recorder case. The data recorders exit to do their job.

    4 PEP

        Ok little guys. Go collect that data.

    5 TEC (V.O.) (INTO PHONE)

        They don't understand you Pep. They are just following their programing.

Family

6 PEP

    You don't know that.

7 TEC

    I programmed the... Alright Pep.

PAGE THREE

The hospital is leaking and cold. There are not safe paths. At any time the ceiling or floors can cave in. Hazards are part of the job. This team has been through similar situations already. It never gets easier, they are just better prepared.

PANEL ONE:

Medium shot. Int. Kobay GOM S081 – Tec's data reception room – Night. Tec looks up at his monitor and screens, reading the information.

> 1 TEC
>> Pep, you have a lobby coming up. Take the stairs to the second floor to the right. The elevator is destroyed.

PANEL TWO:

Medium shot. Int. Wartorn hospital – ER waiting area – Night. Pep is proud of the data recorders she has made her surrogate children.

> 2 PEP
>> See all that data recorded? My little people listen to me.

> 3 TEC (V.O.) (INTO PHONE)
>> You're hopeless.

> 4 PEP
>> Hopelessly in love. With you.

PANEL THREE:

Over the shoulder shot. Int. Kobay GOM S081 – Continued. Tec is sitting at the computer surrounded by screens capturing the data from the data recorders.

5 TEC

    Back at you cute stuff.

PANEL FOUR:

Close shot. Int. Kobay GOM S081 – Continuous. The hospital schematic screen displays data recorders spread through dangerous areas, so Pep doesn't have to.

6 TEC (O.S.) (INTO PHONE)

    Alright. Stay focused Pep. I don't like this place one bit.

PAGE FOUR

The team has encountered so many situations, Tec learned that Padre Ully can see Astral occurrences through digital media as well.

PANEL ONE:

Close up. Int. Kobay GOM S081 – Continued. Tec's expression is that of a person who sees something suspicious.

1 TEC

    Merrio, can you go to the Communication Room?

2 PADRE ULLY (V.O.) (INTO PHONE)

    Sure.

PANEL TWO:

Split shot. Int. Kobay GOM S081/ Kobay GOM 2.0 – Night. Tec puts up the image where the most activity is occurring in the hospital. He looks at the large screen as he points at the anomaly. But Padre Ully, aka Merrio, is looking at another image on his monitor in the Kobay GOM 2.0.

3 PADRE ULLY

    How may I be of service?

4 TEC

    Two of the data recorders are picking up high electromagnetic energy. There aaaaand… There.

5 PADRE ULLY

    Wait, look down the hall. There's something there.

PANEL THREE:

Close shot. Int. Wartorn hospital – Stairway – Night. Pep's face looks sour.

6 PEP

> Raja, there's a stench.

7 RAJA ALI (O.S.) (INTO PHONE)

> I can smell it here on the first floor. Merrio, get over here.

8 TEC (V.O.) (INTO PHONE)

> He's already on his way. He sees something I can't. Get ready.

PANEL FOUR:

Medium shot. Int. Wartorn hospital – Top of stairway – Night. Pep opens her case.

9 PEP

> That's my cue. Good luck Raja. Come back guys.

10 RAJA ALI (O.S.) (INTO PHONE)

> Leave 'em. There's someone else here. GO!

PANEL FIVE:

Group shot. Ext. Wartorn hospital – Front door – Midnight. Padre Ully enters as Pep is leaving.

11 PEP

> Bless you Padre.

12 PADRE ULLY

> And also with you.

PAGE FIVE

Pep rushes to Tec to assist him with anything he needs. Her dedication knows no bounds.

PANEL ONE:

Group shot. Int. Kobay GOM 2.0. – Night. Pep stands in front of the monitors on the shuttle.

    1 PEP

        Where are they now?

    2 TEC

        Second floor.

PANEL TWO:

Over the shoulder group shot. Int. Kobay GOM 2.0 – Communication room – Night. Pep looks over the monitors without a blink.

    3 PEP

        My goodness. Each of the little guys collect so much information. How do you read it all?

    4 TEC (V.O.) (INTO PHONE)

        Pep, I've said it a thousand times.

    5 PEP

        I know, I know. Spider web vision. I still don't get it.

PANEL THREE:

Group shot. Int. Wartorn hospital – 2nd floor – Night. Padre Ully and Raja enter the hallway one of the higher readings occurred.

    6 PADRE ULLY

        Tec, are you getting a good feed on our body cameras?

Family

7 TEC

> Audio... breaking... reason... Visual... clear...

PANEL FOUR:

Peripheral shot. Int. Wartorn hospital – Continuous. There is another hallway leading to Raja Ali's left.

8 NARRATION (CAPTION)

> Raja Ali just misses a hint of movement in another hallway.

PANEL FIVE:

Over the shoulder group shot. Int. Kobay GOM S081 – Tec's data reception room – Night. Pep and Tec watch in dismay as Padre Ully and Raja Ali both seem to see something go in separate directions.

10 PEP (V.O.) (INTO PHONE)

> What are they doing?

11 TEC

> They probably want to cover more ground.

PANEL SIX:

Long shot. Int. Kobay GOM 2.0 – Shuttle ramp – Night. Pep runs to the hospital.

12 PEP

> No. Something's not right. I'm going back in.

13 TEC (V.O.) (INTO PHONE)

> PEP!

14 PEP

> They might need help.

15 TEC (V.O.) (INTO PHONE)

> How the hell are you... Ah! Be careful Pep.

PAGE SIX

NOTE: As Pep enters the hospital, she leads her little helpers to the exit as most are disoriented from the powerful electromagnetic energy coming out of the hospital. There are souls that are mixed good and bad inside, creating a volcanic eruption of paranormal activity.

PANEL ONE:

Long shot. Int. Wartorn hospital – Mother, Baby section – Night. Raja Ali runs into Cultists surrounding a pregnant woman about to give birth.

> 1 WOMAN
>> Let me go, pleeeeease.

PANEL TWO:

Medium shot. Int. Wartorn hospital – Urgent Care section – Night. Padre Ully stops in place as he runs into an entity unlike anything he has ever seen. His eyes are wide, mouth open, and he can't say a word.

> 2 SHARLENE (O.S.) (CAPTION)
>> Where's the bitch and the little shit Priest?

PANEL THREE:

Long shot. Int. Wartorn hospital – Continuous. Pep nearly slips on the floor at what she sees. Her eyes filled with tears from fear.

NOTE: It's Padre Ully hovering in the air, holding his neck, choking.

> 3 PEP
>> Holy... Gotta get Raja. Oh my gosh!

PAGE SEVEN

The child within the woman is seconds away from being ended.

SPLASH PAGE:

Group shot. Int. The woman's womb. An image of a purple demon baby in the womb about to be cut apart by scissors.

> 1 NARRATION (CAPTION)
>> Expecting a newborn male, the spawn of the dark prince was female.
>
> 2 NARRATION (CAPTION)
>> Deemed an unworthy existence, she was set to be sacrificially ended.
>
> 3 NARRATION (CAPTION)
>> Her body would remain an unwilling capsule for the male to come. Petey.

P. Marcelo W. Balboa

PAGE EIGHT

Pep enters the mix but becomes a target of a Cultist as Father Ully and Raja deal with their own issues in the hospital.

PANEL ONE:

Long shot. Int. Wartorn hospital – 2ND floor – Night. Pep gets lost as a Cultist, dressed in a dark brown cloak with a hoodie over his head, sneaks up on her.

>1 PEP
>
>>Shoot. These hallways are like a maze.
>
>2 TEC (V.O.) (INTO PHONE)
>
>>It's... hospital Pep... Everyone... lost.

PANEL TWO:

Medium shot. Int. Wartorn hospital – Continuous. One of the Cultist grabs Pep.

>3 PEP
>
>>Wha...

PANEL THREE:

Medium shot. Int. Kobay GOM S081 – Continued. Tec has a focused expression.

>4 TEC
>
>>Pep, your camera went dark. Can you hear me?

PANEL FOUR:

Long group shot. Int. Wartorn hospital – Mother, Baby section – Night. Just as the Cultist runs into the room with the other cultists, Raja Ali strikes him in the face, freeing Pep from his grasps. The cultists stop trying to kill the woman to get him.

5 SFX

    WHACK!

PANEL FIVE:

Long group shot. Int. Wartorn hospital – Continuous. Raja fights the cultist as Pep runs to the woman.

6 RAJA ALI

    Help the woman Pep.

7 PEP

    You got it.

PANEL SIX:

Long shot. Int. Wartorn hospital – Continuous. The woman is sitting up, holding her newborn infant. NIEKA, a purple two-horned infant with a thin tail, doesn't cry. Her eyes are red, but she looks around calmly. Unafraid. Raja Ali is easily beating the uncoordinated attacks of the Cultists. Pep walks up carefully.

8 WOMAN

    There, there Neika. I won't let any harm come to you my child.

9 PEP

    Uh, miss. You look bad, can I help you and your baby?

PAGE NINE

Raja Ali and Pep come to the rescue but find they're too late as the mother was fatally wounded by the Cultist leader. The newborn infant has survived as Raja Ali discards the glorified extras.

PANEL ONE:

Medium group shot. Int. Wartorn hospital – Continued. The woman hands her infant to Pep.

>1 WOMAN
>>I am ruined. Save Neika. What I tell you next about her tell no one.

PANEL TWO:

Close shot. Int. Wartorn hospital – Continuous. A Cultist gets hit in the face.

>2 SFX
>>CRACK!

PANEL THREE:

Long group shot. Int. Wartorn hospital – Continuous. Pep and Raja have a moment as Neika's Mother lays still in the background surrounded by knocked out Cultists.

>3 PEP
>>Thank you Raja. I'll take it from here. I think Merrio needs your assistance.

>4 RAJA ALI
>>Where is he?

>5 PEP
>>Go straight down the hallway you originally turned left.

PANEL FOUR:

Medium shot. Int. Wartorn hospital – Continuous. Pep consoles the infant.

    6 PEP

        There, there child. I got you.

    7 TEC (V.O.) (INTO PHONE)

        Pep… can't… dangerous.

PANEL FIVE:

Close shot. Int. Wartorn hospital – 2nd floor hallway – Dawn. Raja's face is in shock at what he sees.

    8 RAJA ALI

        ALLAH BE WITH US!

PAGE TEN

The first appearance of Sharlene, the child abuser. Raja Ali rushes to help Padre Ully who is choking to death, hovering in the air. Only Padre Ully can see Sharlene.

PANEL ONE:

Long over the shoulder group shot. Int. Wartorn hospital – Continued. From behind Raja Ali, Padre Ully can be seen points to his flask on the floor as he holds his throat and his feet dangle.

NOTE: Sharlene, a cursed soul walks the hallways looking for a child he would abuse, stands at eight feet with a wingspan of ten feet. His lanky arms and legs have bulging joints. His hair is in an afro and his mouth is long and wide. But to Raja Ali, this pathetic spirit is invisible.

> 1 RAJA ALI
>
> Padre, what must I do?

PANEL TWO:

Medium shot. Int. Wartorn hospital – Continuous. From the perspective of the flask. Raja can be seen from a distance looking at it with the help of Tec.

> 2 TEC (V.O.) (INTO PHONE)
>
> Get... flask... ground.

PANEL THREE:

Long group shot. Int. Wartorn hospital – Continuous. Raja Ali tosses the flask to the hovering priest.

> 3 RAJA ALI
>
> Catch Padre.

PAGE ELEVEN

It is at this point the paranormal cosmic journey takes a turn. An unlikely couple will need to navigate the dangers lurking across the Unworthy Cosmos while traversing the challenges of an unfamiliar addition to their relationship.

PANEL ONE:

Group shot. Int. Kobay GOM S081 – Tec's data reception room – Daybreak. Tec is watching the large screen and switches his microphone to channel two.

    1 PEP (V.O.) (INTO PHONE)

        Um, Tec. Switch to channel two please.

    2 TEC

        You got it.

PANEL TWO:

Group shot. Int. Kobay GOM 2.0 – Shuttle seating room – Morning. Pep is placing a bundle in one of the seats and grabbing a seat belt.

    3 PEP

        Tec… I have a bit of a surprise.

    4 TEC (V.O.) (INTO PHONE)

        Welcome back hero.

    5 PEP

        You have no idea.

PANEL THREE:

Group shot. Int. Kobay GOM S081 – Continued. Tec looks aware of Pep's suspicious tone of voice.

6 NEIKA (V.O.) (INTO PHONE)

> WHAAAH! WHAAA!

7 TEC

> Pep. Why are you crying like that?

8 PEP (V.O.) (INTO PHONE)

> It's a baby.

PANEL FOUR:

Long shot. Int. Kobay GOM 2.0 – Continued. Pep steps back to look at Neika.

9 TEC (V.O.) (INTO PHONE)

> You weren't pregnant when you left Pep.

10 PEP

> It's not ours silly. The mother's dying wish was for me to take her and keep her safe.

11 TEC (V.O.) (INTO PHONE)

> Oh boy!

12 PEP

> It's a girl not a boy.

13 TEC (V.O.) (INTO PHONE)

> That's not what... Alright Pep. Where are we taking her?

14 PEP

> I made a promise. She's ours.

PAGE TWELVE

The priest and the warrior confront the cursed child abuser.

PANEL ONE:

Long group shot. Int. Wartorn hospital – Continued. Padre Ully splashes holy water in the direction of Sharlene.

   1 SFX

       Splash!

PANEL TWO:

Extreme long group shot. Int. Wartorn hospital – Continuous. Raja Ali helps Padre Ully up.

   2 RAJA ALI

       I got you Merrio.

   3 SFX

       CRACKLE! CRACK!

PANEL THREE:

Long groups shot. Int. Wartorn hospital – Continuous. The floor caves in. Raja Ali and Padre Ully crash into the first floor.

   4 SFX

       BOOM!

PANEL FOUR:

Long group shot. Int. Wartorn hospital – First floor waiting area – Day. Raja Ali and Padre Ully emerge from the rubble scraped up.

   5 RAJA ALI

       You good Merrio?

6 PADRE ULLY

    Yes. And you?

Long group shot. Int. Wartorn hospital – Continuous. Before Raja can answer Sharlene runs at Padre Ully.

7 SHARLENE

    WHERE IS HE?

PANEL FIVE:

Long group shot. Int. Wartorn hospital – Continuous. Padre Ully displays his bible as Sharlene tries to shield its gaze from its sight.

8 PADRE ULLY

    May the light of good shine up thee and reveal your decrepit form to all.

PANEL SIX:

Long shot. Int. Wartorn hospital – Continuous. Raja Ali stands firm with his staff in hand.

9 RAJA ALI

    Padre I can see it.

PANEL THIRTEEN

The life partners begin trying to figure out what it means to become surrogate parents to a child born of the prince of darkness.

PANEL ONE:

Close shot. Int. Kobay GOM S081 – Continued. Tec tries to keep a stoic expression as he looks at Pep on the video-com.

> 1 TEC
>> Pep, I could hear portions of the mother's words.

PANEL TWO:

Close shot. Int. Kobay GOM 2.0 – Continued. Pep looks innocent and loving as she looks at Tec in the video-com.

> 2 PEP
>> And you heard what I said too. She's ours.

PANEL THREE:

Split shot. Int. Kobay GOM S081/ Kobay GOM 2.0 – Day. Pep is holding Neika as Tec and she speak.

> 3 TEC
>> I get you Pep. Whatever you want to do I'm by your side. How do we tell the team?

> 4 PEP
>> Look at her. She got out of the seat belt and walked to me.

> 5 TEC
>> Better to apologize than ask for permission I guess.

P. Marcelo W. Balboa

PANEL FOUR:

Group shot. Int. Kobay GOM S081 – Continued. Tec sees the image of Sharlene.

    6 PEP (V.O.) (INTO PHONE)

        Oh Tec, you're the best.

    7 TEC

        Wait! What the hell is that?

    8 PEP (V.O.) (INTO PHONE)

        It's a baby.

PAGE FOURTEEN

Looking away from the light, Sharlene finds what he's looking for. Hearing the noise, LOVETTA, Sharlene's former lover, and PETEY, Sharlene's target of abuse, enter the lobby just beyond the rubble behind Sharlene.

SPLASH PAGE:

Long shot. Int. Wartorn hospital – Emergency exit – Day. Sharlene smiles in delight as he finds his targets. Lovetta and Petey freeze in place after trying to move the debris to escape. Petey is in teddy bear pajamas with a flashlight in one hand and his stitched up limbless white teddy bear in the other hand.

    1 SHARLENE

        There you are. Give him to me <u>bitch!</u>

PAGE FIFTEEN

Parenthood temporarily distracts Tec. He refocuses as he runs back to his computer terminal.

PANEL ONE:

Medium shot. Int. Kobay GOM S081 – Continued. Tec put's his headphones on to listen in on what he sees on the large screen.

   1 TEC

        Padre, Raja are you alright?

PANEL TWO:

Close shot. Int. Wartorn hospital – Continued. Sharlene gazes with his wide grin and impaled eyes.

   2 SHARLENE

        Come here little shit. I'm not finished with you.

PANEL THREE:

Long group shot. Int. Wartorn hospital – Continuous. Padre Ully splashes holy water on Sharlene again. Sharlene turns to Padre Ully as the water now smokes on contact.

   3 SHARLENE (Wince)

        Ahhhh!

   4 PADRE ULLY

        Enough of your confounded chatter. What is your name?

PAGE SIXTEEN

After struggling to find each other, Lovetta and Petey are faced with their most trying moment. Facing the child abuse-murderer, Sharlene.

PANEL ONE:

Long shot. Int. Wartorn hospital – Continued. Lovetta stands strong in defiance of Sharlene's threat as Petey stands strong behind her.

>1 LOVETTA
>>His name is Sharlene.
>
>2 PETEY
>>I'm not afraid of you anymore.

PANEL TWO:

Medium shot. Int. Wartorn hospital – Continued. As Sharlene tried to intimidate Padre Ully, Raja Ali's walking stick struck him in the face.

>3 SHARLENE
>>Your death will be slow and painful Pr....
>
>4 SFX
>>Whack!

PAGE SEVENTEEN

Pep accommodates Neika as the conflict against Sharlene ensues.

PANEL ONE:

Medium shot. Int. Kobay GOM 2.0 – Communication room – Midday. Pep places Neika in a small space in the wall meant to be a desktop space. Neika sleeps peacefully.

> 1 PEP
>> There you go Neika. A perfect little sleeping area. This was daddy's area. He doesn't need it anymore now that you're here.

PANEL TWO:

Medium shot. Int. Wartorn hospital – Continued. One of the data recorders picks up Padre Ully's holy book.

PANEL THREE:

Group shot. Int. Wartorn hospital – Continuous. The data recorder gives Padre Ully his holy book.

> 2 D.R.O.P.A. 05
>> Data dropped.
>
> 3 PADRE ULLY
>> Thank you robot.

PAGE EIGHTEEN

Padre Ully and Raja Ali move in tandem. Raja Ali continues to fight Sharlene as Padre Ully focuses on the innocent by standers.

SPLASH PAGE:

Long group shot. Int. Wartorn hospital – Continued. Padre Ully stands in front of Lovetta and Petey in a defiant stance.

    1 PADRE ULLY

        You will not harm these innocent souls. I call upon the archangels, I call upon the forces of light. In the name of all that is holy, I ask for the discharge of Sharlene from the Physical Realm.

PAGE NINETEEN

The new parents find out Neika is special as Padre Ully attempts to discharge Sharlene from the Physical Realm.

PAGE ONE:

Group shot. Int. Kobay GOM 2.0 – Continued. Pep watches the screens as Neika walks up behind her.

    1 PEP

        What is that? And why is it glowing different colors?

    2 TEC (V.O.) (INTO PHONE)

        It's a ghost. Devonte made this program that can read the electromagnetic pulses. What is invisible to the eye but only Merrio can see.

PANEL TWO:

Group shot. Int. Kobay GOM 2.0 – Continuous. Neika walks up and tries to grab Pep's mouse from his computer terminal.

    3 NEIKA

        Different colors.

    4 TEC (V.O.) (INTO PHONE)

        What the... I thought the baby was newborn. How is she...

    5 PEP

        Well, she is part angel.

PANEL THREE:

Long shot. Int. Wartorn hospital – Continued. Padre Ully recites prayers. Sharlene flails his arms, focusing on Petey, as a dozen black arms reach out from shadows on the ground.

6 PADRE ULLY

>In the name of the one before all I command you to leave.

7 SHARLENE

>I'm not done with you little shit. I'll beat your ass black and blue.

PAGE TWENTY

Sharlene's determination know no bounds. Raja Ali has dealt with abusive antagonists before and takes it personal.

PANEL ONE:

Long group shot. Int. Wartorn hospital – Continued. As Sharlene attempts to flee the black arms and attack Petey, Raja Ali strikes at his knees.

> 1 SFX
>> Pop!
>
> 2 SHARLENE (Weak)
>> Uhg!
>
> 3 RAJA ALI
>> Praise Allah!

PANEL TWO

Medium shot. Int. Wartorn hospital – Continuous. The black arms grab a hold of Sharlene's legs.

> 1 SHARLENE
>> Nooooo!
>
> 2 BLACK ARMS (Whispers)
>> Come with usssss!

PAGE TWENTY-ONE

NOTE: TARTARUS is a place in the Meta-Physical Realm where torture and pain come to those who deserve it.

SPLASH PAGE:

Over the shoulder group shot. Int. Wartorn hospital – Continued. Padre Ully watches as the black arms rip Sharlene apart, pulling him into TARTARUS, a fire infested realm of torment, for judgement.

    1 SHARLENE (Weaps)

        Ahhhh!

    2 PADRE ULLY

        In the name of the creator of all things I command you to depart. May your deeds be remembered in Tartarus.

PAGE TWENTY-TWO

Sharlene is brutally torn apart and pulled into the Meta-Physical Realm in pieces as Lovetta and Petey are sent to ELYSIUM.

NOTE: Elysium is a place good souls go when they have either lived a good life or turned away from evil to live a good life.

PANEL ONE:

Long shot. Int. Wartorn hospital – Continued. As one of Sharlene's arms desperately reach out from the portal to Tartarus, Padre Ully and Raja Ali stand over him.

> 1 PADRE ULLY
>
> May your soul be tormented for your sins for all eternity child abuser.

PANEL TWO:

Medium shot. Int. Wartorn hospital – Continuous. Petey shines a light on the closing portal on the ground as he hugs his limbless bear.

> 2 PETEY
>
> I want my mommy.

PANEL THREE:

Medium shot. Int. Wartorn hospital – Continuous. Lovetta's arm reaches down to grasp Petey as she reassures him.

> 3 LOVETTA
>
> There's no need to worry. Father, can you help Petey get to his mother?

Family

PANEL FOUR:

Long group shot. Int. Wartorn hospital – Nightfall. A light glows around Lovetta and Petey as they go to Elysium. Holding hands, their eyes close with bright smiles.

    4 PADRE ULLY

        I call upon the forces of Light, the archangels, and the great travelers that be. Grant these two souls safe passage to Elysium.

    5 LOVETTA

        Bless you Father. Thank you.

    6 PETEY

        I can see mommy. MOMMY!

PAGE TWENTY-THREE

The mission is complete, and the team reunites in the carrier to head out to their next spooky adventure.

PANEL ONE:

Long shot. Ext. Kobay GOM 2.0 – Ramp – Night. Raja and Father Ully walk up the ramp of the shuttle.

> 1 PADRE ULLY
>
>> I need to research the portal dilemma. Something is off about this mission.
>
> 2 RAJA ALI
>
>> What makes you say that? We've dealt with worse on our travels.
>
> 3 PADRE ULLY
>
>> I feel a presence I can't explain. I don't want to decide anything until I understand more.

PANEL TWO:

Long shot. Ext. Oleciram's atmosphere – Day. The shuttle returns to the carrier in outer space.

> 4 TEC (V.O) (CAPTION)
>
>> Pep, it's Brea on the hologram. Might want to check it out.
>
> 5 PEP (V.O) (CAPTION)
>
>> No worries, I'm going.

PANEL THREE:

Medium shot. Int. Kobay GOM S081 – Briefing room – Night. Pep connects with Brea transmitting the next mission through hologram.

Family

6 BREA (INTO PHONE)

>I received word you had a major success. Great work. Ill send you the next mission.

7 PEP

>I'm reading the coordinates now. Lost Lights. Ok Brea. We're on it.

8 BREA (INTO PHONE)

>Thank you. May you and your team have safe travels.

ISSUE #4

PAGE ONE

The carrier waits as a shuttle lands on a near planet for a scheduled pit stop.

SPLASH PAGE:

Long shot. Int. Unworthy Cosmos – Kobay GOM S081 – Night. The carrier floats just out of orbit of one of the planets in the CHA solar system, DALI.

> 1 NARRATION (CAPTION)
>> Raja and Father Ully take a shuttle to planet Dali for a supply run as Pep and Tec take a break from work to enjoy parenthood.
>
> 2 TEC (V.O.) (CAPTION)
>> Why do I agree to this stuff?
>
> 3 LOCATION (CAPTION)
>> Forsaken Omniverse
>>
>> Cha Solar System
>>
>> Planet Dali

PAGE TWO

Pep and Tec's relationship has evolved to sharing their love for each other with their adopted child, Neika.

PANEL ONE:

Medium group shot. Int. Kobay GOM S081 – Pep and Tec's living room. Pep and Neika are celebrating yet giggling at what they have done Tec.

    1 NEIKA

        Daddy's so pretty.

PANEL TWO:

Close shot. Int. Kobay GOM S081 – Continuous. Tec has a bow and make up on with an annoyed.

    2 TEC

        Pep.

PANEL THREE:

Close shot. Int. Kobay GOM S081 – Continuous. Pep has her hands over her face trying not to laugh too hard.

    3 PEP

        Daddy is pretty Neika. Very pretty.

PANEL FOUR:

Medium shot. Int. Kobay GOM S081– Continuous. Neika joyfully expresses her happiness for her father's make over.

    4 NEIKA

        I love the pretty daddy.

P. Marcelo W. Balboa

PANEL FIVE:

Close shot. Int. Kobay GOM S081 – Continuous. Tec is less annoyed.

    5 TEC

        Thank you baby girl.

PAGE THREE

The Kobay G.O.M. S081 travels passed more breathtaking sights in route to the next mission.

SPLASH PAGE:

Long shot. Int. Unworthy Cosmos – Night. Planets, stars, meteors are all clustered together on one page as the carrier travels through the space.

1 NARRATION (CAPTION)

> Some missions can take weeks to get to even in the great carrier revered for all time throughout Rezandria and the Hall of Legends.

2 LOCATION (CAPTION)

> Forsaken Omniverse
>
> Trian Universe
>
> Deswa Galaxy
>
> Nadac Solar System

PAGE FOUR

Brea reaches out to the team as more pressing information has come to him about a nearby planet. Little does this team know is that by this time more than two thirds of the paranormal teams in existence have been defeated by the forces of darkness. Not one survived.

PANEL ONE:

Extreme long shot. Int. DESWA GALAXY – Day. More planets surround the Kobay G.O.M. S081 as it passes through the USO SOLAR SYSTEM.

> 1 BREA (V.O.) (CAPTION)
>> Pep, are you there?
>
> 2 PEP (V.O.) (CAPTION)
>> I am. What new info do you have for me?
>
> 3 LOCATION (CAPTION)
>> Forsaken Omniverse
>>
>> Trian Universe
>>
>> Deswa Galaxy
>>
>> Uso Solar System

PANEL TWO:

Medium group shot. Int. – Kobay GOM S081 – Briefing room – Twilight. Pep stands by the hologram intercom of Brea as images of the coordinates appear on the large screen above the table.

> 4 BREA
>> A trajectory adjustment. There is a planet directly in your vicinity called Exa.
>
> 5 BREA (CONT'D)
>> Your team is the only one… You are close enough to help. I'll send you the coordinates and intel.

PAGE FIVE

Tec's passion in electronics. Neika would come and sit by him from time to time and hold an extra controller as her father played games. Soon that became their bonding ritual. In time, Tec's job as the data receptionist for missions became a simulation of those moments playing games.

PANEL ONE:

Establishing shot. Int. PLANET EXA's Orbit – Sunset. The shuttle departs across a beautiful outer space expanse as it prepares to land on Planet Exa.

    1 LOCATION (CAPTION)

        Planet Exa

PANEL TWO:

Medium group shot. Int. Kobay GOM – Tec's data reception room – Sunset. Tec speaks to the team through oversized headphones. Neika is tapping him on his arm.

    2 TEC

        Alright everyone, prepare for landing in 5, 4...

    3 NEIKA

        Daddy. Daddy.

PANEL THREE:

Medium group shot. Int. Kobay GOM S081 – Continuous. A close up of Tec as he reacts to Neika.

    4 TEC

        Hey there baby girl. You wanna help daddy work?

P. Marcelo W. Balboa

PANEL FOUR:

Medium group shot. Int. Kobay GOM S081 – Continuous. Neika is in celebration.

    5 NEIKA

        Oh yes, yes.

Family

PAGE SIX

An antlike anthropomorphic being has a park that is haunted. The entity inside has caused a death he is trying to hide. The team's arrival is greatly appreciated.

PANEL ONE:

Medium group shot. Ext. Theme Park – Front gates – Night. Pep meets Zio.

    1 ZIO

        Are you Pep?

    2 PEP

        I am. My team received intel your park may be haunted. I hope we can help.

PANEL TWO:

Long group shot. Ext. Theme Park – Continuous. Zio points to the park entrance in the background.

    3 ZIO

        Please do. Staff said a girl is missing but nothing shows up on my cameras. My park will close down if this is true.

PANEL THREE:

Close shot. Ext. Theme Park – Continuous. Pep opens her case to reveal the data recorders exiting.

    4 PEP

        Go get me data Arthur, Ray, Selly...

PANEL FOUR:

Medium group shot. Int. Kobay GOM S081 – Continued. Tec sits at his computer terminal with Neika sitting on his lap as they look at the readings from the data recorders.

    5 TEC

        You shouldn't have named them Pep.

    6 NEIKA

        Pretty names.

    7 TEC

        Not helpin' sweetie.

    8 NEIKA

        Baby robots talk funny.

PANEL FIVE:

Long group shot. Int. Kobay GOM 2.2 – Analysis Room. Padre Ully and Raja sit at the conference table as they look up at the monitors. Padre Ully has a new tablet that accesses an intergalactic internet created by Devonte called the COSMONET.

    8 PADRE ULLY

        This gadget is unbelievable. I can access religions
        from across the cosmos. Brilliant.

    9 RAJA

        Allah is in the soul. You need no gadget.

    10 PADRE ULLY

        Well said friend.

PANEL SIX:

Medium group shot. Int. Kobay GOM S081 – Continued. Tec's computer screen pics up an alert.

11 TEC

    Alright baby girl, press this button and it will tell the baby robots what information to send us.

12 NEIKA

    Baby robots are smart like me, right daddy?

13 TEC

    You got it sweetie. Yowza mcbowza bebby, we have a winner Pep. Fun house.

PAGE SEVEN

The fun house exterior is colorful with the face of an ant-clown as the entrance doors. The fog has increased as the data recorders enter.

PANEL ONE:

Long group shot. Ext. Fun House – Night. The data recorders of paranormal activity enter the mouth of a large clown.

> 1 DATA RECORDERS (CAPTION)
>> Get data, get data, get data...

PANEL TWO:

Close shot. Int. Fun House – Mirror Room – Night. The first data recorder stops in place surrounded by mirrors.

> 2 DATA RECORDER 08
>> Data get! D-D-Data.

PANEL THREE:

Medium group shot. Int. Kobay GOM S081 – Continued. Tec holds Neika who is falling asleep.

> 3 TEC
>> A couple of the data recorders are malfunctioning, Raja. You may need to help Pep get a visual.

> 4 NEIKA
>> I'm sleepy.

PANEL FOUR:

Close shot. Int. Fun House – Continued. One of the data recorders takes in too much electromagnetic energy.

5 DATA RECORDER 02

    Data overload. A-A-Abort. Abort.

6 SFX

    Bzzzz!

PANEL FIVE:

Medium shot. Int. Fun House – Continuous. The data recorder explodes.

7 SFX

    Zzzz-pop!

PANEL SIX:

Medium shot. Int. Kobay GOM S081 - Tec's computer screen pics up the loss of every data recorder's reading except one.

8 TEC

    Merrio, Raja I have one data recorder still in action, but its readings are really bad.

9 RAJA ALI (V.O.) (INTO PHONE)

    Merrio, its legitimate.

PANEL SEVEN:

Long group shot. Int. Fun House – Continued. The surviving data recorder tries to help recover reusable body parts of the other data recorders.

10 DATA RECORDER 07

    Get data recorders, get data recorders…

PAGE EIGHT

Over the past nearly one hundred quests this team has been on at this point, many variations have occurred. Sometimes the team thinks something is their and its bad electricity. Other times the entity is so hidden they have had to return to deal with it. And then there are side missions like this. Where the risk is high and not everyone is guaranteed to go home.

PANEL ONE:

Extreme long shot. Ext. Fun House – Mouth of the and-clown – Night. Padre Ully and Raja Ali enter the mouth of the funhouse.

> 1 PADRE ULLY
>
>> This dark energy is strong yet different.
>
> 2 RAJA ALI
>
>> I have chills already.
>
> 3 PADRE ULLY
>
>> As do I friend.

PANEL TWO:

Long group shot. Int. Fun House – Mirror room – Night. The mirrors reflect the image of Padre Ully and Raja Ali, but Padre Ully looks ghostly.

> 4 PADRE ULLY
>
>> These mirrors are a mask to take us from the real entity that exists in here.

PANEL THREE:

Medium shot. Int. Fun House – Continuous. Raja starts breaking the mirrors.

> 5 RAJA ALI
>
>> Got it.

PAGE TEN

The exorcism turns for the worse as the entity attacks. The warrior and the priest save the little girl and return to their shuttle unharmed.

PANEL ONE:

Long group shot. Int. Fun House – Continuous. The little girl flies at Raja Ali and Padre Ully.

> 1 LITTLE GIRL
>
> > I am Darmaldu, servant of Karlo.
>
> 2 LITTLE GIRL (CONT'D)
>
> > And I am Nonam, servant of the dark prince.
>
> 3 DARMALDU-NONAM (CONT'D)
>
> > I'm going to tear your flesh off with pleasure.
>
> 4 DARMALDU-NONAM (CONT'D)
>
> > And I will eat your soul.

PANEL TWO:

Long group shot. Int. Fun House – Continuous. Raja Ali's staff strikes the back of Darmaldu-Nonam's neck. As he realized a Demon Tick is attached. The six-armed, tick-like being dislodges it's tentacles from the back of the girl's neck. Padre Ully flinches as it was he who was the target.

> 5 DARMALDU-NONAM
>
> > Ahhhhhh!
>
> 6 SFX
>
> > Whack!

PANEL THREE:

Long group shot. Int. Fun House – Continuous. Padre Ully blesses the possessed child as Raja Ali strikes down at the Demon Tick once and for all.

    3 PADRE ULLY

        In the name of the one before all, with the aid of the power of light grant this child her capsule back.

PANEL FOUR:

Medium group shot. Int. Fun House – Continuous. Padre Ully places his holy book on the forehead of the possessed child as her body tenses up.

    4 PADRE ULLY

        Nonam be gone. Return to your Realm or face the torment in Tartarus.

PAGE ELEVEN

NOTE: The entity doesn't want to leave but has heard of Padre Ully and fears him.

PANEL ONE:

Medium shot. Int. Fun House – Continuous. Nonam's dark energy begins to spill out of the little girls' orifices.

    1 NONAM

        Not… Fair… Priest.

PANEL TWO:

Long group shot. Int. Fun House – Continuous. The little girl cries in the arms of Padre Ully as Raja Ali stands beside them proud of their work.

    5 PADRE ULLY

        Thank you, thank you, thank you…

PANEL THREE:

Long group shot. Ext. Kobay GOM 2.2 – Exit ramp – Morning. Raja Ali and Padre Ully walk up the ramp of the shuttle.

PANEL FOUR:

Long group shot. Int. Kobay GOM – Continued. Tec notices the image still coming from the last surviving data recorder as Neika sleeps with a concept design of an inactive armored data recorder in the background.

    6 TEC

        I'm getting feedback from the data recorder that didn't blow up.

P. Marcelo W. Balboa

PANEL FIVE:

Long shot. Int. Kobay GOM 2.2 – Conference room. Pep snaps that one data recorder survived and runs out to get it.

    7 PEP

        Oh my goodness.

PANEL SIX:

Medium group shot. Ext. Kobay GOM 2.2 – Exit ramp – Daybreak. Pep catches up with the data recorder, who is pulling her case up the ramp of the shuttle.

NOTE: The reusable remains of the other data recorders are secured inside.

    8 PEP

        You brought your friends. Oh my little baby let me help you.

PAGE TWELVE

The Kobay G.O.M. S081 flies through a cluster of colorful uninhabited planets.

PANEL ONE:

Splash page. Int. Unworthy Cosmos – JAMA REGION. The carrier passes through planets of different sizes and colors.

    1 NARRATION (CAPTION)

        The next spooky adventure is far enough away that the team is able to get some rest and relaxation in.

    2 LOCATION (CAPTION)

        Forsaken Omniverse

        Trian Universe

        Deswa Galaxy

        Jama Region

P. Marcelo W. Balboa

PAGE THIRTEEN

Pep and Tec display their evolution as parents.

PANEL ONE:

Medium group shot. Int. Kobay GOM S081 – Pep and Tec's private quarters. Tec is standing over Nieka preparing to change her diaper.

> 1 TEC
>
>> Pep, I'm not good at diaper changing.

PANEL TWO:

Medium shot. Kobay GOM S081 – Bathroom. Pep is in the shower, covered in soap.

> 2 PEP
>
>> Oh you'll be fine yah silly goosalumpkidan.

PANEL THREE:

Medium group shot. Int. Kobay GOM S081 – Pep and Tec's private quarters. Tec takes Neika's diaper off to clean her off with baby wipes.

> 3 TEC
>
>> I guess this isn't so bad.
>
> 4 NEIKA
>
>> Daddy that's cold.

PAGE FOURTEEN

Neika delights in her father changing her diaper.

PANEL ONE:

Medium group shot. Int. Kobay GOM S081 – Continuous. Neika pees as Tec tries to protect himself by hiding his head in his shell.

> 1 TEC
>
>> What the heck? Pep help, she's peeing everywhere.

PANEL TWO:

Medium shot. Int. Kobay GOM S081 – Bathroom. Pep is singing in the shower.

> 2 PEP
>
>> I love body soap and soap loves me. La, la, la-la-la, la, la, la.

PANEL THREE:

Close shot. Int. Kobay GOM S081 – Pep and Tec's private quarters. Neika is giggling.

> 3 NEIKA
>
>> Daddy's funny.

PANEL FOUR:

Close shot. Int. Kobay GOM S081 – Continuous. Tec has an unimpressed expression.

> 4 TEC
>
>> How does a baby know how to talk and walk but not change her diaper?

PAGE FIFTEEN

NOTE: Pep wants to get fixed up for a walk of the ship with the family then a nice pic-nick at the observation deck. Tec's potty adventure exhausts him.

PANEL ONE:

Close shot. Int. Kobay GOM S081 – Bedroom. Pep exits the shower with a towel wrapped around her head.

> 1 PEP
>> Well look at that. The two loves of my life are fast asleep. And I wanted to go look at the stars. Oh well. Maybe…

PANEL TWO:

Long group shot. Int. Kobay GOM S081 – Continuous. Tec is laying down with Neika happily asleep with her butt resting against his head.

> 2 TEC
>> No one's asleep over here. Let's go look at the stars.

PAGE SIXTEEN

The family loves to take trips through different parts of the ship then end their tours at the observation deck.

PANEL ONE:

Extreme long shot. Int. GOLDEN PLANET'S ORBIT - Day. The carrier glides through outer space passing a glowing golden planet.

   1 NARRATION (CAPTION)
       A planet made of pure gold glows as the Kobay G.O.M. S081 passes by.

PANEL TWO:

Long group shot. Int. Kobay GOM S081 – Observation Deck - Day. The family sits on a cloth, having a pic-nick as they look out at the glowing planet.

   2 PEP
       Beautiful.

   3 NEIKA
       Pretty rock.

   4 TEC
       It's a giant ball of pee.

   5 PEP
       Oh stop it!

   6 NEIKA
       Pretty pee.

   7 PEP
       It sure is princess.

   8 TEC
       Seriously?

P. Marcelo W. Balboa

PAGE SEVENTEEN

A threat in outer space confronts the Kobay G.O.M. S081 in route to their next mission.

PANEL ONE:

Splash page. Int. COA KUINU SOLAR SYSTEM. The carrier passes through a system of planets that form a spiraling funnel with a powerful star holding them in place.

> 1 NARRATION (CAPTION)
>> Many areas the team passes through are uncharted.
>
> 2 NARRATION (CAPTION)
>> Some locations are not friendly.
>
> 3 LOCATION (CAPTION)
>> Forsaken Omniverse
>>
>> Daly Universe
>>
>> Adagas Galaxy
>>
>> Coa Kuinu Solar System

PAGE EIGHTEEN

The Kobay GOM S081 is a living machine. When Brea send the coordinates for a destination, the team doesn't have to steer the ship. It knows where to go. But on occasions like this, manual controls are required.

PANEL ONE:

Wide shot. Int. Kobay GOM S081 – Hallway section 64. Tec runs to the CONTROL ROOM as the threat of a MEGA SHIP is visible from the long windows in the background.

    1 SFX

        Alert! Alert! Alert!

PANEL TWO:

Long shot. Int. Kobay GOM S081 – Control Room. Tec is smoking flubberleaf as he puts his headgear on at the navigation station.

    2 TEC

        Testing, testing. Can anyone out there here me? We
        are not your enemy.

PANEL THREE:

Close shot. Int. Kobay GOM S081 – Continuous. Tec sits at the futuristic navigation station with all kinds of buttons, measuring displays and a full view of the warship and its war planes closing the distance on the Kobay G.O.M. S081.

    3 TEC

        Can anyone hear me? We come in peace.

P. Marcelo W. Balboa

PAGE NINETEEN

Tec shows off the transforming capabilities of the Kobay G.O.M. S081.

PANEL ONE:

Close shot. Int. Kobay GOM S081 – Continuous. Tec reaches as he presses a sequence of buttons.

> 1 TEC
>> Hello there. I'm Tec. I'm sorry if we caused any issues. We are travelers that aid planets in need.

PANEL TWO:

Close shot. Int. Mega Ship – Battle Station. A large eyed, gill cheeked, blue-green faced alien with a sack hanging above her face communicates with Tec. Her throat has balls that get in the way of her vocal cords.

> 1 CHINSAK
>> I am the Chinsak Commander. (Glub-glub) You are trespassing. Surrender or die. (Glub-glub)

PANEL THREE:

Close shot. Int. Kobay GOM S081 – Continued. Tec blows smoke and watches the shape it makes.

> 2 TEC
>> Team, please report to your designated crash landings at this time. I repeat, report to your crash landing seats at this time.

PANEL FOUR:

Close shot. Int. Mega Ship – Battle Station. Commander Chinsak's throat balls vibrate when she's angry.

3 CHINSAK

    Do not make Chinsak Commander angry. (Glub-glub) We will destroy your ship if you do not surrender.

PANELS FIVE, SIX, SEVEN, AND EIGHT:

Long shot. Int. Coa Kuinu Solar System. The Kobay G.O.M. S081 transforms into a cube.

4 TEC

    Everyone needs to get into the safety vault.

5 PEP

    Are we crashing?

6 TEC

    No but there's gonna be some turbulence.

P. Marcelo W. Balboa

PAGE TWENTY

A full-on assault is underway as an alien ship extends long arms from multiple exits with claw hands reaching out as the Chinsak Commander demands the surrender of the Kobay G.O.M. S081.

PANEL ONE:

Splash page. Int. Coa Kuinu Solar System. Swarms of dragonfly shaped battle crafts approach the Kobay G.O.M. S081 from the mega ship. The Kobay G.O.M. S081 loads up pulse energy.

PAGE TWENTY-ONE

The communication breaks down from the alien ship.

PANEL ONE:

Close shot. Int. Kobay GOM S081 – Control Room. The Chinsak Commander's video begins breaking up.

> 1 CHINSAK (INTO PHONE)
>> We will eat you fast, (Glub-glub) not slow.

> 2 SFX
>> KSHHHHHH!

> 3 CHINSAK (INTO PHONE) (CONT'D)
>> If you stop this defiant behavior.

PANEL TWO:

Close shot. Int. Kobay GOM S081 – Control Room. Smoke from Tec's flubberleaf cigarette seep out of his mouth as he speaks..

> 4 TEC
>> I'm sorry, you're breaking up. The pulse generator can get a bit shaky.

PAGE TWENTY-TWO

NOTE: The Kobay GOM S081 has the ability to absorb the light energy from stars in it's vicinity. It can store energy for defensive measures as well.

PANEL ONE:

Extreme long shot. Int. Coa Kuinu Solar System. The mega ship extends man metal arms that try to grab the Kobay GOM S081 with pinchers at the end of each. The Kobay GOM S081 seems to explode with a star light energy in all directions.

PANEL TWO:

Extreme long shot. Int. Coa Kuinu Solar System. What remains is a brutal display of the aftermath the pulse generator brings. Parts of the mega ship and battle crafts float in all directions.

PAGE TWENTY-THREE

The Kobay G.O.M. S081 soars past a beautiful spiral of gases and starlight.

PANEL ONE:

Splash page. Int. Unworthy Cosmos – CAMA REGION. Another part of the vast expanse that is the unworthy cosmos is on display as the team continues on toward their next mission.

    1 LOCATION (CAPTION)

        Forsaken Omniverse

        Keya Universe

        KisKis Galaxy

        Cama Region

        Event B12682

PAGE TWENTY-FOUR

The team arrives at their long-awaited destination.

PANEL ONE:

Splash page. Int. Unworthy Cosmos – JAMA SOLAR SYSTEM. The Kobay G.O.M. S081 hovers in space as the shuttle descends onto the planet PORTMO. Gas clouds, odd bubble planets, shining stars, and far solar systems are the decoration in space around this planet of swirling land masses.

    1 LOCATION (CAPTION)

        KisKis Galaxy

        Jama Solar System

        Planet Portmo

Family

PAGE TWENTY-FIVE

The little family embraces as Pep takes on the unfamiliar challenge of an underwater investigation.

PANEL ONE:

Long group shot. Int. Kobay GOM S081 – Pep and Tec's private quarters. Pep and Tec talk as Neika tries to hug the last surviving data recorder, DROPA 07.

> 1 PEP
>> I think you would be better off underwater Tec. This is going to be scary.
>
> 2 NEIKA
>> Neika loves the baby robot.
>
> 3 DROPA 07
>> Threat optimal. System Malfunction.

PANEL TWO:

Long group shot. Int. Kobay GOM S081 – Continuous. Pep and Tec hug as Neika squeezes DROPA 07 with all her heart.

> 4 TEC
>> I made high tec suits for you and the data recorder. You will be fine. Just come back in one piece.
>
> 5 PEP
>> It will be harder to escape underwater, but the rockets you built in will help, I know it.
>
> 6 DROPA 07
>> System failure. Abort! Abort!

PANEL THREE:

Long shot. Ext. Planet Portmo – Surface of the ocean – Day. Kobay GOM 2.4, floats on water on calm waves.

    7 NARRATION (CAPTION)

        After their traditional cuddling moment, Pep and Tec lead the team as they venture onto their next spooky adventure beneath the water covered planet.

PANEL FOUR:

Long shot. Ext. Planet Portmo – Under the surface of the ocean – Day. Pep and DROPA 07 swim underwater to a city of domes.

    8 NARRATION (CAPTION)

        Pep and DROPA 07 swim to an underwater metropolis.

    9 NARRATION (CAPTION)

        The team is unaware, at this point, they are one of a hand full of teams left to deal with paranormal activities across the unworthy cosmos.

ISSUE #5

PAGE ONE

The Kobay G.O.M. S081 sours through a wide view of the Forsaken Omniverse that reveals an unfamiliar existence. Anomalies of different shapes and sizes exist in this region.

PANEL ONE:

Establishing shot. Int. ANMALLY SOLAR SYSTEM – Dusk. The team passes through several planet shaped rocks on their way to the only living planet in the region, MONPOLLY.

> 1 NARRATION (CAPTION)
>> The Unworthy Cosmos are filled with wonders beyond the imagination of any mere mortal. Life exists across countless universes as the great traveler, Brea, creates different teams of various abilities to aid planets in need.
>
> 2 TEC
>> Prepare for landing in 5, 4, …
>
> 3 NARRATION (CAPTION)
>> Of the several hundred paranormal teams he brought together and set out to fend off the forces of evil, only one team survived. This is their origin story.
>
> 4 LOCATION (CAPTION)
>> Forsaken Omniverse
>>
>> Keya Universe
>>
>> KisKiss Galaxy

Cama Region

Anmally Solar System

5 NARRATION (CAPTION)

Enjoy valued reader as you ride along a shuttle carrier that goes by the name, Kobay G.O.M. S081.

PAGE TWO

The team is back in action as they land on a lonely planet among the stars called MONPOLLY. It's a lush green planet filled with unique and colorful life forms.

NOTE: Raja Ali caught the flu on the trip as Padre Ully sprained his ankle on a side mission in route to this mission. Both are sitting back but ready to help if needed.

PANEL ONE:

Medium shot. Ext. Kobay GOM 2.2 – Exit ramp – Sunset. Pep exits the shuttle alone.

> 1 PEP
>> And why is it that I can't take DROPA?
>
> 2 TEC (V.O.) (INTO PHONE)
>> Pep, for the thousandth time, you shouldn't name the data recorders.

PANEL TWO:

Medium shot. Int. Kobay GOM S081 – Tec's data reception room – Sunset. Tec's annoyed expression is a normal occurrence as Pep personalized the equipment again.

> 3 PEP (V.O.) (INTO PHONE)
>> And for the thousandth and one time, I disagree.
>
> 4 TEC
>> They're disposable units. They don't… anyway, the data recorder seems to be heading your way.

PANEL THREE:

Long group shot. Ext. Kobay GOM 2.2 – Exit ramp. D.R.O.P.A. 07 approaches Pep reaching high to give her his present.

5 PEP

    Hey there DROPA, watcha got there?

PANEL FOUR:

Close shot. Ext. Kobay GOM 2.2 – Continuous. D.R.O.P.A. 07 hands the portable data transmitter to Pep.

6 D.R.O.P.A. 07

    Data recorder of paranormal activity has made you a Portable Paranormal Activity Reader to transmit information to technical support as continued upgrades are made to this mainframe.

7 TEC (V.O.) (INTO PHONE)

    To answer your question, they are programed to rebuild and repair themselves. He built a portable tablet for you.

PANEL FIVE:

Medium shot. Int. Kobay GOM S081 – Continued. Over Tec's shoulder tools and parts can be seen behind him that D.R.O.P.A. 07 is working with.

8 PEP

    And who told Dropa to do that?

9 TEC

    Fair enough. And back to your first question, he's building himself some kind of armor from the old data recorders.

PAGE THREE

The Kobay GOM 2.2 departs and lands in a parking lot of a haunted urban community. Tec keeps steady communication as Pep enters an apartment suspected to be the source of the hauntings.

PANEL ONE:

Bird's eye shot. Int. Monpolly's atmosphere – Night. The shuttle flies over water in route to an urban area by the sea.

    1 TEC

        I'm getting some good readings from the portable reader Pep. Looks like everything's working fine.

PANEL TWO:

Long shot. Int. Parking lot – Urban community – Night. The shuttle lands near a broken-down apartment building.

PANEL THREE:

Long shot. Ext. Apartment building – Night. Pep walks up to the front gate of the poorly kept building. The steps are cracked, and the windows are boarded up. There is a strip across the front door stating 'Caution-do not enter'.

    2 PEP

        Yeah, from there it looks fine. This place looks disgusting. There's gunk on the entrance steps let alone the obvious lack of care to the structure.

PANEL FOUR:

Medium shot. Int. Apartment building – Entrance lobby – Night.

3 TEC (V.O.) (INTO PHONE)

    If the place looks like it's gonna fall apart, just leave.

4 PEP

    I'm gonna fall apart. It smells like a toilet overflowed in here.

PAGE FOUR

The team is dynamic. The have learned over the years that they can adapt to anything. With new tech from D.R.O.P.A. 07, Pep's initial investigations have a portable method of reading activity. At first she doesn't understand its value and puts it in her pocket.

PANEL ONE:

Long shot. Int. Apartment building – Continuous. The P.P.A.R. vibrates in Pep's pocket as it collects multiple paranormal readings from the area.

    1 TEC (V.O.) (CAPTION)

        The portable reader is feeding me some crazy information Pep.

    2 PEP

        Whoa! This little guy is rattling.

PANEL TWO:

Medium shot. Int. Apartment building – Continuous. Pep takes out her P.P.A.R. to get a good look at it fully operational.

    3 PEP

        Holy flubberleaf! This thing is glowing with all types of graphics. How do you even understand it all?

PANEL THREE:

Close shot. The P.P.A.R. shows all the diverse activities it can read at once.

    4 TEC (V.O.) (CAPTION)

        Oh yeah! There's motion, sound, electromagnetic, time, heat, you name it this thing can collect the information and send it to me.

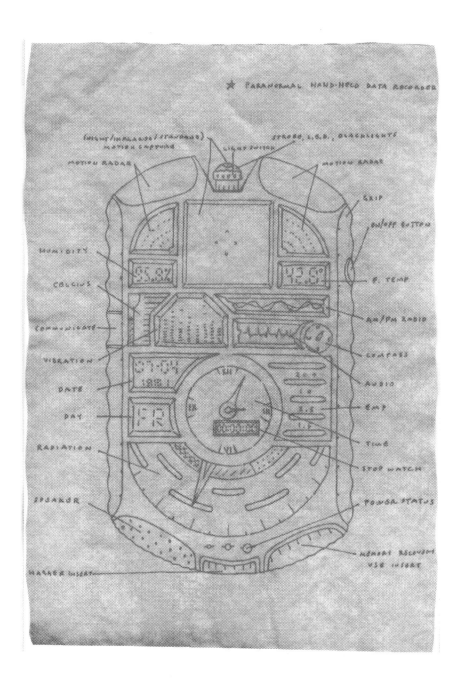

PAGE FIVE

The tension grows as Pep enters the door with the high activity readings.

PANEL ONE:

Medium shot. Int. Apartment building – Continuous. Pep crossed her arms as she quivers from the temperature drop.

    1 PEP

        Tec, it just got really cold. - Brrrrrr!-

PANEL TWO:

Long group shot. Int. Kobay GOM S081 – Tec's data reception room – Night. Tec is at his workstation as DROPA is hard at work upgrading his mainframe.

    2 TEC

        You know what that... Hey Dropa, can you keep it down over there. I'm working here.

    3 SFX

        Bzzzzzt! Bzzzt! Ting!

PANEL THREE:

Medium shot. Int. Kobay GOM S081- Continuous. Tec typing away at his keyboard.

    4 TEC

        Sorry about that. Yeah Pep, there is someone or something in the area ahead of you. Be alert. Raja, Father, better get on standby.

P. Marcelo W. Balboa

PANEL FOUR:

Long shot. Int. Apartment building – Continuous. Pep approaches the door cautiously.

    5 PEP

        Tec, you need to teach me what this reader is saying.

PANEL FIVE:

Medium shot. Int. Apartment building – Continuous. Pep peeks through the door as she slowly opens it.

    6 TEC

        Well, Dropa made it, but I will gladly learn how it works along with you.

PANEL SIX:

Medium shot. Int. Apartment building – Continuous. Pep looks confused.

NOTE: The room is clean, and the foul odor is gone.

    7 PEP

        Never mind. This thing doesn't work at all. The room is beautiful. I can't believe it exists in this rundown apartment building.

PAGE SIX

Pep finds herself in a scary situation as a ghost appears out of thin air and attacks her.

PANEL ONE:

Long shot. Int. Apartment building – Continuous. Pep staggers back as a dark figure grows from the far corner of the room.

> 1 TEC
>
>> Pep, I don't know what you see but I'm getting dangerous levels of electromagnetic activity.
>
> 2 PEP
>
>> I was wrong. Something's here.

PANEL TWO:

Medium shot. Int. Apartment building – Continuous. The dark feminine figure becomes fully realized. Tar bubbles form and pop all over her fully black body. The eyes are frighteningly well-developed eyeballs with a piercing stare.

> 3 BOILING TAR GHOST
>
>> Come here flesh. Tasty soul! Heeheeheehee!

PANEL THREE:

Medium shot. Int. Apartment building – Continuous. The figure, fully formed, chases Pep.

> 4 PEP
>
>> RAJA!

PANEL FOUR:

Long group shot. Ext. Apartment building – Night. Raja and Padre Ully run inside the apartment building.

    5 TEC

        They're already on the way Pep. Get back to the shuttle.

PANEL FIVE:

Long group shot. Int. Apartment building – Continued. The black ghostly figure chases Pep, flailing her limbs around and laughing hauntingly.

    6 PEP

        No DUH! If I make it with this thing on my butt.

PAGE SEVEN

The black ghostly figure fights with Padre Ully and Raja.

PANEL ONE:

Close shot. Int. Apartment building – Daybreak. The black ghostly figure laughs as her limbs flail around. She runs like a floppy wet noodle.

    1 BOILING TAR GHOST

        Tasty souls you have. Let me eat.

PANEL TWO:

Bird's eye shot. Int. Apartment building – Hallway – Daybreak. The black ghostly figure knocks Padre Ully and Raja back with an energy wave.

    2 PADRE ULLY

        Reveal me your nay…

    3 BOILING TAR GHOST

        Noooo

PANEL THREE:

Long group shot. Int. Apartment building – Continuous. The black ghostly figure looks down over Padre Ully.

    4 BOILING TAR GHOST

        I will eat you whole holy man. Soul and all.

PANEL FOUR:

Long shot. Int. Apartment building – Continuous. Raja jumps up and attacks the black ghostly figure.

    4 RAJA

        Not if I can help it.

PAGE EIGHT

The black ghostly figure is hurt by Raja's blessed staff allowing Padre Ully to perform an exorcism.

PANEL ONE:

Long shot. Int. Apartment building – Continued. Raja's staff strikes the black ghostly figure in the head.

   1 SFX

        Whack!

PANEL TWO:

Long shot. Int. Apartment building – Continuous. The figure falls to the ground.

   2 RAJA ALI

        Blessing my staff was the best gift you have ever given me my friend.

   3 PADRE ULLY

        It appears to be a gift we mutually benefit from.

PANEL THREE:

Long shot. Int. Apartment building – Continuous. Father Ully kneels over the black ghostly figure.

   4 PADRE ULLY

        Quickly Raja, get out your rope I blessed as well. This entity may not entirely be ghostly.

PANEL FOUR:

Long shot. Int. Apartment building – The room - Morning. The black ghostly figure sits quietly, tied up.

5 PADRE ULLY

    I command you to reveal your name.

PANEL FIVE:

Long shot. Int. Apartment building – Continued. Father Ully shows his prayer book.

6 PADRE ULLY

    You know what is to come if I should have to call upon the forces of light.

PANEL SIX:

Close shot. Int. Apartment building – Continuous. The ghostly figure reveals no mouth, nose, or ears. Just pure darkness with a clear flame around it's silhouette and piercing dot that seems to float on two pure white eyeballs.

7 BOILING TAR GHOST

    Let us be. You are not wanted here. You are not needed here.

PAGE NINE

The true threat behind the ghostly figure is revealed.

PANEL ONE:

Close shot. Int. Apartment building – Continued. Facial features begin to shine though the darkness of the black ghostly figure's face.

> 1 BOILING TAR FIGURE
>
> I found you again priest. Your life is mine.

PANEL TWO:

Medium shot. Int. Apartment building – Continuous. The eyes of a possessed Pep haunt Padre Ully.

> 2 PADRE ULLY
>
> Remi.

PANEL THREE:

Long shot. Int. Apartment building – Continuous. Padre Ully reaches out to exorcise the entity, placing his hand on the figure's forehead.

NOTE: The tar is melting off revealing the woman under. She has mutilated her face with acid.

> 3 PADRE ULLY
>
> Enough. I know it is not you who possesses this capsule. Tell me your true name and I will make your departure easy.

> 4 BOILING TAR FIGURE
>
> Ahhhhhh! I have no name. I am a lost light that was never born. Let me be. Let me beeee.

PAGE TEN

The entity makes debris from the walls surrounding them fly at Padre Ully.

PANEL ONE:

Long shot. Int. Apartment building – Continued. Padre Ully exorcises the entity as Raja protects him.

> 1 PADRE ULLY
>
>> Your telekinetic tricks cannot save you from the wrath of the one before all.
>
> 2 LOST LIGHT
>
>> Nooooo! This body is mine. I deserve to live.
>
> 3 PADRE ULLY
>
>> I call on the forces of light to cast this lost light back into the darkness from whence it came.

PANEL TWO:

Medium shot. Int. Apartment building – Continuous. Debris is struck by Raja's staff.

> 4 SFX
>
>> Crack!

PANEL THREE:

Close shot. Int. Apartment building – Continuous. More debris is struck by Raja's staff.

> 5 SFX
>
>> Pop!

PANEL FOUR:

Medium shot. Int. Apartment building – Continuous. More debris is struck by Raja's staff.

    6 SFX

        Pow!

PANEL FIVE:

Long shot. Int. Apartment building – Continuous. A close of view of Raja as he strikes the debris.

    7 SFX

        Whack!

PAGE ELEVEN

NOTE: While there are many forms of the forces of darkness such as demons and ghosts, some are of the Physical Realm. Cultists will embrace the possession of their body. Souls that have committed suicide or were taken from the Physical Realm sooner than they wanted will occupy these willing bodies. Where they have intent, the Lost Lights don't. They were souls who were aborted, miscarried, or died from unfortunate circumstances and never knew what is was to be born. Never grew or learned what it was to breath. They are like children with loaded weapons. There is not telling what they will do.

FULL PAGE:

Long shot. Int. Apartment building – Continued. Light glows around the lost light expelling the rest of the tar while pulling the entity out as it fights to stay inside the body of the cultist. The cultist and the lost light share one thought still.

    1 LOST LIGHT-CULTIST

        Stop it! This is what we want. You have no right to do this priest.

    2 RAJA ALI

        Why are there two voices?

    3 PADRE ULLY

        It's the lost light and the cultist. They don't want to separate.

PAGE TWELVE

The lost light is separated from the cultist's body.

FULL PAGE:

Long shot. Int. Apartment building – Continued. The lost light can be seen hovering over the cultist's body as the cultist screams in agony.

> CULTIST:
>> Bring it back. I don't want to live anymore. Let the lost light have this body. Noooooo!

PAGE THIRTEEN

Padre Ully and Raja return exhausted as Pep and Tec are unable to understand what they saw.

PANEL ONE:

Long group shot. Ext. Kobay GOM 2.2 – Exit/Entrance Ramp – Day. Padre Ully and Raja walk up the ramp of the shuttle.

    1 RAJA ALI

        I implore you to do so. You have so much to teach Merrio. Give it to those who are lost.

    2 PADRE ULLY

        I wouldn't know how to start writing a book friend. Perhaps someday.

PANEL TWO AND THREE:

Dual panel close shot. Int. Kobay GOM 2.2 and Kobay GOM S081 – Day. Pep and Tec have stunned expressions as they try to understand what they were watching on the monitors from their respective locations.

    3 TEC

        What in the…

    4 PEP

        I'm so glad they're part of the team Pep.

    5 TEC

        Me too.

PAGE FOURTEEN

The team stop at a nearby planet surrounded by unique stars, uninhabitable planets, and colorful moons.

FULL PAGE:

Long shot. Int. TING-KAI-PO Galaxy – Planet CHI-WA's orbit – Day. The Kobay G.O.M. S081 hovers in outer space as the shuttle descends upon planet Chi-wa. A planet with beautiful beaches and the clearest water in the galaxy.

> 1 NARRATION (CAPTION)
>> The team recovers after a rough battle against a strong adversary by stopping by a nearby planet for supplies and relaxation.
>
> 2 NARRATION (CAPTION)
>> Pep and Tec get a break from parenting as they set out for some relaxation time on the beach.
>
> 3 NARRATION (CAPTION)
>> Raja gets in some weight training while Padre Ully begins journaling his future book, The Unworthy Bible.

PAGE FIFTEEN

Neika has become a surrogate child of the team. She is in everyone's business, absorbing lessons and enjoying the presence of each member as she chooses. Here, she and Padre Ully have some bonding time.

PANEL ONE:

Close shot. Int. Kobay GOM S081 – Padre Ully's Study – Day. On display in a glass casing is a book bound in the flesh of a cultist who willingly gave her life to become the pages and cover. Padre Ully's hand reaches out to grab it.

> 1 NARRATION (CAPTION)
>> A book Padre Ully collected on one of the many spooky adventures he went on with Raja, Pep and Tec.

PANEL TWO:

Medium group shot. Int. Kobay GOM S081 – Continuous. Neika inquiries about what Padre Ully sits at his desk to write in the book with his dip pen and ink waiting patiently.

> 2 NEIKA
>> Neika loves coloring books.

> 3 PADRE ULLY
>> This is no coloring book sweet child. It is a living book that can be felt by the souls that read the words on its pages.

PANEL THREE:

Medium group shot. Int. Kobay GOM S081 – Continuous. The book is opened with Padre Ully beginning to write his first words.

4 NEIKA

    What will people feel?

5 PADRE ULLY

    A worthy existence.

PAGE SIXTEEN

Father Ully's words are brought to life through visuals.

FULL PAGE:

On the pages of Father Ully's prayer book show him fending off a possessed woman. Below is his flask filled with holy water. On the flask is his image splashed the water on an adversary.

   1 NARRATION (CAPTION)

      Padre Ully begins his memoirs.

   2 NARRATION (CAPTION)

      Slowly but surely each word builds the book that he will break down the Physical, Astral, and Meta-Physical Realms and all their glory.

PAGE SEVENTEEN

A breathtaking image of an archangel defeating a demon in the vastness of outer space as Father Ully and Raja watch in their space suits Tec makes them for a future adventure.

FULL PAGE:

Establishing shot. Int. LOTHBRUK NEBULA – Night. A building size archangel defeats a building size demon in outer space as Raja and Padre Ully watch in awe floating at a safe distance in their space suits.

> 1 NARRATION (CAPTION)
>> Padre Ully writes of great battles between angels and demons witnessed with his own eyes.
>
> 3 NARRATION (CAPTION)
>> Neika, intrigued by each lesson, visits Padre Ully throughout the completion of his book to listen to him as he preaches his dogma.

PAGE EIGHTEEN

Padre Ully returns to his private quarters after some quality time with Neika and his new book.

PANEL ONE:

Long shot. Int. Kobay GOM S081 – Living quarter hallway B. Padre Ully walks to his private quarters sorrowful.

> 1 NARRATION (CAPTION)
>
>> Padre Ully will have many more nights like this.

PANEL TWO:

Long shot. Int. Kobay GOM S081 – Room B327 – Night. Padre Ully opens his door and enters his private quarters as he turns on the light.

> 2 NARRATION (CAPTION)
>
>> Returning to his quarters after some time writing his book.

PANEL THREE:

Long shot. Int. Kobay GOM S081 – Continuous. Padre Ully lays down, exhausted and ready for sleep.

> 3 NARRATION (CAPTION)
>
>> Night after night he tries to fall asleep, haunted by nightmares of losing his wife and child. Little does he know there will be more for him to endure.

PAGE NINTEEN

NOTE: Karlo is much older at this point. He has been mutilated and killed. One his journey he has found a way to return to life, but his body is fat, his lower arms are missing with the radius and ulna bones visible and sharpened. His wings are torn off and his bull head is upside down as his neck was broken during his second fight with his fellow fallen brethren Bellosatanicus.

PANEL ONE:

(DREAMED IMAGE) The reincarnated Karlo defeats Raja. The fallen guardian of electrical currents, Karlo, stands in delight as he stabs Raja in the chest.

    1 NARRATION (CAPTION)

        A time will come...

PANEL TWO:

Padre Ully lays on his bed, wide awake, unable to return to sleep as his visions of what may come haunt him.

    1 NARRATION (CAPTION)

        When Padre Ully will be forced to watch his friend
        fall to the fallen guardian Karlo.

PAGE TWENTY

The Unworthy Cosmos are a reminder of how small and seemingly insignificant the team is yet, in this image, they are also made aware of how grand they are to other life forms.

FULL PAGE:

Long Shot. Int. Unworthy Cosmos – Night. Numerous tiny galaxies spin within a swirl made up of gasses and electrical currents that sparkle with beautiful colors.

> 1 NARRATION (CAPTION)
>> The Kobay G.O.M. S081 sours by a swirl of galaxies with life forms the size of atoms on planets smaller than sand.

PAGE TWENTY-ONE

Tec finds Raja, who has been distant lately.

PANEL ONE:

Close shot. Int. Kobay GOM S081 – Observation Deck – Night. Tech has a look of concern as he speaks.

> 1 TEC
>
>> What's up there Raja? You haven't been around the team since that scare on our last mission. Are you alright?

PANEL TWO:

Close shot. Int. Kobay GOM S081 – Continuous. Raja looks bothered as he speaks.

> 2 RAJA ALI
>
>> On our last spooky adventure. The entity grabbed me. It made me see things. Things that were to come. I pray they are just nightmares, but I fear they are not.

PAGE TWENTY-TWO

Raja goes into detail about his visions when Tec asks about them.

PANEL ONE:

Long shot. Int. Kobay GOM S081 – Raja's vision. An image of lost lights. Floating glowing orbs with a clear bluish grey fire around them.

   1 TEC

      What did you see?

   2 RAJA ALI

      Lost lights. An army of them.

PANEL TWO:

Long shot. Int. Kobay GOM S081 – Continuous. An image of cultists. Various beings with acid burned faces dressed in dark garments made of the flesh of the sacrificed.

   3 RAJA ALI

      And an army of cultists ready to be possessed.

PANEL THREE:

Medium shot. Int. Kobay GOM S081 – Continuous. An image of the beautiful prince of darkness. An angel, fallen from the heights of heaven, seated on a flaming throne that does not harm him.

   4 TEC

      That sucks.

   5 RAJA ALI

      Not as much as their leader, the prince of darkness,
      who seeks vengeance upon us.

PANEL FOUR:

Long shot. Int. Kobay GOM S081 – Continuous. An image of demon ticks. Six-armed, bulb bellied, bony limbed, tick headed, grey skinned minions of Karlo.

    6 TEC

        The one I nearly killed?

7 RAJA ALI

        Yes, but his army is but one of other armies we must worry about. A beastly monster named Karlo leads an army of demon ticks. And our paths are unavoidable.

PAGE TWENTY-THREE

Spooky adversaries to come are revealed as this series comes to an end.

PANEL ONE:

Medium shot. Int. Kobay GOM S081 – Continued. An image of an angry Wraith.

> 1 RAJA ALI
>
> Yet it is not the armies I fear most. It is the ones who have no affiliation yet seek the same defilement of the physical beings out there.

PANEL TWO:

Long shot. Int. Kobay GOM S081 – Continuous. An image of a Phantom.

> 2 RAJA ALI
>
> Or the entities that linger at the end of the road. Seeking your demise.

PANEL THREE:

Close shot. Int. Kobay GOM S081 – Continuous. An image of a Banshee.

> 3 RAJA ALI
>
> Be mindful friend. There are evil creatures out there that shiver the spine with just their voice.

PANEL FOUR:

Medium shot. Int. Kobay GOM S081 – Continuous. An image of a ghostly Mare.

> 4 RAJA ALI
>
> Try waking to a beast that sits on your chest, giving you nightmares as you try to sleep.

P. Marcelo W. Balboa

PANEL FIVE:

Long shot. Int. Kobay GOM S081 – Continuous. An image of an Oni.

> 5 RAJA ALI
>
>> I doubt I could defeat even one Oni, let alone the multitudes set loose upon the cosmos.

PANEL SIX:

Medium shot. Int. Kobay GOM S081 – Continuous. An image of the flying skull of a Jinn.

> 6 RAJA ALI
>
>> Let me not forget the Jinn, who work for no one and take pleasure in tormenting our souls.

PAGE TWENTY-FOUR

Raja continues to reveal more threats that are to come.

PANEL ONE:

Close shot. Int. Kobay GOM S081 – Continued. An image of a Yurei.

    1 TEC

        Are they… Will we survive them?

    2 RAJA ALI

        I don't know. Like the Jinn, the Yurei might just torment us.

PANEL TWO:

Medium shot. Int. Kobay GOM S081 – Continuous. An image of a foul spirit.

    3 RAJA ALI

        It doesn't stop there. There are foul spirits who were once us and hate our untainted souls.

PANEL THREE:

Long shot. Int. Kobay GOM S081 – Continuous. An image of a shadow person.

    4 TEC

        We will defeat them.

    5 RAJA ALI

        And what of the people who mimic familiar voices to lure you in only for you to never return?

P. Marcelo W. Balboa

PANEL FOUR:

Long shot. Int. Kobay GOM S081 – Continuous. An image of a Poltergeist.

6 RAJA ALI

> How should we defeat decrepit entities with horrid intentions who can move things in the Physical Realm from the Astral Realm.

PANEL FIVE:

Medium shot. Int. Kobay GOM S081 – Continuous. An image of a Revenant.

7 RAJA ALI

> And below all else are a pure evil at their core.

8 TEC

> Whatever you saw, I respect your concern, but you're not alone. You're part of a team that's down for whatever comes.

9 RAJA ALI

> Good man.

PAGE TWENTY-FIVE

NOTE: This is one of a two page spread.

Stars, planets, constellations, and many other beautiful sights are in view as Raja stands quietly, taking it all in.

FULL PAGE:

Establishing shot. Int. Kobay GOM S081 – Observation Deck – Night. Raja stands at the observation deck.

    1 NARRATION (CAPTION)

        Raja and Tec look out onto the Unworthy Cosmos as they contemplate the threats that are out there, waiting for them.

P. Marcelo W. Balboa

PAGE TWENTY-SIX

NOTE: This is one of a two page spread.

Stars, planets, constellations, and many other beautiful sights are in view as Tec looks out at the Unworthy Cosmos from the observation deck.

FULL PAGE:

Establishing shot. Int. Kobay GOM S081 – Observation Deck – Night. Tec stands at the observation deck.

> 1 NARRATION (CAPTION)
>> As they think to themselves and look out in awe, they are unaware Raja just described the adversaries that are defeating the other paranormal teams throughout the cosmos.

> 2 NARRATION (CAPTION)
>> In due time, their team will be the only team standing against the paranormal forces of darkness.

A word from the Author

Valued reader, if you have ever thought of trying to make a comic book, remember it all starts with a story that you want to tell and drives you to finish. The trick to that is making a story even you want to know the ending to. Start with page one and go from there. You will find it is quite easy once you commit to simply doing it. As for me, I will be working on this and perhaps inspire a few story lines in my role-playing game I plan to play with my family to complete another chapter later in this book. For now, let's take you on a trip through my studio.

My "Studio"

In the beginning… there was a light bulb. Ideas spilled from my thoughts, and I just typed.

I love to watch television & social media outlets while I type on my laptop.

The early days when concept art was all I had to feed a dream, I painted.

P. Marcelo W. Balboa

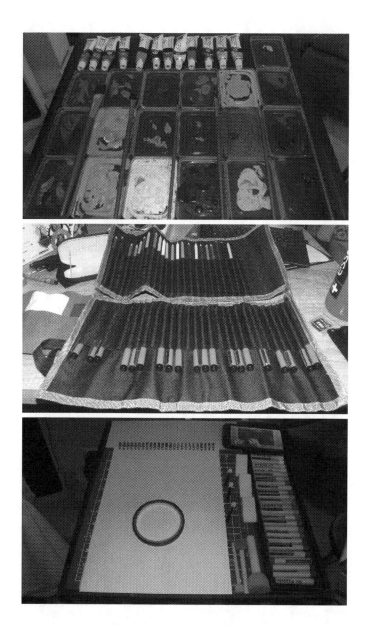

I would only use pencils for majority of my youth. But later in my life I have learned that different tools bring out my imagined work far more. So now I try all art material and let the images I create inspire me.

Family

Scanning the images made it easier to re-collect old inspirational images I forgot from time to time. I need to go on a diet. Motivation photo.

I learned early that a small scanning machine wasn't good enough for my imagination. My art grew from small sketches to full length 10 by 15 images.

I couldn't help but buy any and all the books I discovered that filled my thoughts with more ideas. I WILL NEVER COPY THE WORK OF OTHERS, but my natural urges can't help but extrapolate person, places, and things that came forth from other creative people.

Family

Collectables, memorabilia, movies… It didn't matter. If it sparked a thought that can develop into a story or compliment a character I would dream up, I had to have it.

There were many nostalgic inspirations I regained along the way. Great treasures to hand down to my kids.

Family

I mixed 2-dimensional art with 3-dimensional art to give life to the world and characters I was creating.

Family

My adjustable drawing table was vital but learning to magnetize my pencils and inks turned out to be the game changer.

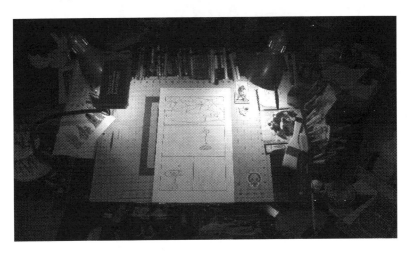

Such work as 'The Munchgalumptagans' found guidance from a conceptual art design like this image I eventually made the original book cover.

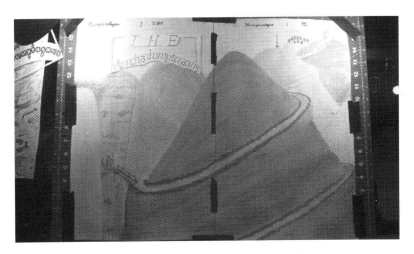

Some images spilled into my mind but never made it to a book. However, they did mold a few faces in my work.

Zero knives, hot glue, sculpting tools, and everything I could find that brought me closer to a physical representation of my creations were in play.

The subsequent "Kit Bashing" inspired by crazy ideas resulted in material I would use to guide the majority of my work. I recommend setting up a table for yourself.

A three-dimensional view of Jokevla, a key city in several of my books has been inspired by this cardboard creation.

I made this mockup dibbuk. It took a year after making it for fun until I finally realized it would be a great character in my book. And I knew just who would need it.

To keep from getting cramped in one area, I collected an assortment of tools that I needed to commit to my art on the go. It's easier to step away for inspiration and even better to have your tools nearby to access when that inspiration kicks in.

Yes, my living room became my studio. It is crazy to look back at what my work area use to look like. Don't pay attention to the trash can. You work with what you got. And in those days, I made sure to horde. Thanks Mom.

I spent many hours with my family trying to create, analyze, and then perfect my role-playing ideas with them.

I bought dice, monster manuals, notebooks, and all other types of material that added to my goal to make a more interactive experience when following my work.

All my family time created what became Cosmic Journey's one-shot collection my family affectionately call, 'The Imagination Game." In this book it called, "Family Edition".

Don't get me wrong. Yes I made an on-the-go pack, but I still made sure to hit the workshop area when big ideas called to me from day and night dreams. Having an area to work on your hobby or personal career is vital, in my view, to feeding that thing that makes life worth living.

With 8 books already carving out the Unworthy Cosmos, this book will delve into the lives of others affected by the ubiquitous occurrences across the universes.

Family

Even as I wrote this book, my work area evolved.

I found new activities that drew my attention. Such as electronics. The Pep and Tec Comic Book series had a lot of tech that inspired me to get into taking apart items like game consoles.

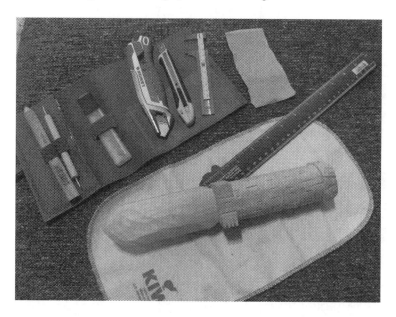

Taking up hobbies is important to relax and stimulate my imagination. I watched a movie with a knife that made me want to whittle my own version.

Family

I recommend finding an activity that gets you away from your writing, as it will help you return refreshed.

I can't tell you how valuable getting out and taking in the view of the world is.

Rise Of The Queen Of Shadow

A Cosmic Journey

Tec visits the resting place of Pep like clockwork. He didn't commit to much after their adventures. But that all changed as Forgotten came to see him. He wasn't in the mood to speak to the person who killed his life partner. "I know you are upset with me, but you have to understand I didn't know she would jump in front as I attacked Neika. I thought she was a demon who snuck on board the ship Tec. I'm sorry." Forgotten said. Tec took a deep breath as he stood up. Still looking at Pep's grave he responded, "I saw what happened. I get what happened. That doesn't mean I have to accept what happened." "Tec, I … I don't know how to repay you for my debt other than to tell you that my gift, that which I attempted to perform on Neika. It allows me to jump into the Astral Realm just as easily as I can push someone into it. I tried to bring Pep back, but her soul was being watched by this entity called Remi. You met her many years ago when she possessed Pep. She took Pep's soul to the prince of darkness who dwells in the Kingdom in Shadow. He waits for you." Forgotten said.

Tec looks at her for the first time since the incident that took Pep's life. "The Astral Realm. To dwell there you must be dead. How is it that you can traverse such a place?" He asked. "I am the daughter of Bello. A guardian on another planet that fell from grace. He did horrible things as I have. I truly deserve death. But his gift gave him the ability to pull souls from the Astral Realm and put them into bodies in the Physical Realm. He forced himself on my mother. He brought my mother back when she killed herself. I was inside her. He didn't care. He buried her alive as an Afterlife. I was born from her and was raised by her. All I knew was darkness until another child of another guardian killed her. Then I was alone. I learned I had inherited

Family

a weaker variation of my father's gifts when I accidentally communed with my mother in the Astral Realm. In pursuit of revenge, I traveled the Physical Realm where I found Karlo, my father's brother. It was my intent to find my father who still resident in the Astral Realm before Brea invited me to join your team after you lost your priest. When I killed… When Pep died I knew I am every bit the child of my father. So I traveled the Astral Realm far and wide to find my father until I came upon the information I just provided to you. Avenging my mother is all I lived for but what I did to you haunts me. What I took away from you two kills me inside. My hate for my father can't be subsided until I at least try to right my wrong. So I ask you to come with me. I will open a gateway for you to save Pep." She said.

Tec thought about it. "You don't come to me to help me. You're selfish. You want to make up for what you did to get it off of your shoulders. But I'm not concerned with you. Your life is what you make of it. Just get me to Pep or as close to this Kingdom in Shadow as you can and leave. I'll consider your debt paid." Tec said. "I can do that." She said. "So what do I need to do?" He asked. "Tonight when you fall asleep I will come for you in your dreams. And when I get you to the front gates I will depart." She said. "Sounds good." He responded. Tec went to his old pad and tucked away into his shell. He looked at some items that reminded him of his time with Pep as he slowly fell asleep. When he opened his eyes Forgotten was standing over him. He sat up confused.

They weren't in his shell. They were in the dark red desert land of the Astral Realm where the souls enter from the Physical Realm. "I take it we're here?" Tec asked as he dusted himself off and rose to his feet. "No. This is the Astral Realm, but our path is long and far. The Shadow Dimension is a place that takes great sorrow to enter." She said. "Then we'll fit in perfectly. Let's go." Tec said. Without a response, Forgotten nodded in agreement and led the way. Ike, the great traveler of the Astral Realm, noticed them. He didn't bother them but kept a close eye.

Forgotten and Tec made it to a cliff overhanging the path that led to the front gate of the Kingdom in Shadow. "What in the hell?" Tec said. "No. This isn't hell Tec. That place is far worse. But it's a close third. The prince of darkness is from hell. He was beautiful and arrogant all the same. He fell from heaven when he defied the one before all. As the realms took shape Hell became a fixed dimension in the Metaphysical Realm." She said. "Physical,

Astral, Metaphysical... how many realms are there?" Tec asked. "That's all I know of. But the Unworthy Cosmos is vast and the void that is the abyss beyond the realms is immeasurable. Only the one before all knows." She said. "Well, whatever the case, that there is an army, and we are just two." Tec said with calm concern.

Forgotten looked at him confused. "You want me to stay?" She asked. "It looks like a hunted castle. I remember when Pep snuck into one. I didn't want to get close to it. Can you help me get in?" He asked. "I can distract these losers. We are alive. They are dead. Our spirits our stronger." She responded. "So...?" He began. "So yes, but my path is not yours. I can't risk dying and not avenge my mother in the process." She said. "I understood you from day one. Get me inside and I'll take care of the rest." He said. "I'll do my best." She said. They descended the cliff and approached the army of suicide souls. "I'll try to find another way in. Can you distract this army?" Tec asked. "I'll do what I can." She said. He didn't hesitate as he ran into the darkness to find another path inside the Kingdom in Shadow. Tec never found another path inside when he returned to a fallen army at the hands of Forgotten. The problem is she was gone. And all Tec had to save Pep was a strong will and his love for her.

In the distance purple flares caught his attention. They were coming closer and closer. Tec was unsure what to do so he prepared to fight. As the flares approached a few feet away he could see a large demon. She looked up at him and stopped. "Daddy?" She said. Tec was confused. "Uh... No. I'm not your daddy." Tec said. The eight-foot demon, with two large bat wings and two large horns that speared out of her forehead, dropped the body of the suicide soul, and stretched her arms out. "Daddy, it's me. Neika." Neika said. Tec stepped back. "Neika? Neika you died a child. How?" He asked. "My body absorbs the life force of the souls in this place. It makes me big and strong." She said. Tec had no words. Neika was still the loving Neika he raised but she looked like the epitome of what a devil in hell would look like.

"My mind is blown Neika. You've grown up... so... big." He said. His face was calm, cool, and collected but his thoughts were moving a mile a minute. "I know daddy. But I'm still you're baby-girl right?" She asked. "Yes, yes. Always. I'm just trying to absorb all this." He said. "Come to think of it. What are you doing here? Oh my goodness. You died daddy?" She gasped. "No. That woman who attacked you and mommy led me here to help find mommy. But now she's gone, and I don't know how to get in this place or home." He said. "Why do you want to go in there. That's a bad place. The prince of darkness is in there. When I saw all these souls just laying here ready to eat I came over, but I would never have come over knowing whose in there." She said.

"Babygirl, you know who that is right?" He asked. She looked at him intrigued. "No." She said. "Many years ago mommy saved you. Your real mother gave up her life to help Pep escape a cult of future suicide souls who wanted to kill you before you could be born." He began. "But you and mommy are my parents. Right?" She asked. "Yes. No doubt. But this prince of whatever found a way to give a part of himself to that woman whose body created you. But when they discovered you were a female they tried to end you." He said. She flopped to the ground, sitting in sadness. "You and mommy are not my parents." She cried. Tec walked up to try and console her, but she was far too large.

"Can I inquire why you are in my realm Tec?" Ike asked. "Ike, long time no see." Tec responded. "Good to see you again friend. But I am still curious. I understand Neika's situation but you and Forgotten shouldn't be here. I saw her leave without you, which concerned me. I am glad I found you, but I'm still left with a lot of questions." Ike said. "She left. Well, she kept her promise I guess." Tec said to himself. "She left you, but you are not dead Tec. Why are you here?" Ike asked. "He said my dad is the prince of darkness. Is that true traveler?" Neika asked. Ike looked at Tec upset. "Why would you reveal such a thing Tec?" Ike asked. Tec felt flustered but remained calm, cool, and collected. "Look, Forgotten killed my wife and child. Then came to tell me this jerk prince took her soul before Forgotten could bring her back to life. Pep is in this place and her soul is trapped as bait for me. Forgotten helped me get her and left because I told her I didn't need her. Then I ran into my daughter who doesn't look like my daughter. I have no idea how to deal with any of this but I'm here. I want to save my wife. If neither of you have a solution, then let me be so I can figure out how to save her." Tec declared.

Neika stopped crying. "Mommy is in there?" She asked. "Yes baby girl. And that fallen angel dead beat father of yours took her, doing who knows what with her, to somehow lure me to him most likely if I died." He said. Ike pulled Tec a short distance away from Neika to speak privately. "You're her real father Tec. You shouldn't call that horrid devilish fiend her father.

He may be beautiful, but his heart is black. She may look like a monster, but her heart is pure. Make amends because she and you will need each other more than you realize." Ike said. "Beautiful? The prince is beautiful? Why did Neika, born from a human, come out looking different?" Tec asked. "Because the prince of darkness has a dark soul. He is cursed to create monsters. But you raised her, and she became a beautiful person. Because of you Tec." Ike said. Tec looked at her then looked down. "Nah. She is a beautiful person because of Pep. Do you have any advice?" Tec asked.

Ike returned to Neika who heard everything. She gave Ike a dirty look for calling her a monster. "I have an idea. It may take a lot of effort, grit, and perseverance from both of you but if you find your way you may be able to save Pep." Ike said. "I'm not a monster." Neika told Ike. "No, you're not. You're my daughter." Tec said. Neika didn't have a reaction. She was so confused. A part of her always knew Pep and Tec were not her parents but to be the unwanted child of the evil prince of darkness made things worse. "Baby-girl?" Tec said. "Don't. I'm not your girl, I'm not your baby. Don't call me that." She said. Tec respectfully backed away. "Neika, I understand you're going through something right now but, whatever you feel, you know Pep is in there. I can gather help, but it will take time. But you have the power inside you to compete with the dark prince like no one else. If you follow the path I set you on, you may not only save Pep but the future of the Shadow Dimension." Ike said.

"For her. She doesn't deserve this. I'll do whatever I can to save her." Neika said. "Good, hold tight." Ike said as he grabbed them and transported them to the edge to the Plain of the Lost Treasures. Neika and Tec were not ready for the ride and began to puke. "That's normal. Just let it all out." Ike said in laughter. Tec looked at Ike. "Why is this large cloud built up like a wall and not moving?" Tec asked. "Many years ago I opened a pathway to you. Since then the place has gotten bigger. Now this is the doorway into the Plain of Lost Treasures. You found what you needed to save Pep back then. Perhaps it can happen again." Ike said. Tec remembered the journey. It almost took his life many times. "Then let's go get another sword." Neika said as she ran into the cloud wall. "NEIKA WAIT!" Tec yelled out as he tried to grab her. "You better get to her before she gets lost Tec. She never traveled far from the land of the falling souls." Ike said. "The area where I came in with Forgotten?" Tec asked. "Yes. Are we really going to have a conversation about this when your…" Ike began but Tec understood what his point was and darted after his daughter.

Tec falls to the ground. The fog wall masked the lower ground level on the other side. Tec returned to his feet and dusted off. A faint whimper could be heard in the distance. Tec walked up to the whimpering child. "Are you alright?" Tec asked. "You know I'm not. DAD." Neika responded. Tec was caught off guard. Neika didn't look like a toddler anymore but was no longer the enormous demon figure she once was before entering the fog wall. Neika was in a dark place in spirit. Her ability to absorb energy in the Astral Realm didn't translate on this plain. The pathetic life forms that sensed her drained her of her sustenance and scattered to sell what they took from her soul. Her memory was foggy and all she could remember is what was in her head just a few minutes ago.

Tec tried to put his hand on her shoulder, but she pulled away. She was confused. She knew he was her father but wasn't sure how or why. "Neika, I'm sorry if I hurt you." Tec began. Neika looked up at him. "Who's Neika?" She asked. Tec paused. "Um, you. My daughter." He said. She started whimpering again. "I can't remember anything. I don't know where I am. I just remember being mad at you, but I don't remember why." She cried. Tec started looking around. There were things lurking about that fed off of sorrow in this plain. "Neika, I need you to trust me right now. We have to find some shelter. We aren't safe out in the open." He said. Something within her trusted him inherently. "Ok." She said softly.

They found a crevice in the terrain several yards away from the fog wall. Neika sat quiet as she watched Tec break a bone and shape them into two short daggers. "How do you know to do that?" She asked. Tec answered without breaking motion. "I've been in the shadow dimension before. Many years ago. Before you were born. I had to survive for what seemed like months." Neika felt confused. "What is shadow dimension?" She asked. "It's a place where things go in the astral realm that belong in the darkness." He said. "We belong in the darkness?" She asked. "We belong in the light, but we came here together to get the equipment we need to face forces of darkness in another plain in this dimension." He said. "What's a plain?" She asked.

Tec paused in slight frustration but realized Neika was just trying to learn. He also noticed the conversation was building a report with her. He gathered himself and said, "I am your father. And your mother is in the astral realm. I came to save your mother who is trapped in the shadow dimension that exists within the astral realm. And within this dimension are different plains. To save your mother many years ago I traveled through the plain of forgotten things within the shadow dimension. When I found out your mother was in need of my help more recently, I returned to the astral realm and found you. But you were different. Bigger, stronger, and fully developed as a…" He paused. Tec chose to be more careful with his words. "You were bigger, but we passed through that wall of fog, and something happed that made you smaller. And the event seemed to have taken a bit of your memory too. I'm making daggers to protect us as we try to find a way to get the equipment we need to save your mother and hopefully jog your memory back." He continued.

Neika thought to herself. 'He seems to love my mother very much. Why do I feel so angry with him?' She looked at him working hard and making weapons to protect them. "You make poking things to fight. What is here to fight?" She asked. "Until I can find better weapons, gear, or whatever I need to keep us safe. There has to be other's here that will provide me with the things we need. We just need to find them. Not all who belong in these plains are bad. But not all who are here are good." He said. Neika pondered for a moment. "So we are good?" She asked. Tec stopped for a second. "You are great. You are the best daughter a father could ever have." He said. The smiled at each other, then Tec finished working on his daggers. "There we go. A couple of well-made daggers. Let's get moving." He said. They exited the crevice in the terrain. Neika followed her father without question.

Tec would face a few small beasts that jumped out of the darker places in the plain of hurtful things. Each time he taught Neika how to strip them of their valuable body parts. After a few days in shadow dimension time, they ran across an eerie old hairy dog faced humanoid. "I see you have much to carry. Sit a spell and perhaps I may have for you what is worth you giving what you have to me." She said. Tec sat on a rock in front of the old female. Neika mimicked her father in silence. Tec pulled several tradable items out of the backpack he made from the skin of one of the monsters that attacked them. The old female tried to reach but Tec put his hand in front of hers. "We have, but you must give." He said. She looked at him with a smirk. "Wise words, wise words. I know this little one beside you. Not too long ago a gang of thieves passed by. They bragged about draining her of her energy. She is special. They planned to return to finish her off. Now give me." She said. Tec moved his hand away. "You had some to say but three things you gave. So three things you take." Tec said.

She looked at him with a smug expression. "I want all." She said. "I have no issue with all, but I want to know where they went." He said. "You seek to... It is your choice. They went in that direction." She said as she pointed directly behind them. In the distance a hill of sharp edges could be seen. Smoke without light reached out to the purple-grey sky. Tec grabbed his backpack, flipped it over and asked, "You can have all, but I would like knuckle poppers." He said. She looked at him with a surprised grin. "You have been here before?" She asked. "No, but I have been in a similar place. Do you have any?" He asked. She looked in her large bag and pulled out a smaller bag. "I will give you what I have. You have given me the same. Karma." She said.

Tec grabbed the bag and placed it into his backpack. "Careful there, I made a very good batch." She said. Tec looked at her, nodded, then continued on. Neika studied her father and copied his actions perfectly. As the two drew closer to the smoke, Tec set his backpack down and kneeled down to talk to Neika. He handed her his daggers then said, "I want you to stay here. If I don't return you will return to that trader. Give her these and ask her to help you return to the fog wall. OK?" He said. Neika looked up in sadness, "Neika help you. You and me go and come back." She said softly. He looked at her and realized he had a decision to make. Protect her from the dangers in existence or teach her to face them at the risk of her safety and security. Neika didn't let him say no as she ran to the smoke. "Neika... Crap!" He said. He put his backpack on correctly and chased after her.

Neika's little legs couldn't outrun her father's. He caught up to her and picked her up. "Hey baby girl. Calm down. I was going to say you can come. Chill." He said as her little legs kept running in place. "Chill Neika. We need to do this right, or we will get hurt or worse." He whispered. She went limp almost instantly. He put her down and turned her around. "They seem to be distracted. I'll provide a decoy. You look for your energy. If you find it run and I'll cover you." He said. "We sneak like in the air vents on Kobay GOM?" She asked. Tec smirked with a giggle at the thought. "Yup. Now we can't make noise so look at me and ill guide you with directions. If my arm goes upward stop. If it points then move in that direction. If I cross my arms don't move. If I point back, run and hide. You got it?" He said. She repeated him perfectly. "Good. Follow me." He said.

The plan went as good as it could as the two crept up to the thieves. They were fixing a soup for an energy orb as they talked and joked going over how they planned to sell the energy in diluted liquid form. As Tec got closer he listened while giving Neika the sign to stop. "We should have taken the other energy orbs. We found the demon first." The tall skinny thief snarled. "Yes but you say this now. Why not when we could have taken them all for ourselves?" The short chubby thief said. "There are five. We have one. There are three of us and two of them. We should go and take from them what is ours. We can take them." The shortest of the three said. Tec took the daggers from Neika and gave her his backpack. He signaled to wait but it wasn't the signals he worked on. He snuck up to the thieves not aware Neika was right behind him.

Tec ran up to the tall thieve who was sitting with his back toward him. As he used his daggers to dismantle the thief, the head of the chubby thief exploded. The smallest thief saw that his two companions in crime had been dealt with quickly and ran away. Tec looked at Neika in shock. She was holding another knuckle popper in hand to throw at the chubby thief before she saw the end result of the initial one in use. "Don't throw another one. I'll get the other thief. Stay here and don't move." Tec said. He took chase after the smaller thief while Neika stood still. She wanted to do as her father instructed but she saw an orb. She looked around to see if anyone was looking. No one seemed to be around. 'One little look won't hurt.' She thought. She walked toward the orb then looked toward the direction her father ran in. There was no movement. She reached for the orb but before she could make contact it flew at her. It spread across her chest after knocking her back to the ground. She opened her eyes to her father kneeling over her. His words were cloudy as she attempted to wake up.

"Bwub bwub bloob. Are you blubb blay?" Tec's vocabulary translated to Neika. Neika could see him, but her senses were weakened for a moment. As she recovered she could hear him clearer as he asked, "Are you alright baby-girl?". She looked at him. A part of her memory had come back. It was of her mother. She felt a great fear come over her. "Where's mom?" She said as she sat up. Tec stood up in shock. "You grew." He said. She looked at her longer legs and arms. "I grew." She responded. He helped her up and her head was to his shoulders now. "You grabbed one of the orbs, didn't you?" Tec asked. Neika was afraid he was going to get upset and didn't answer in fear. He put his right hand on her left shoulder. "I love you. Don't feel you can't be truthful with me." He said. "I did. I'm sorry." She said. He looked around then moved the chubby thief's corpse out of the way and another orb was there. He picked it up and studied it. Neika walked up to the corpse and instinctively absorbed its life energy.

Tec was going to give it to her but, after looking at her, he took a moment to appreciate her youthful appearance. He smiled and remembered all the wonderful memories he had raising her and watching her grow. "You're going to grow up so fast." He said. He looked at the orb then walked up to her. She could see he was saddened and stepped back. "I want all the orbs back. They are my memories, my essence. The one I have back in me makes me remember mommy. I remember you and mommy now. I want to wait until all the orbs are collected before I absorb them. But I do remember something more." She said. "What's that?" He asked. "The faces of those thieves. Every one of them. They had a tool that took these orbs from my chest. They were scary and strong. Stronger than those three. "That's why they have more. These two probably stole their share and ran." Tec said. "Three more. I should have overpowered them, but I think they were waiting for anything or anyone to come from the fog wall." She said.

Tec was impressed that her vocabulary and thought patterns had improved so quickly as well. He was proud but missed toddler Neika already. He chose to be silent and say nothing about his feelings. "Before I disposed of the other thief he told me where the other thieves went. He asked me to take the orbs back from them." Tec said. "He encouraged you?" She asked. "He was being spiteful but I'm fine with that. It got me all the information we need. But since you would like to wait until we get them all I'll hold this orb. We still need to find weapons and armor for the journey ahead." He said while wrapping the orb up with cloth and placing it into his backpack.

On their travels, Tec would slay more beastly beings and teach Neika what was worth using, turning into sustenance, and storing for trade. She participated more and more in the dissection of body parts from slain beasts. He taught her how to make blue fire to cook the sustenance. How to find liquid sustenance from the large grapes that grew everywhere. She learned to make her own backpack from hides, and he gave her some knuckle poppers as well. She learned how to set up a portable shelter and how to clean the area to hide any signs she was present in the area before leaving any camp area. By the time they made it to a great statue of the supreme thief, Neika was well versed in basic survival in their current plain of existence.

Tec put his backpack down and looked around. They were positioned in a safe distance and out of view, but he didn't trust the area in any way. "I think we have been noticed. We should double back and reenter the area from another location." Tec said. Neika followed him. "How can you tell we were seen?" She asked. "There is a scent these thieves give off." He said. "I smell nothing. In fact, I thought there was no scent in this place." She said. He looked at her. "These orbs. They may also be parts of you. Not just you thoughts but your body too. That explains the growth along with the…" He paused at the end. "Along with what?" She asked. He corrected himself before saying brain function. "Your memories." He said. "Oh. So that's why everything tastes the same." She said. "You've been eating without taste?" He asked. "I thought that is what this place tastes like." She said. He pulled out the orb. "Take it. You need your senses. If you grow and get more memories then it can only help us on our journey." He said.

She looked at the orb then him. When she reached for the orb it did the same as the first. Her body responded the same but when she awoke she was her father's height. "Whoa! I don't know how I feel about this." He said. Neika looked around. "This is a scary place." She said. "I take it you couldn't see very well either." He said. "Apparently not. Because it stinks." She said. "That's them. And it's getting worse." He said. Neika reached into her backpack and pulled out some dry tissue to eat. "Nothing." She said. "So you got taller, see and smell better too. What else did you gain back?" He asked. "I remember Padre Ully and Raja. I remember mommy and you in a big ship we lived in. I remember baby Robot." She said before pausing. She teared up. "I remember we lost Raja. Then the water man, Antawn, joined us. He was cool. Living holy water when his body was blessed by Padre. Before we lost Padre Ully. That's as far as it goes. I have nightmares. Now I remember of the dark woman I dream about." She said. Tec didn't have the heart to tell her it was Padre Ully's replacement, Forgotten, who mistakenly thought she was a demon and killed her.

"For now I think we need to focus on our journey. We don't need nightmares making things more difficult." He said. "What's your plan?" She asked. "That statue isn't just the entrance decoration. It's a secret entrance. We need to get in there and use the tunnels to get to your orbs." Tec said. "Wow, that thief wants revenge." She said. "Wanted." Tec corrected. "Right." She responded. Tec continued walking until he found a favorable area to prepare for entry. Just left of the statue. He pulled out his batons he made from a large creature he slaid as Neika pulled out her father's daggers. Tec looked back at her and was reminded she was now his size. It felt comforting and sobering all the same. "No noise. Move quick. Run if things go south." He whispered. She nodded in agreement. They moved quietly, as most Munchgalumptagans do. When they reached the left side of the statue, Tec found the secret door and opened it.

He looked down the dark stairway that had no light whatsoever to help him navigate. "This is going to suck." He whispered to himself. "I heard that." Neika said. Tec smirked as he walked down the stairway. Neika followed, closing the door behind her. Tec chose to walk down the stairway in darkness. Then the pathway was visible. Tec turned around and looked at Neika upset. "Put out the light. We don't know what is here or not here. We could reveal our presence and not even know it." He whispered. "Sorry." She said as she put the hot blue flame out. She didn't need it though. Tec stumbled a few times then hit his head. "Careful daddy. The ground isn't straight." Neika said. "You have night vision?" Tec asked. "I can see you can't see. I never lost any vision when I put out the light. I just thought the light would help you. But that bump on your forehead looks like it hurts. So I guess if it is dark, maybe, uhm, maybe I could lead us." She said. Tec stared at his daughter for a moment. "All of that for a request. Lead the way." He said.

"Right, I love to talk. I remember." She said. "I love you Baby-girl. I got your back." He said. She paused. Tec bumped into her. "Ooops! Sorry." He said. "I'll say stop next time." She said. "And duck if need be." He said. Suddenly a purple red light fizzled revealing the lining of a doorway. The door came loose and Neika caught it. She set it down all while Tec stood in the dark guessing what she was doing. "Where did you get that fire starter?" He asked. I opened a knuckle popper and separated the combustible powder. Tec was silently impressed. "Follow me daddy." She said. "Wait. How do you know we are even going the right way?" Tec asked. "The scent of the thieves. It's weakest beyond this sealed doorway. "Oh. Wow. Heightened smell but no taste. How is that?" He said as they walked. "I would think you would understand the shadow realm and my condition more." She said. "I'm learning along with you. But if you feel good about this direction so do I. I trained you with tracking and seeking games before. I can see you have a little still in you." He said. "Hide and seek in the vents or looking for Robot when he tried to hide from my hugs isn't the same daddy, but I get what you're saying." She said.

They walked up to an area covered in vegetation. Neika set the area on fire, and it revealed two passageways. "There's two doors. One has a circle with a face. The other has a square with a weapon. "The weapon symbol." He said. She opened the door. "It's a long hallway." She said. "Let's go." He said. They walked down the hallway to a large room filled with impressive shields and melee weapons. Neika grabbed her father the most beautiful sword she could find. "Take this daddy." She said. The moment he held it he knew what to do with it. "Wow, it comes with a magnetic sheath. Awesome." He said. She sorted through the shields until she found a light but sturdy one with fancy designs.

She chose a short bow made of something shiny and strong. She gathered different assortments of arrows and put them in a sheath made from the skin of something powerful with scales. "Neika, turn on the light." He said. The blue flame sizzled as it ignited. Tec looked around and filled his bag, and Neika's, with various items he thought may be of use on their journey. After putting on a mixed batch of selected armor that fit him only slightly big, Tec found beautiful armor that he felt Neika could grow into. He tied it up and took it with them as they re-tracked their steps and went to the next room but only found skeletons of different beings restrained and in torturous positions. Neika stopped in place. Tec bumped into her. "You missed a stop." He said. "We should leave. This is a bad place." Neika said. They doubled back and returned to the hallway to the stairs that lead to the exit door they entered. Neika guided them to the right as they exited. She could see there was several doors to the left and right with no door at the end of the hallway. She listened and smelled. All had equally atrocious scents. "I don't know which door to take but there are five on each side." She said. "I hear talking. Where is that coming from?" He asked. She listened with more focus and chose the door. There were stairs leading up. As they ascended the could hear more chattering. "I think we found our way in." Tec said.

Neika pushed the floor doorway open, and some light came through.

Family

They exited into a room filled with treasure. And directly in front of them was one of her orbs. "What are the odds?" Tec asked. Neika ran to it and absorbed it. Tec tried to stop her, knowing it takes her a long time to recover. She opened her eyes as she heard loud noises of someone fighting in the distance. As her vision came to her she could see she was chained within a dungeon of some sort. Her belongings were gone but she was bigger. There was an armed guard facing her at all times and two guards standing on both sides of the only exit. They could hear the ruckus and went to find out what the issue was. More fight could be heard, then silence. The guard, who never looked away from Neika, was unable to react fast enough to Tec who threw two knives at the back of the guards head. One missed but the other landed when the guard turned to look at Tec. Tec rushed over to Neika. She didn't recognize him with his armor on. "Who are you?" Neika asked. "It's me Baby-girl." Tec said. "But you're so much smaller. You shrunk." She said. "No sweetie. You grew. And I found another orb so get ready to grow some more. We need to escape first." Tec said.

He set some crackle stingers against the wall, grabbed Neika's oversized hand, then ran to the exit just before the explosion tore a hole in the wall. He grabbed his backpack. "Let's get out of here. I made a lot of problems for us that will be here soon." Tec said. They ran but Tec couldn't keep up with Neika. She looked back and ran to him. "Keep running Baby-girl. I'll catch up." He said while out of breath. The scent of many more thieves grew worse. "Sorry daddy." She said as she picked him up and ran with him along with all their gear. "Baby-girl. Come on." He said. "Daddy, do you want to escape or die?" She asked. He didn't answer but if she could see his expression she would have thought he'd prefer to die. When she made it to a safe distance she put him down than laid on the ground exhausted. "That was crazy daddy." She panted. He pulled out another orb and placed it on her chest. When she woke up she was almost fully developed and could remember everything. Beside her was the beautiful armor she didn't fit in when Tec initially found it.

Tec was preparing a meal as she sat up quietly. She was very upset. "Hey you. I think you may finally be able to taste something. Try this." Tec said. Seeing he had no idea she was upset snapped her out of it. Her new memories that were happy and loving toward her father were conflicting with her hurt feelings about his insensitive words before they entered the fog wall. She didn't say anything as she reached for the sustenance. She did notice that her arms and hands were fully developed. She took a glance at herself and felt pleased she was almost complete. The armor was still a little big, but it was too beautiful to complain about. As she ate the sustenance, she could taste it and enjoyed it. "You seasoned it? This is delicious. Where would you find seasoning in a place like this?" She asked. "No place in existence is free from the wonders of the fruits of creation. No place, even a dark sad place like the shadow dimension can stop good things from growing. There is a saying. All the darkness in existence can't overtake the strength of even an atom of light." He said. As he enjoyed his meal he noticed she was acting different.

"Your memory came back. Didn't it?" He asked. She nodded yes. "What do you remember?" He asked. "I have two memories. One before and one during... All this." She said. "What's going on in there? You and I were really getting back into our groove and now you're stressing." He said. She looked at him. "I hate myself. I look like the demon my father is. I love you and mommy but I'm this and you two are not. I feel so out of place. So I'm a lot of things in here. But I don't know how to navigate those thoughts and the new thoughts that grew before I got my memory back. It's like, I'm two people." She said. "Do you think the last orb will help you feel more complete at least?" He asked. "I don't know but I can feel it. It is far but I can feel it." She said. He looked around. We should make our way to that large hill. It looks robust with travelers. We might get there in a few hours. Neika looked at her father oddly. "What?" He asked. She stood up and what looked like a shell on her back opened up to reveal two gigantic wings.

They gathered their supplies, stored them in their backpacks and took flight. Begrudgingly, he let his daughter carry him like a baby. "This is ridiculous." Tec said. "You're silly daddy." She giggled. An almost fully developed Neika flew with ease with her father in her arms. She landed just at the edge of the village and set her father down. "Are you...?" She began but he raised his right arm looking at the ground and interrupted her, "Don't. Just don't. Let's go find your orb." He said. An old male who knew the old female recognized Neika. "Well I see you found yourself again." He said. Tec looked at him upset. "You have seen her in this form before?" He asked. "Calm down. I meant her no harm. I was with my wife when we saw the robbery. One of the thieves lives here. But I would be careful. If you are looking for revenge of some sort, this thief is known to be ruthless." The old

Family

male warned. Tec took off his backpack and placed it in front of the old male. "I take it you are a trader like your wife. Is there anyone here that can help us?" Tec asked. The trader looked in the bag and said, "Yes. Here's a map of the village." The trader marked locations and handed it to Tec. "I hope you find what you need." The trader said.

Tec took his Neika's backpack then walked to the edge of the village with Neika. "Neika, stay back for a while. I'll go through the village and collect what we need. I'll return when we're ready to get that last orb." He said. Neika patiently waited this time. She kicked the ground and looked up at the sky. Everything was depressing. No one was happy, celebrating, dancing, or doing anything festive in the village. It was just black-market behavior as far as she could see. She got bored and relaxed on the ground. Tossing rocks and counting glowing eyes looking at her from the darkness surrounding the village. She occupied some of her time learning how to shoot her arrows. Then she tried using her father's daggers which were pocketknives at her size. So she practiced throwing them. Her skill level increased immensely with all the time it took for her father to return.

As she threw both knives at the same time and landed on the same target her arrow did, her father said, "Wow, since when have you been a knife thrower?" "Since you left me to do nothing but throw knives." Neika answered. He took a close look. "Are those the daggers I gave you?" He asked. She smiled, "They shrunk." He grinned. "Is that right?" He asked. "What took you so long? And where's my backpack?" She asked. Tec pulled her backpack around. There was a beautiful knife and a grenade of some sort attached to the sides. He unstrapped a rolled up sleeping mat then opened the bag. Neika was intrigued as her father started digging silently. "I traded my most of our treasures for things we would need on our journey." He said. Then he pulled out a map of shadow, an enchanted necklace, and a pen with a hidden knife. "Here, this necklace is for you. The merchant said it has a spell that protects you by giving you the vision of moments in the future. She said it was made from the lost eye of a great traveler." Tec said.

"Why does your shield look different?" Neika asked. "Because I was able to barter a deal for these two magical gems. One deflects energy projections, and one binds the material, so it never breaks." He said. "Whoa!" She reacted. "No, check this out." He said as he pulled a sparkling hatchet with a flaming handling off of his magnetic sheath. "How are you holding that? It's on fire."

She asked in astonishment. He was just as excited as his eyes opened wide. Normally cool, calm, and collected, he was very proud of this acquisition. "The blade can cut through anything. And only the owner can wield it." He said. "So, it chose you?" She asked. "Yup. Isn't that the coolest thing. The merchant traded it for my sword." He said. "What is the knife on the side of your bag?" Neika asked.

Tec put his hatchet and shield back on their magnetic attachments strapped to his back. Then he reached for the knife carefully to hand it to Neika. "An upgrade. Instead of those shrinking daggers, I want you to have this. It is a vampire blade. The merchant who I traded with said this blade grows when you slay your foes in shadow. Like you it absorbs. You absorb energy from the souls. This absorbs their blood and evolves into something." He said. She looked at it as a child would look at a new toy. "Evolves into what?" She asked. "I don't know. But we will be fighting something very soon. Those thieves are going to want to find us and take this." Tec said. He pulled the final orb out of his bag. "Where? How did you? Daddy you better not have risked her life for this." She said. "Nothing is a risk for my daughter. Take it." He said. She absorbed it without hesitation.

Tec pulled a book out that he traded other treasures for. He sat and read patiently as his daughter grew to her maximum form. The book was about various items in existence that a traveler of shadow came across. After a few pages in, he found his daughter's knife. "The Vampiara Vektra." He recited. It read, the child of a vampire and a vegetation temptress lay slain before her parents. Victim of vengeance. Victim of a woman's scorn. The temptress took her slain child to her family. They cooked her and made a potion from her remains. Her father broke from his body a piece of his bone off. As fast as he healed to full build, the dark witches had the bone marinate in the potion. The witches chanted over the blacksmith as he coated the bone with a special metal only found in shadow. He strapped the handle with the skin of the child as a tribute. "Vampiara Vektra, Vampiara Vektra…" The witches repeated. The temptress went to her child's murderer and gave the knife its first taste. It not only grew in size, but its handle evolved into a glove to protect the hand of the wielder. Over the centuries the knife has grown to full potential, becoming complete body armor.

Tec closed the book for a moment and looked at the knife in amazement. "What the hell?" He said. "What the hell?" Neika repeated. "Don't repeat me Baby-girl." He said. Then he looked up. Neika took much longer when absorbing the other orbs. "What are you doing up?" He asked. She stretched. Her body was frighteningly long. Her wingspan was twice as long. Her purple skin glistened. Her eyes had a white glow in the center. Her teeth were as long as Tec's palm. A chill ran down Tec's spine. For a second he forgot it was his daughter as the armor peeled off her dragon scale skin. "How do you feel?" He asked. "A little upset with myself. I knew I wasn't your child by birth, but you and mommy have been the best parents anyone could have ever had. I just don't like my origins." She said. "There is a remedy to that. Your mother, she needs us. And I think we have the tools to deal with whatever comes." He said.

 He packed up his belongings, grabbed Neika's too, then took a look at his map. He pulled out an ancient compass and studied his surroundings. "The exit is that way." He pointed. They traveled in the direction of the map's revelation. The Vampiara Vekta and Neika grew stronger and evolved together with every attack they overcame along the way. By the time they made it to the fog wall, Vampiara Vekta and Neika were at maximum form. As they walked through they were greeted by Ike who had established a waiting area with staff busy transferring information to each other and soldiers at the ready. "Wow, that was fast." He said. "Fast?" Tec asked. "Time is slower in there but that as fast." Ike said. "We've been gone for months." Neika said. "You look absolutely amazing. You truly made your stay in there worth it. Still, you have been gone only long enough for me to reach out to my sister in the physical realm to spread word across the three realms your situation. The armies of light have just amassed at the Kingdom in Shadow. You jumped in that fog wall a few weeks ago. Now look at you. I see you have traveled far. I pray you are ready for what is to come." Ike said. "What's to come?" Tec asked. "Follow me. I shall tell you on the way." Ike said.

 At the gates of the Kingdom in Shadow stand several armies. All suited to fight off the four kingdoms that threaten the Kingdom in Shadow. As the armies prepare for war, Tec and Neika prepare to enter the gates. "I have told you all I know. Now it is up to you to save Pep. We will fend off the kingdoms as they get word of your journey. Such things can be felt by the darkest of beings that rule the five kingdoms. I will guard these gates, and if we can help, we will follow your trail. For now, be gone. Your fate is in your hands." Ike said. Then he turned to the armies of light and yelled out. "Thank you family. You have answered the call. Our friends have a great obstacle ahead of them. Let us make haste and ensure their success." He said as the armies cheered. He continued his speech as Tec and Neika approached the gates. Neika raised her great sword, the Vampiara Vekta and stabbed between the two great gates. A hairline fracture of the bottom corner of one of the gate doors emerged. Another swing and it cracked. A few more and there was just enough space for them to enter. Dark beings watching at a distance spread to tell the other kingdoms that the great Kingdom in Shadow was under siege. "It has begun." Ike said.

The area is quiet and dirty. Dark soil particles fill the air. The gate's broken portion seals up. "Daddy, something is alive in here." She said. "What do you see? I'm blind." He said. "The ground sealed our way out. Or in. The ground seems to be moving." She said. Tec pulled out his hatchet. The fire from the handle ignited, causing the dirt particles to spray away. The light from the fire gave Tec sight but there was nothing but dirt as far as they could see. "Why is the dirt spreading like a dome around us?" Neika asked. "Because the fire can hurt it. I don't think we are in a room. I think the room is around us." Tec analyzed. "What does that mean?" She asked. Tec raised his hatchet and swung at the ground. It spread before he made contact creating a ripple effect that made a path to a doorway that didn't exist before.

"Leave." The dirt whispered. Tec and Neika ran to the doorway. Tec looked at his map of shadow, unfolded portions and created new folds to reveal a different map. He turned it around and studied it. Ike had told him all he knew of the nine gates they would have to traverse in order to find Pep. "Alright. We have entered the second gate called the Dark Air." Tec said. "Dark Air? What does that.." Neika began saying. Without warning demons made of smoke attacked them. Tec's hatchet tore through them like butter. Neika's sword had no blood to absorb but was fully developed and destroyed the smoke demons with ease. "What are these things daddy?" She asked. "The book I traded for said there are these things called cigarettes that create these smoke demons. The spread tar along your lungs." Tec said as he sliced and diced. "Was that what that dirt was where we entered?" Neika asked as she swung away. "I have no idea what that was baby girl. But I can see an exit up ahead. We need to get there before one of these things gets the better of us." Tec said. They ran to the next gateway.

Family

The area was filled with fire pits and entities made of fire. They turned to the intruders and screamed a scream only fire can scream. The crackles and bursts of air called upon the queen of fire, Catalyn. Her former self gone, all that remained is her inner essence. Coated in a flame that took the shape of a monster with horns and goat legs with six arms. She stood twice the size of Neika. As she walked up to them the fire minions surrounded them. There was no escape. Tec raised his hatchet. Catalyn looked at the axe and recognized it. It was made from her own hands while roaming aimlessly in the Plain of Lost Treasures. It brought back the pain of loss she felt and the regret she felt in her former life in the Physical Realm. She made it to bring pain to those around her while in her sorrowful state but lost it. When she reached out to touch it, Tec stepped back but let her make contact. It grew into a beautiful axe. "I will give you passage. But you will not get another chance. So go. My minions love when things cook alive. Turtles pop." Catalyn said. The minions laughed fiendishly soft. Tec and Neika made their way to the exit.

"What was that?" Neika asked. "I can't really tell you Baby-girl. But I'm not gonna argue." Tec said. For a moment Neika analyzed her father's nick-name for her and saw it was he who looked like her baby boy. Even the way he said her name. Not simply Babygirl, but in two words almost emphasizing she was both at once to him every time he said it. She thought to say something, but she didn't. She loved being her father's daughter, so she just smiled. As they entered the next gateway they had nowhere to step. There was an endless storm with waves crashing. The doorway sat on a stump but as they peeked behind the doorway it was more water splashing in a storm the never ceased. Lightning struck. "There, I saw something." Neika said. "Is it an exit?" Tec asked. "Yes. But there are a couple of them spread out. And you're not gonna like what's in the way." Neika said. "Talk to me Baby-girl." Tec said in his fatherly voice. He pulled out his ancient compass then performed a few twists and turns to unlock the compass that his book said was required to navigate areas covered in water. "It looks like a large serpent and three smaller serpents. I think they're guarding them, or something." She said. "We need to find a way to sneak past them then." Tec said. "Daddy, they're looking directly at us." Neika said. Tec tried to see through the heavy rain, but it was impossible. "I can't see how you see all that, but we need to get to the second of the four doors so pick me up and dart at them. We'll do what we must." Tec said as loud as he could as the thunder drowned their voices. Neika looked at her dad surprised. "Hurry up, I don't have all day." Tec said.

Neika was large enough that Tec could ride her back. That made it easier as she flew at the greater serpent. The other serpents grew fearful as Tec swung his axe. It dispensed flaming projectiles that the storm couldn't wash out. The flames stuck to their scales. At first the serpents acted as if it had no effect, but the flames began to heat the scales up, cooking the meat under. "That's crazy cool Daddy." Neika said. "I know right?" Tec answered as he shot more flame balls at the smaller serpents. The greater serpent didn't flinch. It opened its great mouth and ate the pair. Neika had no fear. Inspired by her father, she sped up and before the greater serpent could close its mouth completely, Neika sliced through the back of its neck. The blood of the serpent soaked into the sword of Vampiara Vekta evolving its armor into an impenetrable scale armor that spread over her body. Tec had to maneuver to keep from becoming encased in the evolving armor. She grabbed her father, closed up her wings and slid through the entrance of the next gateway as the great serpent's body slapped onto the aggressive waves. Tec looked back at what his daughter had just done. He teared up with pride. "Nice job baby girl." He said. She didn't answer. But her body grew a little stronger just from his words.

Tec and Neika would take a moment to think as they gathered themselves. They sat and pondered over what they were looking at. "Which way do we go?" Neika asked. Tec pulled out a small leather notebook with handmade paper. He read through the notes he took of Ike's cryptic directions. He pulled out his compass and made a couple of turns and twists to acclimate the compass to their environment. It could now read directions of this plain. North, east, south, west, up, down, around, under, and so forth. "Ike said the path least taken. Is the path most valuable." Tec said, trying to understand the words he wrote. "Path most valuable." He said to himself. Neika stood up. There are stairs that lead to stairs. And they move every minute. But some don't ever meet others. They just take you in some kind of winding road. I'll fly." Neika said. She put her father on her back and jumped in the air. As she flew across the stairs they moved and changed and adjusted. "There, land there and we can study were we are." Tec said. "There's an exit. I think that's it." Neika said. Once she landed they ran to the gateway and

Family

walked through. It was the same gateway they just entered. On the other side was the crashing waters as far as the eye could see. They backtracked only to find themselves in the same place they were. With one stairway in front of them connected to the platform they were on.

"Well, the only way to the next exit is through these stairs. So let's just figure it out as we go." Tec said. As they expected, the stairs only took them in circles. Every once in a while they made progress. But found themselves back a square one. "Wait Daddy, I think I have it. Downstairs, right stairs, upstairs, left stairs, yellow stairs, blue stairs." She said. The followed her algorithm and the pathway to the exit appeared. "Yessss!" They yelled out, giving each other a 'high-five' in celebration. With Tec on her back she ran through the gateway. On the other side was a dead end. The floor and walls were all made of dark blue bricks. There was no ceiling, just darkness. "Baby girl, look up." Tec said. "Yup." She said as she flew up. The reentered the room through the doorway they just entered. "Crap!" Neika said. "I agree." Tec said. He pulled out his trusty map and compass. It's a labyrinth. We just need to wait but if we go to each door that opens in odd numbers counting up from one, we will find the exit." Tec said. As ten doorways opened up along one wall every few minutes, they followed the sequence Ike told them. With ease they exited the labyrinth. But something sensed them and followed behind them.

The environment was tender and sticky. "What is this place?" Neika asked. "I'd rather not say. But just in case you need to know, we're inside the guts of a giant worm. I think all we need to do is make it through the body and exit." He said. An acid spitting minotaur exited the labyrinth's gateway and saw the two intruders. It roared. Tec and Neika looked back at the beastly minotaur. It was slightly taller than Neika but clearly bigger and stronger. It spit an acid ball at them that missed but made the giant worm react. They flew around, off balance, crashing against the sticky walls. The minotaur thought twice about doing that again but didn't relent. He began chasing after them. Neika's wings were sticky, making flying impossible. Tec hopped on her back, and she ran. It was the slowest chase in the history of chases. I can't write about it because it was so ridiculous. So we will move on to their exit of the giant worm's butthole.

They fall several feet from the ceiling and land on the ground. Their sense of direction had to take a moment to realize their atmosphere had changed. Up and down were rearranged. As they became acclimated to the new environment, the acid spitting minotaur fell. Before he could get his sense, Neika swung once with the Vampiara Vekta, leaving it halfway inside the minotaur's body to soak up all the nutrients. The blade was already long at this point but spread in width, never gaining any weight, but almost stretching like a cat within the bleeding body of the minotaur. As the minotaur's body dropped, they studied the area. "The next gateway. Mind over matter." Tec said as he held the map up, reading his notes. "Chess." Neika said. Tec looked at her then noticed a table rise from the ground. A reaper appeared from the darkness and sat at the table. Neika pulled her blade from the corpse and walked to the reaper with ill intent. The walks of what looked like a dark cathedral separated and vanished as Tec rushed ahead of Neika and sat at the chess table. "Don't baby girl. I doubt killing a reaper will be successful." He said.

Neika looked at her father realizing what was at stake. "Daddy, don't." She whimpered. "A game for a doorway. A life for a loss. Am I right?" Tec said. The reaper made the first move. The darkness that surrounded them gave view to the battle of the armies of light vs the armies in shadow. The Shadow War was underway. Every move Tec made related to the success or failure of the armies that fought for his cause. What the reaper didn't know is Tec had a handheld video game that had chess, braylap, mahjong, doodle bong, tetris, and so many other games from across the cosmos. His favorite, chess. And he was masterful. Neika watched as the wars took place before her eyes. Each defeat frustrated the reaper to the point he began losing faster and easier. The defeat was so one sided that he rose up to slay Tec. Neika blocked the reaper's weapon and grabbed the reaper by the head. She crushed it, absorbing the reaper's energy. Her essence changed as a dark flame surrounded her body. She had absorbed death and became the reaper herself. She could see the pathway to the prince of darkness like a veil had been removed from her eyes.

Her eyes had a yellow, red glow to them. She had nothing to say as she created the opening to the doorway to the great hall of the Kingdom in Shadow where her father sat at his throne. When she walked through she was met by Remi and an army of lost lights. These unborn souls were no match for Pep and Tec's paranormal investigation team in the Physical Realm but in the Astral Realm they were the most dangerous as they never felt the physical world. Ravaged by murders before birth. They yearned for the taste of the souls that once lived. There was no stopping the torment that was to come. Remi pointed at Tec and Neika. The lost lights shot at them in their glowing bulb forms. Neika and Tec fought for their lives as the prince watched just a few yards away. Pep's soul remained caged beside him. As if by heavenly design, just as the lost lights were about to overwhelm them, Ike and the five armies had united and followed after the duo. They came to their aid just in time, leaving Ike and Remi to fight in their long-awaited moment.

"I watched you and studied you. Now I get my chance to..." Remi began. Ike attacked with sword and shield. "Be silent you retched thing. You're words are useless, and your life is a waste. I will send you to hell where you belong." Ike said as he fought Remi. Neika and Tec ran to save Pep, but the dark prince stood in front of them. "Get Mommy." Neika said. "Baby-girl, I can..." Tec began. "Daddy, this is my fight." She said. "You think you can defeat me? I am the Prince of the Shadow Dimension. The most beautiful angel in heaven. You are a demon. An underling to me. What is your name that I may lay claim to it when I send you to Tartarus." The Shadow Prince said. "Tell me your name angel of darkness and I will tell you mine." Neika said. Their conversation gave Tec the opening to help Pep escape her cage. "I am Lucifer the beautiful. And you are?" He said with a smug arrogance. "I am Neika, daughter of Pep and Tec. Bloodline of the prince of darkness, Lucifer." She said. Lucifer didn't flinch. "I sensed angelic blood within you. Come. Let us finish you off the way it should have been done when you were unborn." He said.

Their fight was so glorious and powerful that the lost lights stopped fighting. Remi lay in defeat as Ike ended her existence in Shadow. Ike would look up in awe at the sight of the fallen angel, so beautiful and fair fighting his daughter, a purple demon. So horrid and foul was her appearance that anyone could have mistaken her for the devil himself. Yet it was she who represented the forces of light in her frightening form and he who represented the forces of darkness in his beautiful form. Still, it was the magical energy that exploded from each of their attacks that caught everyone's attention. No one in the Astral Realm possessed such power. Neika had no idea what she was capable of until all the pain and rage bottled up over who her father was spread throughout her body through the form of hate for him and love for Pep and Tec all at once.

The power of their strikes shot waves of energy that knocked the lost lights and the army of light back. Everyone had to duck low as they watched the two fight. Tec was unable to free Pep until the cage shattered from the waves the fight was making. By the end Neika had emerged the victor, slaying her father with his own sword and sending him to Hell. Her victory broke the lost lights who scattered to the depths of the Plain of Sorrow. The army rose up and cheered. Pep's soul became consumed by a light that appeared from within her. Tec and Neika hugged her before she left for Elysium. "I love you both very much. Neika, you will rule this place. Lead it with the love we showed you and teach the lessons you learned from Padre Ully and Raja Ali. Tec. I love you. Always have. Always will. Live while you're alive. Stop hiding in that shell. Go on a journey and find yourself. I'll be watching over both of you." Pep said. They embraced again. "Wait, Mommy. What do you mean rule?" Neika asked as Pep transported to Elysium. "Daddy, what did she mean?" Neika asked.

"It means you are the Queen of Shadow, Neika." Ike said. Everyone in attendance dropped to a knee. As Neika looked at her father drop to a knee she put her hands on her mouth. "What? Me? But I'm a mistake. I wasn't even supposed to be born. I'm no ruler." She said. "That is why you must lead this kingdom. Theat lack of thirst for power is what this place needs." Ike said. "Why not you Ike? Are you not the great traveler of the Astral Realm? Do you not have the bloodline to contact any realm?" Neika asked. "It was always meant to be you. It's why we found you, why Pep and I raised you, why you learned from Padre Ully and Raja's religious discussions. You have lost and gained so much just on our journey alone. Baby... I mean, Queen of Shadow, it is your time." Tec said. He bowed his head. "Now take the crown of your predecessor and ascend the throne. Your kingdom awaits." Ike said. Neika gave the crown to her father and kneeled to him. "Daddy, would you?" She asked. Tec stood up and placed the crown atop her head. Holding hands, he walked his daughter to the throne, and she sat with dignity. Tec's body began to glow. "You may be the Queen of Shadow, but to me, you will always be my princess." He said before the light consumed him and he returned to the Physical Realm.

The Forgotten Path

Valued reader, there is a story I need to tell. Forgotten had left Tec and I needed to find her path. Running across these items at a thrift store, I mixed and matched them until I found inspiration.

This terrible tale begins in the depths of the earth. Wait, hold on. Let's begin further back. Let me take you as far back as the 'Unworthy Existence', the book, time frame. There was a fiendish felon by the name of Bello. He was the guardian of souls and had an honorable duty to look over the souls of those who passed away in the Physical Realm. He felt little for the souls over time as he found some to be great but others to be sickening. When he turned against his creator to find new purpose, he sought to find a beautiful female to plant his seed. When the sacrificial lamb was found, he forced a conception the beautiful female detested.

Trapped and alone, the mother killed herself. This didn't sit well with Bello who forced her soul back into her body. He had a large underground room dug out for her to be buried in while forever remaining in this state of being dead and alive. As an Afterlife, her soul and body were attached but not in sink like before. Her basic cravings took over. Worms and soaked soil were her sustenance. She dug paths blindly, creating an underground labyrinth to have a place she felt safe enough to have her child. When her child was born she did all she could to keep her alive. Months alone in the dark drove her mad. Her daughter's breathing pulled the living part of her back.

Nevertheless, nothing lasts forever. Another person was buried where she was originally buried. He was far more dangerous. When she went over to see what the sounds were about she could sense him. He was chained up, so she dug more intricate paths to make it harder for him to find her daughter. Everything was fine until another person was buried who was left unrestrained. He seemed to enrage the chained man who transformed into a bear from time to time. This made the mother very defensive. She remained hidden but her nightmares revealed her presence. When the free man tried to find her, she became protective of her daughter. She attacked the man who was not a man but a descendent of the guardian of travel, Brea.

She was a descendent of a guardian bloodline as well, but she was half-dead. Afterlives were a broken version of the living. The defense of her child was valiant but all for not. The man and the bear man would find a way out while a child lay forgotten. When the forgotten child felt the loss of her mother in her dream, she chased her. What she didn't realize is she inherited a spark of her father's gift. She first learned she could traverse the Astral Realm in her dreams at an early age. This was just the tip of the iceberg. Her mother was not as blessed, leading to an entry into the Astral Realm that was violent and abrupt as she did little in the Physical Realm to earn a soft landing. When the forgotten child found her mother, she was broken. "Wuh?" The forgotten child reacted. "My child. Forgotten by the world. I pray you are not dead like me." Her mother said. "Me. Child. Forgotten?" The forgotten child asked. Her beauty was clear as the eyes could see. A beauty her mother didn't see in the dark. "My world. The world that forgot you never deserved you." Her mother said. "World forgot me. Forgotten. Me." The forgotten child said. "Yes but you will be the one who no one forgets when all is said and done. Leave me my Forgotten. Find your path and make the world remember you." Her mother said. Her broken soul seemed to decay into a red hill of dust and coagulated blood. Her destination was to the Plain of Sorrow. Forgotten only saw the red hill of dust and coagulated blood. She dropped to her knees in tears, grasping at the remains of her mother.

Forgotten looked around and noticed many hills like her mother as far as she could see. Her sadness drew dark things, but she opened her eyes when the two men escaped. She was very powerful and fast as a descendent of a guardian herself. With one jump, she broke through the exit the two men escaped from moments before. She was nude but her body was covered with mud. Raised in the darkness, she had no idea she had an attractive body with a beautiful face as her mother once had before Bello defiled her. She looked around and just walked forward. Wherever she ended up was her fate. Yet in the back of her mind, she remembered her mother's words. "Forgotten. Me. Forgotten." Forgotten said to herself.

She walked through rough terrain, brutal weather, and did it all nude as the day she was born. Fools tried to attack her. Without a second thought, she tore their limbs off one by one. The meat was good, but her gift connected her with the souls of the departed bodies. She saw their families and their loved ones in an instant. She opened her eyes. Laying on her back, she sat up. The world was still the world, but she was different. She saw the blood on her hands and cried. "Never again." She told herself. With a wipe of her hands on the ground to get some of the blood off, she continued to walk until there was no more land. Then she swam. She didn't know how to swim but for some reason she continued to enter the deeper part of the ocean. With a valiant effort, she would still drown. When she awoke, she was in a net with fish of many types. As the net was slung over a fishing boat, she spilled out with the fish. The fishermen sounded the alarm. "There's a woman in there. Get her out of there. Bring her inside." The captain yelled.

Forgotten fell back into the Astral Realm where she would catch the attention of Ike. When her body recovered, she awoke in the Physical Realm a hundred years the wiser and driven to find her father, Bello. There was nothing the men could do to stop her. She jumped out to sea and swam like she had been doing it all her life. In the Astral Realm Ike, the son of Wollis, son of Elliom, son of Brea, learned about the rise of Forgotten but kept his distance and studied her. When he found out that she had returned to the Physical Realm on her own, he was baffled. He knew of the guardian of souls, but it didn't make sense. "How can a child be birthed from Bello? He was enormous." Ike asked himself. He would continue on learning more about the Astral Realm as he too traversed the Realm and let whatever should come his way do so without resistance.

As time in the Physical Realm moves slower than time in the Astral Realm, Ike became a wise man of the Realm when Forgotten returned. She had come with vengeance on her mind. On her travels in the Physical Realm, she learned of the rest of her bloodline and the fallen guardians. She made her way back to the Astral Realm to hunt for the one they called Karlo. Karlo was making a name for himself in the Shadow Dimension within the Astral Realm. Killing a warrior who fought by the side of a priest. In doing so his name spread like wildfire. That sealed his fate, as Forgotten was able to find him and tear him apart, limb by limb. Her exploits would gain the attention of all the rival kingdoms in Shadow. But her most valuable ally came at the hands of Ike, her cousin. He would connect her with Brea, brother of Bello but one of the good guardians. She had nothing better to do so she joined one of his paranormal investigation team but killed a member in an unfortunate misunderstanding.

She returned to the Astral Realm where much had changed since her last visit. The fall of Karlo left the dark prince with far more power than the kingdoms that rivaled him wanted. As he was still healing from an injury, he received from the Munchgalumptagan Tec, his castle was restructured into an impenetrable fortress. When she found out the soul of the one she killed was captured by the dark prince, she returned to the Physical Realm to find Tec. Tec was not happy to see her as she was responsible for his child and life partner's deaths, but he relented when she informed him of the captured soul. She pulled his soul into the Astral Realm where he would be given guidance by Ike. In Tec's attempt to find entry, Forgotten obliterated the guards at the front and was confronted by the dark prince's general, Remi. Forgotten unleashed her wrath on Remi. To prevent a gruesome annihilation of her soul, Remi gave Forgotten information on her father. Forgotten had earned such a name that the prince of the shadow dimension took note.

Forgotten forgot all about Tec in her rage. She sought out Ike for answers. He was not hard to find. "I saw you with someone upon your return, yet you walk alone. For someone who has been here before you look lost. Still, you look inspired to find something. May I asked what is wrong, Forgotten?" Ike asked as he descended upon her. "You know how to travel. I need to

Family

go the Metaphysical Realm. I have business to attend to." Forgotten said. There are only the Physical and Astral Realms within my reach. For what reason do you seek aid. You clearly pass through Realms without issue." Ike responded. "Look, you ... I simply need access to the third Realm. Can you help me?" Forgotten struggled to say as her fists clinched. "You are your own worst enemy. I am not your ally or foe. What you seek I cannot give you. If you want the Realm beyond the two you traverse then you must become something you are not." Ike said. "What the f-... Something I'm not. What does that mean?" Forgotten asked. "This Realm is attached to the Physical Realm. Shadow is its glue. But the Realm you seem to be seeking is beyond choice. You must earn it. Why do you seek such a path?" Ike asked. "My father, Bello. He raped my mother, then buried her while pregnant with me. He left us to rot." Forgotten said. "I am sorry for my insensitive inquiry." Ike said. He paused in deep thought.

"You know something. Tell me. I don't have time to play around." Forgotten said. "Patience. There is a woman in the Physical Realm. She is very experienced in portals. I learned a few things from her, but I am sure she has evolved her gifts since then. She may have the answer to your dilemma." Ike said. "Where can I find her?" Forgotten asked. "Seek Brea. He can lead you to her. Her name is Scin'd." Ike said. "Look... I, uh... You know..." Forgotten stuttered, realizing Ike remained helpful as she was rude. "I understand. You're welcome." Ike said. "Yeah... Ummm can you do me a solid?" Forgotten asked. "I can try. What is the issue?" Ike asked. "I came here with Tec. His life partner's soul was captured by Remi." Forgotten said. "Remi. That means the prince of..." Ike thought aloud. "Yes. And I left him there when I defeated Remi, and she gave me information about my father to save her soul." Forgotten said. "I will find him and help." Ike said. "That means a lot to me. I won't forget your help." Forgotten said. The two separated without goodbyes.

Brea was already informed by Ike when Forgotten reached out to him. He was kind enough to take Forgotten on a cosmic journey to meet Scin'd. "Why would you bring her here Brea? What she did. Devonte told me everything Tec told him." Scin'd said. "You don't know what happened. I never meant to hurt anyone. I thought there was a demon on the ship and Pep jumped in the way. How was I supposed to know they made friends with a demon? I never meant to hurt her. I asked Brea for help but if this is the help then I'll find Bello on my own." Forgotten said. "If I may? Scin'd, you're wrong about her situation. I was there and it was an accident. Tec is hurt. He wasn't in a good place when Devonte talked to him." Brea said. "How is it that Tec would come with me to the Astral Realm to save Pep if he was still angry with me? Look… Whatever. I need to find my father and Brea thinks you have the path to get me to him. I just need to know what that is, and I'll be out of your way." Forgotten said. "I'm sorry for my judgement. If Brea says you are good then I accept you're good. What path are you talking about?" Scin'd asked.

"My fallen brother, Bello, is her father." Brea said. Scin'd knew the story of the unworthy existence. "Oh shit." Scin'd said. "What does that mean?" Forgotten asked. "I'm sorry. I didn't mean anything. I'm sorry. I just know of Bello." Scin'd said. "He took her mother against her will and buried her alive while pregnant. It's in the Hall of Legends archive." Forgotten said. "What does all this have to do with me? I have my own issues to deal with." Scin'd said. "I'm done Brea. I don't need her. Take me to the Hall of Legends. I'll find my way to my father on my own." Forgotten said. "Very well." Brea sighed. "Scin'd I'll return to you in due time. I have some literature that may be of interest to you. I'll bring it to you for safe keeping." Brea said.

Brea took Forgotten to Rezandria. There, she took her own path as Brea returned to Scin'd with the Unworthy Bible written by Padre Merrio Ully. "Here you are my dear. I hope it helps you find your daughter. Be careful though. Whatever you put into it gives every word power. I am unsure what that power is or how it came to be. But it is strong." Brea said. "I will study it and let you know what I can do with it. If anything." Scin'd said. "Good. Very good. I will see you again someday. May your travels be accurate and successful. Until then, be safe." Brea said before traveling off into the Unworthy Cosmos. Scin'd opened the book and began reading. The book expanded and added its own empty pages. Scin'd could feel it calling to her to fill it with her knowledge of the dark magic. She went to work, researching and documenting everything she knew into the Unworthy Bible.

Forgotten was doing her own research. She had come to a decision to seek her father through death. She stole a shuttle and flew off to a planet not too far away where there were known low lives. When she landed her plans went as she hoped as she was surrounded and attacked. But this group was not interested in killing her. She was very beautiful with long black hair and pale white skin. Her eyes were baby blue but looked like the water on a clear blue shore as the sun sparkles on the waves. She had absolutely no idea as her self-esteem was never developed underground with her Afterlife mother. They spent weeks having their way with her. She had no idea what wanting to truly die was before. Originally, she planned to fight villains until they overcame her and took her life. This torture and degradation was unexpected and haunting. Yet, she knew at any time she could overtake them. Watching them, studying their sinful nature, she saw herself in many ways. Feeling their assault with utter disregard for her safety made her contemplate her selfishness and lack of empathy. The experience was horrifically therapeutic. Almost cleansing.

When Brea found out what Forgotten had done he went to look for her. She was hidden well. He assigned a fresh team just out of training on Rezandria to assist. This team was made up of a psychic, a private investigator, a doctor, and a telepath. As a safeguard against potential threats, Slug Shot was added to the team. Forgotten's body was found in a dumpster, deteriorating for several days. She was taken to Rezandria to be buried but Scin'd was in Rezandria at the time. When she caught word of the death of Forgotten she went to visit her during the preparation. "Stop. You can't burry this woman. She is not dead." Scin'd said. "I have checked her, and I assure you, she is dead." Doctor Waiden said.

"Yes. By medical standards, you're right. Her body is not alive, but her soul is at work somewhere else and still connected. You must take care of her capsule. I feel her still here. While I feel her somewhere else, she is powerful and can return. Treat her as if she will." Scin'd said. "You are ridiculous. Death is permanent. This is real life, not a game." Doctor Waiden said. "Brea, you brought her to me to help her. Did you believe that she could help me too?" Scin'd asked. "I did. I believe the Astral Realm traveler Ike can help. But I am only dominant over the Physical Realm. As you showed, you can open links to these two realms. She can travel in her dreams. There has to be something there that can help both of you and many more in need if we can find a way to make this potential discovery an asset for us." Brea said.

"I need a place to work Brea. Have you come across a planet with high energy? Makes the hair on your arms rise?" Scin'd asked. "Understood." Brea said. He took the team, inserting Scin'd as the new member, to the planet of Kalimani in the Shonar galaxy. He brought Libel and Doggle. Warlocks who lost their way. They promised to answer Brea's call. But they killed each other. The shadow people were onto Brea's team building and wouldn't have such a powerful witch like Scin'd receive any aid. They drove each of the team members mad. Scin'd was on her own. Fearing the Demon-ticks, Scin'd armed herself with dark magical weapons. A short sword made from the spine of a toddler Slenderman. Unholy water to draw evil spirits in, much like urine for a deer. And two daggers made from a haunted tree that were forged by a great weapons smith who was robbed the day after they were made. They traveled a great distance from person to person until they found Scin'd. They have been content with her ever since.

Scin'd prepared her space with a blood sealed circle and protective symbols facing north, east, south, and west. As she recited her blessings, she could feel something different. In a flash she was in front of Forgotten. They were not in the Astral Realm. Far worse. They were in hell. "Why have you followed me?" Forgotten asked. "You died. I was trying to help you." Scin'd said. "Help me? Help… You followed me to Hell. This path is not for you." Forgotten said. "Hell?" Scin'd asked. "Yes. My father is here. He is a hell knight for one of the fallen angels. I have to find him. But with you here, now I have to get you back before your body decays." Forgotten said. "Like yours has?" Scin'd asked. "I wanted to die. Is that what you want too?" Forgotten asked. "I want to find my daughter. She was taken away. I just want…" Scin'd teared up. Forgotten paused for a moment. She thought about her mother. She thought of what her mother must have felt for her. For a moment, the darkness in her soul subsided. "I'm sorry. I don't have social experience. I … I'm sorry." Forgotten said.

"What do we do?" Scin'd asked. Forgotten thought to herself but got frustrated. "I'll help you and in exchange you help me." Scin'd said. Forgotten looked at Scin'd and studied her for a moment. She admired Scin'd's elegant confidence. "Deal. We need to find somewhere to hide. The dead are sensing your life." Forgotten said. They would find an area to lay low. But there was no rest as this dimension of Hell was infested with war and chaos. The weak worshipers were always bullied and beaten. They had little to no rest as every Demon and Sub-demon that sensed their delicious souls would taunt them at every corner. The women took weeks before they found Bello. He was a beast at dominating Sub-demons and found himself in the higher ranks of the Devil, Beelzebub.

Forgotten remembered her promise and helped look for someone or something that might lead to Scin'd's daughter. As luck would have it, a man killed in a forbidden forest spoke of a child killed by her childhood friends. Forgotten freed him from his hanging cell. "What was her name?" She asked. "Judith. The bitch's name was Judith. We went to find missing girls but there was nothing but blood. We heard rumors of a witch in the woods. We had to kill her. But she was part of the forest or something. She turned the tables on us and some of us ended up here." He cried. "What was the name of your planet?" Scin'd asked. "The forbidden forest is in Jokevla." Forgotten said. "What?" Scin'd asked. "She has been right under your nose all along. "I'm sorry Forgotten but I must find her. Please forgive me if I haven't met my part of the deal." Scin'd said. "Leave me. I never asked for you to be here anyway. And I have my eyes on the prize already." Forgotten said. Scin'd hugged Forgotten. She flinched but gave in. She felt the love of her mother. "Thank you." Scin'd said. Forgotten almost said thank you too but Scin'd left Hell to find her daughter in the Physical Realm.

Forgotten was focused. She joined the group of weak worshipers but when a Sub-demon tried to attack her, she overpowered her. The fight was shocking as no one had ever seen a weak worshipper so strong. Killkill, a more powerful Sub-demon, did what Dienow could not then brought Scin'd too Bello. He knew instantly she was of his bloodline. "You are a child of the Guardians, are you not?" Bello asked in a grand deep voice. Forgotten refused to respond. Killkill forced her to her knees. "Answer wench, or I'll rip your soul apart and put it back together for two generations." Bello said. "What does it matter to you? Do you not kill your own? Be done with it." Forgotten said. Killkill readied her claws. "Let her be. She will come around." Bello said.

Bello had her enslaved. Treated like the pathetic souls who thought worshiping devilish characters was profitable. Her arrogance was crushed out of her. But she never gave up. Bello kept a close eye on her and as he rose in ranks, he brought her out of the ashes and into his ranks. Forgotten played the part as she rose in rank. Rumblings of the return of 'Death Incarnate' caused a ruckus in Hell. The disturbance riled up a civil war that lasted several generations. Bello became so powerful, other Devils began referring to him as Bellosatanicus. His place was next in line to reign over Hell. The story of his rise would find its way into the Hall of Legends on Rezandria.

P. Marcelo W. Balboa

Not because of its inspirational purposes but his fall at the hands of his daughter. By removing his head unexpectedly, she became next in line. And her position gave her access to many gifted Demons and Sub-demons who helped her perfect her gift. She would trap her father's soul in a dibbuck to keep it as a trophy. Her friendship with Scin'd grew as well. They helped each other and felt an incredible appreciation for one another. Forgotten would open Scin'd up to all the secrets of Hell creating a power within Scin'd that made her the most powerful dark witch in the Physical Realm. Yet both women had no evil in their heart. They planned to change things from the inside. Some day.

Scin'd And The Forbidden Forest

P. Marcelo W. Balboa

Scin'd Mcbufduk had not words as she walked up to the living forest. She could feel the unsettled energy pulsing from the edges of the outer trees. Almost taunting her to come in while simultaneously repelling her away. The hairs on her arms and the back of her neck rose. The long quest to find her kidnapped daughter seemed to be at its end yet it also felt like it was a beginning of some sorts. Many thoughts ran through Scin'd's head. Will she hate me? Am I worthy of her? Is she even here? The trees moved. Scin'd could see a path in the distance opening. She walked forward hoping this path would lead to Judith.

Family

You are Amazing

Could it be that my daughter is you?
No longer the new version of me.
What a glorious entity you have become.
Such grandeur, so many colors to see.

Yet with no words, I fear you feel sour.
Towards me no doubt for not being around.
I can feel the discomfort in the trees.
My heart breaks like the dead leaves on the ground.

But you do not have to burden yourself any longer,
For I am here my daughter.

To Scin'd's astonishment, the path continued to evolve, leading her to her long-lost daughter. But not as she had hoped. The acts of others forced Judith to join with nature to avenge those who had committed wrong to her. She then trapped them in this living forest which she was now in control of. Her essence transcended the physical restraints of her former capsule to spread to the forest itself. Now, within her stood the woman she was once within. Judith presented herself in a child's form on the tree she was slain at. Scin'd knew it was her daughter. She walked up to the tree and reached out but a gust of wind from nowhere yet everywhere pushed her back. Suddenly the wind whispered.

P. Marcelo W. Balboa

Life's Cradle

What is a mother if not the reason I was born?
Is she not the one who raises the sun?
Is she not the one who raises the moon?
Who am I to grieve her disposition?

If I should lose her due to separation,
Perhaps mental before it becomes physical,
To whom should I provide such discrepancies?
Am I supposed to remain silent, maybe even grateful?

I get that I am alive.
Therefore, she did not take me out while in her uterus.
I am truly pleased she allowed me the chance,
To face this world on the terms God has given us.

Still, alone is the fate my journey has provided me,
However, do not misinterpret my description.
For in hard times, I have learned a lot about myself,
Moreover, I know who I am without any confusion.

Would I prefer a life with my real parents there?
To protect me or just be there to cry on their shoulder.
Of course, but these were not the cards I was dealt.
So, I have learned to accept what is and move forward.

Family

P. Marcelo W. Balboa

What About Me

I was the first one.
Before me, there were none, right?
Yet I count more than one now.

I count from afar.
Because you let me go mom.
For what reason is this so.

That I must watch you,
Live life without me with you.
And you seem happy.

For too many years,
I grew up in need of you.
Nowhere to be found.

Then you just pop up,
In my life, out of nowhere.
And expect what? A big hug?

Family

P. Marcelo W. Balboa

Out of My Hands

What would you want me to do?
What happened was because of me not you.
One day you were born,
The next day you were gone,
In the end our lives got misconstrued.

There are no words that will change a thing.
No matter what song I try to sing.
What is done is done,
Every tear has run,
All that is left is what we have come to be.

If you honestly believe that I am a charlatan,
Due to you or others professing why I was a villain,
That is fine with me.
I just want you to see,
All I want is to be a part of your life again.

I do not assume to understand the life you endured,
Nor should you feel I have judged you, rest assured.
It is up to you,
Tell me what to do,
I do not expect it will be easy, I am sure.

Family

P. Marcelo W. Balboa

Waking up into a Dream

You speak so well good mother.
As if you had time to think.
Maybe you prepared this speech.
Repeating each word in sync.
I could be wrong about it.
What good are your words anyway?
You were never there when it counted.
So, it does not matter what you say.
I admit you speak to my heart.
The broken child in me mourns.
But what I am is because you were gone.
I loathe the day I was born.

Go ahead! Say more pretty things to me.
As if your vocabulary could change a thing.

But before you waist your breath to pursue,
The sweet little thoughts that might alter my view.
Know that I am not the child you came for,
Nor will I ever be that little girl you knew.
Because of the hate of others my flesh was tore,
And I became everything around you.
I can never be what I was anymore.

Family

P. Marcelo W. Balboa

I Never Expected it to be Easy

I would not and could not pretend to be,
A mother or friend or anything close to you.
I agree with all your words because they speak truth.
All I ask is that you open your eyes and see,
What you have always meant to me.
No matter what you feel know this to be true.
You can hate me all you want but my love will never undue.
I pray you forgive me for not protecting you sweetie.

Who can prepare for such a conversation?
There are no manuals that guide someone in such ways.
I hold no animosity toward you for such rough communication.
I can only blame myself for not being there for you during the hard days.
Just slow down and give me a chance to prove my salutation.
I am sure it would be better than just letting what could be decay.

Family

P. Marcelo W. Balboa

The hurt keeps hurting

Do you know what it is to be,
Born first yet knowing how you replaced me?

I have imagined the life I could have had,
If I was able to live like my brother.
To be raised by a loving dad,
To be able to call you, my mother.
Knowing you're here for you makes me mad,
You're intent is not real, so why bother?

Still, there is no getting away,
From an undying pain that lingers.
A pain that I feel every day,
And you coming here is a stinger.
For every word that you say,
Provokes a flame in me you should not tinker.

Family

P. Marcelo W. Balboa

Face the Truth

The only way out of a maze
Is to learn from the wrong ways you went.
I can not and would not try to erase,
The memories in your life while I was absent.

My daughter, you had to accept no one repents,
For the life they hurt on their path of hate.
The real issue is your lack of content,
Allowing others to disrupt your mental state.

Yet I see you have found your way.
You do not need to explain yourself at all.
You were strong in the face of those who desecrate.
So feel no shame when those warmongers fall.

Remember, you only feel shame when being bullied.
But you showed resolve and found you are freed.

Family

P. Marcelo W. Balboa

<u>Inside My Head</u>

This bliss makes me clinch my fist as this stranger reaches in my heart with a mother's kiss.

My defense says her previous offense of years of absence cannot be undone with verbal recompense.

Every night that I cried she was not there to hold me tight when there was no light in this life of mine.

Yet she expects me to forget her debt as if my heart could reset the upset mindset born from her regret.

Though the pain remains in my brain a part of me yearns for a chance to obtain just a grain of love again.

I can not ignore anymore what could be in store for the core of my being by ending this forsaken war.

For me to grow I must let go of the slow flow of heartbreak only I know which happened years ago.

What path I thought was shut I should at least try to rebut and trust my gut that I can get out of this rut.

This day has halted my spirit's decay as this mother of mine seeks to sway away the pain I openly display.

Still, I feel blessed to possess a mother willing to invest in a being compressed by unbearable distress.

I pray she does not play with the trust she earned today that has swayed my vengeful reign.

Family

P. Marcelo W. Balboa

<u>Reunited</u>

Birthday
Hurray

Admiration
Capable
Expectation
Irresistible
Abduction
Horrible

Tears,
Mother.
Fears,
Daughter.
Persevere,
Together.

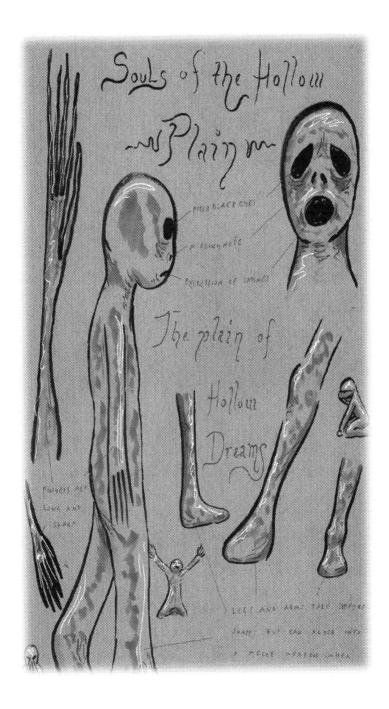

The Plain Of Hollow Dreams

Deep within the Shadow Dimension, within the Astral Realm exists plains of sorrow. One in particular is the Plain of Hollow Dreams. Here exists the domain of the souls that are trapped. They are not good or bad. Just pinned down by the failures of their past. Accomplishments that never came to be haunt their souls. They can't let go of their lost opportunities. This plain manifested from the stench of sorrow brought about by the souls of poor lifeforms who lived full lives yet never became what they knew in their hearts they were meant to be.

They sulk in woulda, coulda, shoulda declarations. Dark patches cover their souls like leprosy. It serves to remind them, with constant throbbing pain caused by the patches, that they never fulfilled their purpose in life. The same embarrassment they felt when alive now stained their souls. Their fingers are still formed with long arms as a reminder of their inability to grab onto their dreams and follow them. Their feet have no toes or ability to curve as if to taunt them for their lack of taking steps that would benefit them when alive. Each soul lives in a state of stillness. Destined to contemplate what could have been. They can as they always could change their mind set but instead, they all choose to self-inflict unworthy guilt for not achieving what they knew they could have.

The plain itself is cruel as it figures out the failures of the souls and recreates their most desired pursuit. Almost to taunt the souls to create a stronger guilt. The plain feeds on the memories of the souls and the sadness that creates the black patches on them. There are those who have limits to their self-inflicted way of existing. They often times seek to punish themselves. Others simply want to find a lazy escape from the guilt. Not in the plain of sorrow. Death is too good for them. No matter the degree of self-inflicted harm, they always return to their original state. Patches included.

Still, in the darkest of places, light is still stronger. And one soul found refuge in helping other souls find their passions and at times experience successful outcomes. Despite the plain trying to derail them at every opportunity. His guilt still anchored him to the plain but his attempts to fight off his guilt distracted him. He searched inside himself long enough to feel something better. Helping others made his head rise up. He could see others just standing and swaying in front of obstacles. So he moved. One step at a time. Helped one soul at a time. Few if any succeeded but helping them was enough. He became known as Redeemer. The darkness of the plain would not take this lightly. It searched for another soul who wanted to stay in the state of guilt just as much as Redeemer wanted to overcome it. His guilt made him forget any little he may have succeeded in when in the Physical Realm. The Redeemer tried to help him.

There are those stuck in their ways. They will not take help, benefit from encouragement, or absorb positivity. They wallow in their discontent. They seek only an existence of eternal sorrow. They are resistant but every once in a while, they're aggressive. When the Redeemer soul met him, he knew right then and there what his purpose was. And it was then that the Rival soul came to be. For every soul the Redeemer tried to help, the Rival would pull another down lower. But the Rival was growing in his guilt. He was not as hard working as he could be in competition with the Redeemer. So he decided to fight the Redeemer. But he didn't believe in himself so when they fought, the Redeemer won.

From that fight forward he spent every second contemplating destroying the Redeemer. He learned to turn his limbs into melee weapons. This caught the Redeemer off guard, damaging him, but he had it in him to adjust and overcome this adversity. The Rival learned to use the plain as an asset. It too couldn't stand the Redeemer anymore. Finally, the Rival was able to overcome the Redeemer. And as the Plain helped the Rival thwart the existence of the Redeemer, something amazing happened. Everyone of the souls the Redeemer helped now found it in themselves to help him. The plain weakened, causing a crack to form in the middle. On one side now existed those who could come back from guilt and on the other side remained the souls driving to self-inflict their guilt for eternity. The Rival would act as a transporter for those who wanted to dwell in that domain. While others who didn't have the necessary guilt, regret, or sorrow would not be allowed to pass. The plain inverted the domain to make it more difficult to cross then allowed the tears of sorrow to spill as an endless waterfall creating a still river that marked the separation of the two domains in the plain of hollow dreams. One of the sad souls who leaned toward the Redeemer and the other for the sad souls who leaned toward the Rival.

Kit Bash Projects

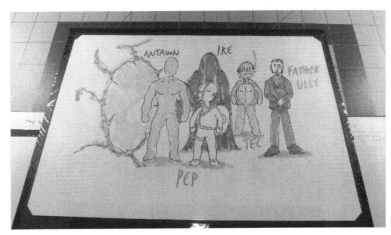

I highly recommend creating concept art. Here is a finished piece that I used to help me as I created and developed Pep and Tec's Spooky Adventures.

Here's my kit bash of Tec and Nika that I really drew from. To make the separate parts I hot glued together look like one piece, I painted them with a grey base coat.

Padre Merrio Ully and his brother in arms Raja Ali in a kit bash presentation that I took glimpses at from time to time. The weapon in Ali's hand was clear. I even thought of making his weapon in the comic books something magical because of this physical image.

Pep and D.R.O.P.A. in a kit bash I made before the rest. Although they look far different in the comic books, I was able to extrapolate key parts into the finished work.

With this team created and the initial team drawn, I had to create more of a story to explain why the team changed. That taught me how art both 2d and 3d can help inspire a developing product.

And of course… I needed baddies. The top is the Scorched One, from left to right is the Starved One, the Mutilated One, the Rotted One, the Boiled One, and the Damned One. Notice they inspired the kingdoms in my family game.

Red Snow

An Unworthy Existence

Following his first defeat at the hands of his fellow fallen guardian Bello, Karlo would remain hidden in shame for many years. His shame, however, was not strong enough to prevent him from spying on the growing child he forced into this world. The boy was strong and wild but loved his mother. He and his sibling would sneak out deep into the forest against his mother's instructions. "Kennith, Daymon, you better not be far off." Andrea called out. When there was no answer, there was hell to pay. She would make them cut wood, work the garden, or repair the fences. Point is, they were in trouble again.

"Daymon, I don't want to cut wood today. I just want to relax. We shouldn't go so far from home." Kennith said. "You're lazy brother. We can't stay pinned down to a small area. We need to explore." Daymon said. "But mom…" Kennith began. "But mom nothing. We have seen all kinds of cool places. If we stayed near the house we would never know about the water fall or the fishing spot by the crystal river." Daymon said. "Yeah. I guess you're…" Kennith began. "Shhhhh. Did you hear that?" Daymon interrupted.

In the distance were a few deer that made their way through the forest. Daymon pulled out his bow and prepared a custom-made arrow. The brothers took their time tracking the deer. As Daymon broke ground, he found a perfect opportunity to release his arrow. The deer scattered as the arrow hit its target. The brothers followed the blood until the deer was in sight. They took what meat they could carry and returned home. "See, what a great kill. We will have a feast fit for a king." Daymon said. "Yeah, what king has to repair fences? You know there's a broken part of the back fence, right? Mom's gonna kill YOU AND ME." Kennith said.

The day had turned into night. The boys were almost home when something big ran through them. They were caught off guard. As they sat

Family

up in shock from the initial blow they looked for each other. "Kennith?" Daymon whispered. "I'm here. I think my arm is broken." Kennith said. "Shut up. Whatever that was took our dinner. I'm going to catch it. Mom can't make us fix that dumb fence if we bring home a memorable meal." Daymon said. "Mom can't make dead kids do anything Daymon. Let's just go home. Whatever that was is not going to be hungry if it is eating that deer. I don't want to be food. Plus my arm is broken." Kennith said.

Daymon looked at his brother's arm. "Crap. You're gonna get us in trouble." Daymon said. "ME?! How am I gonna get us in trouble? I didn't…" Kennith said. Daymon covered Kennith's mouth. "Shhh. It's still here." Daymon said. The brothers looked in the direction of the sound of crackling sticks. The unseen threat was fast, circling around them swiftly. "We need to get home now. Move Kennith." Daymon said. They ran as fast as they could as the sound of crackling branches chased them. The brothers made it home and rushed inside. "Where were you two?" Andrea asked.

The heavy breathing and fear in the brother's eyes said everything. "What happened? What's wrong with your arm Kennith? What did you see out there Daymon?" Andrea asked. "I don't know what it was mom. It was big and it's dark out there." Daymon said. "That's why you shouldn't be going out so far. There are things out there I can't protect you from. That's why we have the fencing. That's why I don't want you out after dark. Why won't you listen to me?" She yelled. The boys had no answer. Andrea feared what was out there for a reason. But she blocked it out of her mind at an early age. The trauma was too much. She knew it was Karlo chasing the boys. What he did took her will. Nightmares consumed most of her life. Her love for her brother and empathy for her son gave her reason to live. But the day would come when she would have to face her past. "Not today." She thought to herself. She boarded up the windows and doors. "Get to the secret space now." She whispered. The boys fell asleep under the floor that night.

Years would pass. Daymon and Kennith would grow into strong men. But their paths took them in two directions. Kennith sought the city life while Daymon sought to perfect his craft of outdoor survival. He built his own cabin in the woods on his own. Karlo was one to hover around the cabin but never enter. He too was haunted by his past. It would take years to finally confront his shame. One snowy night he watched from afar, as Daymon enjoyed himself with his fiancé, Cailan, and friends. Karlo landed on a tree to watch through a window. He could not stand the man Daymon had grown into. Jealousy and envy filled Karlo's thoughts. On the first anniversary of their marriage, Daymon and Cailan invited their closest friends to stay at their cabin to celebrate. Upon their arrival, Cailan put their dog outside to accommodate one of their friends. She had no idea Karlo would make a meal of him. It was just the beginning.

The evening was filled with drinking and laughter. By morning, Daymon would wake up to blood and body parts all around him. "Cailan." He screamed. Slipping on body parts and blood, he searched in tears. He ran outside and cried in the red snow. Far off he could hear a scream. "Cailan?" He yelled out. The death around him was heartbreaking but a chance to save his fiancé took precedence. He ran until he realized he was being drawn to his mother's cabin. When he arrived his fiancé was passed out, covered in blood on the roof. "Mom." He yelled. Andrea came out in a hurry. "What happened?" She asked. "That's not any way to say hello." She began. "Mom, Cailan is on the roof. Everyone at my cabin was kill. Whatever it was killed Spartan too. The only one alive is me. Cailan's on the roof. How did she…?" He said. "Get the ladder in the back. I'll lock the front. Take her down so we can bring her in through the back door." Andrea said. "Yes mam." He said. Daymon carried Cailan inside and set her on the guest bed. Andrea looked for any wounds. "This isn't her blood." Andrea said.

He teared up in happiness, brushing Cailan's hair out of her face. Andrea looked at him and how gentle he was with his wife. "I need to tell you something." Andrea said as she began making a meal for her guests. Daymon looked at her confused. "Did it try to attack you too?" He asked. Andrea paused for a second. She teared up, clenched her fists, and stopped cooking for a second. "Karlo. Your father's name is Karlo. He did this." Andrea said. Daymon wasn't trying to understand. "Why are you? You're in shock mom." He said. "Stop. Just stop son. You need to hear this. Listen. Ok?" She said. Daymon could see his mother's body language. "Why did he do this? Why? What do you mean my father? Has he… Has he always been here?" He asked.

"Yes. He is a king, but he has kept his eye on you." Andrea said. "Why didn't you tell me? Why would he do this?" Daymon asked. "I was raped Daymon. But I love you. And I kicked that monster out. I was ready to die. He must have seen that and left." She said. "But he never really left, did he?"

He asked. "No. I don't know why he is doing this. But it is him. And only you can finish this." She said. She pulled out a small box she kept in her closet. Before she opened it Daymon said, "The horn?" She looked at him confused. "You know about it?" She asked. "I used to sneak in your room and play with it." He said. She pulled it out of the box. "After killing my parents and older siblings, I stood in front of my baby brother, ready to die to protect him. Even after being ravaged by... Karlo. He broke a portion of his horn off and told me to stab him. I think he felt bad. I don't know. I don't care. But I believe it can kill him." She said. Daymon was confused. "Kill him? It a bone can do it then a gun can too." He responded. "NO. No it can't. Like I said, he's a monster. This horn was his. He broke it from his head. He is one of the fallen guardians. You are his son. Weapons won't hurt him, but you can. Find your father, confront him, and if you need this use it." She said.

He was overwhelmed inside but didn't show it. He grabbed the horn. "Be careful, it's sharp." She said. He giggled. "I know. The scar on Kennith's forehead is from this." He said. Andrea gave him a familiar look. Daymon was in trouble. "Come on Mom. Your secret versus mine." Daymon said. She went back to cooking, rolling her eyes. "Ouch. Shots fired. I'm still your mother Daymon." Cailan responded. Cailan began to moan. "Cailan, thank goodness. Oh, my goodness I thought I lost you." Daymon said. "What?" Cailan reacted. "Calm yourself down Daymon. Let the woman wake up before you fill her in with all that." Andrea said. "Fill me up with what?" Cailan asked. "With this good food if you know what's good for you." Andrea said. Cailan looked at Daymon. "Why are we at your mother's. And, I'm sorry Andrea, it's good to see you." Cailan said. She looked at Daymon. "What are we doing here?" She whispered.

"It's a long story. Mom will fill you in. I'll need to leave for a while. There's something out there. It hurt everyone but you and me." He said. She began to cry. "Everyone. Oh no." She said as she covered her face with both of her hands. "I will make sure she is safe. But you must move quickly. The hunter is the prey. You will need to change that." Andrea said. Daymon kissed his mother on the forehead then kissed his wife on the lips. "Get that son of a bitch Dray. I know you can." Cailan said. He ran to the door and opened it. "Lock all the doors. I won't be back until I have this things head." He said. The door closed as Andrea and Cailan looked at each other in silent confidence.

Karlo knew he had made an impact. It was enough to settle his envy down. He returned to his royal quarters. Blood stained. His followers were unsure who he killed this time. He reigned with fear. It was how he took his new empire in the first place. When Karlo had just ran from his shame, he went as far as he could. He hid in caves while a war was taking place in the Iceland Region where he chose to hide in shame. It was separate from the world war created by him and his brethren. Karlo stood over a cliff and watched. What caught his attention was a wizard. Sparks flew as the attacking army was pushed back. The wizard changed the war. The attackers were winning, led by the infamous Legend Killer. As a youth, if he heard legends about a bear, or snake, or wolf out in the wild that revealed themselves to be dangerous, he would return with it as the victor. Soon enough, his name was solidified.

Everyone on the battlefield respected him. But the wizard was unexpected. The wizard did things that had never been seen before. Karlo knew this. So he swooped down and took him from the fight. At that point the tide turned, and Legend Killer inspired his army. They won the fight. By nightfall the empire was Dito's, the reigning emperor, once more. But he saw what happened. Defenses were set in place should Karlo return. As expected, he did, along with the wizard who condemned all those in royal positions. They were cursed to be turned into bears. This transformation was volatile. None of them had any control over when they transitioned at first but slowly learned to over time. Legend Killer bided his time but knew some day he would be the one who took Karlo down. Until then, he chose to be his general.

A good choice considering he could have been cursed along with the royals. Fast forward to present day, he had slain multiple assassins, warriors on quests, and other legendary beasts. It would be fitting that he was about to be tested by a warrior greater than any he faced before. Daymon walked up to the front gates. "KARLO." He yelled. Legend Killer came out. "You are the son of Karlo?" He asked. "Where is the monster?" Daymon responded. "I am Legend Killer. I would like to help you. Put your weapon down and we will go inside." Legend Killer said. "KARLO." Daymon yelled again. "You're disappointing me. I would think the son of a king would act better." Legend Killer said. Daymon pulled out his father's horn. He had carved a wooden handle to turn the bone into a dagger. "Come out and face me you coward." He said as he raised the dagger with his right hand.

"It is only right that I explain your father has given me permission to execute you. I seek peace." Legend Killer said. Daymon put his backpack down and repositioned into a ready stance. Legend Killer smiled. "I accept." He responded. They ran at each other and fought valiantly. But Daymon was the son of a Guardian. And as the son of the Guardian of Electrical Currents, he was a walking battery. Legend Killer was far more skillful but when he stabbed Daymon in the chest with his own dagger, Daymon's body fought for its life and burst like a light bulb. Legend Killer lit up like a match, screaming as he cooked for all to see. They fell together. Neither rose up. Cailan woke up the next morning and found Daymon's body at the front door. Cailan was inconsolable for weeks. Finally, Andrea had it. "We have to move on darlin. We have to live on for him." She said. Cailan looked at Andrea and said, "I'm pregnant."

Itty Bitty World

In the private quarters of the Guardian of Metal, Kobay, floats a planet unlike any the universe had ever seen. To make sure none of his brethren would discover his blasphemy, Kobay created a planet out of metals the size of a baseball. He created a platform that encapsulated the planet but made the life forms think they were floating in outer space. Kobay created the initial life forms of this Itty-Bitty World, but their synthetic body types were able to procreate with no male or female identity.

Watching the planet he was assigned by his creator to look after, Kobay came to understand that intervening in the daily lives of his creation would not benefit them. So he watched them grow on their own from a distance. One day, one of his brethren, Sol, came to check on him and discovered the creation. He too understood the value of creation but chose to be seen. After Sol became just as invested as Kobay. "So whatcha been up to now Cutie-Puh-Tooties?" The Guardian of dirt and soil asked. His feeling toward them in that moment transmitted to their life energy and they began to refer to themselves as "Kutipatuties" almost instantly. These visits also created an awareness of a greater power in their lives. The Kutipatuties began to create places of worship and live their lives in accordance to what they believed would make their greater power happy with them.

The fallen brethren along with the world war below the Kingdom Above the Clouds, where Kobay resided, reduced Sol's visits to none. The Kutipatuties were very intelligence, advancing their technology to a point they sought to meet their creator. Within a few years they were flying. Every year after that they were getting closer to breaking through the atmosphere to experience what they thought was outer space. This time lapse was a day for Kobay who would come to visit again. "Well what do we have here. You've been up to? And why does the land look fresh and fruity?" He asked as he peeked. "Sol, you didn't." He said. To his dismay, they had created a civilization of the planet in the sphere they were trapped in. Construction was underway to break the encapsulating structure as he entered his private quarters.

"What are you doing?" He asked them. They were so devastated by his revelation of self that many citizens passed away from shock. His heart broke from experiencing so much death. He created them from his energy, connecting his life light to theirs. "I so sorry." He said as he brought them back to life. "Don't do this. I can keep you safe and happy. There is nothing out here." He said. "I am Beek, one of many Gihblets on my Fresh and Fruity planet. I am commander of this unit. I come in peace. Please forgive us for offending you great one. We simply wish to find the creator, Sol. And, perhaps, explore." Beek said. Beek's words solidified Sol's involvement, who would get an ear full upon his eventually long-awaited return to the Kingdom Above the Clouds. Kobay chose to separate himself from their minds to let them grow but there was still enough connection to influence. But he chose not to as he still believed intervening would hurt his creation more. So he relented. "Very well. I wish you well on your cosmic journey. May you find all you are looking for. I am your creator, Kobay. But know that you are the product of your own journey. Live free." He said tearfully. For he knew the horrors that were out there. But he knew the great life forms and beautiful sites to see as well.

Inspired by his own creation, Kobay would go on to help Brea with space transportation for the teams formed on the planet Rezandria. The Kutipatuties created a base at the opening of Kobay's capsule and flew out to explore Kobay's home. They expanded their exploration to the planet the Kingdom Above the Clouds looked over then took the path of true outer space. Their exploration would draw the attention of Nuwa, the supreme creator, and Adonai, the one before all that exists and does not exist. As Tec, a Turtlumpkidan from the planet Flubberboober, continued to rack up accomplishments, Adonai decided to challenge both life forms with the protection of the Unworthy Cosmos.

A story to be told on another day.

Wisdom of the Golden Guardian

The path of avoiding avoidable stress

This recording of the words of the Golden Guardian I wrote shall remain without an author name as it is not about the author but the message. I am of the survivors of the universal merge. As a witness to the heavenly sights that took place, I fully understand how insignificant I am while simultaneously understanding how valuable life is. But the way of life is complex and not all ways are the right way. Where many had no path as they fell victim to the reality we are dust in the wind, others sought to find truth. At some point in our rebuilding of a new society we were visited by a beautiful angel called the Golden Guardian. Many of us witnessed the Golden Guardian's great deeds. So the day the Golden Guardian came to visit, everyone had questions. Here were the answers…

I Entering Existence

1 The birth of anything is the beginning of the death of anything in the physical realm 2 Life is now 3 Take for granted a moment and memory will haunt you 4 Live life to the fullest while you are here 5 There is no fixed path so choose the one that makes you feel most fulfilled 6 Absorb life from start to finish as if it was your first day alive 7 Embrace all things that improve your existence 8 Only the dead stop growing so if you are still breathing then get out there and do something awesome 9 You are born then you pass away but in between is a lot of space to do some things that make living worth it 10 Live a life worth remembering with a smile

II Fear of the Future

1 The mind is powerful and beautiful while horrifying and detrimental 2 Release yourself from what you cannot control and embrace what you can control at this moment 3 Planning for the future is constructive but worrying about the future is deteriorating 4 Focus on what is most important today and make sure it makes you happy, then what is not today will no longer take precedence over your life 5 There is nothing tomorrow that can ever affect today that you haven't allowed 6 Do what you know you should do and don't do what you know you shouldn't do 7 No one worries about the bad things that could be when they are focused on making a reality of the good things that can be 8 Make a deliberate attempt to seek peace in the present 9 The sick only worry about getting healthy while the healthy worry about everything else 10 Those with no future would give anything to have a future to fear

III Regret of the Past

1 Rest in peace in life not just death 2 Let go of what holds you back from growing happier 3 Anything negative that was that hasn't destroyed your ability to dust yourself off and rise back up is never worth the energy of holding onto 4 If you don't want to endure the haunting thoughts of regret, you must work toward a disciplined life that avoids avoidable stress 5 Everything that was can never be undone so take all things that happened as a seed to grow from not a pill to be poisoned by 6 Release yourself from the bond you have with the thoughts of yesterday as today presents an opportunity to create memories worthy remembering 7 Move forward every day as you will find, even if others may not be proud of you, you can find pride in many new things you have done 8 Free yourself from the weight of yesterday as today is the start of the rest of your life with limitless opportunities to make better decisions than before 9 You should not regret all things you experienced as much of it only proves what you have overcome 10 Life is not like a book that can be edited or rewritten, moreover, it is like clay that can be remolded into a new image that what it was

IV A Worthy Existence

1 Look into yourself and find what makes your life worth living 2 Seek any and all information that gives you the path to making what makes your life worth living possible 3 Build goals that make you want to get up in the morning 4 If you believe in your goals you have no need to prove yourself to anyone 5 Enjoy the journey of life for too many seek happiness in the future and miss all the years they could have been happy now 6 Someday you will wake up just glad you were given another day as the last day draws near and you will look back thinking about what you did when you had all the days in the world to do it, so go do it now 7 If you aren't at a stage in your life where you are willing to fight to protect someone with your life then you still have something missing worth living for 8 If you haven't taken a deep breath and smiled after doing something meaningful to you and only you then you haven't lived yet 9 Find what pleases your soul in a way that dilutes the issues of the world around you 10 Take in everything that exists around you while you are still here and you will understand what living means

V Social Values

1 Living in rivalry with others takes away from the benefit accomplishing greater things together 2 Surround yourself with supportive people and you will build a foundation that will strengthen you under any pressure 3 Surround yourself with idea people and you will find life more fruitful 4 Discard toxic people for you and them as you will find that you are less stressed in thoughts than when they are in your life 5 Don't worry about what others think because there is a strong chance no one was thinking about you 6 Give your energy to those that love you… All your energy 7 Anyone that builds you up wants what is best for you and anyone that breaks you down does not want what was best for you, know the difference 8 You don't need to be in an environment where others make you feel down so leave 9 Take care of those that care for you 10 Life is awesome but sucks without others to enjoy it with, find the people that enjoy what you enjoy, and you will multiply that awesomeness

VI Work Life

1 No task is a burden when the occupation is something you love doing 2 Nothing that is worth doing is without bad days, find solutions instead of marinating on the problems 3 Many jobs require the coexistence of people with separate thoughts and lifestyles so understand all the people around you and learn the best way to coexist with them 4 Too many point the finger at others instead of taking responsibility so learn to take responsibility and your work life will take on a different experience 5 Tell no one your secrets as it will be used against you 6 Work hard to achieve higher success, not to defeat others or tear others down 7 Know the jobs of everyone around you and you will understand your role in the business you are a part of 8 Plan fun things for your days off and work with integrity when you're on the clock 9 If you want to be something in life and you don't have a plan to get there then you never wanted to be that in the first place 10 Two things are true in the workplace; No one is going to do things for you and you need to work hard to get anywhere

VII Anxiety

1 It is not wrong to fear danger because danger is a real threat but fear of what could be or may have been is not real so therefore it is not worth a single thought 2 A man sits on a boat fishing to get away, a man sits on a boat lost at sea wishing he could get back… perspective 3 The lack of control of what is occurring in your life pales in comparison to the choice to control your reaction to what is occurring in your life 4 Know what is making you anxious, break down the issue logically, understand why this makes you anxious, embrace a mature outlook of the situation, then give yourself the permission to agree with thoughts of solidarity 5 Thinking positive in negative times can change the entire scope of your current existence 6 Sometimes we find ourselves in a place that makes us upset and once we realize we can remove ourselves at any time we are no longer a prisoner to that stress 7 Learn to accept that things are not as bad as you think they are then learn to release yourself from the cycle of self-defeat 8 Give nothing power over you that doesn't make you stronger 9 You must come to accept that not every thought you have has validity in your life 10 Everything in

your life begins and ends inside your brain so take control of your mindset and focus your thoughts in positive character building directions

VIII Perseverance

1 There is nothing as fulfilling as challenging yourself, pushing through adversity, and growing from the lessons gained from the experience 2 Suffering in the moment is an experience everyone has to endure but knowing that everything that is now will soon be a memory is forgotten by too many 3 The most difficult times may seem to make you stronger but they exist only to show you how strong you already were 4 Every obstacle conquered will prove to lead to another opportunity to endure another obstacle that will lead you to a more accomplished life 5 Some of the hardest times make for the best memories, keep going and you will find the deepest treasure that is self-accomplishment 6 Giving up is such a relief but never rewarding 7 Keep fighting… it may seem like the world is caving in but if you just keep pushing till the end, you will always love yourself for hanging in there when you thought you couldn't endure anymore 8 Worrying finds a reason to give in where warriors find a way to break through 9 Don't kill yourself over something that you can be replaced at rather construct yourself through adversity that will turn you into someone that cannot be replaced 10 Do whatever you must do to get to a point where you are doing what you always wanted to do

IX Be You

1 Some will try to say you changed and mean it in a negative way but you have the right to became the you that you were always meant to be regardless of the perception of others 2 Know that most people will reflect themselves onto you so don't dictate your life by the thoughts of others, what you want to be is your right to be 3 The happiest you shines in places where you matter most so get to where you matter most 4 Never feel self-conscious for being the you that makes you most happy 5 Do you as you feel you understand yourself to be and not what others think you are or should be as it is you who has to live with you your entire life 6 The only thing you can truly change in your life is you but that change can be everything in your life 7 Others

will have things to say about a life that isn't there's yet they can never enjoy the life you live for you 8 If you don't try to find who you are you will never know who you could have been 9 Don't fear change; if you stay where you are then you never go anywhere 10 You can be surrounded by all the right people and not feel good about you and yet you can be around all the wrong people and feel good about who you are… You are the most important key to finding happiness with who you are

X Let it Be

1 Think about it… why are you worrying about what you're worrying about? 2 You are where your mind is so be where you always want to be 3 Everyone experiences life in their heads so make that place a place worth living in 4 If something good should enter your life, remain in your life, or leave your life… Let it 5 Not everything requires a response so build up your self-control 6 The past, present and future are always changing so stop trying to grasp them and just live content you exist in all of them 7 The stress of frustration is a stain on the spirit that can be washed away with the simple act of accepting what frustrated you was never worth worrying about in the first place 8 The things that drain your spirit are often times temporary which makes that temporary drain of your spirit a waste of your temporary time in existence 9 Some people will not listen no matter how logical, right, or convincing you are so don't make an effort to justify yourself to those that don't value your words 10 Some decisions you have to make will hurt your heart on the path of protecting your soul

Family Edition

Where adventure awaits!

Take your PC anywhere you wish to as your CG provides gentle nudges toward a fulfilling completion of memorable cosmic journeys. Feel free to read Cosmic Journey, the book, for references to the origin story.

Family

COSMIC GUIDE JOURNEY AGENDA

CREATE & USE WORLD AND DETAILED LOCATION MAPS

- **START HERE, IDENTIFY LOCATION AND MAIN QUEST** -THROUGH CRYPTIC MESSAGING CAN ALSO BE AQUIRED HERE
- ITEMS CACHE IN AREA
- ARMOR AND APPAREL MARKET IN AREA
- WEAPON BLACKSMITH IN AREA
- ENCOURAGE OPEN WORLD EXPLORATION WITH OPPORTUNITIES TO EARN NOTES. (PREPARE MAPS FOR WORLD, EACH CONTINENT, AND SPECIFIC AREAS)
- **SECOND LOCATION**
- ISSUES IDENTIFIED, MULTIPLE DILEMAS SHOULD SEE SEPARATE BUT SHOULD GUIDE PLAYERS TO THE ULTIMATE GOAL, COMPLETE THE MAIN QUEST.
- MISLEADING ISSUES PRESENTED. DROP THUGS, MONSTERS, COMPLICATED SCENARIOS TO CREATE DISTRATIONS.
- **THIRD LOCATION**
- SOLUTIONS IDENTIFIED IN NON-OBVIOUS BUT ALWAYS AVAILABLE WAYS. PERHAPS USE CODED MESSAGES WITH RUNES, CHARACTURES, OR BILINGUAL INTEL.
- TRAPS PRESENTED THAT CREATE A SENSE OF DISCOMFORT. LIFE AND DEATH CHOICES ARE ALWAYS AN OPTION TO BUILD UP THE TENSION.
- **MULTIPLE CHOICE LOCATIONS**
- EASY WAY TO VICTORY HIDDEN BY COMPLICATED CHOICES, A1
- HARD WAY TO VICTORY ENHANCED BY CAPTIVATING OPPORTUNITIES, B1
- WINDING PATH THAT ONLY LEADS BACK TO SQUARE ONE, C1
- **RESULTS OF THOSE CHOICES**

- A2…HARD CHOICES LEAD TO GREAT REWARD ALONG WITH SHOCKING REVEALS.
- B2…STALLING SITUATIONS, DEAD END SITUATIONS, AND SITUATIONS THAT HOLD THE PLAYER CHARACTERS BACK
- C2…PUZZLES, RIDDLES, AND TRICKERY DISTORT THE WAY TO C3
- **(C) LONG PATH TO VICTORY**
- C3…LOCATIONS LEADS TO LOCATIONS LEAD TO LOCATIONS LEAD TO A3
- **(B) LONG PATH TO VICTORY**
- B3…SIDE MISSION 1 LEADS TO SIDE MISSION 2
- B4…PLOT TWIST SIDE MISSION 2 LEADS TO SIDE MISSION 3 OR 4
- B5…SIDE MISSION 3 OR 4 SOMEHOW LEADS TO A3
- **(A) QUICK PATH TO VICTORY**
- A3…THE STORY IS TOLD IN FULL.
- THE SERIOUSNESS OF THE QUEST IS BROUGHT TO LIGHT.
- THE MISSION IS MADE CLEAR.
- THE TEAM IS GLORIFIED AND REWARDED IN PREPARATION FOR ACCOMPLISHING SOMETHING WORTH EXPERIENCING.
- **CALM BEFORE THE STORM LOCATION**
- ALL PATHS LEAD TO THIS MOMENT.
- ALL THINGS LEARNED, GAINED, AND IMPROVED UPON NOW FIND FULL VALUE IN AT THIS TIME.
- END RESULTS LEADS TO FINAL STAGE.
- $((((((\text{FINAL STAGE})))))) $

Session Control

Brea's Guild has called upon you to be the Cosmic Guide, CG, for the Unworthy Cosmos. You must build a team of cohesive members to thwart adversaries that exist across multiple universes. Dice of any type will be needed for the non-player characters, NPC, and player characters, PC, to perform a selection of actions that will arise during the game. Be mindful the CG is the dreamer of and reference to an imaginary world filled with limitless locations, scenarios, and NPC. The CG will need to create quests, missions, and actions for every session. Custom builds are welcome but if the CG chooses to utilize these reference guides for world building, that's fine too. As long as the PC go on epic adventures and find memorable bounty along the way. Adventure awaits!

Destination Creation – D3

1. Physical Realm
    a. *Underground*
        i. Caves
        ii. Catacombs
        iii. Tunnels
        iv. Sewers
        v. Dungeons
    b. *Land*
        i. Forest
        ii. Desert
        iii. Urban
        iv. Arctic
        v. Open grassland
        vi. Mountain range
        vii. Island
        viii. Swampland
    c. *Ocean*
    d. *Deep Sea*
    e. *Air*
    f. *Space*

            i. Planet
            ii. Meteor
            iii. Sun
            iv. Supernova
            v. Blackhole
            vi. Spaceship

    2. Astral Realm
        a. *Limbo*
        b. *Shadow*
        c. *Purgatory*

    3. Metaphysical Realm
        a. *Tartarus*
        b. *Naraka*
        c. *Hell*
        d. *Elysium*
        e. *Valhalla*
        f. *Heaven*

Map Location and Symbol Identification

- Create a World Map.
    - Create Continent Maps.
- Create State or Country Maps.
    - Develop
        - Politics
            - Taxes
            - Voting
            - Service to the people
            - Corruption
            - Revolutions
        - Military powers
            - Bases
            - Training facilities

- - - Weapon manufacturing
  - Economic positions
    - Markets
    - Jobs
    - Wealthy vs poor
    - Corporations
    - Small businesses
  - Illegal activities
    - Gangs
    - Mafias
    - Drug-lords
    - Common thugs
  - Religion(s)
    - Holidays
    - Influence
    - Ceremonies
  - Society
    - Medical professionals
    - Education facilities
    - Firefighting facilities
    - Police stations
    - Legal facilities
    - Utilities
      - Water
      - Gas
      - Electricity
      - Trash
- ➢ Create Settlement Maps.
  - Create custom markers to identify;
    - Quest related locations.
    - Side quest related locations.
    - Miscellaneous action locations.
    - Different terrain in the area.
    - Locations of items and memorabilia.

P. Marcelo W. Balboa

In Cosmic Journey, Family Edition, the maps, gear, weapons, armor, and holy grails are not acquired at the start. The CG should create opportunities for the PCs to locate, discover, etc. all the items needed to complete the journey as they traverse the initial stages of the quest. The CG should always keep in mind that the acquisitions will be useless or simply for entertainment if they are not needed frequently once acquired. In some cases spontaneous puzzles, obstacles, etc. should be created and require the items each PC has attained throughout the session. It is a benefit to the CG that the item utilized be in an impactful moment. Not just to be used for uses sake. The CG should make the item feel memorably valuable.

Location and Settlement Options

Places – Roll D60

1. *Dungeon*
2. *Ghost Ship*
3. *Deserted Island*
4. *Radiation Plant*
5. *Spaceship*
6. *Farmland*
7. *Desert Town*
8. *Ghost Town*
9. *Sanitarium*
10. *Hospital*
11. *Theme Park*
12. *Gothic City*
13. *Prison*
14. *War Camp*
15. *Village*
16. *Cabin*
17. *Castle*
18. *Mountain Terrain*
19. *Railroad Station*
20. *Sewers*
21. *Underground Tunnels*

22. *Lakehouse*
23. *Plantation*
24. *Wild West*
25. *Ghetto*
26. *Urban Community*
27. *Shipping Yard*
28. *Elementary School*
29. *High School*
30. *University*
31. *Light House*
32. *Graveyard*
33. *Cemetery*
34. *Forbidden Living Forest*
35. *Observation Tower*
36. *Arctic Station*
37. *Mansion*
38. *Dreamworld*
39. *Secret Lair*
40. *Behind a Waterfall*
41. *Catacombs*
42. *Inside a Volcano*
43. *Eden*
44. *Temple*
45. *Shrine*
46. *Battlefield*
47. *Jungle*
48. *Magical Secret Place*
49. *Morgue*
50. *Museum*
51. *Theatre*
52. *Structure floating on water.*
53. *Underwater*
54. *Underground*
55. *Structure in the Sky*
56. *Black Hole*
57. *Cult Settlement*

58. *Camp Site*
59. *Ancient Ruins*
60. *Wherever the players agree they want to go.*

Atmosphere and Environment Options

Weather Adjustments – Roll D6

1. *Did occur in area.*
2. *Has occurred nearby.*
3. *Would have occurred.*
4. *Will occur in area.*
5. *Could occur nearby.*
6. *Should occur in area.*

Weather Report – Roll D12

1. *Cloudy with strong winds*
2. *Hot*
3. *Hurricane*
4. *Foggy*
5. *Blizzard*
6. *Clear sky*
7. *Thunderstorm*
8. *Tornado*
9. *Hail*
10. *Tsunami*
11. *Snowy*
12. *Earthquake*

Main Quest Genres – Roll D12

1. *Action*
2. *Comedy*
3. *Crime*
4. *Drama*

5. Fantasy
6. Horror
7. Romance
8. Thriller
9. Outer Space
10. Western
11. Eastern
12. Open World Discovery

Side Missions – Roll D24

1. Find an artifact
2. Attempt to escape
3. Monster hunter
4. Suicide mission
5. Return a cursed item
6. Protect the fort from a horde
7. Something dangerous is stalking
8. Emerge from fallout shelter
9. Run and hide from life threatening being
10. Solve a murder
11. Prevent life threatening conflict
12. Traverse a dangerous gauntlet
13. Last one to survive
14. Last one not infected by virus
15. Something is here with us
16. Buried alive
17. First to find exit
18. Capture the flag
19. Exorcism case
20. Find a missing person
21. Captured and separated
22. Beat the clock finding shelter
23. Team up to confront dangerous villains
24. Transport valuable item

P. Marcelo W. Balboa

Miscellaneous Actions – D30

Temporary Stall PC and/or NPC – Roll D10

1. Dead end
2. Looping path
3. Obstacle course
4. Multiple choice path
5. Evolving stairway
6. Evolving pathway
7. Suspicious pathway
8. Door leads to another door in a different area
9. Character is blinded
10. Confusing discovery

Hold PC and/or NPC Back – Roll D10

11. A riddle must be solved
12. A puzzle must be solved
13. A trivia question must be answered
14. Assemble an item
15. Arrange an item
16. Build something that allows progression
17. Present two hard paths with death looming
18. Seal all doors around character
19. Trick character into a trap
20. Introduce an NPC in need… Or are they?

Damage Assessment for PC and/or NPC – Roll D10

21. Assortment of pitfalls
22. Gas chamber
23. Shrinking room
24. Avalanche
25. Breathable air decreases
26. Floor activates projectiles

27. *Floor tiles fall into void*
28. *Room seals and floods*
29. *Proximity explosives*
30. *Whirling and swinging blades in area*

        Direction danger is coming from – Roll D8

1. *North*
2. *Northeast*
3. *East*
4. *Southeast*
5. *South*
6. *Southwest*
7. *West*
8. *Northwest*

The CG is always free to add onto and/or create fresh scenarios and their locations. The CG should create unique and personal symbols to identify each area or item location on the maps to make sure everything is easy to locate.

P. Marcelo W. Balboa

Character Development Categories

Armor is 50 max and health is 100 max, but there is no need to roll for value. All PC will start with full health and no armor before beginning their quest. Armor, if needed, will be acquired by the PC as the CG sees fit during game play as the PC are on their journey. The CG can roll a D50 to provide value to the Armor.

Character Origins – Roll D50

1. *Angel*
2. *Celestial*
3. *Arcangel*
4. *Demon Prince*
5. *Demigod*
6. *Guardian*
7. *Humanoid*
8. *Minion*
9. *Afterlife*
10. *Witch*
11. *Warlock*
12. *Wizard*
13. *Hoodoo*
14. *Priest*
15. *Nun*
16. *Shaman*
17. *Monk*
18. *Rabbi*
19. *Sorcerer*
20. *Cursed Being*
21. *Ghost*
22. *Poltergeist*
23. *Demon*
24. *Lost Light*
25. *Spirit*
26. *Shadow People*

27. *Wraith*
28. *Phantom*
29. *Banshee*
30. *Jinn*
31. *Mare*
32. *Revenant*
33. *Shade*
34. *Yuri*
35. *Oni*
36. *Demon Tick*
37. *Occultist*
38. *Black Cat*
39. *Hell Hound*
40. *Hell Knight*
41. *Ethereal Spirit*
42. *Soldier*
43. *Firefighter*
44. *Police*
45. *Doctor*
46. *Nurse*
47. *Dentist*
48. *Hairdresser*
49. *Chef*
50. *Whatever the CG can imagine.*

P. Marcelo W. Balboa

Character Life Form Inspiration – Roll D120

Land Life

1. *Plant Kingdom Lifeform*
2. *Insect Kingdom Lifeform*
3. *Arachnid Class Lifeform*
4. *Rodent Class Lifeform*
5. *Reptile Class Lifeform*
6. *Animal Class Lifeform*
7. *Homo-Sapient Lifeform*
8. *Ice Being*
9. *Fire Being*
10. *Liquid Being*
11. *Goblin*
12. *Ghoul*
13. *Clown*
14. *Gihbolet – Read the Itty-Bitty World Chapter*
15. *Gnome*
16. *Munchgalumptagan – Read the Munchgalumptagans*
17. *Troll*
18. *Mummy*
19. *Zombie*
20. *Minotaur*
21. *Centaur*
22. *Maglurian – Read the Munchgalumptagans*
23. *Afterlife – Read the Unworthy Existence*
24. *Yeti*
25. *Sasquatch*
26. *Giant*
27. *Titan*
28. *Dinosaur*
29. *Satyr*
30. *Robot*
31. *Ogre*
32. *Orc*

33. *Gremlin*
34. *Werewolf*
35. *Hyena*
36. *Dirt Being*
37. *Rock Being*
38. *Mutation*
39. *Mixed Animal*
40. *Whatever the Cosmic Guide can imagine.*

Sea Life

41. *Bacteria Class Lifeform*
42. *Fungus Kingdom Lifeform*
43. *Fish Class Lifeform*
44. *Acid Jelly*
45. *River Monster*
46. *Serpent*
47. *Nymph*
48. *Nixie*
49. *Lagoon Creature*
50. *Mermaid*
51. *Living Sludge*
52. *Alligator*
53. *Crocodile*
54. *Scylla*
55. *Charybdis*
56. *Shark*
57. *Water Horse*
58. *Dolphin*
59. *Water Demon*
60. *Crab*
61. *Whale*
62. *Octopus*
63. *Afterlife*
64. *Piranha*
65. *Stingray*

66. *Jellyfish*
67. *Lionfish*
68. *Barracuda*
69. *Sea Snake*
70. *Eel*
71. *Triggerfish*
72. *Putter fish*
73. *Stargazers*
74. *Thorned Starfish*
75. *Stonefish*
76. *Sea Slug*
77. *Munchgalumptagan*
78. *Flower Urchin*
79. *Prehistoric Sea Creature*
80. *Whatever the Cosmic Guide imagines.*

Air Life

81. *Bird Class Lifeform*
82. *Pterosaur*
83. *Dragon*
84. *Eagle*
85. *Crow*
86. *Bat*
87. *Dragonfly*
88. *Chicken*
89. *Duck*
90. *Fairy*
91. *Vampire*
92. *Pegasus*
93. *Unicorn*
94. *Alicorn*
95. *Phoenix*
96. *Griffin*
97. *Hippogriff*
98. *Munchgalumptagan*

99. *Unidentified Flying Object*
100. *Vulture*
101. *Owl*
102. *Raven*
103. *Afterlife*
104. *Lammergeyer*
105. *Ostrich*
106. *Hawk*
107. *Swan*
108. *Seagull*
109. *Mosquito*
110. *Cockroach*
111. *Flamingo*
112. *Hummingbird*
113. *Parrot*
114. *Hornet*
115. *Honeybee*
116. *Gargoyle*
117. *Transforming Plants*
118. *Cham Rosh*
119. *Tengu*
120. *Whatever the Cosmic Guide imagines.*

Optional Names – Roll D26

A (1)
Roll a D50 for this letter option.

1. Aaron
2. Abbie
3. Abigail
4. Abner
5. Abraham
6. Achilles
7. Adamo
8. Aduana
9. Adela
10. Adeline
11. Adria
12. Agatha
13. Aidan
14. Aileen
15. Akeem
16. Alastair
17. Alec
18. Alessandra
19. Alethea
20. Alex
21. Alexandria
22. Alfred
23. Alisa
24. Allegra
25. Allie
26. Alycia
27. Amber
28. Amy
29. Anabel
30. Anastasia
31. Anatoly

32. *Andrea*
33. *Angelica*
34. *Angelo*
35. *Anika*
36. *Annemarie*
37. *Antoinette*
38. *Antonio*
39. *Archer*
40. *Aristo*
41. *Artemus*
42. *Ashton*
43. *Audrey*
44. *Austin*
45. *Avery*
46. *Aviva*
47. *Axel*
48. *Azalea*
49. *Azaria*
50. *Azis*

B (2)
Roll a D40 for this letter option.

1. *Bailey*
2. *Balboa*
3. *Baldwin*
4. *Barclay*
5. *Bartholomew*
6. *Basil*
7. *Bayley*
8. *Beatrice*
9. *Beaumont*
10. *Bedelia*
11. *Bella*
12. *Belle*
13. *Benedick*

14. *Benjamin*
15. *Benton*
16. *Bertram*
17. *Bethany*
18. *Beverley*
19. *Bijorn*
20. *Billie*
21. *Blair*
22. *Blakely*
23. *Blossom*
24. *Bobbie*
25. *Bonita*
26. *Boston*
27. *Bradford*
28. *Bradley*
29. *Brandon*
30. *Brandy*
31. *Brea*
32. *Brett*
33. *Brianna*
34. *Briar*
35. *Brice*
36. *Britany*
37. *Bronwyn*
38. *Brooke*
39. *Burton*
40. *Byern*

C (3)
Roll a D50 for this letter option.

1. *Caesar*
2. *Cain*
3. *Caitlin*
4. *Caleb*
5. *Calista*

6. *Calypso*
7. *Camelia*
8. *Cameron*
9. *Candace*
10. *Candy*
11. *Caprice*
12. *Carina*
13. *Carmelita*
14. *Carter*
15. *Casey*
16. *Cassody*
17. *Cassius*
18. *Catalyn*
19. *Catriona*
20. *Cecilia*
21. *Cedric*
22. *Celeste*
23. *Chadwick*
24. *Chanelle*
25. *Charity*
26. *Charmaine*
27. *Chase*
28. *Chastity*
29. *Chauncey*
30. *Cheryl*
31. *Cheyenne*
32. *Chloe*
33. *Christoph*
34. *Christabel*
35. *Clarice*
36. *Clayton*
37. *Clyde*
38. *Cody*
39. *Conan*
40. *Conner*
41. *Constance*

42. Constantine
43. Consuela
44. Coralina
45. Corey
46. Cornelius
47. Cosette
48. Crispian
49. Cristian
50. Cynthia

D (4)
Roll the D40 for this letter option.

1. Dahlia
2. Daisy
3. Dakota
4. Dallas
5. Dale
6. Dalton
7. Damaris
8. Damon
9. Danae
10. Daniel
11. Darius
12. Daphne
13. Darrel
14. David
15. Dawn
16. Deandre
17. Deangelo
18. Delicia
19. Delilah
20. Delwyn
21. Demarko
22. Demetrius
23. Denis

24. *Denzel*
25. *Desdemona*
26. *Desiree*
27. *Devin*
28. *Diamond*
29. *Dianna*
30. *Diego*
31. *Dillon*
32. *Dirk*
33. *Dominique*
34. *Dorean*
35. *Dottie*
36. *Drew*
37. *Duncan*
38. *Dunston*
39. *Dwight*
40. *Dylan*

E (5)
Roll D36 for this letter option.

1. *Easton*
2. *Ebony*
3. *Eddie*
4. *Eden*
5. *Edith*
6. *Edmund*
7. *Edward*
8. *Eldon*
9. *Eldridge*
10. *Elena*
11. *Elibay*
12. *Elisa*
13. *Ella*
14. *Ellis*
15. *Eloise*

16. *Elvira*
17. *Elwyn*
18. *Emelia*
19. *Emerald*
20. *Emmett*
21. *Enoch*
22. *Erica*
23. *Erik*
24. *Erin*
25. *Esmee*
26. *Esmeralda*
27. *Esteban*
28. *Esther*
29. *Ethan*
30. *Evaline*
31. *Evan*
32. *Evangelina*
33. *Everett*
34. *Evonne*
35. *Ezekiel*
36. *Ezra*

F (6)
Roll D28 for this letter option.

1. *Fae*
2. *Fabian*
3. *Faith*
4. *Fallon*
5. *Farquhar*
6. *Fawn*
7. *Fedor*
8. *Felicia*
9. *Felicity*
10. *Feodora*
11. *Ferdinand*

12. *Ferguson*
13. *Fernando*
14. *Ferris*
15. *Filep*
16. *Finella*
17. *Fiora*
18. *Flo*
19. *Flower*
20. *Fortunia*
21. *Frank*
22. *Fred*
23. *Frederic*
24. *Freya*
25. *Fritz*
26. *Fufu*
27. *Fulton*
28. *Fyodor*

G (7)
Roll D34 for this letter option.

1. *Gabriella*
2. *Gahiji*
3. *Gaia*
4. *Galahad*
5. *Galway*
6. *Garnet*
7. *Garrett*
8. *Garrison*
9. *Gaston*
10. *Gemma*
11. *Genevieve*
12. *George*
13. *Gerald*
14. *Germain*
15. *Gerry*

16. Gervase
17. Ghislain
18. Gibson
19. Gigi
20. Giles
21. Gill
22. Gillian
23. Ginette
24. Ginger
25. Glen
26. Glynis
27. Grace
28. Graham
29. Granja
30. Gregory
31. Gunn
32. Gustav
33. Gwenyth
34. Gwynne

H (8)
Roll D26 for this letter option.

1. Haidee
2. Hakeem
3. Halima
4. Hamilton
5. Hank
6. Hannah
7. Harding
8. Harley
9. Harmony
10. Harriet
11. Harry
12. Heather
13. Heathcliff

14. Heidi
15. Helena
16. Heloise
17. Henry
18. Hercules
19. Herman
20. Hilary
21. Hilton
22. Honoria
23. Hope
24. Horatio
25. Hudson
26. Hunter

I (9)
Roll D16 for this letter option.

1. Ian
2. Idalia
3. Ike
4. Ignatius
5. Illona
6. Imara
7. Iola
8. Irwin
9. Isaac
10. Isabel
11. Isaiah
12. Isidor
13. Ives
14. Ivory
15. Ivy
16. Izzie

J (10)
Roll D36 for this letter option.

1. Jack
2. Jackie
3. Jackson
4. Jacob
5. Jacqueline
6. Jade
7. Jaime
8. James
9. Jamila
10. Jamison
11. Janelle
12. Janice
13. Janine
14. Japheth
15. Jayden
16. Jeanna
17. Jen
18. Jeronimo
19. Jerry
20. Jessica
21. Jessie
22. Jewel
23. Jillian
24. Job
25. Jody
26. Jonathon
27. Jordan
28. Joseph
29. Josiah
30. Joslyn
31. Joy
32. Judith
33. Julianna

34. *Juliet*
35. *Justin*
36. *Yosef*

K (11)
Roll D32 for this letter option.

1. *Kai*
2. *Kailey*
3. *Kaitlyn*
4. *Kali*
5. *Kamilla*
6. *Kane*
7. *Kareem*
8. *Karissa*
9. *Katie*
10. *Kaye*
11. *Kaylyn*
12. *Keifer*
13. *Kelly*
14. *Kelsie*
15. *Kemp*
16. *Kent*
17. *Kendall*
18. *Kendra*
19. *Kenya*
20. *Kevin*
21. *Khalil*
22. *Kiara*
23. *Killian*
24. *Kinzy*
25. *Kirsten*
26. *Kitty*
27. *Konrad*
28. *Korenia*
29. *Kreese*

30. Krystoffer
31. Krystle
32. Kurt

L (12)
Roll D30 for this letter option.

1. Lakeisha
2. Lafayette
3. Laird
4. Lalia
5. Lahna
6. Lancelot
7. Larissa
8. Lateef
9. Latoya
10. Laura
11. Lauren
12. Lavender
13. Layla
14. Leah
15. Leandra
16. Lee
17. Leilani
18. Lennox
19. Leo
20. Lesley
21. Lessa
22. Lia
23. Lilian
24. Livia
25. Logan
26. Lonny
27. Lucinda
28. Ludwig
29. Luna

Family

30. *Lyn*

M (13)
Roll D50 for this letter option.

1. *Mace*
2. *Mackenzie*
3. *Madelyn*
4. *Madison*
5. *Madoc*
6. *Madonna*
7. *Magdalena*
8. *Magnolia*
9. *Magnus*
10. *Mahalah*
11. *Malcolm*
12. *Mallory*
13. *Mandy*
14. *Marcella*
15. *Marchelo*
16. *Marco*
17. *Marcus*
18. *Mariella*
19. *Marilyn*
20. *Marisol*
21. *Mark*
22. *Marshall*
23. *Marquita*
24. *Matilda*
25. *Mavis*
26. *Max*
27. *Maximillion*
28. *Maxine*
29. *Megan*
30. *Mell*
31. *Melanie*

32. *Melody*
33. *Mercedes*
34. *Merlin*
35. *Mia*
36. *Micah*
37. *Michael*
38. *Michelle*
39. *Mikka*
40. *Milly*
41. *Mindy*
42. *Miranda*
43. *Miriam*
44. *Mitchell*
45. *Modesty*
46. *Monica*
47. *Montague*
48. *Mortimer*
49. *Munroe*
50. *Murphy*

N (14)
Roll D20 for this letter option.

1. *Nadia*
2. *Nahum*
3. *Napoleon*
4. *Nancy*
5. *Naomi*
6. *Natalya*
7. *Nathaniel*
8. *Ned*
9. *Nellie*
10. *Nessa*
11. *Nichole*
12. *Nick*
13. *Nikita*

14. *Nila*
15. *Nina*
16. *Niobe*
17. *Nita*
18. *Nixie*
19. *Nolan*
20. *Nowell*

O (15)
Roll D10 for this letter option.

1. *Obadiah*
2. *Octavia*
3. *Odelia*
4. *Ogden*
5. *Olivia*
6. *Olympia*
7. *Oprah*
8. *Orion*
9. *Ottis*
10. *Owen*

P (16)
Roll D30 for this letter option.

1. *Padraig*
2. *Paige*
3. *Palmer*
4. *Paloma*
5. *Pamela*
6. *Pandora*
7. *Parker*
8. *Patience*
9. *Patricia*
10. *Patton*
11. *Patrick*

12. *Payton*
13. *Pearl*
14. *Pedrina*
15. *Pedro*
16. *Penelope*
17. *Percival*
18. *Peregrine*
19. *Perpetua*
20. *Persephony*
21. *Persia*
22. *Phebe*
23. *Phylicia*
24. *Pierce*
25. *Pip*
26. *Pixie*
27. *Pollyanna*
28. *Porter*
29. *Prescott*
30. *Priscilla*

Q (17)
Roll D6 for this letter option.

1. *Queenie*
2. *Quincy*
3. *Quinn*
4. *Quintessa*
5. *Quintana*
6. *Quinton*

R (18)
Roll D40 for this letter option.

1. *Rachael*
2. *Rafael*
3. *Raja*
4. *Rashida*

Family

5. Raven
6. Ray
7. Raymonda
8. Rebekah
9. Red
10. Regan
11. Regina
12. Reginald
13. Reinhold
14. Remington
15. Rex
16. Rheanna
17. Rhonwen
18. Rick
19. Riva
20. Robair
21. Robyn
22. Rochelle
23. Rocky
24. Rodrick
25. Roland
26. Romano
27. Ronan
28. Rosabella
29. Rosaline
30. Rose
31. Rosetta
32. Roslyn
33. Ross
34. Rowlandson
35. Roxie
36. Royston
37. Rudy
38. Rutger
39. Rutherford
40. Ryan

S (19)
Roll D50 for this letter option.

1. Sabas
2. Sabian
3. Sabrina
4. Sadie
5. Sage
6. Sahara
7. Salvatore
8. Samson
9. Samuel
10. Samantha
11. Sandra
12. Sapphire
13. Sarah
14. Sasha
15. Savannah
16. Schuyler
17. Scott
18. Sebastian
19. Selena
20. Selma
21. Septima
22. Seraphina
23. Shae
24. Shannon
25. Sharidan
26. Sharon
27. Shawn
28. Sherlock
29. Shirley
30. Sidney
31. Sierra
32. Siegfried
33. Sigmund

Family

34. *Sigrid*
35. *Simon*
36. *Sinclair*
37. *Skyler*
38. *Sly*
39. *Sofia*
40. *Stanley*
41. *Star*
42. *Stefan*
43. *Stephanie*
44. *Steve*
45. *Sterling*
46. *Strom*
47. *Stuart*
48. *Summer*
49. *Suzanna*
50. *Sylvia*

T (20)
Roll D32 for this letter option.

1. *Tabitha*
2. *Talia*
3. *Tamar*
4. *Tanisha*
5. *Tanner*
6. *Tanya*
7. *Tarquin*
8. *Tasha*
9. *Taytum*
10. *Taylor*
11. *Tecumseh*
12. *Terrance*
13. *Tess*
14. *Tex*
15. *Thaddeus*

16. Thaine
17. Theo
18. Theodoros
19. Tobias
20. Tiara
21. Timothy
22. Tina
23. Tisha
24. Tito
25. Tony
26. Tori
27. Trenton
28. Trinity
29. Trixie
30. Trudy
31. Turlough
32. Tyson

U (21)
Roll D8 for this letter option.

1. Ulric
2. Ultan
3. Ulysses
4. Uma
5. Unity
6. Uri
7. Ursula
8. Uriel

V (22)
Roll D20 for this letter option.

1. Valentina
2. Valeria
3. Valary

4. Valetta
5. Vance
6. Varrick
7. Vasili
8. Vergil
9. Venetia
10. Venice
11. Verena
12. Veronica
13. Vicky
14. Victoria
15. Vienna
16. Viktor
17. Violet
18. Vittorio
19. Vivian
20. Vodka

W (23)

Roll D18 for this letter option.

1. Wade
2. Waine
3. Walden
4. Walker
5. Wallace
6. Walter
7. Warrick
8. Welby
9. Wendy
10. Wentworth
11. Weston
12. Whitney
13. William
14. Winifred
15. Winston

16. Winthrop
17. Wyatt
18. Wyndham

X (24)
Roll D6 for this letter option.

1. Xandria
2. Xanthe
3. Xavier
4. Xenia
5. Xeno
6. Xerxes

Y (25)
Roll D12 for this letter option.

1. Yale
2. Yasir
3. Yasmin
4. Yolanda
5. Yorath
6. Yorick
7. York
8. Yosef
9. Yuri
10. Yves
11. Yvette
12. Yvonne

Z (26)
Roll D6 for this letter option.

1. Zacchaeus
2. Zaid
3. Zelda
4. Zeena
5. Zenobia
6. Zephyrine

P. Marcelo W. Balboa

NPC Difficulty Levels

In the event an NPC or PC find themselves in conflict with an antagonistic NPC, these are the base levels the CG can use to identify the damage assessment. Although the Cosmic Journey Armor is set at 50 max and Health is set at 100 max, Family Edition will expand the NPC conflict levels.

Level 0 Resistance
The character has 0/50 Armor and 1/100 Health. Rolling a D20 can achieve success or failure at no risk to the PC.

Level 1 Resistance
Flip a coin for Armor and Health.

Level 2 Resistance
Roll a D3 for Armor and a D4 for Health.

Level 3 Resistance
Roll A D6 for Armor and a D8 for Health.

Level 4 Resistance
Roll a D8 for Armor and a D10 for Health.

Level 5 Resistance
Roll a D10 for Armor and a D12 for Health.

Level 6 Resistance
Roll a D12 for Armor and a D14 for Health.

Level 7 Resistance
Roll a D14 for Armor and a D16 for Health.

Level 8 Resistance
Roll a D16 for Armor and a D18 for Health.

Level 9 Resistance
Roll a D18 for Armor and a D20 for Health.

Family

Level 10 Resistance
Roll a D20 for Armor and a D22 for Health.

Level 11 Resistance
Roll a D22 for Armor and a D24 for Health.

Level 12 Resistance
Roll a D24 for Armor and a D26 for Health.

Level 13 Resistance
Roll a D26 for Armor and a D28 for Health.

Level 14 Resistance
Roll a D28 for Armor and a D30 for Health.

Level 15 Resistance
Roll a D30 for Armor and a D32 for Health.

Level 16 Resistance
Roll a D32 for Armor and a D34 for Health.

Level 17 Resistance
Roll a D36 for Armor and a D40 for Health.

Level 18 Resistance
Roll a D40 for Armor and a D50 for Health.

Mini Boss Level
Armor 50/50
Health 75/100

Boss Level
Armor is 50/50
Health is 100/100

The CG can customize the Armor and Health level as these are just assisting reference guides, not mandatory applications. This Family Edition alters conflict from the original game by implementing the D110 damage assessment roll. Any time the PC has the chance to defeat the NPC or PC they may be in conflict with, the corresponding player may choose to roll their D20 to fulfill a finishing action to add icing to the cake.

Player Character Occupations – Roll D12

1. The Scholar, *who approaches everything with a think first mentality.*
2. The Priest, *who approaches everything with faith in a higher power.*
3. The Warrior, *who fights for glory and honor with an undying loyalty to fellow warriors.*
4. The Area 51 project *is a troubled mind with post-traumatic stress after being dissected and altered piece by piece.*
5. The Engineer *obsesses with measurements, blueprints, planning, and inventions.*
6. The Medic *will risk their own life to save those so others may life.*
7. The Jack of all Trades *is skilled at many things but a master of none.*
8. The Sorcerer *can perform extraordinary acts with spells, potions, and magic.*
9. The Mercenary *will shoot or blow up anything if the pay is right.*
10. The Scientist *questions everything while seeking more than what the eye can see often times* discovering new things that can build or destroy.
11. The Hacker *thinks in terms of the digital world.*
12. The Survivalist *enjoys nature, all that grows from it, and is at an advantage in any minimalist atmosphere.*

CG can create another Occupation that flows cohesively with the gameplay. NPC are Occupations are unlimited.

P. Marcelo W. Balboa

Character Contributions

Each PC must have qualities that are beneficial to the team yet unique among the members of the team. While the Occupation defines the PC, their purpose in the game is defined by their Contributions. Cosmic Journey, the book, details the rules and regulations pertaining to Contributions. In this, Family Edition, modifications will be made to encourage a more personal attachment to the player and their character. Contributions have been split between Attributes, or characteristics, and Capabilities, or superpowers. At the start of the game, players can choose five Attributes and an individual Capability from the selections broken down within these two categories below. Players can record their choices in their hall of legends entry log which should be filled before any quest begins. All Contributions must correlate with the PC Occupation. All Attributes and Capabilities are valued at +1 each and are only applicable when the appropriate Contribution is needed. Although only the needed Contribution can be applied, if there are multiple Contributions that are applicable, they can be added to the result of the number value rolled simultaneously.

CG, do not control any player's PC. Allow the players to influence the game while not letting any player control it. If a player wants their PC to try something that they can't, try to find a way to test the boundaries of each player's PC to help make them more than they were. The actions of and NPC or PC should at some point impact the story. Through gameplay, a CG can help players learn the value of failure and the rewards of enduring then pushing themselves to overcome the adversities that follow. Provide a satisfactory experience of doing good with their occupations. Study the players and their characters and find a happy medium to ensure a pleasurable experience. Be positive and supportive while guiding the players.

Character Attributes

D20 rolls are optional for players that are new or just want to have a fresh character to play with. Feel free to reference Cosmic Journey, the book.

Education

1. *Inventor*
2. *Programmer*
3. *Nutrition Expert*
4. *Tech Expert*
5. *Living Calculator*
6. *Rocket Scientist*
7. *Hacker*
8. *Robot Expert*
9. *Exorcism Expert*
10. *Psychology Expert*
11. *Map Maker and Navigator*
12. *Expert Operator*
13. *Astro Physicist*
14. *Mechanical Expert*
15. *Medical Expert*
16. *Gun Modifier*
17. *Optical or Dental Expert*
18. *Nuclear Physicist*
19. *Chemist or Alchemist*
20. *Spell Reader*

Intuition

1. *Enemy Detect*
2. *Accurate Gut Feeling*
3. *Investigator*
4. *Trap Expert*
5. *Problem Solver*
6. *Puzzle Solver*
7. *Riddle Solver*
8. *Tracking*
9. *Jury Rigging*
10. *Pick Pocket*
11. *Lock Smith*
12. *Demolition Expert*
13. *Rifleman*
14. *Night Awareness*
15. *Perceptiveness*
16. *Accurate Long-Range Aim*
17. *Code Breaker*
18. *Strategist*
19. *Camouflage*
20. *De-Javu Reader*

Charisma

1. Leaves no one behind
2. Party planner
3. Influencer
4. Skilled barter
5. Skilled trader
6. Healer (Clean and wrap wounds)
7. Reviver (CPR)
8. Attention to detail
9. Courageous rescuer
10. Empathetic
11. Mimics sound
12. Romancer
13. Animal friend
14. Local leader
15. Inspires thoughts
16. Linguist
17. Intimidator
18. Debater
19. Ear hustler
20. Socially skilled

Strength

1. Large vehicle, air, and spacecraft expert
2. Knockout striking power.
3. Heavy melee carry and usage.
4. Heavy armor carry and usage.
5. Heavy projectile weapon carry and usage.
6. Can carry more storage for self or others.
7. Carry others along with their inventory.
8. Pushing and pulling seemingly immovable objects.
9. More control in gravity weakened environments.
10. Welder
11. Blacksmith
12. Armor builder
13. Weapon builder
14. Weapon repair
15. Tool builder
16. Ammunition maker
17. Wand builder
18. Key maker
19. Book maker
20. Medicine maker

Endurance

1. *Powerful stomach*
2. *Poison immunity*
3. *Strong bones*
4. *Tough skin*
5. *Long distance swimmer*
6. *Long distance runner*
7. *Mountain climber*
8. *Self-Healer (Basic Nursing Skills)*
9. *Healer (Wound Care, CPR, AED, First Aid Expert)*
10. *Silent sufferer*
11. *Torture & emotional damage perseverance*
12. *Intestinal fortitude*
13. *Grit under pressure*
14. *Depression resistant*
15. *Outdoorsman*
16. *Hunter*
17. *Tracker*
18. *Minimalist*
19. *Basic fire expert*
20. *Hard to kill.*

Athletics

1. *Martial artist*
2. *Contorting ability*
3. *Parry attack*
4. *Sneak*
5. *Reflexive dodge*
6. *Escape ability*
7. *Superior gun slinger speed*
8. *Tactical Espionage*
9. *Moving target accuracy*
10. *Super speed*
11. *Weapon suppression skills*
12. *Parkour expert*
13. *Superior battlefield movement*
14. *Obstacle passing expert*
15. *Terrain trekking expert*
16. *Acrobatic*
17. *Super physical quickness*
18. *Sleight of hand ability*
19. *Agility*
20. *Dexterity*

Good Fortune

1. Lucky guess
2. Good luck
3. Out of luck
4. Blessed path
5. Karma is a ...
6. Helpful strangers appear when in need.
7. Helpful animals appear when in need.
8. Item finder
9. Item salvager
10. Random luck
11. Critical hit luck
12. Accidental healer
13. Can kill antagonists with accidental ricochet.
14. Accidental damage avoidance
15. The enemy feels pity.
16. Hoarder of surprisingly useful items
17. Scrounger of useless items that can be combined into useful items.
18. Recycler of used items to find new purpose.
19. Easier path finder
20. Beginners luck

P. Marcelo W. Balboa

Character Capabilities

Here are optional D26 roll choices categorized by their first letter but feel free to reference Cosmic Journey, the book. Better still, keep in mind as the CG that superpowers have no limit. If the player and CG agree to a power, go with it. It will make the game more fun. Just make sure the abilities are unique to the team.

A

1. Animal senses
2. Auto healer
3. Alteration of form
4. Animal communication
5. Animal summoning
6. Astral realm travel

B

1. Bless objects
2. Bless characters
3. Breath underwater
4. Breath in outer space

C

1. Charge objects
2. Chemical immunity
3. Create illusions.
4. Crawl/Climb – Anywhere/Anything

D

1. Disease immunity
2. Drain energy
3. Disappear, reappear.

E

1. *Energy absorption*
2. *Energy projection*
3. *Energy deflection*
4. *Environment manipulation*

F

1. *Firework blast*
2. *Flight*
3. *Force blast*
4. *Force field*

G

1. *Growth*

H

2. *Heal acceleration*
3. *Heal others*

I

1. *Invisibility*
2. *Illusion creation*
3. *Image projection*

J

1. *Jump unnaturally High.*
2. *Jump unnaturally Far.*

K

1. *Keen Super Senses of taste, smell, sight, sound, and touch.*

L

1. Limitless contortion

M

1. Magic expert
2. Magical travel
3. Master of elements
4. Metaphysical realm travel
5. Mind control
6. Mind reader

P

1. Phase through
2. Physical realm travel
3. Plant creation
4. Plant control

Q

1. Quickness mastery

R

1. Radar senses
2. Radiation absorption
3. Radiation immunity
4. Regeneration

S

1. Shape shift
2. Shrink
3. Slow time
4. Sorcery

5. *Stretch (Lengthen limbs and or torso, etc.)*
6. *Summoning*
7. *Sun ray absorption*
8. *Superior lightning speed*

T

1. *Telekinesis*
2. *Telepathy*
3. *Teleportation*
4. *Transform (Into something/someone that is touched)*
5. *Transform (Those touched into something/someone else)*

V

1. *Ventriloquism*
2. *Vision enhancement (Player and Cosmic Guide can agree upon what that enhancement will be)*

W

1. *Wand expert*
2. *Witchcraft expert*

Any particular gift/talent can be created or chosen by the player for their character. The PC are only limited by their occupation, prevention of PC team member contribution repetition, and the final decision agreed upon by the CG. Be open to finding items, gear, etc. on a cosmic journey that will provide more contributable abilities. Rolling the D20 during the selection phase of character development is still optional but not necessary.

P. Marcelo W. Balboa

Cosmic Journey Travel Pack

Before travel, make sure the team is prepared for a journey. Make the experience feel real. Go over the survival pack checklist of everything they will need before heading out on their quest.

The Survival Basics

- Fire
    - Matches
    - Kindling
    - Lighters
    - Candles
    - Ferro rod
    - Magnifying glass
- Cover
    - Tent
    - Thermal blanket
    - Sleeping bag
    - Pancho
- Cutting
    - Multitool
    - Axe
    - Saw
    - Combat knife
    - Machete
    - Nail clippers
- Container
    - Canteen
    - Pot
    - Pan
    - Bottle
- Repair
    - Tape
    - Sewing needles
    - Cotton material

Family

- Cordage
    - Rope
    - Sewing sting
    - Paracord
- Storage
    - Backpack
    - Trash liners
    - Zipper locked bags
- Food
    - Rations
    - Hydration filter device
    - Utensils
- First Aid
    - Pain and sinus pills
    - Pill for a running stomach
    - Wound bandage
    - Wound creams
    - Sanitizer
- Navigation
    - Compass
    - Map
    - Binoculars
    - Lamp
    - Flashlight

P. Marcelo W. Balboa

Player Gameplay Dice Rolls

CG, flow with each player, work cohesively with their PC.

50/50 Odds – Flip a coin (C2)

- Before the coin is flipped, the player claims a side.
- Success is identified by the claimed side facing up.

Establish turn order – Roll D4

- The lowest number rolled leads turns.
- The highest number is last in turn rotation.
- Ties require another roll until order is set.

Good, Bad, or Neutral Fate of Character – Roll D6

- These rolls apply when a roll equal to an opposing roll of dice and when success or failure in undetermined.
- Rolling a 1 or 2 will lead to a bad fate.
- Rolling a 3 or 4 will lead to a neutral fate.
- Rolling a 5 or 6 will lead to a good fate.
- CG chooses fate when the roll is neutral.

First dibs (and - or) Not it options – Roll 2D6

- This roll permits the winner to acquire a targeted item but can be reversed to not be the one chosen to enter an area or be the first to commit to a suspicious action.
- 7 or 11 confirms success and the player can decide to put this successful action into play.
- Another player can nullify this roll with a successful roll of their 2D6.
- Rolling 2D6 with a result of two ones will give the CG full control over the fate of the PC.
- Failing to roll a 7 or 11 will also nullify the roll, forcing a roll of fate.

Communication with NPC – Roll D8

1. *Fail, distrustful reaction provoked. Will require another PC to communicate at this juncture.*
2. *Failure, defensive reaction provoked. May have to come back later.*
3. *Fail, may roll again next turn.*
4. *The C.G. can choose a story of barely succeeding or failing which is determined by the fate roll.*
5. *Results in a wipe of the forehead success.*
6. *Results in a respectable story of success.*
7. *Results in a satisfying story of accomplishment.*
8. *Results can positively affect the mission or quest.*

Revival – Roll D10

1. *Results in a ghostly apparition. The player can choose if their PC will pass away, be a friend or foe, possess an NPC, or reincarnate as another PC with the same soul next session.*
2. *Results in a revival with only 10 health but the PC is possessed. Only an exorcism can give them a chance to return to who they once were.*
3. *Results in revival with only 20 health but the PC is living dead for the rest of the session. The player can determine if their PC will be a friend of foe while in a living dead state.*
4. *Results in revival with only 30 health but the PC is traumatized resulting in hallucinations for the rest of the session. At the start of the next session, if the main quest is still on going, the PC can recover.*
5. *Results in revival with only 40 health but the PC will not be able to remember anyone or anything for the rest of the session. At the start of the next session, if the main quest is still on going, the PC will have recovered when the CG decides it is the right time.*
6. *Results in revival with only 50 health. The CG can choose if the PC will be in a coma and if another PC can save them.*
7. *Results in revival with only 60 health and the player character will be ill for the rest of the session.*
8. *Results in revival with 70 health and a possible nightmare in the near future.*

9. Results in revival with 80 health with a headache.
10. Results in revival with 90 health.

Terrain Perseverance – D12

1. Player must roll for fate to prevent the loss of an item, weapon, gear, etc. as chosen by the CG.
2. Player must roll a D110 to avoid unnecessary injury along with a fate roll to establish if it is major or minor.
3. Player must roll a D110 to overcome conflict.
4. Player must roll a D110 to endure terrain damage.
5. Results in Cosmic Guide declaring success or failure depending on the fate roll. With damage assessment.
6. Results in Cosmic Guide declaring success or failure depending on the fate roll. Without damage assessment.
7. Succes but player must roll a D20 to evade negative effects from weather issues.
8. Results in a successful journey.
9. Results in success with the ability to help a player character with a low roll.
10. Results in success with the ability to help all player characters with a low roll.
11. Results in success with the ability to help all low rollers and a chance of finding a new item as well.
12. Results in the accumulated success of all rolls resulting in 8 and up with the addition of the Cosmic Guide rewarding notes.

Any PC with the correlating items, gear, attributes, or capabilities can have the appropriate modifier applied to their dice roll if it should apply. CG has final say.

Armor rebuild or repair – Roll D50

- The armor value is only valid if the player has gear in their inventory that defends against damage.
- Combine any dice to add up to 50.

- Once the value is determined, it must be honored until the gear is repaired, destroyed, or replaced.
- The Cosmic Guide determines whose, when, where, and why armor is affected.
- For the purpose of this game armor is maximized at 50.

Healing – Roll D100

- Only PC with the occupation, gear, or item that allow healing self or others can perform this action
- Healing others or self-healing requires the roll of a D100 with a maximum result of 100 health no matter the amount of health the player healed already has.
- The CG determines when and where (Location of place not body) healing is permitted. Players determine who, what, and how the body is healed.
- The CG can allow players to trade, gift, etc. the necessary items or gear that allows for the player in need of said item or gear to heal self or others.

Cosmic Guide and Player Dice Rolls

All rolls that can be affected by the acquisition of correlating contributions, items, gear, etc. can be modified. Said modifications should be adjusted by defining their worth with a corresponding roll of the appropriate dice.

Initial Roll – Modifier

D8 – (+/- D2)
D10 – (+/- D4)
D12 – (+/- D6)
D20 – (+/- D8)

In order to create an experience worth remembering, situations must arise the player characters will be forced to overcome. There are specific regulations the CG must follow when engaging in any situation where damage assessment takes place. Each dice rolled are for a specific reason that takes personal intention out.

Each conflict, terrain perseverance, and other health threatening events the CG see fit to provoke will require damage assessment. There is only one damage assessment roll required per encounter unless the CG chooses to require rolls in response to the event in progress. If the damage assessment is in response to an attacker, then one roll is all that is required. If the attacking NPC is a boss, then the CG can require multiple damage assessments. The CG will be required to roll D110 against the D110 roll of the player. The end-result will determine if the player or the threat is damaged, as well as to what extent.

Initial Roll – Modifier

D100 (percentage dice) – {+/- (*Low* D20, *High* D50)]
D110 – {+/- (*Low* D20, *High* D50)]
D50 – {+/- (*Low* D10, *High* D20)]

The CG is always in control of the value of all items, gear, and all other acquisitions. Still, it is important to know how the player feels about certain improvements made to their player character. The player is the most valuable part of the CG experience, but it must be remembered that the PC is the most valuable part of the Cosmic Journey. The CG is only the sparks where the PC is the one who creates the fireworks. Have an agenda to direct the players but let the epic tales of overcoming conflict be challenging yet positive influences on the overall experience. Not all D110 rolls need more than one roll as the higher number can gain victory. The player can describe what they want to do in conflict, at this point, without a D20 roll for success. It can help a smoother experience and the story won't slow down.

The player attacked, chosen, etc.
by order the established – Roll D4

1. As determined at the start of the quest.
2. As determined at the start of the quest.
3. As determined at the start of the quest.
4. As determined at the start of the quest.

Family

Fate Roll – Roll D6

1. Any dice rolled resulting in one of the middle two number values will ensure hair line success.
2. Any dice rolled resulting in one of the middle two number values will ensure hair line failure.
3. Any dice rolled resulting in one of the middle two number values will ensure the CG will decide the player character's fate.
4. Any dice rolled resulting in one of the middle two number values will ensure hair line success.
5. Any dice rolled resulting in one of the middle two number values will ensure hair line failure.
6. Any dice rolled resulting in one of the middle two number values will ensure the CG will decide the player character's fate.

Direction of approaching conflict – Roll D8

1. North
2. Northeast
3. East
4. Southeast
5. South
6. Southwest
7. West
8. Northwest

Targeting area potential damage may occur – Roll D12

1. Head
2. Fingers
3. Toes
4. Throat
5. Left arm
6. Left leg
7. Right leg
8. Left leg
9. Stomach

10. Chest
11. Back
12. Groin area

Damage Assessment – D110 vs D110 Rolls

- Damage assessment is the process of the player rolling D110 against the value of the CG rolling D110 for any particular event that may result in injury or death.
- The dice roll number values are set against each other once per event.
- The number value left after the lower number is subtracted from the higher number is the damage applied to the PC with the lower roll value.
- If the event there is terrain damage, and the PC has the higher valued roll then the terrain can be damaged as described by the CG.
- All damage assessment affects armor then health.
- Damaged armor, weapons, & items along with PC health will be tracked by the CG throughout the entire quest.
- PC that receive little to no damage will have the option to choose to continue to fight or evade.
- PC that receive significant damage can choose to evade or remain stunned until the event is over or another PC comes to their aid.
- PC that receive life threatening damage will only have the option to run away or concede the session.
- A PC may seek revival from any PC willing to perform the task if the D20 roll is successful.
- Death is only a word in this game. The CG can define it and its results however they choose.
- Any player that is protective of their PC can opt out of death by choosing to stalemate the rest of the quest.
- Health can only be healed, and Armor can only be repaired when PCs are in areas clear of damage assessment situations.

Remember CG, instant win, and extra rolls for another opportunity to overcome small conflicts is an option. The goal is fun gameplay, not over analyzed altercations with minor to non-story progression encounters.

Family Edition Success Check – Roll D20

Rolling a D20 is necessary when failure to attempt something is a possibility for a PC or NPC. Here are the results of rolling each number.

1. Absolute fail: *May also affect missions or quest.*
2. Haunting fail: *May also affect story down the line.*
3. Ridiculous fail: *May also affect nearby NPC or PC.*
4. Embarrassing fail: *A story of humbling failure.*
5. Comedic fail: *The failure has a silly result.*
6. Valiant fail: *Courageous display in failure.*
7. Heartfelt fail: *The failure provokes empathy.*
8. Inspiring fail: *The setback still motivates others.*
9. Subject to fate roll: *Player progression is hindered.*
10. Subject to fate roll: *Success or failure, no benefit.*
11. Wipe of the forehead success: *Should have failed.*
12. Confusing success: *The result doesn't make sense.*
13. Self-satisfying success: *Failure simply didn't occur.*
14. Honorable success: *Could have failed but wouldn't.*
15. Pat on the back success: *Success well earned.*
16. Respect success: *Impressive display of success.*
17. Determined success: *Failure has no chance.*
18. Awesome success: *Definitively successful result that could benefit the player character progression.*
19. Undeniable success: *Player progression is ensured but the NPC and PC nearby may also be positively affected.*
20. Legendary success: *May also positively affect character progression, other characters, the environment, side missions, or the main quest.*

P. Marcelo W. Balboa

Memorable Treasure Acquisitions

CG, this item generator for random treasures, not only creates items but spells can be created as well and accessed by the D20 roll for success.

D20- Weapons

1. Gem
2. Amulet
3. Knife
4. Nunchaku
5. Baton
6. Dagger
7. Kukri
8. Kama
9. Sickle
10. Machete
11. Short Sword
12. Long Sword
13. Hatchet
14. Axe
15. Hammer Axe
16. Pickaxe
17. Mace
18. Flail
19. Spear
20. Scythe

D10- Weapon Modifiers

❖ Roll D4 to determine the damage assessment value, DAV, which is applied to the D110 roll.

1. Of the Demon Tick (Eats a portion of opposing character's soul) Decrease opposing character's damage assessment roll result by (____).

2. Of Shadow's Sorrow (Makes opposing character paranoid and afraid) Decrease opposing character's damage assessment roll result by (____).

3. Of Limbo's Curse; (Gives visions of terror to opposing character each time they are struck successfully) Decrease opposing character's action success check roll result by (____).

4. Of Purgatory's Jinx; (Makes opposing character insecure and depressed) Decrease opposing character's action success check roll result by (____).

5. Of Tartarus' Wrath; (Penetrates Armor) Decrease opposing character's life by (____) per successful damage assessment roll.

6. Of Naraka's Vengeance; (Turns opposing character's attack on them) Decrease opposing character's damage assessment roll result by (____) then add that number to the damage assessment roll result of the character in possession of weapon.

7. Of Hell's Horror; (Gives opposing character nightmares) Decrease opposing character's life by (____).

8. Of Valhalla's Glory; (Character is invigorated with the warriors spirit) Increase damage assessment roll result by (____).

9. Of Elysium's Blessing; (Character gains life) Increase life by (____) every successful damage assessment roll.

10. Of Heavenly Radiance; (Character and allies gain life) Increase the life of character and allies participating in conflict by (____) every successful damage assessment roll.

D10- Armor

1. Crown
2. Helmet
3. Gauntlets
4. Arm Armor and Breastplate
5. Chainmail
6. Leg Armor and Sabatons
7. Bracelet
8. Ring
9. Necklace
10. Shield

D10- Armor Modifiers

❖ *Roll D16 to determine the DAV.*

1. Of Light- (Strengthens the character's soul) Increase life of character each turn by (____) when damage assessment is rolled regardless of results.

2. Of Darkness- (Weakens the opposing character's soul) Decrease life of character that attacks player character by (____) each unsuccessful damage assessment roll of opposing character.

3. Of Protection- (Fortifies item) Increase damage assessment roll result by (____).

4. Of Defense- (Improves character's ability to defend against attacks and dangerous terrain) Decrease opposing damage assessment roll result by (____).

5. Of Strength- (Increases ability to withstand terrain) Increase damage assessment roll result in opposition to terrain damage assessment by (____).

6. Of Security- (Withstands most harsh weather conditions) Increase damage assessment roll results in opposition to harsh weather damage assessment by (____).

7. Of Energy- (Character is powered up) Increase action success check roll result by (____).

8. Of Power- (Character contribution is enhanced) Increase action success check roll result by (____) when character is performing an action that requires their contribution success.

9. Of Magic- (Magic of character is increased) Increase action success check roll result by (____) when character with an occupation and contribution that relates to magic.

10. Of Endurance- Increase character and allies D20 roll by (____) when in conflicts involving bosses or mini bosses.

D20- Projectile Weapons

1. *Boomerang*
2. *Dart*
3. *Shuriken*
4. *Throwing Knife*
5. *Bomb*
6. *Potion Bottle*
7. *Slingshot*
8. *Blowpipe*
9. *Wand*
10. *Staff*
11. *Bow and Arrow*
12. *Crossbow*
13. *Revolver*
14. *Pistol*
15. *Shotgun*
16. *Semi Auto Rifle*
17. *Automatic Rifle*
18. *Sniper Rifle*
19. *Grenade Launcher*
20. *Rocket Launcher*

D10- Projectile Weapons Ammunition

❖ *Roll D12 to determine the DAV.*

1. *Blinding Flash*
2. *Freeze*
3. *Incendiary*
4. *Acid*
5. *Smoke*
6. *Poison*
7. *Heat Seeking*
8. *Proximity Combustion (This ammo will explode when near targeted opposing character)*
9. *Sticky Combustion (This ammo attaches to target then explodes)*
10. *Armor Piercing (These rounds damages life)*

Be mindful of the occupation of each PC as they are subject to the limitation of their contributions to the team. Rest assured, where certain discovered items are not usable by the PC, they are tradable. The PC with the attribute or capability to modify or improve an item can do so at the appropriate time deemed by the CG for a more immersive and pleasing gameplay experience. Any and all items are subject to usage limitations set by CG. But the modifications are not limited to dice rolls of numbers. Percentage dice are a fine choice to modify the effects of a particular item. Once DAV is applied to enchanted item, that item is permanently forged.

P. Marcelo W. Balboa

Treasure Acquisitions

Cosmic Journey is nothing without leaving with more than you came to the table with. Purposeful spontaneity provides the player with a sense of unscripted freedom while freeing the CG's unlimited imagination. Here is an optional category if the players seek to acquire new things that they have the option to enhance with their own modifications. Simply roll the dice, choose an option, and ask the player what power they would like the item to provide. The CG names the item and provides it to the PC during gameplay. The item may not affect the roll value but the satisfying application to gameplay will make for a joyfully memorable experience.

Sustenance, D24

1. Item player would like.
2. Broth of _.
3. Tea of _.
4. Mead of _.
5. Root of _.
6. Leaf of _.
7. Meat of _.
8. Vine of _.
9. Stew of _.
10. Salt of _.
11. Life blood of _.
12. Honey of _.
13. Vitamin of _.
14. Pie of _.
15. Soup of _.
16. Roast of _.
17. Water of _.
18. Bread of _.
19. Milk of _.
20. Beans of _.
21. Rice of _.
22. Pill of _.

Family

23. Serum of _.
24. Item CG would like.

Holy Grails, D100

1. Item player would like.
2. Accursed Idol of _.
3. Blessed idol of _.
4. Seed of _.
5. Lantern of _.
6. Mask of _.
7. Whistle of _.
8. Skull of _.
9. Stone of _.
10. Book of _.
11. Pen of _.
12. Ashes of _.
13. Hand of _.
14. Paw of _.
15. Compass of _.
16. Flower of _.
17. Pearl of _.
18. Bag of _.
19. Instrument of _.
20. Tears of _.
21. Mirror of _.
22. Hat of _.
23. Coat of _.
24. Shoes of _.
25. Underwear of _.
26. Eye of _.
27. Brain of _.
28. Fang of _.
29. Cloth of _.
30. Orb of _.
31. Shroud of _.

32. Quilt of _.
33. Metal of _.
34. Purse of _.
35. Belt of _.
36. Ink of _.
37. Cauldron of _.
38. Box of _.
39. Bell of _.
40. Leather of _.
41. Talisman of _.
42. Key of _.
43. Candle of _.
44. Thorns of _.
45. Quill of _.
46. Parchment of _.
47. Doubloon of _.
48. Vessel of _.
49. Cape of _.
50. Carpet of _.
51. Hair of _.
52. Pendant of _.
53. Heart of _.
54. Medallion of _.
55. Card of _.
56. Token of _.
57. Charm of _.
58. Coin of _.
59. Thread of _.
60. Wax of _.
61. Corsage of _.
62. Scroll of _.
63. Tool of _.
64. Doll of _.
65. Cream of _.
66. Incense of _.
67. Anvil of _.

68. Locket of _.
69. Map of _.
70. Clock of _.
71. Shawl of _.
72. Rope of _.
73. Sandals of _.
74. Sea chest of _.
75. Scarf of _.
76. Gloves of _.
77. Portrait of _.
78. Backpack of _.
79. Pouch of _.
80. Basket of _.
81. Glasses of _.
82. Vial of _.
83. Mug of _.
84. Plate of _.
85. Tome of _.
86. Hide of _.
87. Powder of _.
88. Chain of _.
89. Venom of _.
90. Lipstick of _.
91. Dice of _.
92. Chalice of _.
93. Oil of _.
94. Perfume of _.
95. Cologne of _.
96. Scepter of _.
97. Ointment of _.
98. Bottle of _.
99. Fragment of _.
100. Item the CG would like.

Exploration, D32

1. Item player would like.
2. Passage of _.
3. Bite of _.
4. Kiss of _.
5. Tree of _.
6. Mark of _.
7. Curse of _.
8. Blessing of _.
9. Trap of _.
10. Maze of _.
11. Riddle of _.
12. Puzzle of _.
13. Shadows of _.
14. Bubbles of _.
15. Vapor of _.
16. Wind of _.
17. Spores of _.
18. Dust of _.
19. Sand of _.
20. Oasis of _.
21. Element of _.
22. Void of _.
23. Prophecy of _.
24. Spark of _.
25. Bridge of _.
26. Land of _.
27. Luck of _.
28. Light of _.
29. Flame of _.
30. Doorway of _.
31. Ora of _.
32. Item the CG would like.

Tracking Gameplay

A notepad is fine but if you want to create a spreadsheet that can be printed when a new quest with multiple sessions is scheduled then do what works for you. Keep in mind that any damage assessment will require simultaneous note comparison of damage attained if conflict between PC and NPC arise.

Locations

- Note coordinates on map by way of latitude (1-2-3s) and longitude (A-B-Cs).
- Note name of every location as it pertains to the order the player characters are traversing them.

NPC Armor and Health

- Identify any notes acquired during the session.
- Keep up to date status reports of health level.
- Keep up to date status report of armor strength.
- And keep a log of all NPC introduced throughout the entire quest.

PC Armor and Health

- Identify any notes acquired during the session.
- Keep up to date status reports of health level.
- Keep up to date status report of armor strength.
- And keep a log of all NPC introduced throughout the entire quest.

NPC Acquisitions

- Identify any item, gear, etc. acquired during gameplay.
- Identify the location of any item, gear, etc. that has been overlooked.
- Identify location of any item, gear, etc. that was lost, dropped, or mishandled but can be regained.

PC Acquisitions

- Identify any item, gear, etc. acquired.
- Identify the location of any item, gear, etc. that has been overlooked.
- Identify location of any item, gear, etc. that was lost, dropped, or mishandled but can be regained.

Hall of Legends Records

While the Cosmic Guide creates a world that is inclusive, allowing for input on minor world events, the Player's Character progression should always be in mind. Cosmic Journey is about playing with familiar faces to catch up, reminisce, or simply have a good time with. The Family Edition exists to create new memories and tighten relationships. The Hall of Legends creates that sense of acceptance and belonging throughout a community of coexisting players around the world. It is the CG and player's choice how they set up their categories, columns, rows, etc. Keep track at all times. Know that the Hall of Legends was initially meant to keep track of the history of an underwater community called Rezandria. As Brea's Guild evolved and Cosmic Guides have come to lead countless teams, there is no limit to the experiences that have occurred. All Cosmic Journeys completed within the Unworthy Cosmos will always be considered valid and will be recognized by the Hall of Legends.

It is safe to say that the Unworthy Cosmos is a vast existence that reaches beyond the imagination of a mere human being. That being said, there are limitless cosmic journeys that have taken, are taking, and will take place. But none are below the recognition of the Hall of Legends Records. In Cosmic Journey, Family Edition, players input their character's information into the HOL Entry Log. A universally recognized information system that qualifies all participants to be placed in the Hall of Legends on Rezandria. Below are the details needed to complete the HOL Entry Log.

P. Marcelo W. Balboa

The HOL Entry Log

- Player name
- Player character name
- Player character alias
    - Before gameplay (possibly no alias)
    - After gameplay
- Player character occupation
- Player character contributions
    - Attributes
    - Capabilities
- Player character back story
- Team affiliation(s)
- All quests completed.
- Experience points, XP
    - Cosmic Journey gameplay time
        - Years
        - Months
        - Weeks
        - Days
        - Hours
        - Minutes
        - Seconds
- Quest XP
    - All quests attempted.
    - All completed quests.
- Side Mission XP
    - All side missions attempted.
    - All completed side missions.
- Any notable items PC acquired overall.
    - Gear, weapons, armor, etc.

Cosmic Journey

Family Edition supply list

1) Roll results reference sheet.
2) Stationary
    a. Scissors
    b. Tape
    c. Markers
    d. Index cards
    e. Calculator
    f. Sticky notes
    g. Pens
    h. Pencils
    i. Notebooks
    j. Dry erase board and markers
    k. Glue
3) Dice
4) Dice tray
5) Cosmic Guide screen
6) Play mat (with grid)
7) Terrain
8) Player minis
9) NPC minis
10) Monster minis
11) Treasures (prizes or memorabilia to take home)
12) Snacks and beverages

P. Marcelo W. Balboa

Cosmic Journey

A commentary from the creator

Cosmic Journey has always been the glue that allows valued readers to live alongside the characters that exist in the Unworthy Cosmos. Family Edition brings all that intent and expands to a more experience friendly application. Games of similar imagination requirements collect the minds and bodies of a community of characters that understand how important quality time with others is. No matter the location, groups gather to create experiences together on special nights that fulfill similar interests. Of course, the Player Characters are just as important as the Players themselves. A Cosmic Guide should always look for an opportunity to reward them for making the world better. Every Cosmic Journey, Family Edition, should be a platform for players to interact on a healthy social level. It should pay attention to the value of people enjoying each other's presence. Having an agenda is important but games should feel encouraging, especially under difficult circumstances. Empathy and support from the CG is vital as many players are developing social skills in the process. Talking to the players and coming to agree on like-minded ideas in order to make things fun and easy flowing while at times challenging is important. There must be assumably impossible situations that players must join together and in some cases help others to overcome. Adjusting to the varying personalities and learning to coexist with perhaps unfamiliar personalities, is what the Family Edition is all about. Getting to know each other can provide more fuel for a more engaging story with humor, suspense, survival horror, and many other experiences that may corelate with the audience. All alongside the never-ending exploration, discoveries, obstacles, and character progression. Cosmic Journey is about getting out there and going to places uncharted only to come back with souvenirs, stories, and memories with other players to remember.

Thank you…

To my beautiful, loving, precious little family of five.

The story of Tec's Quest

*Told through a storied version of a Cosmic Journey Quest
I played with my family as their Cosmic Guide.*

Tec, a small Turtlumpkidan who lives on the planet Flubberboober, runs desperately to aid his life partner Pep. She too is of the same humanoid body type but of the Squirlumpkidan lineage. He was visited by her one morning to participate in yet another paranormal adventure. But they didn't know that the prince of darkness was trying to enter the physical realm by defiling an innocent body. Pep, in her ever-present need to find proof her fallen friends still existed, entered a castle where a young boy went missing. What she found only confirmed suspicious activity. What's more is the boy, and his predator were still in the castle. She would find the boy in foul conditions but the predator, an elderly Elfilumpkidan, found her. Holding a recorder, Pep was seen by Tec as she ran for her life only to be captured.

Pep was initially afraid to enter the seemingly haunted castle but the thought of losing Pep inspired the courage in him. He broke in and ran the halls. "Pep. Pep, where are you?" He yelled over and over. His nerves grew tighter as he felt something following. As he made his way through the maze of hallways throughout the castle, he ran into the spirit of the boy who went missing. Tec almost fell to the floor in shock. "Oh, golly what the flippin'…?" He reacted. A blue transparent energy pushed the air around to create sound. "I take it you are the hero. Your friend is about to be sacrificed." The spirit said. "Where is she?" Tec asked. "It matters not. You must kill the entity within the Elfilumpkidan named Schika. For not doing so will only guarantee your friend's death and yours. And the doorway for the prince of darkness will be open to roam the Physical Realm." The spirit warned. "Where is such a tool? I have nothing but my shell and what's inside. There are electronics and such but nothing to kill a prince of darkness." Tec replied.

The spirit moved the air, creating what sounded like a spooky laugh. "That's not what I am saying at all. I know you have nothing you silly Turtlumpkidan. I am coming to you to take you to the one who can help you." The spirit said. "How?" Tec asked. "You have to come with me to the Astral Realm to meet a wise man." The spirit said. "Whatever it takes to save Pep. I'm in." Tec said. The spirit lunged at Tec and absorbed into him. Tec fainted. As his eyes opened he found himself in an unfamiliar place. Reds of differed tones surrounded him. His sight was unfamiliar. The scent of the place was gone. The sounds were bone chilling as souls fell to the ground and splattered. "What the hell is going on?" Tec reacted. "This is not hell my friend. It is the entrance way into the Astral Realm." The spirit said.

"Wait. You're not a ghost anymore. Are you the boy Pep was talking about?" Tec asked. The spirit now took the form of his original body once he was in the astral realm. "I am. And you must hurry. Your path is grim, and you may not make it out with all your soul." The boy spirit said. "What does that mean?" Tec asked. "It means that there are things in the shadow that should never have existed. And they will not be happy with your presence." A grand voice answered. "Ok, hold up. I need a moment. Who are you and where did you just come from? Spirit kid. This place, whatever you did to me. This huge dude. I need answers." Tec said. "Sorry about that. Your friend is in danger and her soul may be the key for the prince of darkness to enter the Physical Realm. I'm Troy by the way. And I asked the great traveler to meet you as you would need help in rescuing your friend's soul." Troy said.

"The prince of darkness is involved? This is bad." The great traveler said. "And who are you?" Tec asked. "I am the descendant of the great traveler, Brea, and if your friend is correct, you have no time to waist. I will open a path for you to get where you need to be as I seek aid from my father." The great traveler said. He opened a portal for Tec who paused for a moment. "Wait. Hold up. How do you even know this guy? You just went missing. How do you know anything about this place? I'm not going to do anything until I know what's going on." Tec declared. "I'm just a kid. I don't have all the answers, but I learned that this time works different from the Physical Realm time. Months could pass here in the Astral Realm and only a moment

Family

would pass in the Physical Realm. I learned of the great traveler by way of roaming this realm on my own for too long of a time." Troy said. "I am Ike, the great traveler of the Astral Realm. I came to be in this realm from a surprise attack from my uncle. He overtook our kingdom, and I was killed. My father's, father's father Brea was a great traveler of the Physical Realm. I inherited his gift. I have been here and have come to be a guide for all who are lost. Including Troy and yourself. Now hurry, you mustn't wait any longer. The fate of the Physical and Astral Realms may be dictated by your success. I will be off to find aid in these matters. I bid you farewell and good journey." Ike said before flying away at an intimidating speed. "I hope you have the information you need." Troy said. "I do. I am Tec by the way." Tec said. "You should hurry Tec. And it was nice to meet you. I wish you all the luck." Troy said. Tec turned to the portal and entered.

Ike would reach out to his sister Elliana, a gifted mental traveler. "Sister, I am in need of Brea. Can you let him know the prince of darkness is on the planet Flubberboober trying to enter the Physical Realm? I have a warrior on his way to retrieve the cursed sword of Ednedria. But I fear he will not make it out without the aid of one of our great grandfather's teams." Ike transmitted. "I hear you my brother. Fear not, I have already let him know as you messaged me." Elliana transmitted cerebrally. "Thank you. How have you been?" Ike asked. "We are still rebuilding but there will be a day when we can smile at what we have overcome." She responded. "This is good to hear." He said. "And what of your circumstances? Are you alright?" She asked. "I fear a great war is coming. But it is hard to tell who and where this will happen. So I continue to keep watch. Still, I fear the shadow holds more than anyone understands. It may be too late by the time anyone figures it out." He said. "Stay safe my brother. I sense much of what is occurring in the Physical Realm will inevitably lead to that revelation in the Astral Realm." She responded. "Hmmm. Understood. Well, I must be off. May your days be plentiful and wonderful sister." He said. "Likewise my brother. I love you." She said as they lost connection.

Elliana had almost instant connection with her bloodline no matter their position across the cosmos. "Thank you for the information Elliana. I will do my best to help Ike in any way I can." Brea, the great traveler, transmitted. Brea reached out to his most successful team who just finished a cosmic journey against a great wizard. Jack Ryan, a mercenary who loves guns and explosives of all types. He's earned a reputation for being a cold-blooded skillful gun for hire in his past but his bond with his current team as softened him up... just a little. Booker Dewitt is a warrior who is loyal to his friends and fearless. Melee weapons are his specialty, but he has attained many other gifts on his cosmic journey. Blossom, the medic of the group, has a deep love for nature and its sustenance. She can make healing formulas out of any herb. Still, it is her steadfast will and willingness to go anywhere to save the life of a friend that separates her from healers of her kind. Last but not least is Hashimira, a sorceress with spells, magic and powers attained over her long cosmic journey, who has only tapped the devastating potential she can bestow upon anyone who may threaten the team. As individuals they may have chosen to look the other way at most issues like this, but together they would answer the call.

They met up at a tavern, yes reader... a tavern, they were accustomed to visit to recollect memories. They enjoyed some beef stew, corn bread, and alcoholic beverages while they waited. After a couple of hours enjoying the stories of other travelers, something happened to Blossom. Elliana guided Ike's essence to find Brea's team and Blossom was receptive to his energy waves. "Blossom, I am Ike and I called on Brea to reach out to you and your team to help a warrior on a great quest. I can bring you all to the Astral Realm to aid him, but it will require your souls to leave your body. I can't guarantee you will get your soul back or even all of it still whole. If you decide not to help, I will understand. If you do, I must know now for the little hero may already be in need. Know that the fate of the Physical and Astral Realms may be affected by your decision." Ike transmitted. Blossom snapped out of her connection.

For some reason, Booker put a cloth over his head and a jacket over his shoulders and began speaking in a light girly pitched voice, "Alright guys I'm now in character." He was clearly very drunk. Hashimira began creating little plant creatures who were babbling incoherent words as they too were a bit tipsy. Jack stopped everyone as he noticed Blossom wasn't her normal self. No one said it but they all seemed to know she had gone somewhere and came back while sitting in her chair. "Look lads." Jack said. Everyone looked toward Blossom. She repeated what she was told and insisted they make their choice at once. No one hesitated. They had already been through so much they were confident they could overcome anything together.

Family

With Hashimira's help, Blossom faded back into the Astral Realm, accepting the challenge to help Tec on his quest. Ike immediately opened the doorway for the souls of Blossom and her companions to fall into the Astral Realm. Then he created a portal that would lead to the place within the Shadow Dimension where Tec went. "May your journey save the realms." Ike said. All four entered the portal and were suddenly surrounded by darkness. Their bones chilled from the negative energy that seemed to drain the life from them. Just as time is slower in the Astral Realm than the Physical Realm, Shadow slows time even more. If there were any paths to follow it would take time for their sight to get acclimated to the sheer darkness. Booker and Jack put their night vision equipment on. Hashimira took out her black light which caused many hidden beings all around them to scream in fear, fleeing in all directions. Booker pulled out his sun blade. The light itself is so powerful it shatters the land. He put it away before the land tore apart. Blossom then pulled out her crossbow and released a magical arrow. It could reveal the path they need to go anywhere else, but its light is consumed by the darkness, and it returned scared and traumatized.

Jack activated his small robot to scan the area. With a radius of thirty feet in any direction, Hashimira took out her black candle and lit it creating a blue glowing light. "There are unidentifiable threats in large numbers surrounding our perimeter. They appear to be afraid." The robot said. Hashimira then tried to use her gem of true path, but the darkness began to eat the light as soon as it cleared a few feet out of the blue light into the pure darkness. Still, there was enough revelation to lead them at least thirty feet in the right direction at any time. Blossom pulled out her crystal staff of light and said, "Tah, tah." Which activates its power as long as she is in a fighting stance. As it has the same effect as Booker's sword, she deactivates the light. Little by little, they are learning what they can and can't do. Clearly, this place is like nothing they have ever experienced but they are also like nothing this place has experienced.

All the commotion draws the attention of an elf princess lost in shadow for eternity. "What are you doing here?" She asked. They don't answer. "Who are you? And what.." She began. "We were sent here by a message that was given to our friend." Hashimira answered. "What friend?" She asked. "Oh, um, what was the name he told me?" Blossom said. "Answer or I will smite you where you stand." The elf princess yelled. "Our friend was given a vision." Hashimira said. "And what was this vision you speak of?" The elf princess asked. Blossom and Hashimira look at each other. "Um, we were picked after our last journey and were asked to help a friend." Blossom said. "You keep repeating nonsense. Who sent you and why are you here?" The elf princess yelled as she repositioned to fight them. "If it's a fight you want then so be it." Booker declared. "What was the name?" Blossom said. "I do not wish to fight you but if you want to then so be it." Booker said. Jack said nothing but as Booker spoke, he was already creating explosives for the fight. "Brea sent us. We were given a choice to come and help our friend or not and we chose to come. There's your answer." Hashimira cried out.

"The great traveler is your friend? Oh my, I didn't… I'm so sorry. I … How can I help you? My name is Moliasha. I was the ruler of this Plain until I was overthrown. I have little power now, but I know these lands very well and can aid you." Moliasha said. "Where are we gonna go?" Jack asked his teammates. "Where are we supposed to go?" Booker asked. "Where are you from?" Hashimira asked. "I am from the land of Kupa Ning. I was betrayed by my sisters who wanted power over peace. They damned me to this Plain within Shadow. One of my sisters was betrayed later on, just as I was, but she tracked me down then overtook my throne. So I roam alone as my companions have been captured and are most likely destroyed." Moliasha responded. "Have you seen a little green guy that looks like a turtle?" Booker asked. Moliasha looked at him with grave concern. "Tec. You're here for Tec?" She asked. "Yes mam." Jack said. "Indeed." Booker said.

"Come with me. He is in very dangerous places." She said. They followed her but she was too fast. Soon she was out of sight. Then the ground became a sticky sludge and began to grab them. Their bodies vibrated and vanished into thin air. The elf princess had used her power to scatter the team into different points in time in the Astral Realm. Each would find themselves at a pivotal turning point on Tec's journey to find the curse sword of Ednedria. For Tec this experience was one on going flow although his soul is separated into multiple pieces. For each of the members of Brea's team, their journey would be singular and separated by time. Their only chance of success is to rejoin Tec's soul and find the path to the sword of Ednedria. For the purpose of this story, loyal reader, you will take a journey through each of the team members' moment they meet Tec. Let us continue.

When Tec entered the portal he landed in the same place Brea's team would sometime after. "Where did you come from? Are you a spy for my sister?" Moliasha asked Tec. "What? No. I don't even know who that is. I'm Tec and I just need to find a special weapon to fight off a dark prince." Tec said. "Lies. Be gone insect. I was tricked and lost my most loyal soldiers. Now my sister haunts me with tricksters and laughable stories. I'll show her. You want a quest maggot? Let your soul be torn apart as my warriors have been torn from me. Let time separate your soul and may the shadow spread the torn pieces. You will be lost in darkness for eternity." Moliasha said. The ground turned to sludge and grabbed a hold of Tec. His body started vibrating then he vanished into thin air. When he recollected his senses, he found himself in a new place. The scent of boiled flesh made him nauseous.

In an instant, the part of his soul that held his most defining memories was met with Blossom. Tec is cool under pressure and stands firm. "Who are you?" He asks. "I'm Blossom. I was sent here to help you." Blossom said. "What? I just got here. Is this some trick that elf lady is playing on me?" He asked. "No, we came here to help you." Blossom said. Tec looked around. There was no one but them there. He looked at her like she was crazy. "We? It's just you." Tec said. "Well, I have a team with me, but we were separated. I don't know where they are, but I know we are here for you." She said. Tec looked at her for a moment. He noticed that her hair was mixed with braided and straight hair. She was wearing a skirt but her outfit itself was like armor. She held her medical tools in her combat ready vest jacket. She was not as tall as the elf lady, but she was at least a foot taller than him. As most Munchgalumptagans are between two to three feet full grown. He stood a grand three feet easily.

"Where do you come from?" He asked. "I currently reside on the planet Rezandria where my friends and I take refuge, train, and go on cosmic journeys to help others like you." She began. But sounds of little things began to close distance on their location. "Um, I think we need to get somewhere safe." Tec said. "Yeah." Blossom responded. They take a moment to look around. There are rocks covered with plants and the ground is saturated with a mucus-like substance coating weeds of a dark grey tone. The sounds of something coming seems to be to the east. They decided in an instant to run west. They are met with a hill of rocks covered with slimy grey grass.

More sounds are heard from the north. "I guess we have to find out what is coming." Tec said. "Yup, let's go see what's making all those rumbling sounds." Blossom responded. They turned to the east and returned to their original spot. Before they could get there they were attacked by tiny blue monsters with four arms and two legs. They were in countless numbers with only one intent; to dive into their victim's throat and suffocate them. Blossom started to stomp relentlessly. The little monsters tried desperately to dive in her mouth, but her parries are enough to block them. Tec had a more difficult time due to his size. If Blossom hadn't been there he would have been consumed.

He was mesmerized by her as she stood in a fighting stance, revealed her crystal staff of light, and yelled, "Tah, tah." The light was toxic to the little Sufficaters who melted instantaneously. The sounds of all their screams at once drew the attention of the Blobber. She loved her babies and knew every one of their voices. Hearing their screams infuriated her. The ground rumbled as she ran to the area their screams came from. Tec and Blossom tried to keep a straight face as Blobber appeared. Her body was decorated with the limbs of the fallen victims her babies killed. Each one was simply stuck to her sticky boiled flesh but responded to her will. Tec and Blossom couldn't tell where she started or ended. Her face was covered with faces of the tortured faces of victims. Her fat greasy body slid toward them.

Blossom pulls out her double-bladed boomerang and targets each of the limbs stuck to Blobber's body. "You fools. I can't die. You will pay for your stupidity." She gargled. But the impact of the boomerang removed all of her stolen limbs. As she attacked, they fell off revealing she had two skinny, flimsy, pathetic arms, and tiny hands. As she tried to pick her fallen limbs up, Blossom pulled out her bow and shot arrows at all the limbs, sealing them to the ground. "Ahhhhh." Blobber yelled in frustration. Her fat body jiggled as she jumped up and down like a spoiled child. Her little arms flailed around uselessly. "Leave my home murderers. Leave." She cried. Neither knew the way out. "Well which way is the way out." Blossom asked with a sarcastic expression. "South. There is a path south you can go. Leave me. NOW." Blobber gargled.

Tec picked up some daggers that looked like small swords in his grasp. "Wow, look at these." He said. Blossom waited patiently as Tec sorted out the bounty of the fallen limbs. He noticed there was a cape with holes. "Look

Family

at this. It's cloth but shines like diamonds. I'm taking it." He said. "Great. Let's go." Blossom said. They ran south, but they kept their guard. Many of the little Sufficaters were following them, waiting for a mistake. They knew they had escaped the Blobber when the steaming environment changed to a dry crusty one. "What is that?" Tec asked. Blossom heard it too. There was a conflict in the distance. Explosions erupted that were familiar to Blossom. "Is that Jack?" Blossom asked. She ran to see if her friend was in need of help.

Around the same time Blossom had arrived near Tec, Jack appeared near Tec in another timeline. As Blossom arrived in the Kingdom of the Boiled in the Shadow Dimension, Jack was transported to a time later in Tec's lifeline somewhere in the Kingdom of the Scorched. This portion of Tec's soul was not aggressive. So much so that as he and Jack appeared, Tec immediately befriended Jack. "Oh, hello there. I'm Tec. I have no weapons and have nothing to fight you if you so choose to rob me. Could you tell me where I can find a cursed weapon to defeat the dark prince?" Tec said. "I don't know where the cursed weapon is at." Jack said. "Oh. Well that's fine. Are you from around here?" Tec asked. "No." Jack said. "Did you run into an elf lady by chance?" Tec asked. "Yup." Jack responded.

Their conversation was interrupted as they were elevated by dark grey rock hands that burst upward directly under them. Tec thought the hand looked so friendly he lied down on his face and hugged it. "Get your face away from the hand." Jack said. "But it's a high five. Is this not a gesture of love and respect for Humalumpkidans?" Tec asked. As Jack tries to figure out what to do, the rock hands take them to a golden nugget structure in the shape of their master, the Molten Rock Lizard. The rock hands break apart into thousands of small rock goblins and seal off any chance of escape for Jack and Tec. Their only choice is to enter.

Tec is so moved by the tiny creatures that he tries to hug one of them. "Don't do anything dumb. Just stay next to me or I'll slap you silly." Jack said. "But they're so cute. Can I have one?" Tec asked. "Did you not hear…" Jack began. He grabbed Tec's arm like a child and took him with him as they entered the structure. "Awwww. They're so cute." Tec said. The entrance was long and the further they walked the hotter it became. In the distance the entrance opened up to a large cavern. There were multiple holes leading to countless areas in Shadow. "Do you know this place?" Jack asked. "Nope. I just got here. I met a nice elf lady who was excited to meet me. She felt it necessary to send me on this wonderful site seeing tour. But I guess she must have gotten lost." Tec assumed.

He looked up at Jack with an innocent expression. Jack knew he was telling the truth or at least his perception of it. "Let's take one of these paths. Don't do anything dumb." Jack said. Tec hugs Jack's leg. "You love me don't you friend?" Tec asked. Jack just begins to walk as Tec is attached to his leg. Their attempt to escape is thwarted by the appearance of the Molten Lizard King, Fuknok. He spits lava spit, cutting off the pathway they were going. "Who enters my home?" He asked. They turn to the great voice and look up as if he were the size of a building. Tec lets go of Jack to hug the Molten King. "Oh my goodness. It's a lizard. I love lizards." Tec yelled as he ran with open arms at the Molten King.

Jack grabbed Tec before he touches the Molten King. "What are you? And what are you doing in my home?" Fuknok asked. "We're here to look for a cursed sword." Jack said. "The sword of Ednedria? Lies. Everyone knows this is the murderous weapon that can kill anything in any realm. You seek to destroy me?" Fuknok said. Then he began to spit hot coals at them. Jack's right arm is struck by debris. Tec is knocked out by the large debris exploding everywhere. Jack tried to avoid the debris but slightly sprained his left ankle. Jack pulled out a rocket launcher and aimed at what looked like Fuknok's eye. A direct blow leaves Fuknok blind. With Fuknok weakened Jack began shooting at the Molten King with his rail gun. The bullets tore through the body of Fuknok. "Stop. I don't want to die. Get out of my home." Fuknok cried out. "Where's the sword?" Jack asked. "Take the second pathway. Leave me." Fuknok said. Jack grabs Tec and takes the second pathway. Fuknok seals the path leaving no other choice for Jack but to continue on. As they emerge from the new path, thousands of rock goblins await them.

Jack unleashes a round from his bazooka. The explosion can be heard from miles away. The rock goblins attack them mercilessly. They grab Tec and try to tear his limbs off. Jack attempts to shoot them with his revolver but the goblins overwhelm him and try to tear him apart as well. Blossom and Origin Tec begin to see Jack and Loveable Tec in the distance. As they approach, Blossom yells out in relief, "Heyyyy, Jack, it's you." Jack turns to look at Blossom to make sure it really is her. "Help me please. I'm about to die here." Jack says. "No problem. That's what I'm here for." She said. Origin Tec pushed Blossom out of the way of a swarm of rock goblins that dove at

Family

her. She falls over and hits her head. Origin Tec tries his best to fight them off but is overcome. The rock goblins focus on the two Tec's and Jack. Blossom looks dead.

As she opens her eyes, she takes out her boomerang and starts knocking goblins off of the two Tecs and Jack. Both Tecs do their best to fight off the hordes as Jack pulls out his shotgun and rains terror on the defenseless goblins. Blossom compliments Jack's attack with arrows but the arrows break on the bodies of the rock goblins. Pop! Kaplow! Crash! The bodies of the rock goblins explode everywhere as Jack unloads numerous bullets with his rail gun, giving both Tec's a chance to retreat behind him. Blossom finally unveils her demigod killer sword and swings for the fences. The rock goblins had the numbers, but fear took over once they realized they had no chance of defeating the duo. And just like that, they were alone. The atmosphere was dry and dusty. Origin Tec and Loveable Tec didn't see each other. Something in their psyche wouldn't allow them to recognize the other as their soul as they are a part of one soul. Loveable Tec finds refuge in wrapping his arms and legs around Jacks right leg. "I love you friend." Loveable Tec said. Jack says nothing but doesn't fight the little guy off. Blossom walks over to Origin Tec. "Good teamwork." She said.

Origin Tec nods in agreement. He looked at the group and noticed everyone was exhausted. "Let's find a place to recover. We have no idea how long our journey will be and there are more mouths to feed." Origin Tec said. The group makes their way through a winding path surrounded by hills of dry dusty rock on either side no matter the route they take. Origin Tec would find a good hiding spot in the distance. Blossom and Jack follow. Loveable Tec never lets his body grip go, remaining glued to Jack's right leg. Once they were all safe, they settled in to recuperate. Origin Tec remained sitting up as Jack passed out, healing from near death as Blossom fell asleep from pure exhaustion. Loveable Tec remained close to Jack as Blossom remained near Origin Tec. Both teammates were too tired to realize neither Tec's recognized the existence of the other. After a good rest, Blossom woke up first. She looked around, paranoid that she or the others may be in danger. Everyone was asleep except Origin Tec. Tec was sitting on a small rock keeping guard over his new companions. Blossom noticed her armor was repaired. As a healer, she was able to help everyone with their injuries. Jack received medical attention from Blossom, but his injuries were serious and would take time to recover from. Loveable Tec took to her kindness and let her fix chips on his shell. After a couple of days, Origin Tec went out to survey the land.

As Blossom arrived in the Kingdom of the Boiled and Jack landed in the Kingdom of the Scorched, Booker arrived in the Kingdom of the Starved. The Tec he appeared with was the angry rage of Tec. The part of him that remembers losing his entire family every day. The part of Tec's soul that seeks revenge for the loss of any opportunity to grow up with a mother and father. The Tec that is antisocial and awkward with others due to the lack of siblings in his life. As Booker and Mad Tec appeared, Booker appeared outside a structure while Mad Tec appeared inside. What's worse is Mad Tec was now trapped in a prison cell with several tortured souls, including the last three of the elf princess's surviving warriors. Their souls were too drained to react. They stared at Tec in shock. He just appeared before them and didn't look like any being they had seen before. Mad Tec turned to them. Although they were far larger than he was, his angry expression frightened them.

Mad Tec noticed this and didn't take it well. He looked around to see what was making these prisoners so fearful. His size allowed him to slip between the bars. He was quiet in his movement while cautious of getting spotted from any direction. More prisoners began to notice him. Their spirits rose as they could see he was making his way without incident. Then a rumble shook them to their core. Mad Tec watched them as they ran to the back of the cells in fear. They shivered and wet themselves. Some cried in terror. Mad Tec looked around and saw nothing that would cause this type of reaction. He slid into a cell then hid under a bed so low only someone his size would fit. A few minutes passed. Clank! A door along the hall opened. All the prisoners freaked out. They fought each other to get to the back of the group. Mad Tec wasn't so mad at this moment. A dark figure in a long trench coat and hat walked up to one of the cells. Her boots smacked the ground with a deep thud every step.

As she opened the cell doors, the prisoners screamed as if they were being set on fire. She grabbed a woman and dragged her. Mad Tec kept his distance as he followed. The prison was mediocre, lit by candles and foggy from the smoking kitchen. Soul-flesh was cooking every second in this Plain of the Shadow Dimension. The Starved One craved the quality sustenance that was the souls of the greedy, the over eaters and the cannibals of the Physical Realm. His pimple monster collected them while his demon chef prepared the meals. Mad Tec was unsettled when he entered the kitchen. 'How the hell are souls chopped up like bodies? What is this place?' He thought. His size made it easy to hide. The guards were so useless, Mad Tec was able to get the prison keys from one guard passed out on duty.

He returned to the prisoner cells and set everyone free. They were weak but ready to escape. He led them carefully through the hallways. The spark of fear in Mad Tec's soul vibrated in Origin Tec's soul. He ran in the direction of the prison with all he had in him. Small, weak beings hiding in shadow tried to attack him on his way to the prison, but Origin Tec would not be denied. He knew somehow he was in danger even though he wasn't the part of his soul there in person. 'Why do I feel like I'm going to die?' He thought as he ran. 'What is this place? That elf witch did something to me. This can't be real.' He thought. Deep in thought and driven to get answers, he didn't pay attention to Booker who could hear him approaching quickly. Origin Tec tripped a wire that wrapped him inside a crudely made net. As he struggled, Booker revealed himself.

The fear felt by Mad Tec and the worry felt by Origin Tec acted like a siren within Loveable Tec. He bounced up and yelled out, "Something is wrong. We must help me. Please. Wake up. We must go now." Blossom and Jack sat up startled by the commotion. Jack only knew this version of Tec to be kind, docile and loving. He grabbed his gear and set out. Blossom did the same. While all this is happening Hashimira appears before the fourth version of Tec. He is the even keel part of Tec. The strongest influence of any part of his soul. When Neutral Tec caught a glimpse of Hashimira he tried to speak but their bodies were swept into the air. Both felt their throats squeeze as they hovered. "Whatever you are here for you had better explain why you have a witch here little thing." A cloaked stranger said. Neutral Tec was allowed to speak.

"I have come only to retrieve a weapon that will save my life partner. I mean you no disrespect." Tec said. "How is it that you possess the magic to teleport?" The cloaked stranger asked. "I am not sure who this is or how she came to end up here with me, but I came from another world. The great traveler Ike aided me. I was sent to the location of my desired item then ran into an elf lady who cursed me and sent me away. Now I feel less myself and I'm lost. Plus I have a stranger by my side whom you are obviously uncomfortable with. Let alone you yourself with this terrible magic you took by breath away with. I assure you magical woman, I am here only to find the tool necessary to save my life partner and depart immediately." Neutral Tec said. The cloaked stranger thought deeply for a moment. "Elf lady you say?" She responded. Then she looked at Hashimira with disdain. She could see Hashimira was educated in high levels of magic. "Tell you what. If you take me to your elf lady, I'll take you to your weapon. That is what you are seeking? Am I correct?" The cloaked stranger said.

Neutral Tec didn't trust her, but he was left with few options. "Deal." He said. "Good. And as for you. You can find your way out of the Dungeon of the Damned." The cloaked stranger said. She closed her eyes, chanted a spell and Hashimira vanished. Neutral Tec landed safely on the ground. "Well then… What is your name little thing?" The cloaked stranger asked. "I'm Tec. What's your name?" He asked. "Betra. Now that we have that out of the way, off we go don't you think?" Betra asked. Something within Neutral Tec shook his senses. He suddenly had the feeling he was in danger. He used this opportunity to trick Betra and find himself, even though he was already there. With her ability to read his energy, she rose with him and flew in the direction he desired to go. While they were in flight, Mad Tec almost escaped with the prisoners. The chef returned to the cells to find them empty and gave chase. The rumble of his steps frightened the prisoners who began fighting each other as if they were still within the cells. "Stop. You're being ridiculous. We need to run, or you will surely be caught." Mad Tec said.

His confidence triggered a lost courage within the elf princess's three surviving warriors. "He is right. We must gather ourselves." The eldest of the three said. "We have nothing to fight with Dargoth. Bregg is still very weak. We couldn't fight this little guy if we tried." The youngest of the three said. "Nectal, if you wish to die here then so be it. I'd rather fight if it is to be my last breath." Dargoth said. "I will fight with you brother." Bregg said, as he stood as sturdy as he could on his own. "Brother, no. You must gather your strength. I will fight." Nectal said. "I agree with Nectal. You look weak Bregg. But you can help by getting the prisoners to a safe place." Mad Tec said. He held up the keys and offered them to Bregg. "They will be safe with me." Bregg said. He took the keys and led the prisoners out of the prison. Dargoth,

Family

Nectal and Mad Tec turned in the direction the rumbles were coming from. "Well hero. Lead the way." Nectal said.

"Crap. What else can go wrong?" Origin Tec asked. Booker cuts Origin Tec down. "Oh thank you. I hope you're not going to eat me stranger." Tec said. "I don't eat turtles." Booker said. "That's a relief. Look, I need to find a way in that prison. Something is drawing me there. I think the weapon I need might be in there." Tec said. "Alright, let's go." Booker said. They make their way around the prison, looking for an entrance. After a long pointless attempt to find a way in they are met with Neutral Tec and the cloaked stranger. "What are you doing outside this prison?" She asked. "We need to get into this prison. There is a great weapon that may be in there." Origin Tec said. The cloaked stranger laughed. "There is nothing in their but the Pimple Monster and the pathetic souls that are fed to the Starved One by his chef. You don't want to go in there. As for you, you deceitful little rat, I'm done with you." The cloaked stranger said. She raised her hands causing Neutral Tec, Booker, and Origin Tec to rise off the ground.

As they choked, the prisoners exited the prison with Bregg. But the Pimple Monster was on their tail. Luckily for the two Tecs and Booker, the group ran in their direction. The Pimple Monster closed ground and forced the cloaked stranger to release her grip on the two Tecs and Booker. "What a wonderful surprise. I'll leave you to the horrors that are sure to come." The cloaked stranger said. She flew away as the Pimple Monster began eating the prisoners. Bregg does what he can to fight it off but needs help. Booker comes to the aid of the prisoners as he pulls out his sun blade. The land begins to crack apart, forcing Booker to put the blade back into its sheath. Booker then tried to hit the Pimple Monster with his sledgehammer but one of its pimples opened up, and splashed puss, damaging the hammer and injuring Booker's right leg. Booker opened a cloth that had a storage portal sown into it. "Get in the hole if you want to live." Booker said. In desperation, the prisoners run into the whole. Their fate was already horrible, so they didn't have an issue with dying instantly. To their relief, the hole was a large space that was similar to the space in their cells.

With everyone safe, Booker tries to injure the Pimple Monster with poisonous twin blades, but it is immune to poisons and the blades are parried by the Pimple Monsters awkward extended limbs. Booker pulls out his vampire sword and jumps at the monster. He stabs the Pimple Monster in its biggest pimple causing the puss to splash. The puss almost completely destroys Booker's armor but the blood that follows is drained from the monster by his vampire blade. The Pimple Monster squeals and spins before falling over and deflating. Popping bubbles of puss and farting sounds get weaker and weaker until all that is left is twitching flesh. And like clockwork, Blossom, Jack, and Loveable Tec arrive just in time to help.

The prisoners exited the cloth room once the threat was gone. "Holy crap. You just killed the Pimple Monster. No one has ever survived an encounter with the Starved One's shadow hound." Bregg said. "This is not the threat that haunts me." Loveable, Neutral, and Origin Tecs said simultaneously. Everyone looked at them. They were there but couldn't see each other. No one knew this as they looked at each other in confusion. All three Tecs are all experiencing this moment at once as a simultaneous perception. Mad Tec's experiencing their experience as much as they are experiencing his. Yet none of them know of each other as they are all one soul. "You must be the friends of the female sorcerer." Neutral Tec said. "There is a threat to me in this prison that must be confronted." Loveable Tec said. "You should save your friend as I save myself." Origin Tec said. Even though Blossom, Jack, and Booker never revealed enough details, the accumulated experiences of Tec's separated soul instinctively knew they were connected and understood their paths needed to go different ways.

"I don't know what path you must take because I was magically transported here by a cloaked stranger. What I can say is we came from that direction and your friend was sent to some place called the Dungeon of the Damned." Neutral Tec said as he pointed in a specific direction. "Oh boy. This is a horrid place. And I have seen horrors in this prison. You must hurry for your friend's soul will be ravaged mercilessly." Bregg said. The Tecs ran to the prison with Bregg as the prisoners fled in multiple directions. Blossom, Jack, and Booker ran in the direction Neutral Tec pointed. It didn't take long before Brea's fractured team got lost. Machinery of all ages and types surrounded them. Vehicles, planes, trains, and so on. But they were all rusted and forgotten. There is a mist that fills the air that smells like engine fluid and gasoline. It is dark but the trio's eyes have become accustomed to it at this point.

Jack activates his robot. It's electrical waves wake up the energy accumulated by the forgotten machinery. The ground begins to shake

Family

as a helicopter, tank, spaceship, and other vehicles rise from the ground and float to the energy source. Metal clashed as mega machinery fused together as one. Blossom, Jack, and Booker turn to the source and witness a metal giant standing several stories high looking directly at them. The monstrosity raised its right arm made up of a helicopter with heavy machine guns. Thoop! Thoop! Thoop! Fifty caliber bullets flew at the trio with the intent to kill. Blossom's left leg is hit with shrapnel. Jack's Right arm is just missed by two bullets. The trajectory of each bullet that flew by their heads whistled so loud they stung their hearing. Booker's right foot was hit by a bullet. It would have ripped the foot off if it hadn't just clipped the outside.

Blossom tries to help Booker with his injured foot as he morphs his right arm into a shield to protect them. Jack, a half vampire, uses his speed to shoot the monstrosity up what should have been the butt hole. But the bullets that are flying are numerous enough to cause oil and gas to blind him. The monstrosity raises its left leg and attempts to stomp on Jack. Blossom is quick and is able to clean and bandage the wound as Jack narrowly escapes death. Jack's super speed helps him dodge the tank food of the monstrosity. The ground crumbles under the impact but Jack is able to keep his balance and pull out his revolver. With deadly aim, he shoots at the shin of the monstrosity. A perfect shot at the gas tank of the truck that connects the tank foot causes an explosion. The monstrosity falls to one knee.

A cry much like a little weakly baby comes from the Jet head of the monstrosity. "Ehhh!" The sound is painfully high. Blossom throws her double-bladed boomerang at its chest causing the top of the Jet to dislodge from the torso of the monstrosity. "Ehhhhh!" It cries out in pain. Booker uses this distraction to run up at the right leg of the monstrosity and attack with his twin axes. The first axe swung makes contact with the metal of the jeep portion of its right leg and freezes it. Booker's second swing is with the ash axe that turns the monstrosity's right leg into black dust. "Ehhhhhhhh!" It cries as it falls on its back.

Jack lands awkwardly from the blast of the stomp. Booker is consumed by the avalanche of black dust. The monstrosity is overcome with confusion allowing Blossom to pin down it's helicopter arm. The monstrosity flails its left space-ship arm in any direction, trying to get up but failing. Blossom frees the right arm with the gun to pin down the flailing arm, allowing the monstrosity to begin shooting at them. Jack pulls out his big ass bazooka and fires at the monstrosity's helicopter arm, tearing the limb off. "Ehhhhhhhhhhhhhh!" It cries out. As Booker continues to dig out of the pile of ash, Blossom attempts to tranquilize the metal being and fails. The attempt tickles the monstrosity as it squeals. It cries out in anguished laughter in response to Blossom's confusing behavior.

Jack jumps atop the monstrosity's vulnerable chest, runs up to its face and unloads an explosive shotgun round into its metal mouth as it cries. The explosion ends the cries as the monstrosity's body lays limp. Booker also lays limp from the energy put into escaping the ash pile. Jack and Blossom ran to help Booker and pulled him free, but he remained unresponsive. Blossom checked his vitals and looked for any life-threatening wounds. "He's fine. Just sleeping. He's exhausted." She said. "Do you have water?" Jack asked. "Um, I think I have…" Blossom said. "You don't have water do you? I'll just slap him." Jack said. "I can provide care to him. I thought I had something." She began as Jack attempted to wake Booker up. Jack pushed Bookers face, waking him up. "Hey Booker, you were under dust. You missed the whole fight." Jack said. "Say that to my rolls." Booker said. (I realize as a writer this made no sense to you as a reader, but my son broke the fourth wall upset with his brother for waking him up as he fell asleep during this part of the game. His rolls resulted in low numbers reflecting Booker's lack of participation. Now let us continue.)

The trio dusted themselves off and continued on. It took days to clear the machine cemetery. The darkness grew thicker and colder the further into the ice plain they traveled. In the distance, they could see a structure that looked like a frozen waterfall with a bridge that crossed in front of it. From their perspective, it was a pathway. From a wider view, it was actually a giant, frozen troll holding a stick. Its soul froze as it puked. Jack activates his robot to scan the area. "Perimeter secure. Pathway clear to move." It communicated. The trio walked across the bridge, enduring the stench of the frozen puke waterfall. Jack grabs Booker and Blossom before the frozen troll wakes up. Just as they make it to the other side, the troll breaks apart. The sound of the crumbling ice wakes up the Icicle Giant.

They placed Booker in a safe spot before confronting the Icicle Giant. Blossom unleashed two arrows from her duel arrow bow. "Was this thing the bridge?" Blossom asked as the arrows flew into the Icicle Giant's mouth. It began choking on the toothpick like objects. This gave Jack the opportunity

Family

to unleash another round from his big ass bazooka. The impact tears the Icicle Giant's torso apart, creating a snowy sky. The Icicle Giant began to break up into large ice rocks. Jack grabs Booker and Blossom then runs as fast as he can to escape getting buried under thousands of ice rocks three times their size. The wind pressure from the falling rocks thrusts him further away as he carried his friends in his arms.

As the ice dust settles, the trio find themselves in the darkest environment they have experienced yet. They can barely see their hands stretched out in front of them. Jack, exhausted from his efforts, lays next to Booker. "What should I do?" Blossom asked as she looked over her friends. "Oh, I know." Blossom thought aloud. Blossom positions herself in a fighting stance, stretches out her staff and said, "Tah Tah." The crystal on her staff lights up revealing a Tar Goblin sneaking up on them. Jack already fell unconscious as it attacked. Booker put himself in harm's way. With one swing of her spine axe, the Tar Goblin almost killed Booker. Blossom hesitates as the Tar Goblin attacks her. She throws her double-bladed boomerang at its face. It dodges the initial fly by but is cut in the back of the head when the weapon returns to Blossoms outstretched hand.

Booker jumps at the Tar Goblin, cocks his heavy hammer back and thrusts it at the Tar Goblin's injured skull. The impact crushed its head like an anvil landing on an egg, splattering its brains everywhere. The Tar Goblins arms drop as its body falls like a rag doll onto its axe that falls with the sharp end facing upward. The Tar Goblin's body twitched, only helping the axe slice it in half. Before heading on, Blossom makes a shelter to help aid her friends in recovery.

On the other end of things, the three Tec's separate from the group and as they run they become one. Tec's essence becomes stronger but is still weak without Mad Tec. Little does Stronger Tec know, Mad Tec is in a battle against the Chef or, as she affectionately calls herself, Soul Slicer. Nectal and Dargoth breathe hard as their weakened state leave them unable to handle the blows of the Soul Slicer. Mad Tec is just as exhausted, but his rage drives him forward. Soul Slicer stands in shock as Mad Tec runs at her. She kicks him like a soccer ball. His body spears across Soul Slicer's chop shop.

"You little shit. I remember your mother. She never loved you. That's why she gave you away." She said. Mad Tec wasn't sure how to react to her words. His nerves tensed up. He repositioned himself to prepare for another attack. The Nectal struck her across the right cheek. Dargoth grabbed Soul Slicer's cooking fork as Nectal attacked. He lunged at her as she dropped to one knee. With all the strength he had left, he stabbed her in the neck. Mad Tec watched all this and perfectly timed a flying knee that helped shove the cooking fork all the way through Soul Slicer's neck. She reached out for help as purple, green blood squirted out of the open wound. "Helpp.... Kchhhhh... GGeeluhhhhh..." She gargled.

The three warriors stood over her twitching body. "What did she just say?" Nectal asked Dargoth. "Halkugeluhhhhhhh. Then she died." Dargoth said. They chuckled at the imitation. "How is it possible to die in the place where death leads to?" Nectal asked. "Maybe there is another dimension or realm beyond this." Dargoth guessed. With a clean swipe, Mad Tec cuts Soul Slicer's head off then throws it at her butt to make sure she dies with shame. "Whoa." Nectal and Dargoth reacted simultaneously. "What was that about?" Dargoth asked. "For my mother's memory." Mad Tec said as he took Soul Slicer's set of keys. "Let's find out where these lead." Mad Tec said. Nectal and Dargoth look at each other in agreement then follow Mad Tec excitedly.

Elsewhere, Brea's fractured team would get the necessary rest to continue in good health. They are much more cautious in their travels as they finally approach a cliff with the view of an open field that leads to a dark dungeon-like structure. "This is suspicious my friends. I should probably use my robot Snake to check the area." Jack said. "Um, don't I have something?" Blossom asked herself out loud. "These lands feel suspicious my friends. Remain cautious." Booker said. As Snake took readings of the area, Booker checked his compass. The dial vibrated, pointing south. Blossom attempted to use her lantern of revealing but the flame quivered as if it was afraid. Snake returned dizzy and confused. "Readings, corrupt, readings, detrimental to health." Snake said before shutting down.

"Let's go." Jack said. Their friend needed them. It didn't matter what dangers may come. Hashimira was in danger. The open field has a radius of over a thousand yards. There are no sounds, nothing alive, just cracks on the ground and fog in the air. "Oh dear. Spooky." Blossom said. They don't realize it but that open space made it easy for the dungeon guards to watch them approach. The trio had nowhere to run when the dungeon mile high front gate opened and five guards, eight foot tall each, exited

Family

to capture them. Cloth sacks get put over their heads as their hands are secured behind their back. The guards take them inside and beat them until they fall unconscious. Jack wakes up as if from a nightmare. He has been tortured before as a mercenary. This was nothing new to him. Shortly after, Booker opens his eyes. He's dizzy but a warrior himself, pain is just a part of life. Grilled cheese and pain are what he eats for breakfast. Blossom and Hashimira are not as welcoming of the treatment. Blossom has a concussion and Hashimira has been tortured so brutally she is dead.

(I must intervene my valued reader as it has been brought to our attention by my wife who is playing Blossom that someone needs to wake her up so she can save her people. This was not my fault as she rolled an eleven, but the fate roll was negative, so she is knocked out. But for some reason she thought she could revive our daughter's character, Hashimira, while still unconscious. Happy wife, happy life. So she wakes up.) "Yayyyy. I wake uuuup." Blossom said. As they look around, they can see many other cages much like the cages they are in. Hashimira and Blossom are in a cage with a dead warlock. Booker and Jack are in a cage all to themselves. There are other species, beings, etc. in other cages alive, dying, or dead. Some cry, some scream, but all are afraid. The trio watch as a fearful soul is removed from the cage she was in so she can be tortured in front of the rest of the caged souls.

Blossom reads Hashimira's vitals and can feel that she is dead but warm. She performs CPR on her friend as perfect as it can be performed. Two breaths, thirty pumps to the chest, repeat, repeat, repeat. Hashimira opens her eyes, but she is not the same. Everything that held her back from becoming the greatest sorcerer who ever lived was gone. The human part of her had died but the magical part of her is what kept her body warm and her blood moving slowly. With Blossom's revival, Hashimira rose upright with glowing eyes and sent out an energy wave that ripped apart everyone in the dungeon. All except her friends and a few prisoners she watched get tortured alongside her. The cages were released from their bondage and set on the ground safely. Then they opened from the top like the outer layer of a banana before it is consumed. Still, this newfound energy that always existed within her had never been used. So she passed out, though her health was almost fully recuperated.

As the free souls looked around at the area, they could see little due to the large pit at the center about two football fields wide. From their caged position, they could see that there was an exit not but a few kilometers away from them. The vaporized giant torture ghouls were now twenty foothills of dust they had to traverse just to get to the other side where two-mile-high doors remained shut. "What do we do?" Blossom asked. "Let's go get our stuff." Jack said. Lucky for them, the bottom of the doors had just enough space to crawl under. As guards prepared the next batch of souls to be tortured in a chamber to the right, Brea's team looks around and can see large doors in front of them and in the opposite direction of the screaming. "Let's go to the doors on the right." Booker said. "Booker!?!" Blossom said. "You never know. We could make new friends." Booker said. "You better be right or I'm gonna slap you." Jack said.

Booker slaps jack. "Cause I feel like it." Booker said. Jack wiped his cheek and nodded in acceptance but knew he would get his revenge for that slap. As the team walked in the direction of the screaming, they crawled under the mile high doors to find mountains of armor, weapons, magical items, and many more things getting ripped from the new arrivals who were getting prepped for torture. The team got their first view of the ghouls who looked like humanoid goats with disfigured bat wings. Each ghoul stood the height of an eighteen-wheeler upright. Jack saw this as the perfect time to slap Booker. While the two scuffled, Blossom retrieved their stuff from the pile. By the time the two were over it, she had already brought their stuff to them and helped Hashimira heal and wake up.

"We have to go help Tec now." Blossom said. "Let's save these souls. Maybe we can get information." Booker said. Booker attempted to attack one of the ghouls, but it sees him, grabs him, then places him in a cage. Hashimira runs up to help him and is also grabbed. She is different than before. Every atom that makes up everything the ghoul is made of is under her control. She focuses her energy and projects a wave that is focused on the ghouls head. The atoms separate creating the image of the ghouls head popping like a balloon filled with green powder. The other ghouls scream in horror and run to their dungeon master Ednedria. "We need to go help Tec. We have to find him and help him so we can return back to the Physical Realm." Blossom said. The group follows her. Hashimira pulls out her gem of true path and leads the way to the exit. They are practically unseen as they crawl under the mile high front gates and escape.

Family

But halfway across the open field the ground shakes. There are loud screams that ring out like sirens from the dungeon. Suddenly a horde of demons start tearing from the ground like moles. In seconds the group is surrounded by hundreds of thousands of demons of all varieties. But they do nothing but seal the group in place. The front gates of the dungeon fly open as the Dungeon Master exits to confront the ghoul murderers. Ednedria, the Dungeon Master, is twice the size of the largest ghoul and possesses a sword made from the pit of tortured souls. It can kill anything in any realm. It's length is twenty-three feet four inches, and its width is six feet ten inches. The blade tears the air as Ednedria swings it skillfully, charging intently at the stunned group. The demons move out of the way as fast as they can, but many are squashed under each of Ednedria's steps.

Hashimira elevates in the air and attempts to tear apart the sword of Ednedria. But Ednedria is still too far away. Booker pulls out his horn of Volhalla and blows on it causing heroes of old to enter the Shadow Dimension and fight alongside the group against the demon hordes. Blossom revealed a whistle then blew on it calling upon a giant ghost girl along with a hawk, a minotaur and an alicorn who would join the fight. Jack pulled out his rocket launcher and fired a round at Ednedria's legs. A perfect hit caused Ednedria to stumble but it wasn't enough to prevent him from advancing. Even with a limp, he never lost focus of his objective. Kill Hashimira. But Hashimira had different plans. She focused all her energy on Ednedria's head. With all she had in her she projected the energy.

Ednedria's stumbling and arrogant sword play happened to land his sword in front of his head just as the energy wave made it to him, shattering the blade. The explosion was devastatingly large. Broken pieces sprayed all across the Plain. Luckily, a small machete size piece of the blade landed in front of the prison where Tec and the three loyal warriors of the elf princess were camping outside. Ednedria falls backward from the burst of energy but never sits up. A large piece of the blade speared through his left eye. The horde runs in terror at the sight of Ednedria's death. In seconds the team is all alone as they once were when they first arrived.

As Mad Tec and the elf princess' loyal warriors exit the prison, Strong Tec runs into Mad Tec causing a vibration in space that warps the air around Tec's body like ripples in water. Bregg, Nectal, and Dargoth stare in shock. "Did those two-turtle people just become one?" Dargoth asked. "Yup."

Nectal said. "Yep." Bregg said. Tec rose a few inches off the ground as his soul became complete. In an instant he fell to one knee. "Are you alright there little warrior?" Dargoth asked. Tec stood up, stared at the men with a smirk and said, "Oh yeah... I'm doing alright." The loyal warriors walked past Tec, trying to act as if they weren't in shock. "We need to get away from this place and find a place to camp." Nectal said. "Agreed." Bregg said.

They were able to find a perfect spot on a hill with a full view of anything moving around them in any direction. An explosion so strong it shook the air in shadow woke them up. Tec was on guard duty and looked back to see if anyone else felt what he did. That turn of his body was all he needed to avoid a broken piece of Ednedria's sword stabbing him in the throat. Nectal ran to the broken piece of metal and grabbed it. "Ouch." Nectal said. Just a touch broke skin as Nectal began bleeding from the small cuts the blade caused. "Crap that thing is sharp." Nectal said. "Here." Bregg said after ripping part of his long jacket. Tec wrapped the scrap cloth around the metal and kept it with him. The group set out to help Tec, but Bregg became curious. "Tec, you said you were sent to the prison by transport. Who did that?" Bregg asked. "A cloaked stranger. She wanted me to lead her to the elf princess, but she turned on me when I didn't." Tec said.

The men looked at each other. "Where did you last see the elf princess?" Dargoth asked. "Before she transported me, we were on what looked like floating islands. She was down about losing all her warriors. I think she thought I was a spy or something." Tec said. "She thinks she lost us all." Bregg said. "We must find her." Nectal said. The group set out to find her but when they arrived on her island there were no signs of her. "Where could she be?" Tec asked. Everyone stayed silent. "I dare not say." Nectal said. "Say it." Bregg said. "We must locate the Plain of Sorrow. If she believes us to be all dead then she must carry a heavy burden. That area is a magnet to all in depressed states." Dargoth said. "And if we are wrong? What do we do if we are caught in sorrow's web?" Bregg asked. "Is it not worth it? I would go wherever it took to save my life partner Pep." Tec said. "Well said my friend. Let's go." Dargoth said.

On their way Dargoth stops everyone in place. "What is it?" Nectal asked. "That smell." Dargoth said as he turned around. The group turned around in turn. "What?" Tec asked. "It's a Stickypoo." Bregg said. Tec chuckled. "A what?" Tec asked. "There are all types of life forms in the cosmos. And many were never meant to see the light of day. This one is a travesty to the senses without light. With light..." Dargoth tried to explain but was interrupted by an attacking Stickypoo. This fifteen-foot double horned poop Minotaur was strong and fast. He collided with the warriors, scattering them in all directions. Dargoth attacked its left leg as Bregg attacked its right leg. Nectal fell to the ground, ill from the paper cut caused by the broken metal that almost killed Tec. Tec noticed Nectal, remembered the incident with the metal, unveiled a portion of the metal and ran at the Stickypoo.

The Stickypoo was weak at the knees and fell on his face. Dargoth and Bregg climbed the disgusting depiction of deadly demented defecation. Dargoth drove a stick into the spine of the Stichypoo. Bregg wasn't as lucky as the hostile heap of horrid hatred grabbed him and slammed him into the ground. Tec took that distraction as an opportunity to drive the broken piece of metal into the face of the sickening cesspool of sour stickiness. The Stickypoo squealed and tried to flick Tec off. Tec jumped out of the way of the voluptuous venom of vulgar villainy. Diarrhea blood spewed from the wound. Dargoth tried to run up to the Stickypoo's face to stab his eye but was swatted away when the gross gunk of ghastly gruel rolled over. Tec changed his route as he ran toward the Stickypoo's neck and jumped as high and far as he could with metal weapon in hand. A direct insertion into the back of the neck ended the conflict in an instant.

But Tec didn't stop. He chopped and chopped at the neck of the flagrant festering of funky fart-knock. "Tec. TEC." Dargoth yelled out. "Tec, it's over my friend. Let up already." Bregg said as he tried to hold Tec back. With a final swing, the Stickypoo's head separated from the flapping body. "That's sick." Bregg said. "Yup." Dargoth said. Tec ignored the sour smell of the flapping body. He turned to Nectal and ran to him. Bregg and Dargoth followed. Nectal was half awake and speaking gibberish. "Nectal, it's Bregg. What happened to you? Tell me so I can help." Dargoth said as he checked his supply bag for medical aid. "Can your princess help him?" Tec asked. "The princess. Right." Bregg said. He lifted his friend and began running to the Plain of Sorrow. Dargoth gathered his things. "Wait for me Bregg." Dargoth said. Tec wrapped his metal weapon and followed Bregg along with Dargoth.

After finding a place to recover, Brea's team gathered whatever supplies they had and cooked a meal. Each took turns standing guard as the others rested. When it was Hashimira's turn to stand guard, she noticed an armored warrior running in the direction of the Dungeon of the Damned. She rushed to each of her teammates to wake them up. "What's wrong?" Booker asked. "There's a weird looking armored guy coming our way. It was a … there was a…" Hashimira said. "You ruined your line. Give it up." Jack said. (Valued reader, I feel I am yet again obligated to explain myself. My daughter, Hashimira, was fumbling on what to say. One of my sons, Jack, was as supportive as you would expect a brother to be. It was funny because they are in character, so I just kept typing as they spoke. Let's see what they have to say next.) Jack pulls out his revolver and aims it at the armored warrior. "Stick em up… Who are you?" Jack asked. The warrior stopped. "Stick what up?" Dargoth said. "You people talk weird." He continued. "Sorry, I thought you were an enemy that wanted a piece of thine prettiest sexiest revolver." Jack said. (Don't ask valued reader.) "Oh, my bad." Hashimira said. "Uh… Can you put the damn gun down asshole?" Dargoth insisted.

Jack puts the gun down. "Where's Tec?" Booker asked. "That's why I'm here. I came to get you. He may be in danger yet again as he and my brothers went to find our leader, the Shadow Princess. But they haven't returned. I fear they are all lost." Dargoth said. "Take us." Hashimira said. They follow Dargoth to the entry way to the Plain of Hollow Dreams. "Here we are. It pains me to ask that you go without me. I fear what that place can do. And what it represents." Dargoth said. Each of them stood equally before a wall of moving waves of black liquid. "Is this like a portal?" Booker asked. "It is and it is not. This is the path of sorrow. My dear friends may have thought it was the Plain of Sorrow. They are the tears of the depressed souls that are haunted by something in their past lives. On the other side exists multiple paths but it's impossible to say which path my brothers took to find our leader. You may very well get pulled into sorrow yourself. All I know is it is most likely that our leader has lost herself in the Plain of Hollow Dreams. Tec has pain. And this place feeds off pain." Dargoth said.

"Well… I guess we should walk in." Booker said. Upon entry, Booker and Jack are split from Hashimira and Blossom. They emerge from the liquid wall in a raining colorless forest. Booker attempts to use his night vision and spots Tec with Bregg. They are sitting over Nectal who is laying down motionless. Booker runs over to them to get a closer look. Jack follows. Bregg is crying over Nectal who is neither moving nor breathing. Tec looks up at

Family

Booker and Jack. "You found us. We have been lost for weeks." Tec said. "This is a nightmare." Jack said. "It's a mind game. Show yourself BEAST." Booker said. Tec looks at Jack confused. "You idiot. This place isn't a beast. You are the beast, and it feeds off you. If you feel pain it will drive you into the sorrow you have within. Nectal killed himself. He was raped as a child. Sold into slavery and beaten all his childhood. His pain never left him. Here, it took over his mind. This place… It is a mirror of all that is wrong with you. We are lost. You are too. You just haven't figured that out." Bregg said. Then he turned to his brother and hugged him.

Hashimira and Blossom were not so unfortunate in their travels. They were taken to a hollow grave. In it was a shovel. Brick walls surrounded them. A crow stood atop the wall directly in front of them. It looked at them but didn't make a sound. "Is this a cemetery?" Hashimira asked. "You are where you were when you died." The crow said. "What is this place?" Hashimira asked. "It is what should be should you do what you shouldn't have when you did it." The crow said. "What happened here?" Hashimira asked. "What happens here is up to you as here has no understanding of what is to happen should you do or not do what you could or would not do." The crow said. "We're inside a brick wall. Where are we?" Blossom asked. "You are friends with that turtle? Are you not?" The crow asked. "Yes we are." Hashimira said. "Yes. We're here to save him." Blossom said. The crow laughed. "Save him. Is that what you came for? You can't save yourselves. I couldn't save my warriors just as you can't save yours." The crow said.

"Are you the lost princess that the warriors came to look for?" Hashimira asked. The crow flew down to them and began to transform. "What warriors?" She asked. "Were there not warriors that have come to look for you?" Blossom asked. The elf princess rose up, taking her true form. "Stop wasting my time. What warriors do you speak of?" She demanded to know. "I believe one of your warriors is outside of the liquid wall we passed through." Hashimira said. "Who? What is his name?" Moliasha asked. "Dargoth." Hashimira responded. Moliasha suddenly dropped to her knee in tears. "Are you lost here? How long have you been here." Blossom asked. The elf princess rose to her feet. "I am not lost. You are. I took refuge here as I thought I lost my warriors. That's why the grave sits there. It taunts us as we live with the thought that they died, and we still live. The guilt of any survivor. Come, we must see to it that I reunite with my loyal warrior." The elf princess said. She opened a hole and walked through, exiting the path of sorrow back into the open range of the Shadow Dimension. Blossom and Hashimira followed right behind her. "Dargoth." She yelled out as she ran to hug him. They embraced and cried in happiness.

The tearful embrace of Bregg was far less happy. Nectal's soul had seeped into the colorless grass and become its fertilizer. Bregg cried as his brother left him alone. Tec tried to console Bregg by placing his right hand on his friend's left shoulder. Bregg placed his right hand on Tec's consoling hand and stopped crying. "Thank you my friend." Bregg whispered tearfully. A hole opens and Dargoth runs through. "Bregg, Nectal, I found the princess." Dargoth said. Blossom, Hashimira and Moliasha emerge behind Dargoth who sees Bregg in tears. "No." The elf princess said. "Moliasha? Is that you?" Bregg asked in disbelief. "It is my darling." She responded. He ran to her and bowed but she reached for him in warm embrace. He cried. "Nectal killed himself. He's gone. This place. It consumed him." Bregg cried. "Worry no longer. I will take you two and we will go to a better place." Moliasha said. "Before you do, can you help me. I am in need of a path back to my life partner. I am afraid she may be in grave danger, and I may be too late." Tec said. "I'm so sorry. I should have helped you all at the start. The metal you carry will do what you need. If you can find a weapon smith to create a handle you can use it without hurting yourself. I will take you to a path that can lead you out, but I must warn you. The Tear-bath Creature will not take kindly to trespassers." Moliasha said.

With that, Moliasha kept her promise and helped Tec along with Brea's team locate the tear lake that possessed the pathway out of the Plain of Sadness. "The path is under this lake of tears. But what lives down there will devour your soul to feed its creation. Be safe. Your only chance of escaping this place is through the hole at the bottom." Moliasha said. The team stands together in deep thought as a waterfall spills tears endlessly into a lake that never overflows. "Did you hear a big explosion some time back?" Booker asked Tec. "Only when this sharp metal nearly killed one of us. Nectal tried to grab it, but it cut him, and he died slowly. Bregg thought he killed himself, but I fear it was simply this metal." Tec said as he unwrapped an object to reveal it was a broken piece of Ednedria's blade.

"I can craft that metal into a weapon you can wield if you want." Booker said. "I do." Tec said as he handed the piece of metal to Booker. As Booker gathered items to build the handle for the metal, Hashimira manipulated the metal to reshape it into a beautiful sword. Jack and Snake pulled out all their supplies, took them apart, then engineered a harness that works like a magnet for the blade. Tec is blessed with a sword and sheath that stick together yet he can grab it at any moment and immediately wield it in conflict. Tec dove into the lake with sword in hand. The rest follow him. Underwater waited the Tear-bath Creature. It was a humanoid fish that towered over the trespassers. Beside him was his creation. A plant that took a humanoid form as he fed her the souls of trespassers to bring her to life. The only problem with her creation was, to stay alive, she would need to be fed souls consistently. As she came closer to death, the Tear-bath Creature was grateful to see fresh food for his love.

"Welcome. I am so pleased to see you. Come to me. I have a surprise in store for you. All of you. Thank you for coming to visit my wife and me. I am Shay. This is Tulip. We are so pleased you are here. Come to me." Shay said ever so softly. Hashimira attempted to use her gem of truth but the liquid in the lake distorted the path, knocking Tec off course. He quickly regained his composure. "I'm going to kill you with this blade and go through that hole. My life partner needs me, and you will not stop me." Tec said. Shay swam at Tec. Tec swam at him just as fast, proving a turtle can move just as smooth underwater. Shay didn't expect this, swimming face first into the blade of Ednedria. Tulip screamed in horror and deteriorated. Hashimira grabbed Jack who was drowning, Blossom grabbed Booker who passed out, and Tec led the way into the hole at the bottom of the lake of tears. Once they shot out of the other end of the tube, they swam to the top and crawled onto the dry land.

A boat floated up with a figure covered in a trench coat. Tec stood up, removed much of the gear he and his other selves acquired, and gave it to the dark figure. It was accepted as payment to cross over. Although the lake looked the same as they passed over, the dark figure had actually taken them through an unseeable exit. It was at this time that Ike sensed them then traveled at the speed of thought to snatch them from eternal darkness and remove them from the Shadow Dimension. "I was sure you were all gone. It has been several months since I last saw you. I take it you have completed your task." Ike asked. "Yes we have." Jack said. "We have." Blossom said. "Very good. I will send word to Brea that you are on your way home. Thank you for all you have done. You may very well have saved the Physical Realm from the prince of darkness. As for you Tec, I will return you to the moment you left the Physical Realm. Or at least as close to it as I can." Ike said. And that was that. Tec returned to save his life partner and Brea's team returned to their bodies fully intact. (Valued readers I am privileged to say that my family and I had a wonderful time. We ate and danced and celebrated as their quest came to an end in victory. Thank you for taking the time to go on this cosmic journey with us. May you become the hero you were always meant to be.)

Family

Behind the Scenes

Building family memories

After escaping the dungeon of the damned then defeating the horde of demons, it was only right that the heroes have a meal that celebrated their success.

To celebrate helping Tec get the sword of Ednedria and return to his life partner in time to save her I bought fireworks for the family to enjoy.

P. Marcelo W. Balboa

It was a great memory for my family.

Then they were rewarded with a fabulous meal fit for a king.

Cosmic Journey

The return of the Princess

If you are wondering what happened to the princess and her loyal warriors, I took my family out to play a continuation of the role-playing game I adapted into a chapter of this book. I decided to make an event of it at a comic bookstore we visit often. They were kind enough to let us use their tabletop gaming area. This was a family memory we all enjoyed.

The family took control of the Princess, her loyal warriors and her long-lost familiar, Star. Star is the fox that battles the dragon in the comic book idea I let you in on earlier in this book. I had my family play out the origin-story of how Star ended up fighting a dragon.

P. Marcelo W. Balboa

I went all out creating a physical world my family could play in. They fought great foes and made new allies along the way.

I did my best to keep track of everything as the Cosmic Guide. Pencils and calculators go a long way when tracking health and armor during multiple conflicts.

Family

I am pleased to let you in on the success they had finding Star which ensured the elf princess, Moliasha, could battle her evil sister, Betra, at full strength.

By the end, the fight tears open a hole in space that sucks the evil queen, fox, and dragon into outer space. You know the outcome from reading the comic book sneak peek.

Vincent's Life

Layla Hudson grew up with wonderful parents in a safe neighborhood. She was the only child until she was separated from her father when her parents divorced. He would go on to have three more children with a new wife many years later. When she would visit, she could see they were much happier than her. Moving from place to place with constant abuse at the hands of new boyfriends her mother met, Layla grew resentful. She would come to a point where she couldn't take anymore and ran away. But the great planetary war that ravaged the world began as she was on her own. Although she originally chose to stay with her mother in the divorce, she instinctively went to her father's house for solitude. But he was gone.

She would find her siblings safely hidden in his fallout shelter. To her, they were spoiled brats with a life she should have had. In spite of them, she took the mantel of provider until they could find out what happened to their father. But years passed. And her siblings remained in the fallout shelter as she went for supply runs all that time. They made a promise to wait for their father or depart the shelter only when supplies ran out. That day would come when Layla didn't return from a supply run when she got trapped among the ubiquitous occurrences in the Forbidden Forest.

The siblings would finally exit the shelter and travel to their uncle as their father instructed. Their adventure was life threatening, leaving them damaged by the experiences. Though Layla would find her way out, track her siblings down, and save them, she too was haunted by her experiences. Regardless, she would go on to build a resistance against the political powers that be. In the process, two of her siblings would be lost. The youngest, Vincent, was kind and loving but when he lost his beloved siblings he shut down. Layla would rise from rags to riches as she became the queen of Rezandria. But it came at a cost.

She mistreated her siblings and when Vincent remained the only survivor, he wouldn't go with her. She promised him the world, but he

Family

refused to accept her as she was always so mean to them. He felt all alone in the world. But he didn't realize that her experience during the war changed her. The new paradigm effect opened her eyes. Still, Vincent experienced his own paradigm effect. His kind loving personality became protected. He would choose to only reveal his living kind self to a select few for the rest of his life. It would take decades for him to open up to Layla once more.

To get him to come with her from the ashes of their uncles destroyed home proved to be the most difficult moment. She would plea with him, but he resisted. When he gave in it wasn't without a struggle. As queen, she would give him a mansion to grow a new family in. One he could change the cycle their parents had made. And her role ensured protection. So he could heal at his pace. Before this could be she needed to start the path to closure between them. As they drove to the mansion, she looked at Vincent who was staring out the window quietly.

"Vincent, I know you're trust for me isn't what it was for Risa or Jay, but I want you to know my love is as strong for you as theirs was." She began. "Pffff!" He responded. "Life doesn't come with a manual. Each of us have to figure out how to live by the standards of our perceptions. And at times, our reactions can be uncalled for." She continued. "I remember a lot of uncalled reactions you had to their love." He said. "Though there are memories that put a frown, there are also those that put a smile on our face." She said. "All you ever did was push us away when all we wanted to do was pull you in." He said. "No one is perfect. People sometimes commit to actions that bring regret. I admit to my faults. I am truly sorry for my transgressions toward you. I am blessed to have you in my life. And I will always cherish your existence in my life. I pray you find it in your heart to forgive me, but I will not require it. My love for you is pure and needs no return of said love." She said.

He turned toward her with a curious expression, yet he said nothing. "You simply being you in my life is good enough. I value you deeply. I may have created regretful memories, but you have given me so many good ones. Thank you for all the happy memories. I hold no grudge for any of your shortcomings." She said. He stood up strong. "What shortcomings?" He asked. She giggled. "You're perfect as you were and are. I love you very much. I hope that there will be a day when we can sit together, enjoy a delicious meal, and laugh or cry in happiness together. Until that day I will love you still. I will cherish you still. May your days be blessed until your last breath." She said.

Vincent didn't say anything, but he was listening. He would go on to meet a kind, loving, God fearing woman. They would raise two children. One would pass away from cancer but the other would meet a nice young lady who would give him three wonderful grandchildren. He tended to be firm with his son but when his grandchildren would come to stay the night he would become that playful childlike character he once was before the great war. Through the visits from his grandchildren he would find his most satisfying happiness. Every visit or sleepover would give him the opportunity to recapture his childlike qualities. He loved his grandchildren like he loved Risa and Jay. And to entertain them, he would tell the story of how a superhero named Layla came to find him and help save the world.

World Peace

On the planet Flubberboober, two brothers would rise in power as they fought for liberation on opposite sides of the planet. Both thought they were fulfilling a prophecy that said the son of a great king would rise up and bring world peace. As the two became the remaining powers that be, they met with each other only to find that they were brothers of the famous king, Connell Mcbufduk. Joining forces, they were able to bring peace to the world as the prophecy said they would. And it was in good time. The fairies that attacked their planet, years before their truce, were exposed by magical beings from a magical island who were now welcomed to spread across the world.

Up until then, fairies had eaten their prey and taken their identities all around the world. Friends turned on friends, family rose against family. Descension within the ranks of military and political hierarchies threatened the stability of peace when the magical beings revealed fairies were among them. The now royal brothers would choose to combine forces to expose every fairy. As many citizens across the world went missing, the brothers prepared their soldiers for the war to come. King Conner, the Humalumpkidan, and his brother Emperor Kane, the Alicorlumpkidan would inspire all races to set their differences aside for true world peace. In their success, they would lead their combined armies in a magical war against the fairies that covered the planet. The war was as sight to see from outer space where the creator of the planet and the native life forms on it watched.

She feared for this day and pushed her Munchgalumptagans to become stronger just for this moment in time. Their existence was threatened, and they were ready to answer the test. Magical explosions of all colors illuminated the skies. The creator was worried for them but felt satisfied she had provided enough hardship for them to persevere. The war took valuable lives from both sides. Lasting nearly a decade, neither side would relent until the other was eradicated. The final battle came to pass when the leader of the fairies attempted to overtake Conner. They knew of Kane's magical abilities but didn't know that Conner was the son of the dark witch, Scin'd.

She blessed him with a protective spell. The fairy was stunned, waking Conner from his slumber. The fairy, Ninajay, was imprisoned causing the remaining fairies to focus on her location. They refused to stop trying to free her no matter the cost. And the cost was great. Ninajay never spoke, shed a tear, or ate. She passed away in solitude. The war had ended. The planet celebrated their victory in unison. Conner and Kane remained in power until their final days. Their lands would be split between their children who would go on to maintain the peace their forefathers created. And Connell Mcbufduk would go on to be the foundation of world peace for all ages. Their impact on the Unworthy Cosmos would reach Brea's Guild and the Hall of Legends. Leading to the rise of the great-great-great grandson of a fallen Humalumpkidan King, Shem. Artimus Igtaup Madnanimus was born out of wedlock to the great-great granddaughter of a stained royal lineage. But his story is for another time. For this stories ending I leave you, my valued reader, is that of the home of kind, happy, loving, squishy Munchgalumptagans living in world peace as it was always meant to be.

Hall Of Legends

Hustle and bustle crowded the plane of Rezandria. Home of the renowned establishment of Brea's Guild. A fortified basic training center responsible for creating some of the most impactful teams to save countless lives across the Unworthy Cosmos. Their stories are held in the great Hall of Legends. Yet it is one story that stands out more than most. It is that of Gregory Hudson. Adopted child of the King and Queen of Rezandria. Blessed with long life they feared watching their child grow old and pass before their eyes, so they made their kingdom their child. Until the grandchild of Karlo emerged. When they caught word they offered themselves as parents to raise this child.

Unsure of what he would become they gave all their resources to training, educating, and protecting him. It was frowned upon when he befriended the Munchgalumptagan Artemus. Raised in a bloodline of failed kingship, Artemus sought only to redeem his father's legacy. Leader of a small community on the planet Flubberboober, though everyone was kind, there was this aura of distrust in the communities surrounding theirs. It drove his father to drink his life away. His mother carried the ranks. She was the true bloodline of the fallen king, Shem. It was her burden Artemus carried while on his quest to become a hero of legend on Rezandria.

They joined many teams but never separated. That was until they came upon Sharlene, the child abuser. Finding a way to escape Tartarus, Sharlene began to reign hell upon unsuspecting children. Gregory and Artemus along with a Rabbi and a ninja, sought to end his murderous campaign. Artemus was the one supposed to die beside the Rabbi and ninja, but Gregory sacrificed himself to save his friend and brother in arms. Returning alone broke the hearts of everyone in Brea's Guild. It struck fear into all who saw Gregory as the perfect representation of Rezandria and the Hall of Legends.

By this time everyone felt Artemus was like family to Gregory and understood he felt the loss more than anyone but the King and Queen of Rezandria. Artemus had his named changed to Artemus Gregory Shem as he wished to redeem his bloodline and carry on his brother's story. He began studying the Munchgalumptagan of old. Inspired by Pep and Tec's spooky adventures and Connell Mcbufduk's epic tales, he requested any and every side missions to build his story of the warriors of tomorrow to read about him. Every thought, action, and mission he took was with the realization that he would pass away some day and wanted to be remembered well.

In the end all the side missions drew the attention of the Heavenly Courts. They called him to the Gates of Heaven for a personal request. The challenged him with the quest to change the fate of the Unworthy Cosmos. What was could never have been had it not been for the rise of the Queen of the Planet of the Guardians, Ellianna. Her role was essential in many pivotal moments in the history of the Unworthy Cosmos. Her impact on the Metaphysical, Astral, and Physical realms was immeasurable. To earn this quest Artemus was tested in a survival horror experience against a creature that represented the physical form of his subconscious sorrows, failures, and regrets. It stalked him across the Plain of Hollow Dreams until Artemus could run no more. Again, at near death he was saved. An unexpected hero aided Artemus in slaying the beast. Artemus was frustrated in his failure to overcome the adversary on his own.

"Why do you fret? Are we not in victory?" The Redeemer asked. Artemus put his hands on his hips and walked around. "This was my mission. Overcome my past. I failed. I needed someone's help to succeed. I couldn't do it on my own. That's exactly how my brother died." Artemus said. "Gregory was here for some time. He knew you would carry his death on your shoulders. But his burden was to let you go so you could grow. Now he's in Elysium." The Redeemer said. "He was here? You know me? What… How…?" Artemus stuttered. "Relax friend. You must focus on you. No one can succeed without help. I could not overcome my Rival without the help of your brother. You could not overcome this challenge without me. You must pay it forward. Help others overcome in the present and you will find more value that trying to overcome figures of the past. Now go, your father, grandfather, and great grandfather are in need of you in this horrid place. I wish you well on your journey." The Redeemer said. Artemus tried to get

Family

more information, but the Redeemer departed to aid others. As it is written in the Hall of Legends, Artemus would go on to redeem his bloodline, overcome his self-inflicted mental woes, and earn the right to join the most important team to be called upon by the Heavenly Courts.

Well, my valued reader, we have come to the end of this unworthy anthology. I pray your read has been a fulfilling journey. Until the next book, be safe and may God Bless every one of you.

Thank You All

UNCONDITIONALLY

Family is written as a compendium of all the relationships in my life. As I have gone on this journey to complete this book my life has gone through life altering experiences. Each fashioning my book more and more. But it was the memories of my loved ones that fed the family in each of my stories. For that, I thank you all.

First of all, the parents that raised me Cecilia and Adolph Balboa, and the family members they were the glue to… Lupe, Sam, and Vicky – Goldie, Mike, and Micole – Uncle Richard – Joseph, Rosie, and Melanie – Cindy and Amanda – Marcelo and Marcelo Jr. – Jennifer, Christopher, and Tanya – Carlos Jr. – Stephanie – Aaron – and the woman who birthed me, thank you for any part you played in motivating me to succeed.

Second of all, the friends that I care for like family whether we see each other each day or once a decade. Valerie – Steve – Juan G. – Chris P. – Alex, G. – Cynthia, G. – Larissa L. – Prince M. – Adegboyega A. – Lissette, G. – Norma B. – Bobby K. – Jerry C. – Robert P. and Kristen P. – Jesse, B. – Elaine, M. – Arturo, B. – Jonathan, F. – Keedah, F. – Tony, W. – Caleb C. – Ned, C. – Erica, M. – Martha, R. – and my father figure, Richard Benford. Thank you for the valuable roles you played in my life.

And last but not least, every martial arts champion I coached along with every parent that came to train or brought their child to train, client I had as a personal trainer, as well as my hired artists. Thank you all forever.

P. Marcelo W. Balboa

LEGACY OF THY FATHER

A post war world has found world peace through the fulfillment of the prophecy of the rise of the son of a great king of old. There are factions and separatists here and there but overall the greater whole are built on strong foundations of loyalty to the higher powers that be. Order had been restored. But in a few places there were secluded members of the defeated. One territory was that of the Humalumpkidans. Their neighbors were a small group of surviving Maglurians. It was the Maglurians, a metal worshiping culture, that overtook the Humalumpkidans, who enslaved and exterminated other Munchgalumptagans many wars ago.

Some families found forgiveness as a path and intermingled then created families of their own. But both cultures were stained by their actions. And those who were not happy with the intermingling decided to end the growing territory of Interminglers. A young couple, Dilyla and Archelio happened to be a new couple on a romantic journey to see a famous waterfall several days away. When they returned home they were not ready to see their community crumbled, highlighted by flames. Dilyla, the daughter of the bloodline of the fallen king of the Maglurians ran to her people. Archelio, the son of the bloodline of the fallen king of the Humalumpkidans, ran to find any survivors of his people. They would meet no less than a day later as the sole survivors. Holding hands they stood atop a hill looking down on the remnants of their bloodlines. "It's all over. Our lives are all over." Dilyla said. "Never. We will build a new legacy from these ashes. We will live on for them." Archelio said.

About the Book

Family can be complicated. Some are blood relatives and others are so close they are a stronger relation than blood. In Family, An Unworthy Anthology, each chapter delves deeper into these various relations while some reveal the impact the previous books written by P. Marcelo W. Balboa have had on the regular people of the world.

About the Author

The Unworthy Cosmos is vast. Life exists in countless forms. Each existence has a story to tell. Driven by the need to define family from his point of view, P. Marcelo W. Balboa has accumulated characters and stories that cover the complex relationships that family creates.

Printed in the United States
by Baker & Taylor Publisher Services